# TORTURED TEARDROPS

# TORTURED TEARDROPS

---

TAMARA'S TEARDROPS #3

P.D. WORKMAN

ISBN: 9781989080191 (IS Hardcover)

ISBN: 9781989080184 (IS Paperback)

ISBN: 9781989080153 (KDP Paperback)

ISBN: 9781989080160 (Kindle)

ISBN: 9781989080177 (ePub)

pdworkman

# ALSO BY P.D. WORKMAN

*Reg Rawlins, Psychic Detective*

What the Cat Knew

A Psychic with Catitude

A Catastrophic Theft

Night of Nine Tails

Telepathy of Gardens

Delusions of the Past

Fairy Blade Unmade

Web of Nightmares

A Whisker's Breadth

*Auntie Clem's Bakery*

Gluten-Free Murder

Dairy-Free Death

Allergen-Free Assignation

Witch-Free Halloween (Halloween Short)

Dog-Free Dinner (Christmas Short)

Stirring Up Murder

Brewing Death

Coup de Glace

Sour Cherry Turnover

Apple-achian Treasure

Vegan Baked Alaska

Muffins Masks Murder

Tai Chi and Chai Tea

Santa Shortbread

*Zachary Goldman Mysteries*

She Wore Mourning

His Hands Were Quiet

She Was Dying Anyway

He Was Walking Alone

They Thought He was Safe

He Was Not There

Her Work Was Everything

She Told a Lie (Coming soon)

He Never Forgot (Coming soon)

She Was At Risk (Coming soon)

*Kenzie Kirsch Medical Thrillers*

Unlawful Harvest

*High-Tech Crime Fighters*

Virtually Harmless

*Stand Alone Suspense Novels*

Looking Over Your Shoulder

Lion Within

Pursued by the Past

In the Tick of Time

Loose the Dogs

AND MORE AT PDWORKMAN.COM

*To those who have reached the end, and hung on.*

ONE

TAMARA AWOKE WITH A hand gripping her shoulder. She sat bolt upright, her eyes flying open, hands coming up to protect herself.

"Take it easy, French," Kirk snapped, pulling back from her. "What are you doing still in bed? Reveille went a long time ago. You're missing breakfast."

Tamara swallowed and looked around. She was in juvie. Where else would she be? Her most recent taste of freedom seemed to have broken her body's entrainment to the rigid schedule. It had been years since she had failed to wake at the reveille bell. She was alone in the cell, but it took a few long seconds for her to remember that she was odd man out with no cellie. Which explained why she hadn't been wakened by her cellie when she failed to rise at reveille.

Kirk stood back, watching her, waiting for her to get her head on straight and get out of bed. Tamara lowered her hands from the defensive position in an attempt to show Kirk that she was fine and wasn't going to attack him the first chance she got. As if she could have taken him on anyway. She was smaller than most of the other girls, certainly no threat to one of the men guarding the block. Tamara pushed her blanket off and scrubbed at her eyes with her fists, trying to wake up fully. The threads of her dream were still clinging to her brain like wisps of fog. She'd been running from some threat, but she'd lost who or what it was.

"Just... didn't hear it, I guess," she offered lamely.

Kirk shook his head. "We don't have the time to be babysitting you. You know the schedule and the rules. You don't get some special pass because you've been on TV lately. No one cares about your celebrity or what you did when you were out. It's just the same here as it was before. You're just the same as you were."

A ball of fire lit in Tamara's gut. She breathed slowly, trying to keep it from igniting further. Everything Kirk said was true. She wasn't anyone special, just because she'd been taken hostage and had ended up the suspect in an assault and kidnapping. Never mind that she'd been trying to protect the baby from what Tamara and the baby's two sisters had gone through. She didn't want any little girls having to deal with Mr. Baker's lecherous advances ever again. He was in jail. He wouldn't be getting out again any time soon with Mrs. Baker testifying against him. He wasn't going to walk this time.

"French!" Kirk snapped.

Tamara startled and focused on him again. He seemed like he was far away, much farther than the few feet the cell would allow. Tamara rubbed her eyes again, as if her only problem was vanquishing the drowsiness.

"Yeah. Yessir." She massaged her forehead and face. "I'm up. I'm coming."

"You don't have time for showers, breakfast is already on. Get your days on and get to canteen."

"I will. I'm up."

She swung her feet over the edge of the bed to demonstrate that she was awake and aware and on her way to breakfast.

Kirk gave her one last glare and left the room, pulling the cell door shut behind him. Tamara moved as quickly as she could, stripping off her pink night uniform and pulling on her orange day jumpsuit. She glanced at the observation window in her door before using the toilet and splashing some water on her face. She opened the door to make her way to the canteen. The smells of breakfast floated down the hall to her, even less appetizing than usual.

Kirk was still standing there, waiting on her, making sure that she didn't go back to sleep again. He looked her over and shook his head.

"What?" Tamara demanded.

"Comb your hair and tie it back. You're not going into breakfast looking like that."

Tamara patted her sleep-tousled hair down self-consciously. She turned around and went back into the cell to get her comb from her kit and drag it through her hair a few times, until it no longer snagged. She stretched an elastic around it in a ponytail and returned to the hallway.

"Sorry. All ready."

He shook his head again. Tamara hadn't been trying to act like a princess, but she knew that was what he was thinking. That she thought she could just do whatever she wanted because she was better than everyone else. She didn't know why she couldn't get back into the regular schedule and felt so tired and foggy.

Dr. Sutherland said it was perfectly normal. She had been through a traumatic experience. She had barely slept or eaten. Her body was just trying to heal, and that took resources. Her attention and alertness were suffering simply because her body only had so much energy to draw on.

She could have asked him to write her a sick note until she started to feel better, but she knew how well that would go over with the staff and the other girls. They already resented her for how much attention she was getting. She didn't need a bigger target drawn on her back. She wanted to go back to being invisible, someone that nobody cared about.

Kirk walked her all the way to the canteen to make sure that she got there. Like if he left her side, she might wander off down the wrong hallway and never make it to the canteen. The way that her brain had been behaving since she got back, maybe he had a point.

"Shape up," he warned as he prepared to leave her to her breakfast. "I don't want more of this 'diva' behavior from you. We're going to start cracking down."

They had been giving her a little leeway since her return. Not writing her up every time she broke the rules or forgot where she was supposed to be. Not reporting infractions to the administration or Dr. Sutherland. Not imposing all of the consequences they were authorized to.

Tamara swallowed hard and nodded her understanding. "Yessir. Sorry. I'll try harder."

He watched her enter the canteen and was still standing there when she looked back. Tamara had been expecting to have to get in line with the other girls as usual, but everybody had already dished up and was sitting at their tables eating. She was *really* late. Everybody watched her enter the room. So much for staying invisible. Tamara grabbed a tray and hurried over to the serving counter.

She didn't really want anything, but she knew she would get sent to Dr. Eastport if she refused to eat. She was underweight and they were keeping a close eye on her to make sure that she put back on the pounds she had lost during her brief stint on the outside. She stopped to get a soupy bowl of oatmeal and a piece of toast, turning down reconstituted eggs and whatever the squares of breakfast meat were supposed to represent. Tamara felt dangerously nauseated by the smells, but there was nothing in her stomach to throw up. She would feel better once she had eaten. Hopefully.

Tamara added a portion of apple juice to her tray and turned around to face the tables, scanning for a safe place to sit. Most of the tables were either full or were declared gang tables. There were few who, like Tamara, managed to stay independent after the first few days. In the beginning, she'd had Glock to prevent the gang recruiters from *persuading* Tamara to join up. After three years, they just accepted that she was independent. Or at least, that had been the case before the prison break. There had been increasing pressures for Tamara to join the Sharks or TMJ since her return. She resisted, but resisting meant she had to constantly be on her guard. And there was no one watching her back for her this time.

Tamara drifted toward the wall. She could just stand there and scarf down what she could of her breakfast and not have to sit down and risk the ire of either of the gangs or one of the smaller factions.

As soon as Tamara leaned back against the wall to make herself comfortable to eat standing up, Millican moved toward her. Tamara looked at the nearby tables to see if she could squeeze into one of them before he reached her, avoiding the lecture on following mealtime rules. But there was nowhere safe.

"French," Millican rumbled, "you can't stand here to eat. You know that."

"I'm just... I just want a bite of toast, I'm not going to be staying..."

He grasped her arm. The opportunity to make her own choice of a safe seat was gone. Millican pulled her away from the wall, his iron fingers uncompromising. He steered her toward the nearest empty seat. Tamara tensed, pulling back, but he didn't let her resist. He pulled her up to the table, indicated the seat, and when Tamara didn't cooperate by sitting down, he pressed her into it.

"No nonsense from you," he commanded. He stood there for a moment, his eyes going over the rest of the girls seated at the table. "And there had better not be any trouble from the rest of you."

They continued to stare down at their meals as if they hadn't even heard him. No attitude. No hint of a threat.

"Lewis," Millican pressed.

"Do I look like I'm causing trouble? Just eating my breakfast."

Millican stood there for a moment longer. Tamara picked up her piece of toast and nibbled a corner. There was no word from any of the other Sharks at the table. Tamara didn't try to tell Millican it was too dangerous for her to be there. He knew the political situation as well as she did, or he should.

Millican nodded and walked away, pacing up and down the wide aisles between the tables, watching for any sign of trouble.

Tamara dipped her toast into her oatmeal. She kept her eyes at middle distance. Not looking submissive and weak staring down at her meal, but also not challenging anyone at the table. Her body straight, shoulders back, alert and aware of every movement around her, every eye that flicked in her direction.

"Nice of you to join us," Lewis said in a growl that was barely above a whisper.

"Can't help what the bulls do." Tamara took a bite of her toast. She pulled the tab on her apple drink and ripped it off.

"Why aren't you in here when everybody else is, so you can sit where you belong?"

Tamara took a gulp of the apple drink to try to wash down the balled-up bolus of toast that was sticking in her throat. She couldn't eat while trying to avoid a fight with Lewis and her girls, but if she didn't eat, she would attract the attention of the security staff again. Millican was keeping an eye on her. He was bound to notice if she just sat there staring at her meal. Tamara dreaded taking another bite, but she had to. She wasn't sure how much time was left until the end-of-breakfast bell but, considering the half-empty plates of those around her, it wouldn't be long. If she hadn't finished most of her meal by then, it would mean a trip to see Dr. Eastport.

Then again, so would aggravating Lewis.

"Missed reveille," Tamara explained. "I know, it's dumb. Been here long enough to know better. My body's all screwed up since..." Tamara shrugged and glanced at Lewis briefly, "you know."

"Oh, don't we feel sorry for you. So sad you lost track of the schedule while you were on the outside."

"It's stupid," Tamara reiterated. She took a couple of bites of her toast, chewing it aggressively. She had to be able to get something down before the bell rang.

"You been back for a week. That's long enough to get your head on straight."

Tamara made no response. It didn't matter whether she agreed or disagreed; either response was just going to wind Lewis up.

Lewis kicked Tamara sharply under the table, making her jump. "Frenchie! Hey!"

Tamara's world turned red. Protocol called for a measured response; a protest, getting to her feet, maybe a curse or a threat. But there was nothing measured about Tamara's response. She was on her feet instantly. She grasped the edge of the long table and flipped it into Lewis's lap.

There was instant chaos.

"What the hell!" Lewis shouted. She tried to jump to her feet, but it was too late, the remains of her breakfast were in her lap and the weight of the table pinned her down. The Sharks went to her aid instead of going after Tamara.

"Get off of me!" Lewis was screaming, slapping everyone's helpful hands away while simultaneously trying to throw the table off to free herself.

One of the guards had hit the general alarm and the guards stationed in the canteen hurried over to put a stop to the fight before it could get going. The sound of the alarm blaring in Tamara's ears just infuriated her more. She couldn't think straight.

Lewis was free and on her feet, yelling at the Sharks to get Tamara. They finally clued in and were turning toward her. Rather than turning tail or seeking protection from the security staff, Tamara drove straight at Lewis, the fire inside her erupting in molten red lava.

Lewis was bigger, stronger, and more skilled than Tamara. Most of juvie was bigger and stronger than Tamara. But Lewis had been taken off guard and was still reeling from having everything dumped in her lap. Driven by her rage, Tamara threw herself at the bigger girl and did her best to inflict maximum damage before she was stopped by the guards and the Sharks. She knew she would be stopped, it was just a matter of how much she could do in the seconds that she had.

She went directly for Lewis's face, the most vulnerable place available, but Lewis was taller than Tamara, so when she covered her face and pulled back, Tamara took advantage of her lower center of gravity, throwing her shoulder into Lewis's soft middle while her face was covered, managing to take her to the ground.

That in itself was a victory. Tamara had no chance of beating Lewis in a fight. Getting her on the floor would at least boost Tamara's rep. A shower of blows rained down on her from behind while she tried to keep Lewis down to get another strike or two to her face, and to keep from getting grabbed or flipped by her.

"Stand down! Break it up! French!"

By the time the guards started pulling girls out of the dog pile, Tamara was regretting her choice. She was no longer in a position of power. She took several blows to her face and head before the guards started to get control.

Millican was the one to grab Tamara and pull her to her feet. "What just happened here?"

Tamara held her hand to her bleeding nose, not bothering to answer.

"What happened?" he repeated. "I look away for one second and everything suddenly goes all to hell."

Tamara still didn't give him any answer. She wasn't about to commit to a story and get caught in a lie. Not being gentle, he wrenched her hands behind her back and restrained them with a zip tie.

"I don't know what's gotten into everyone," Millican growled. "Brawling at breakfast? You know better than to get involved in something like that."

Tamara gave a grunt in response. Sure, she knew better. He didn't even know she was the one who had started it. Lewis had instigated and Tamara could have just eaten it, but that would just make her a target the next time. She had to show her teeth.

Millican pushed Tamara a couple of feet away. "Just stay there." He resumed pulling other girls out of the fight, until everything was quiet again. By the time the backup got there, the guards posted in the canteen already had it under control. With all of the participants handcuffed, they started returning girls to their cells or diverting them to the infirmary or isolation. The blood streaming from Tamara's nose meant she was routed to the infirmary. She was one of the first to be treated.

Dr. Eastport poked and prodded Tamara's nose. "Doesn't look like it's broken," he said. "Just bloody." He wrapped a large piece of gauze over Tamara's nose and squeezed it tightly. "Hold it like that. Fifteen minutes. No peeking, no blowing your nose."

"Okay." Tamara put her fingers beside his to pinch it.

"Anything else?"

Tamara shook her head.

Eastport was studying her, trying to read her. "You sure, dear? Nothing else?"

"No. I'm fine."

"All right. Stay here. Don't move." He left her on the gurney and went on to the next patient. It was Gomez who had escorted Tamara to the infirmary and was supervising her and a few others. He stood with his back to a wall, watching her. Tamara looked away from him and focused on the middle distance, contemplating her situation.

She closed her eyes to try to rest and relax, but that was a mistake. With her eyes shut, she could still see the infirmary even more clearly. She was thrown back in time to her initial intake three years before. Dr. Eastport leaning close to discuss his findings, the smile that usually adorned his face gone. He sat on a little round stool and took off his glasses.

"So you're sexually active," he observed.

"No."

"You can lie to me, but your body can't."

Tamara opened her mouth to argue but stopped, meeting his steady gaze. "Yeah, I guess."

"You also have not been using protection."

Tamara's jaw dropped. "No way you can tell that!" she protested.

"Unfortunately, I can."

Suddenly, she understood. "Don't tell me he gave me something!"

He nodded gently.

"Is it mono? I've been so tired."

"You're pregnant."

The room spun around her and Tamara felt like she was going to throw up. "I couldn't be pregnant! He said I couldn't get pregnant."

"A boy will tell you whatever he thinks he has to."

Tamara wrapped her arms around her belly, the tears starting, her throat closing up.

"No, no, no. I can't be pregnant. It could be a mistake, couldn't it? Those tests aren't always right."

"It's not a mistake. I'm sorry."

Tamara sobbed, feeling the last vestiges of control slip away from her. Rivers of tears ran down her face. She had done what she had to to get away from the Bakers, to be free to live her own life instead of being a slave, and she was going to again be responsible for another life, another baby.

"Here, none of that," Eastport comforted. "Take a deep breath and settle down. It's not as bad as all of that."

"I can't be pregnant! I don't want a baby! I can't do this!"

"No, it's okay. We'll take care of it."

Tamara felt a scream rising from inside her. Her speech dissolved into unintelligible crying. She started to shake violently and she could no longer understand what the doctor was trying to say to her. It was as if he were talking to her from somewhere else. She just put her hands over her face and screamed and screamed. Eastport eventually gave her an injection that made the whole nightmare dissolve into oblivion.

"French. French!"

Tamara focused on the voice and was dragged back to the present. Her intake had been three years ago. It was in the past. Long since taken care of. Gomez clutched her shoulder, shaking her and trying to snap her out of the flashback.

"What's the matter with you? Get a grip on yourself!"

Tamara wiped tears from her face. She rubbed her aching head and scrubbed her eyes, trying to focus on the present and find a way to explain it away to Gomez.

Dr. Eastport hurried back into Tamara's curtained cubicle, brows down, concern written all over his face. "What's wrong? What's going on?"

Gomez dropped his hold on Tamara's shoulder. "Hell if I know. She was just sitting here and started bawling. Wouldn't answer me." He stared into Tamara's face. "Seems to be back know. You think it was some kind of seizure?"

Dr. Eastport took Tamara's pulse, smiling reassuringly. "Hey, there. You okay?"

Tamara nodded. She didn't know what to say to him.

"Are you in pain?"

"No. I'm okay. It was just... nothing."

Dr. Eastport looked at Gomez. "You want to give us a minute?"

Gomez's eyes narrowed, not liking it. "I need to keep an eye on her."

"Go keep an eye on one of the others for a minute. Tamara's not going to go leaping up and getting into mischief, are you?"

Tamara shook her head. "I'll stay here," she promised. "I won't move."

Gomez reluctantly moved away from the end of Tamara's bed and went out of sight to check on the others. Tamara knew that the curtains only provided the illusion of privacy. The other girls and Gomez would still be able to hear what she said to the doctor.

He pulled the blood pressure cuff from its cage on the wall and put it around Tamara's arm. He pumped the bulb.

"You want to tell me what's going on?" he asked.

"No... just... I don't know. I'm fine."

He put the stethoscope into his ears and released the valve on the cuff, listening. "Your pulse and blood pressure are very high. I'd expect them to be down, now that you're away from the fight. You were calmer a few minutes ago. Now you're wound up again. What happened?"

"I don't know." Tamara wasn't about to confess to having flashbacks. She needed a reputation for being tough, not crazy. "Maybe like Gomez said, a seizure."

He shone a penlight into her eyes, shaking his head. "I don't think so. Did he do something to you? Hurt you or touch you?"

Tamara looked in the direction that Gomez had gone. Dr. Eastport raised his hands in a questioning shrug, indicating she could answer the question nonverbally. Tamara shook her head. "No. He didn't do anything. He's never done anything."

Dr. Eastport gazed at her steadily, waiting for further confirmation. She again shook her head. *No.*

He took her pulse again and nodded. "You need something to relax you? Having anxiety?"

"I don't take meds. I don't need anything."

"There's no shame in taking appropriate medication. Nothing wrong with getting help when you need it."

"No. Don't want anything."

"I'm keeping you here until I'm sure that you're stable," he warned.

Tamara rolled her eyes, but the only one who could see the gesture was Dr. Eastport. He patted her shoulder, smiling.

"Have a rest. You're going to be here a while."

Tamara sighed and closed her eyes. She was tired, still feeling like she hadn't had enough sleep. She might as well get what sleep she could, given the opportunity.

TWO

SHE WAS BACK OUT of the infirmary a couple of hours later, Dr. Eastport unable to find any other reason to keep her there. It was Millican who escorted her back to the main wing. He walked briskly beside her, saying nothing to start with. As they got closer, Tamara's gut started to twist and clench. What had she been thinking, getting physical with Lewis instead of looking for a way to get out of the line of fire?

She had taken Lewis to the floor, which was an accomplishment, but Lewis was not going to let it go. She was going to be pissed. Instead of staying neutral, Tamara was now an enemy. She couldn't fight the entire gang.

Millican noticed Tamara starting to lag behind, looking back at her. He slowed his pace.

"Come on." His tone wasn't irritated. Maybe he sensed her anxiety.

"Where are they all?" Tamara asked. "Lewis and the others. Who's in isolation?"

"Pretty much all of them are either in iso or their cells, separated. Let everybody cool down."

"They're on restrictions?"

"We're taking care of it. You're going back to your cell too. Don't need you making more trouble."

"Oh." Tamara nodded and took a deep breath, trying to calm her anxiety. She didn't have to face the Sharks. Not yet. Maybe it would all blow over if it were a day or two before Lewis could talk to her soldiers. Maybe it wouldn't be as bad as she thought. "Okay."

"You've never been one to make waves," Millican said. "I don't know what's been going on with you since before the prison break. If you want to get another crack at parole, you'd better tone it down."

Tamara bit her lip. He was right; she had been angry ever since she had discovered the Bakers hadn't had to serve any time for what they had done to her. But what she'd been feeling since her return to juvie was different. Not just anger at the Bakers, though it still ground at her that Mrs. Baker was free to do whatever she liked. At least Mr. Baker was in prison pending his trial. It was a start. She couldn't attach her new anger to any event or trigger. It just came out of nowhere.

Millican frowned at her. "Well...?"

"Yeah. I'll try."

"Try? You know how to behave. You've done this before. Just get your head on straight and quit stirring up trouble."

"Yessir."

He looked like he had more of a lecture to give her, but agreeing with him took the wind out of his sails. He gave a nod and continued on. Tamara kept pace with him again. There was nothing to worry about. Not until Lewis and the Sharks were out again.

* * *

SHE SPENT the rest of her time in her cell sleeping. She felt like she could sleep forever and still not get enough. Twice, guards brought her meals and Tamara roused herself enough to eat sufficient food that they wouldn't report her back to Dr. Eastport or Dr. Sutherland. Then she curled up on her bunk and fell back asleep.

She didn't lie awake at night after having slept most of the day. The lights went down and she fell into a deep sleep.

But she didn't sleep through the next morning's reveille bell. She woke up abruptly before first light, her heart pounding in her chest. She lay there for a moment, frozen on her bunk, sure that some sound had awakened her.

Tamara turned over and looked swiftly around her cell. She didn't have a cellmate, there was no one else in the cell to make noise. She looked at the door. A guard entering when he wasn't supposed to? A noise in the hallway that was out of place? She slipped out of her bunk and turned quickly to reassure herself there wasn't anyone in the cell with her, even checking under the lower bunk.

She looked at the closed cell door, watching the doorknob to see if it was turning. It was still. Tamara took a couple of steps over to it and twisted to see if it were unlocked. It was still locked as it should be. So what had wakened her?

Tamara peered out the observation window into the hallway. There was no one there. She strained to look as far as she could in either direction, but couldn't see so much as a guard on patrol. No sign of what had awakened her.

She started to pace. She knew she should try to go back to sleep, but she couldn't settle down, so she paced back and forth across the cell. Just a few steps one direction, pivot, and a few steps the other way. Her skin was crawling. She didn't know if they would let her off restrictions, or if they would keep her in her cell another day. If they let her out, would they also let Lewis and the Sharks out?

Tamara bit her nails. She didn't want to deal with the aftermath of the fight with Lewis. Dissing her in front of her gang had been a terrible move. And she hadn't just dumped Lewis's break-fast, but the breakfasts of all the Sharks sitting at the long table.

Tamara clenched her fists and dug her fingernails into her palms. Anger welled up in her again, obliterating the anxiety. Lewis had been picking a fight. She knew very well that Tamara was only sitting there because Millican had forced her to. So why not take it up with Millican instead of Tamara? She'd just been looking for an easy target, but she'd found that Tamara was not as defenseless as she looked.

Tamara swore to herself and continued to pace.

One of the most difficult things about juvie was filling the time. Learning to do nothing and just let time pass. Following the imposed schedule when you had to and just sitting around the rest of the time.

Finally, the reveille bell sounded. Tamara washed her face and combed her hair, putting it back into a ponytail. It was strange seeing her hair dark, when normally it was almost white. Just one more thing that was wrong and disorienting. Was it possible that she had changed herself so much that she wasn't even the same person anymore?

As soon as the doors unlocked, Tamara grasped the handle and pushed her door open violently. She was sick of being cooped up in the room. She needed to be out. She needed air. Space.

Kirk was in the hallway walking toward her. He raised his eyebrows. "You out already? No missing reveille today!"

"No. Been awake for hours."

"You may as well hit the showers before it gets busy."

"I'm going outside."

Kirk squinted at her. "What?"

"I'm going out. To the yard. I need some air."

"You can't go to the yard right now."

Tamara marched toward it anyway. Who was he to tell her she couldn't go out to the yard if she wanted to?

"French. You can't go out to the yard."

"I can go if I want to," Tamara insisted. "I'm not on restrictions."

She walked past him, ignoring his protests. The halls were quiet. None of the other juvies were out of their cells yet. She walked past a couple of other guards who looked at her with puzzled expressions, but none of them stopped her. As she had told Kirk, she wasn't on restricted movements.

She found herself not in the little courtyard, but in front of the library doors. Why had she gone there? She didn't have any desire to go to the library. She'd read every book she was interested in. Some of them several times over. She wasn't going to go on the computers and find out more about Denny and Christina Baker. She didn't want to know that the police case against them had fallen apart and they had, once again, been released into the public.

Tamara tried to push open the door to the library, but the door wouldn't budge. It was dark inside. Where was Mrs. Ruth? Had they fired her and closed the library? They were always complaining about budget cuts, saying that they couldn't afford to run programs anymore. Had they decided the books or the computers weren't being well enough utilized? The ancient computers were slow and cranky, but they did afford one small window to see what was going on in the real world.

She kicked at the door and slammed her hip against it, trying to force it open. They couldn't shut it down. If they were going to cut a program, it should be one of the arts and crafts program, making ugly clay ashtrays or kindergarten-like drawings, not the library program. Didn't they know how important literacy skills were?

Tamara tried to twist the handle and push open the door again, fury building. Glock had always told her only sissies went to the library and Tamara couldn't afford to be seen as weak by the other girls. But Tamara liked Mrs. Ruth and liked to be able to escape into a book now and then, even if it were one that she'd already read three times.

"French!"

Tamara's head whipped around and she spotted Millican walking toward her. She banged into the door once more, as if the third time she was going to be able to force the heavy door open.

"What the hell are you doing?" Millican demanded.

"I wanted to go to the library," Tamara growled. "Who shut down the library?"

"Nobody shut down the library. It's not open until free time. Or if one of your classes goes there. What's going on with you?"

Tamara turned to face him fully. Millican stood facing her with one hand on his taser.

"I just want to get a book. Or get onto the computer." Tamara tried to remember why she had gone there in the first place. Had it been to look up the Bakers on the computer? She hoped they stayed locked up the rest of their lives, the sadistic perverts.

"French, stand down. Chill. You can get a book later. When Mrs. Ruth is here. What are you so wound up about?"

"She should be here now! Why isn't it open?" Tamara kicked backward against the door behind her. "You could use your code to get in. Open it up for me. Just for a minute."

"I said *stand down.*"

Tamara realized that her fists were clenched, held up high to defend herself. The world turned suddenly around her and she had a sense of vertigo. What was she even doing there? She knew the library wasn't open first thing in the morning, during breakfast and showers. Why had she expected to find Mrs. Ruth there?

She forced herself to unclench her fists and she put her hands out to steady herself, not sure she was going to be able to stay on her feet.

Millican eyed her, moving his hand away from the taser. "That's right," his voice was pitched low and soothing, like she was a spooked horse. "Now why don't you tell me what's going on? Kirk said you were insisting you were going out to the yard, and then I find you trying to break down the library door. What's up?"

The yard. That's where Tamara had been trying to go. Not to the library. She didn't want to go to the library. How had she ended up going the opposite direction?

"Did you move it?" Tamara asked, looking at the library door. It was the library, wasn't it? They could have moved it to another section. Sometimes the administration did things like that for no discernible reason. Decided that the English room was more suited to be a crafts room. That the enrichment programs should be in a different wing, nearer the isolation unit. There was no explaining their logic.

"They didn't move the library."

"But I wanted to go to the yard. Why isn't it here?"

"This isn't the yard. Neither one is open right now," Millican's soothing voice was taking on an irritated edge. "You need to hit the showers and change into your days. Then breakfast. You can get some yard time later on, during free time."

Tamara looked down at herself, realizing that she was still in her pinks. The yard wasn't open until later. Neither was the library. She put her hands on the door behind her, trying to steady herself.

"I don't... I don't understand."

"You been sniffing or what? What's wrong with you?" Millican grabbed Tamara's arm, startling her. She tried to jerk out of his grip, but he held on to her.

Tamara closed her eyes for a moment, hoping the fog of confusion and vertigo would lift. It didn't work. She opened her eyes again and blinked at Millican. "I'm... maybe I was sleepwalking," she suggested. "I just... didn't know where I was going or what time it was. I was having a dream." She shook her head. "It's nothing. I'm okay now."

Millican slowly let go of her. Tamara pulled back and rubbed where his fingers had been.

"Back to your room or to the showers," Millican said. "You get yourself changed and ready for breakfast. Understand? Or I'm going to put you on restrictions."

"Yeah, I get it." Tamara nodded. "Yes, sir." She clenched her teeth shut, keeping herself from apologizing to him. When she'd had a shower, she'd be fully awake and feel better. It would wash the confusion away.

Tamara looked up and down the halls to get her bearings and managed to choose the correct route back to her unit and the shower room. There were a few tired voices, there before the main crowd made it in. Getting into the showers early was best. Not that there was any hot water, but a person at least stood a chance of avoiding harassment by any of the other inmates.

She entered and, without looking at anyone else, stripped off her pinks and stepped into a shower stall. The blast of cold water was enough to wake up anyone. Tamara breathed in quickly and held her breath, standing still for a moment and hoping against hope that the water would either warm up or her body would get used to it.

"Hey, it's Frenchie," said a teasing voice. She sounded far away, slightly muted. Tamara grabbed the soap and started to lather up. She was careful not to show any concern over the attention. She needed to just focus on the job at hand and get in and out quickly. But as she moved, she turned and glanced around to see who had spoken to her. It was Tabby. Tabitha Smith. TMJ, not a Shark, so maybe she would be inclined to be friendly toward Tamara. Tamara had, after all, gotten half a dozen Sharks thrown into isolation, which was good for TMJ.

"Frenchie, oh Frenchie..." Tabby crooned, trying to get Tamara's attention.

Tamara pushed her face under the freezing stream of water. Despite the shock of the water, she still felt removed from herself. The fog didn't entirely lift.

She quickly rinsed off the suds and shut off the water. She grabbed a thin, dingy towel and wrapped it around her body without drying off first. Her hair dripped down her back.

"Where ya goin', Frenchie?"

Tabby was moving across the room toward Tamara. Tamara flashed a glance around the room, looking for any potential weapons. It was bare of anything but soap, towels, and fresh uniforms.

"Stay away from me," Tamara warned.

Tabby laughed. A guileless, childish voice. She might be able to fool people on the outside into thinking she was a simpering, harmless halfwit, but Tamara and the other girls at juvie knew better. Tabitha sounded like a sweet little girl, but she was a tough gang chick with a cruel streak and her skill with a blade of any kind was legendary.

Dumas, one of the few female guards, was on shower duty. She always got roped into it, since, if possible, the girls were supposed to be guarded by a woman when in such a vulnerable position. It didn't take long to lose all modesty in juvie, and Tamara didn't really care whether they were guarded by a woman or a man. She would have preferred Kirk in there. He was a better guard and didn't get flustered easily. Or Zobel. She hadn't seen him since her return to juvie. It was a few seconds before Tamara remembered he'd been injured during the prison break. Had he been killed? Or was he just recovering from his injuries or taking a vacation?

"No talking in the showers," Dumas warned.

A useless rule. No one needed to talk or make verbal threats in order to start a fight or abuse another inmate.

Tabby was still walking toward Tamara, grinning like a Cheshire cat.

"I said stay away from me," Tamara repeated, raising her voice.

Dumas could have no doubt that there was trouble brewing. If she didn't act, it was because she wanted to see Tabby and Tamara mix it up.

Tabby slowed and took a glance toward the guard, measuring her chances. Dumas's attention was on them, no longer bored and casual in her supervision.

"Tabitha, get showered. French, get dressed and move on."

Tamara wasn't about to turn her back on Tabby to pull a fresh uniform and whites from the neatly labelled shelves. Tabitha kept up her saunter in Tamara's direction, as if she too were only concerned about getting a uniform to change into after her shower. Tamara planted her feet and balanced herself, ready for a fight.

"French, get your clothes," Dumas ordered, taking a step toward them. Her voice was getting higher, which meant she was nervous. Tamara wanted a guard who was calm and in control, not one who was going to panic.

"Keep her away from me," she countered, nodding toward Tabby.

"What am *I* doing?" Tabby protested in a voice that was all innocence.

"I want you both to stay away from each other," Dumas warned, starting to walk toward them.

"There's no reason I can't say hello to a friend," Tabby protested.

"You know the rules. There's no talking in the showers." Dumas's hand hovered over the panic button on her uniform, waiting for Tabby's next move.

Tabby stared at Tamara, eyes hard and cold as ice. Nothing like the sweet girl persona she was affecting. She dropped her voice to a near-whisper that Dumas wouldn't be able to make out.

"You got involved in a fight that wasn't yours," she told Tamara. "Don't think I've forgotten that."

Tamara stared at her, baffled. Then it started to come back to her. It was Tabby who had stabbed Zobel during the rumble that preceded the prison break. Tamara had prevented Tabby's initial attack on Zobel as he was trying to get another fallen guard out of the way. Tamara hadn't been able to stop the second attack, and that was when Zobel had gone down, spouting blood like a geyser.

Instead of feeling anxious about Tabby, Tamara was angry. Tabitha had had no business attacking a guard in the middle of a gang fight. She was supposed to be fighting Sharks, not guards. Not the people who were there to protect them and keep the peace. That was against the unwritten rules for a gang fight in juvie, unless Tabby had something personal against Zobel, which Tamara didn't think she did. Zobel was a good guard, not one that took advantage of the inmates or was a bully.

Tamara shoved Tabby away from her, into the metal siding of the nearest shower stall.

"Stay away from me!"

Dumas hit her panic button and an alarm sounded. Tabby's face flushed red, but she had no opportunity to hit back. Dumas had jumped between them and was keeping the two of them apart, baton out and her other weapons within easy reach.

"Cool it, you two. Both of you take three steps back."

Tamara didn't move. Tabby couldn't; she already had her back against the wall. She had her teeth clenched and if her eyes were lasers she would have vaporized both Tamara and Dumas.

"She shoved me! She put her hands on me, I didn't do a thing."

"Just shut up. You were both in violation. French, I said to get back!"

"I need my uniform. I gotta get my clothes."

"Do what you're told, now!" Dumas's voice rose in a scream.

Tamara wanted to punch her right in the nose. Dumas's panicky voice got under Tamara's skin like fingernails on a blackboard.

Dumas could see Tamara's defiance and poked the baton at her, driving her back. "Back up like I told you!"

"Don't touch me. I didn't do anything. Just protected myself. Tabby started it."

"I don't care who started it. You're both in violation. Both of you. Back up."

Tamara still resisted, pushing back against the pressure of the baton. Dumas pulled the baton back and Tamara thought for a split second that she had seen reason and was withdrawing. But Dumas whipped the baton back with a crack against Tamara's arm. Tamara yelped and grabbed her arm. She instinctively took a few steps back from Dumas. She pulled her hand back from her arm to look at it. A scarlet stripe stood out along the skin, and it wasn't just a surface bruise, either. She could feel it right down to the bone.

"What'd you do that for?"

"You listen to the security staff, or you're going to get hurt," Dumas yelled back, still a hysterical undertone in her voice.

The door crashed open and a couple of the other guards hurried in. They slowed when they saw that there was no fight in progress.

"What's going on?"

"These two can both go straight back to their rooms!"

Tabitha affected a pout as one of them grabbed her by the arm to escort her back to her cell. Gomez looked at Tamara, then back at Dumas.

"Take her back to her cell," Dumas repeated.

"I need my clothes," Tamara growled, impatient with Dumas for being so dense. She wasn't parading back through the unit in a towel.

"Uniforms are right there. Grab one."

Tamara had been undressing and dressing in front of guards and other inmates for three years. She should have known she wasn't going to get even a semblance of privacy after having an altercation in the showers.

Still seething, Tamara looked over the labeled shelves and pulled out a small uniform and whites. She did her best to pull them partway on before divesting of the towel to finish clothing herself. Gomez stopped her to look at the welt on her arm. Tamara glared at Dumas. "*She* did that."

Gomez shook his head. "I'd recommend being cooperative, then. You going to cause me any trouble?"

"I wasn't causing any trouble. It was Tabby. She was the one who was talking and threatening, came over here to give me hassle. How come I get punished for Tabby breaking the rules?"

Dumas opened her mouth to defend her actions, but Gomez motioned her to silence. "You don't get punished for Tabby's behavior. You got punished for yours. You listen to what you're told and you won't end up black and blue."

Tamara pushed her arms through the sleeves of her uniform and buttoned it up, scowling. She hadn't properly toweled off, and her hair was already soaking into her fresh uniform. It would end up being clammy and cold half the day. And she was going to have to be back in her cell again. Forget any chance at fresh air when they were finally allowed out to the yard.

Gomez took her by the right arm, the opposite side from the bruise, and escorted her out of the showers.

"She didn't need to hit me," Tamara maintained.

"I'm not second-guessing a coworker. I've seen for myself how you've been lately. If you want to get your old privileges back and be trusted, you need to shape up. Lose the attitude that we owe you something, be respectful, follow the rules. You want to act like a wild animal, you're going to be treated like one."

Tamara slowed and resisted his grip as they went down the hall toward her cell. "I don't want to be shut in again," she protested. "I was locked down most of yesterday. You're going to have to write it up if you isolate me again today."

She knew the security staff hated all of the paperwork that was associated with reporting to Dr. Sutherland every time an inmate was put in isolation, and the constant reporting back to ensure that no one was left segregated long enough to cause psychological damage. The guards could get away with not filing paperwork the first day if the inmate were in her own room instead of the isolation unit, but a second day in her cell would require a formal report to Dr. Sutherland.

Gomez scowled.

"I don't want to be locked up again," Tamara repeated. "I'm jumping out of my skin. I need to get out."

"Dumas said put you in your room."

"She didn't say to lock it."

Gomez looked sideways at her. "I don't need to be told that."

"I wanna see Sutherland."

He sighed. "Seriously, French? You know the drill. You keep getting in trouble, you get to go to your room to think about it and cool off. If you don't want to have to chill in your room, then you quit getting into fights and behave yourself."

"It wasn't me, it was Tabby. She's got it in for me because I tried to stop her stabbing Zobel. I didn't start anything, all I did was defend myself."

Gomez stopped walking. He stared at Tamara, eyes intense. "What did you say?"

"She's got it in for me." Tamara stopped there, an uncomfortable feeling in her stomach. Had she blabbed too much? She didn't think she was saying anything they didn't already know. But Gomez's eyes made her second-guess herself.

"After that. About her stabbing Zobel."

Tamara shifted. She rubbed her sweaty hands together and glanced around the hall. There were girls starting to come out of their cells, headed to showers or breakfast. Most of them still bleary-eyed and grumpy, not ready to have a conversation or take note of what was going on with Tamara and Gomez.

Tamara shrugged and didn't answer.

"It was Tabitha Smith who stabbed Zobel?"

Tamara wanted to ask about Zobel. About whether he had survived and, if he had, how he was doing. Was he dead? Still healing? Reassigned to another position or looking for another job?

"French." Gomez's hand closed around Tamara's arm. The left one this time, right on top of the baton bruise. Tamara flinched and tried to pull away. He took no notice of the pain he was causing her and pressed her back against the wall of the corridor. "It wasn't caught on camera and everyone claimed they didn't know who did it. But you..."

She had never been questioned because she had been taken hostage during the prison break. They had asked her about the prison break and about what had happened while she was out, but the police hadn't asked her about the gang fight that preceded the prison break, or who it was that had stabbed Zobel. Tamara had almost convinced herself that it never happened.

"I don't know anything."

"Don't feed me that line now. You just said it was Tabby."

"You misheard. I *stopped* her from hurting Zobel. That's why she's targeting me."

"Zobel was stabbed. You didn't stop anything."

"There was... it happened more than once. I stopped Tabby the first time, when Zobel was rescuing one of the other guards. That young guy, who just ran right into the fight. I forget his name."

Gomez didn't supply it.

"And then something happened, and... he got stabbed. I couldn't stop it the second time."

"Then you saw who did it. Who was it?"

"No, I didn't see. I just saw that he was hurt and tried to stop the bleeding."

"You were right there. They should have questioned you. They should have followed up. *Tabby*."

"Everybody thinks she's this sweet little girl..."

Gomez gave a snort. "Nobody believes her sweet innocent little girl act. You think we're that stupid?"

Tamara tried to find her way to her goal. She wanted to be free. She wanted to be able to leave her room and to get out to the yard during free time. Not sleep the day away again or pace the whole time.

"I'm no snitch. All I know is she was harassing me today. So why am I getting locked up?"

"That's the way it works. I wasn't there. Dumas saw what was going on. And Dumas said you both were to go back to your cells. So that's what we do."

"I was locked up yesterday," Tamara insisted. "You can't lock me again today."

"All I have to do is file the paperwork."

"If I'm asking for Sutherland, you have to tell him."

"I will tell him. I'll also tell him that you're only asking for him to get out of an appropriate consequence. And that your safety is in question because you know something about another inmate and they might retaliate and you were in a fight already."

Inmate safety was one of the few exceptions to the isolation rules. If an inmate had to be segregated for her own safety, it was different from just doing it to punish her. They might even talk about transferring her to another facility, and Tamara was not eager to get transferred. With Glock upstate and Vernon in the women's prison, there weren't a lot of places where Tamara would not be known. Even if there were somewhere she didn't have a direct acquaintance, the inmates and staff would still know who she was through the media. Her name and face had been on too many news reports.

"It wasn't Tabby," Tamara insisted. "I didn't see who it was. It was chaos in there. You saw. You came into the middle of it. I couldn't see what happened. I just saw Zobel was hurt and I tried to help him."

Gomez let out a long sigh. "I don't know what's happened to you, French. We could always rely on you before. What's changed?"

"Maybe before, I thought if I did all the things I was supposed to do, it would all work out in the end. Just like everyone kept telling me. But you know what?"

She waited for his answer, her question dangling. He avoided her eyes. He knew that it didn't work that way. Even if that was what they always told the inmates. They said that inmates obeying the rules and doing what they were told would get them what they wanted, freedom and their own lives back. But inside, they knew very well that it wasn't true. Most of the inmates in juvie would never get those lives. Those normal lives on the outside, working honest jobs and raising families and not being dragged down into the mire over and over by poverty, old gang associations, and addiction.

Without a word, Gomez started to escort Tamara down to her room. He didn't try to answer her question or to justify himself. If he lied to her, she would know it, and if he told the truth, he had to tell her she was doomed to spend most of the rest of her life doing time in one facility or another, between short stretches on the outside.

But Tamara knew the truth. Things wouldn't go in her favor just because she tried to follow the rules and do the right thing. Things would only go in her favor if she made them. She had to look out for herself and her own interests and stop expecting everyone else to do right by her.

Because no one was going to act for her but herself.

Gomez stopped at Tamara's cell. They both stood there for a moment, looking in through the open door. Gomez motioned

Tamara in. She reluctantly walked back into the small, claustrophobic room.

"I want Sutherland," she reiterated. "I gotta talk to him."

"I heard you."

Gomez swung the door shut.

Tamara renewed her restless pacing.

THREE

K IRK BROUGHT TAMARA HER breakfast. Tamara looked at the tray of greasy, unappetizing reconstituted foods. Her stomach turned. She gagged just looking at it. There was no way she was going to be able to get it down. Maybe the piece of toast.

Maybe.

"I want Sutherland," she told Kirk, just as she'd told Gomez.

"It's already on your sheet. You'll get a session with him today."

"When? I can't stand being cooped up here anymore!"

"When he gets to you. You're not the only one in this facility who needs help."

"How many of the rest are being segregated? I should get first crack, before the sessions that are just routine."

"It's up to Sutherland to schedule his appointments, not me. I don't have any say over it."

"Tell him it's urgent."

Kirk rolled his eyes. "You're not special, French. He'll get to you when he gets to you."

"He'll want to see me first. If you tell him it's urgent."

"Sorry. You'll get him when he decides the time."

"If you don't tell him it's urgent, I'm gonna tell him that I told you to, and then he'll write you up for not passing it along."

Tamara didn't know if this was true. She knew Sutherland was very strict about the proper reporting being done. He would have to have some kind of consequence in place if the security staff neglected to follow the rules, leading to inmates potentially being traumatized. They didn't want to cause permanent psychological damage and turn them into worse, more hardened offenders. Glock and Vernon were ten times worse than Tamara was. Did the guards want her turning out like them?

Kirk shook his head, letting out a breath. "You're a piece of work, French."

She didn't know whether that meant he would tell Sutherland she needed to see him urgently or not.

* * *

TAMARA WAS STILL PACING, her breakfast meal mostly untouched, when one of the newer guards opened Tamara's cell door.

"You've got an appointment with Dr. Sutherland," he announced.

"About time!"

He raised an eyebrow. It probably wasn't the usual response to having an appointment with Dr. Sutherland. Tamara and the other inmates didn't generally look forward to sessions with him digging around inside their brains and dictating everything from when they should sleep to what they should think and how they should breathe.

Tamara walked to the door. She paused, unsure of whether he was going to insist that she be handcuffed for the escort to Dr. Sutherland's office. But he just motioned for her to continue and walked beside her on the way there.

Tamara walked into Dr. Sutherland's office and was assaulted by a rush of memories and sensations. She paused in the doorway, trying to get her bearings. Neither the guard nor Dr. Sutherland noticed anything wrong. Tamara staggered to the designated chair across from Dr. Sutherland's desk.

"Tamara French. Good to see you again." Dr. Sutherland smiled. "Have a seat," he encouraged, when Tamara didn't immediately sit down. He made a sign to the guard, who was still standing by, and the guard withdrew, pulling the door shut.

Tamara sat down slowly. She hadn't thought through what she would tell Sutherland once she got in to see him. She hadn't considered what it was he would need to hear in order to convince the security staff and administration that Tamara should be free to follow the usual routine instead of being locked in her room. But Dr. Sutherland took up the slack in the conversation.

"Since you came back here... you seemed a little... distant. Not quite the same Tamara French that we are used to here."

"Yeah. It's been... weird."

"From the reports I'm getting, you are having a significant amount of difficulty settling back in to the routine. Would that be accurate?"

"Yeah."

"And why do you think that is?"

"Because..." Tamara trailed off. She had no idea what to tell him.

Dr. Sutherland waited for a while, seeing if she could formulate an answer, before proceeding any further.

"Maybe you could tell me a little bit about what happened when you were... away. I know that a lot must have happened in a very short time. You're still trying to process that."

Tamara nodded.

"Maybe you could tell me about how you felt being with Vernon. Was that something you had planned on and expected?"

She knew that he wasn't allowed to tell the administration or the police any of the details that Tamara divulged, but she was still leery about giving him any details. Especially when it made her feel so vulnerable and raw.

"I didn't know what was going to happen. Not any of it. I wasn't in on it. Not on the fight, and not on the prison break. I was... just a bystander. I was as shocked as anyone."

"Probably more so," Dr. Sutherland suggested.

"Yeah. I wasn't expecting any of that."

"And so you found yourself a hostage of Olivia Vernon. I don't imagine that was a pleasant experience."

Tamara shook her head. Her face warmed. Her feelings toward Vernon and Sly were so confused, she couldn't put them into words. They had held her at knifepoint and gunpoint. They had abused and threatened and beaten her. But they had also taken care of her, had given her advice and helped her. She didn't know whether they were enemies or friends. None of it made sense.

Sutherland nodded, watching her, waiting for her to elaborate. Tamara shrugged.

"You can probably guess most of it," she said as casually as she could manage. "They kept me until they were sure the cops weren't on their tail, then they let me go. Then..."

"Then you didn't turn yourself in."

"No."

"Didn't you think that was the right thing to do?"

"Yeah... but... I had to find out about the Bakers." Tamara looked down at her feet. What exactly had made her think that coming to talk to Dr. Sutherland was a good idea?

"What about the Bakers? I would have thought that you would want to stay as far away from them as possible."

"They never served a day," Tamara snapped. The heat of her anger suddenly flared through her chest, so substantial that it hurt to breathe. "You said that they were punished for what they did to me, but they weren't! They never had to serve a day for what they did. They just went on, having another baby to abuse and letting him hit on the babysitters. How is that right?"

"Unfortunately, the justice system doesn't always impose what we would consider to be justice, does it?"

The answer was just a little too glib. How long had he been waiting for her to return to recite it? How many other girls had he said it to? Dr. Sutherland didn't care one bit about justice.

"They beat me and got me pregnant and neither one ever served a day!" Tamara raised her voice in outrage.

Dr. Sutherland studied her. "That wasn't fair to you, was it? But you were responsible for killing their children. I imagine the judge took that fact into account."

"They didn't care about those babies. They didn't care that they died."

He took a while to answer her. Tamara kept repeating the words to herself, justifying what she had done. She had saved Julie and Amy from the same fate as she had suffered. It hadn't been the best choice, she admitted, but she'd had her reasons. And Mr. and Mrs. Baker didn't care about them. Not really.

"Were you around when Mr. and Mrs. Baker found out about their children's deaths?" Dr. Sutherland asked.

"Him, not her. She was still out stripping. He was the first one to get home. In the evening, when he knew it would be just me and him and she wouldn't be around."

Dr. Sutherland either didn't catch her insinuation, or he ignored it. "And how did Mr. Baker respond when he found that his children were dead?"

"Only Corrine was dead. Julie wasn't, but she was sick. He attacked me, hit me and swore at me."

*As soon as she put it into words, she was back there.* As the cops had come back into the bedroom where Tamara was, there was a ruckus downstairs. Mr. Baker's voice, angry at the police for not letting him in, not telling him what was going on. Outraged and self-righteous.

Tamara gulped, frozen in place, looking at the policemen, Harney and Fram. "That's him. Mr. Baker. He's gonna kill me!"

"Nobody's going to hurt you," Harney, the cop who had been first on the scene, reassured.

"Let him up," Detective Fram called down the stairs. "I'll talk to him."

Tamara held on to the side of the crib to steady herself, terrified.

Mr. Baker came charging up the stairs. "What's going on here? What did that little tramp do?"

He pushed into the bedroom, restrained by Fram's hand on his arm.

"What did you do?" he demanded, seeing Tamara. "I leave you alone for a few minutes and come back to a house full of cops! What the hell is going on?"

Of course, he hadn't just left her for a few minutes; that was for the benefit of the police. Tamara had been there taking care of the babies since she had gotten out of school and Mrs. Baker had left for work.

"Mr. Baker," Fram said, pulling him back and trying to get his full attention. His voice was low and grave. "Mr. Baker... there's been a tragic accident."

The florid color drained from his cheeks. "An accident? What kind of accident?"

"I'm afraid that Corrine..."

"What? Where is she? What did she do to Corinne?"

Fram tried to hold Mr. Baker's attention. "Corrine drowned, sir. I'm very sorry."

Baker lunged towards Tamara. Fram held him back. Harney grabbed for him as well, pinning him between them.

"Get your hands off of me!" Baker shouted, trying to jerk

free. "I'm not going to hurt the little whore. I won't touch her. I want to make sure the baby's okay!"

"Julie's sleeping," Tamara whispered.

"I'm not talking to you. Let me go pick up my baby," he growled at Fram.

Fram and Harney slowly let him go. Tamara backed away from the crib, getting out of his way. Mr. Baker leaned over the crib and pulled back the blanket Tamara had covered Julie with. He let out a startled exclamation.

"What did you do to her? What's wrong with Julie?"

Harney jumped forward and looked at the baby. She lay there as Tamara had left her, flaccid, eyes dilated, lips blue, spit and vomit dripping out of the corner of her mouth.

Harney swore. "Are the medics still here?"

Fram shook his head. "I'll call them."

Then Mr. Baker went after Tamara with an incoherent shout of rage. Fram and Harney were too slow to stop the initial blow from connecting, but managed to pull him back after. Fram shouted for an officer to help and had Baker put in cuffs and taken back downstairs. Tamara was once again left alone with the police.

*"And you think that was an act?" Dr. Sutherland asked. "You think he didn't care?"*

Tamara tried to pull herself back to the present. She was shaken by the images and tried to push them away from her consciousness.

"Maybe he cared he wasn't going to have anyone left to abuse," she posited. "Or maybe he wanted to put on a good show for the cops. Maybe he just wanted to hit me one last time."

"When we talked about this before, you said that you believed he had some feelings for his little girls, but maybe not as deep as they should be."

"I thought... because he liked to cuddle them, and changed

their diapers and all... I didn't remember... that he... did that to them."

"Molested them."

Tamara's stomach turned. She tried to swallow back the acid rising in her throat. She did not want to throw up in front of him. She pressed her hand over her mouth, trying to keep her breakfast down.

"Why do you think you didn't remember that part?" Dr. Sutherland asked.

"It's..." Tamara shook her head. "It's awful. I couldn't believe it. I didn't want to think that he... did that to babies."

"Why didn't you tell the police?"

"The police didn't believe anything I told them. Why would I tell them that? If I said he did that to the girls, they might think that he... did that to me."

"He did."

"But I didn't want to tell. I just wanted them to let me go so I could get away. I still thought that they were just going to put me into emergency respite and I could run away, and then I could just be on my own and not have to worry about any parents, any home."

"You must have realized at some point that they had arrested you and were not going to let you go free."

"Yeah."

"But you still didn't tell them."

Tamara rubbed her head. She had sat in that dully painted room, no one to speak for her or support her, her thoughts so foggy and confused... she couldn't remember anymore what she had and hadn't told them. Maybe she'd told them everything and they just chose not to use any of it.

"I don't know."

"You don't know why you didn't?"

"I don't know if I did. Maybe I did. Maybe I told them."

"No. I don't think so."

"You don't know," Tamara protested. "You weren't there!"

"No, I wasn't. But I've been present at a lot of interrogations. And I don't think that you gave them that information."

"Would it have made any difference if I did? What would they have done? They still would have let the Bakers go scot-free."

"You don't know that."

Tamara slumped back in her chair, giving Dr. Sutherland full-on bad attitude. He ignored her body language and smiled politely.

"You are here because you wanted to see me today," he said. "Urgently, I understand. Here I am, controlling the conversation and not giving you the chance to talk. What was it you wanted to see me about?"

Tamara kept her silence for a full thirty seconds, but couldn't manage any longer than that. What if he signaled the guard to take her back to her room because she refused to talk?

"They've locked me up two days in a row," she complained. "I'm going crazy! I gotta walk around, get some air. They're not supposed to lock me up two days in a row, are they?"

Dr. Sutherland looked down at the folder in front of him, and Tamara wondered how much information he had about what had been going on the last few days.

"It's not my fault," she tried to head him off, "it's other girls threatening me. What am I supposed to do, wait for them to beat me up?"

"Why do you think these other girls are getting on your case? Why would they be threatening you?"

"I don't know. Maybe they're jealous, thinking I was having a good time on the outside. They gotta attack whoever is different. I don't know. You're the shrink."

"What happened today?"

"Tabby was threatening me in the showers. Dumas throws a

fit over it. Look what she did to me." Tamara pulled up her sleeve to show Dr. Sutherland the black bruise.

Dr. Sutherland grimaced. "Ouch. That looks painful. Did you go to the infirmary to have it looked at?"

"No. I've been locked in my room all day!"

Dr. Sutherland's eyes went to the clock on his wall. Tamara realized it was not even noon. While morning started early at juvie, 'all day' was obviously overdramatizing.

"All day yesterday and all morning today," she clarified. "I'm only here now because I kept telling them to let me see you right away."

"Yes. That was clever of you. So today, because Tabby was threatening you—with what? What did she have to say?"

Tamara shifted uncomfortably. "She didn't say what... she was getting in my face. Came over to me. She's not even supposed to talk to me in the shower and Dumas didn't stop her. She hit me for defending myself. I got the right to defend myself."

"The security staff are here to deal with any problems you might have. If Tabitha had attacked you, they would have defended you."

"So I should just take it? I should let myself get beaten up?"

"You were not beaten up."

Tamara pressed her lips closed. She wasn't getting anywhere with Dr. Sutherland. What she needed was for him to lift her segregation. Instead, he was focusing on all the wrong things. She covered her face with both hands and summoned tears. They came even more quickly than usual, as if they were waiting just under the surface, waiting for her to break.

"I want out," Tamara sobbed. "I can't stand being locked in my cell any longer. It's driving me crazy. I feel like... I'm going to fall apart."

Dr. Sutherland pulled a tissue from the box on his desk and handed it to her. He nudged the box closer to her so that she could take her own when the first wasn't enough. He waited for her to get control of herself before continuing with the session.

"Why don't you tell me what happened yesterday?" he suggested.

"Yesterday?" Tamara tried to reach back through the fog to remember what had happened the previous day. I seemed like it had been years ago. "It was... yesterday..."

Dr. Sutherland was looking down at the notes on his file. "I understand there was an incident in the canteen at breakfast."

Tamara tried to grasp it. Just a day before... it shouldn't have been so hard to remember.

"I was..."

"You apparently got into a fight with Lewis."

It came back. How could she have forgotten so quickly?

"They made me sit down at Lewis's table. I don't belong at her table, I'm not in her gang. She didn't like me being put there." Tamara shrugged. "I didn't start the fight, she did. Wouldn't have happened if they hadn't stuck me at that table."

"So *that* was the security staff's fault too."

Tamara didn't like the edge to his voice. "I didn't say it was their fault. It was Lewis, she wouldn't leave me alone. Didn't like me sitting there."

"You need to take responsibility for your part in these incidents, Tamara. You have been here for three years. You know how to handle these tensions. You never used to get into these kinds of fights."

"I used to have someone watching my back."

"I see."

He made a note on her file. Tamara tried to see what he was writing. What observation had he made that was so important it needed to be committed to paper? Was he making note of something that was wrong with her? His decision on whether to take her out of segregation or not? Something to follow up with the security staff about?

"I'm not going to get into one of the gangs," she told him, worried he was taking her words the wrong way. "I'm not looking to join up with someone. It's just... what am I supposed to do when someone is giving me grief? Just take it? Get beat up?"

"Maybe talk to a guard. Let them know what's going on. You can't just fly into a fight every time someone looks at you sideways."

"I'm not! But I'm sure as hell not going to wait until someone's got me pinned down before I fight back."

Silence drew out between them.

"Why do you think you're experiencing so much more opposition right now?" Sutherland asked finally. "Has that changed? Or has your reaction toward it changed?"

"You're acting like it's my fault," Tamara said sullenly.

"I'm inviting you to examine your own reactions. Is this something that has changed externally or internally? Are you being targeted or are you reacting differently?"

Tamara folded her arms across her chest. Things were not going as she had expected. Knowing how Dr. Sutherland felt about putting juveniles in isolation, she had assumed that it would be no challenge to persuade him to overrule the guards and order that her restrictions be lifted. But he wasn't acting like an ally. Instead of seeing she was in an untenable situation and needed to be let out of her cell, he was accusing her of being the problem. When all she had ever done was defend herself against others.

For the first time, she saw Dr. Sutherland as an enemy. Not just someone she had to meet with occasionally to prove her mental health. Not just an inconvenience. All this time, he had been her enemy and she hadn't even seen it. She stood up.

"Guess I'll go back to my cell, then."

Sutherland leaned back in his chair, eyebrows up. "I think we still have some more work to do here, Tamara. We're just starting to investigate what the problem might be."

"I see what the problem is." Tamara's face twisted into a sneer even though she tried to keep is smooth and impassive. It was no wonder the other girls were behaving toward her like they were, if Sutherland was feeding them his lies. He had been poisoning them against her.

"Are you sure you're ready to go?" Dr. Sutherland glanced in the direction of his desk drawer, where he kept the sweet treats that were a reward for finishing a session with him. He obviously intended to withhold her reward, since she was leaving of her own accord instead of waiting until he said they were done.

She wanted to grab the edge of his desk the same way she had grabbed the table in the canteen, and flip it right into his lap. That would show him. He'd see that she wasn't a little girl who could be pushed around and manipulated. She'd had men lie to her and manipulate her before. She wasn't going to fall for it again.

But the desk was big and solid, not a cheapie little particle board thing. It probably weighed two hundred pounds. She would cut a ridiculous figure trying to grasp the edge and flip it like the light canteen tables. Instead, she just stood like a statue, arms folded across her chest, waiting for him to release her.

"I am sorry you are having such difficulty, Tamara," Dr. Sutherland said in a soft, persuasive voice. "I wish that you would stay and work it out with me. I think we could make some progress on getting to the bottom of these issues and helping you to find another way to deal with your problems. But if you're not willing to..."

"You're not helping me. That's obvious."

"I would like to help, if you would let me in."

Tamara shook her head.

Dr. Sutherland made a motion and the door opened behind Tamara. She turned and walked out with the guard, seething, to return to her room.

TWO DAYS IN HER cell was more than enough for Tamara. She was up and waiting for the reveille bell again the next day. A junior guard who was patrolling the hall when she opened her door shadowed her. Tamara glared at him, irked by having someone in her space. He didn't pull back. Tamara didn't know the names of all of the new guards. Turnover was high and she only paid attention to the names of the guards who stayed there more than just a few weeks or months. She looked at his name bar.

"Back off, Calver."

At first, it looked like he was just going to pretend he hadn't heard her, but then he gave a little shrug and spoke. "I've been given my orders."

"To dog me?"

"To keep an eye on you, yes. Make sure that you're not harassed."

Tamara narrowed her eyes at him. She had her suspicions that he was not following her to make sure she wasn't harassed, but to make sure she didn't get herself into any more trouble. But there was no way to prove it one way or the other.

"Give me some space," she snapped. "I don't need you right on my heels. I got personal space, you know?"

He slowed, letting her get a little farther ahead of him. A knot tightened in Tamara's gut. The anxiety that had been building in her during her two days in her cell was not getting any looser with a guard on her heels. They might be able to prevent her from being bothered for a day or two, but once they backed off the personal guard assignment, she was going to be an even bigger target than she had been before. The other girls were not going to appreciate the staff showing special attention to Tamara by assigning her personal security.

She was lucid enough not to go to the library or yard before showers and the canteen again. She focused on keeping the schedule fixed in her mind so that she wouldn't do anything stupid. She went to the showers and glared at Calver again when he followed her in and stood by to watch her strip and shower.

"You mind?"

He shrugged and didn't leave or turn away. The little brown-noser had been given his instructions and he wasn't going to deviate one inch. Tamara was going to have his eyes on her all day. She couldn't assert that she wasn't going to start any trouble or be targeted in the showers, because that was just what had happened before.

Tamara turned her back to him to strip down and kept it to him as she stepped into the shower. She could have skipped her shower for one day, but then the staff would be flagging the change in behavior and wanting to know what was wrong with her.

There were whispers from the other girls as they observed that Tamara had a guard on her. She had an even quicker shower than usual, barely skimming the soap over her limbs and body. She stepped back out of the shower to grab a towel and dress.

There had not been a lot of girls in the shower, since she had been ready when the reveille bell had rung, but the canteen was another story. Everyone was either already there or would be once they finished dressing. After grabbing a piece of toast and juice, Tamara chose a seat away from anyone else and away from the tables where the gangs typically sat. She stared down at her tray, her jaw clenched, as everyone stared at her.

Lewis and the rest of the Sharks were out of segregation, as Tamara had expected. Lewis went out of her way to walk by Tamara, eyeing her and nodding. The rest of the Sharks followed suit, winding around the tables so that each one of them could walk past Tamara and glare at her. Tamara wasn't sure who it was, but one of them whispered to her as they filed by, and the others snickered.

Tamara turned her head to look at Calver and see if he had heard, but his eyes were elsewhere. He had one job and he'd already fouled it up, failing to hear the threat. Tamara banged the leg of the table she was sitting at, which drew Calver's attention back to her. He raised his eyebrow, wanting to know what was up. Tamara glanced to the side, at the Sharks who had just passed her. He studied them for a few moments, but they didn't appear to be a threat, so he shrugged it off and continued to watch elsewhere in the canteen.

Tamara coughed and again indicated the Sharks with her eyes, but he still didn't see any reason to be concerned. Tamara looked around for one of the more senior guards, someone who knew the political structure of the inmates and would know to keep an eye on the Sharks, but she couldn't catch anyone's eye. They all knew that Calver was supposed to be assigned to Tamara. Tamara put down what remained of her toast and sat back, watching and waiting for the end-of-meal bell.

By free time, it was obvious that Calver was already bored with his job. He yawned several times and whenever Tamara looked at him to see what he was doing, he was gazing off in the other direction, paying no attention to her. He was checking back in on her every few minutes, but he didn't see any threats and she wasn't starting any fights, so he didn't see any reason for concern.

Tamara walked toward the yard with him trailing several steps behind. She made an effort to keep her head up and be alert for any threats. She knew better than to stare at her shoes and just curl up within herself. She had to be tough and vigilant.

In the yard, she found her own space, away from the gangs, milling around the other independents, even though she wasn't friendly with any of them. Just because they weren't in the gangs, that didn't make them close. They didn't share or watch each other's backs. Tamara picked up a cigarette butt that someone else had left behind and walked over to Millican to have him light it for her. His brows drew down.

"Why not have Calver light it? He looks like he needs something to do."

"He's useless. He thinks this is all a game. That nothing is going to happen."

Millican took a slow look around the yard before returning his gaze to Tamara. "All quiet right now. You see or hear something?"

"The Sharks. They want me for dissing their boss. You think Lewis is just going to let that go?"

Millican glanced at Lewis, but didn't keep his gaze locked on her, didn't make it obvious that he was evaluating her. His eyes flicked back and forth to the other Sharks, the higher-ranking members.

"I'm not saying you're wrong," his words were carefully considered, "but I don't see anything. So Calver isn't derelict..."

"So maybe they don't do anything today. Maybe they wait for another day or two, until everyone lets down their guard." Tamara took a deep drag on the cigarette, knowing it wasn't going to satisfy her craving. Her heart was racing, but it wasn't because of the nicotine. "That doesn't mean the threat isn't real."

He gave a conciliatory shrug. "We can't read what's on

anyone's mind here. We can't tell what they're thinking or planning."

"Yeah. Exactly."

Calver realized that his protectee was talking to another guard and drifted over, his jaw clenched. "What's going on?" he demanded.

"Just doing a threat assessment," Millican advised. "Tell me what you see."

"I don't see anything."

"Really?" Tamara challenged. "Nothing?"

"Take it easy," Millican told her, before turning his attention back to Calver. "Come on. What do you see?"

Calver looked over the yard, teeth still clenched. Tamara didn't like the look in his eye. She moved away slightly, just an infinitesimal readjustment, orienting her body away from his.

"I see inmates in the yard," Calver announced. "No special threats. The same as always."

"Go on."

"With what? Who's here?" Calver was impatient. "Sharks, TMJ, other kids."

Millican raised his brows.

"Okay, yeah, French too," Calver said impatiently. "And you and me and two other guards."

"Threats?"

"One of the inmates could be armed. A shiv or some other homemade weapon. Or they could just use their bodies. Hands and feet. Several attack at once, overwhelm her."

Millican nodded. "Anything else?"

"No one is going to get over the fence. French isn't going to go after anyone, are you?" he sneered at Tamara.

"What's happened lately? What's likely?"

"Fight in the canteen. Fight in the showers. What of it? Neither one was in the yard."

"Who? You have to think about what happened."

Tamara reached the end of the cigarette and dropped it to the pavement, stepping on it and grinding it out. Both guards watched her, waiting. Tamara stared back at Calver.

"You don't think there's any real threat?"

"No. I don't see anything to be concerned about."

"You always need to be concerned in the yard," Millican warned. "If there's going to be a problem, this is one of the places it's likely to break out. Lots of people in a small place. Not much to do. Wanting to burn off some energy." He looked back toward the building. "Only one way in and out, that means it's a bottle-neck if something happens. Harder to get more guards in and the inmates out efficiently. Tempers boil over out here. Someone steps on someone's toes. Nudges someone. Decides to do something when it's harder for us to see."

Millican and Calver scanned the inmates again. Calver not so casual about it anymore.

"The fight in the canteen was with the Sharks," Millican said.

"And the one in the shower was with a TMJ," Calver said. He shrugged. "So what? What does that tell you?"

"It tells me the Sharks are the bigger threat."

Calver frowned. "Why?"

Millican raised his eyebrows. "Why? One girl versus a large portion of the gang. Fighting the leader of the gang where everyone else can see. Dissing her by dumping her breakfast in her lap and putting her on the ground. What do you think?"

"Oh." Calver cleared his throat. "Sure."

"They threatened me," Tamara tried to speak quietly and without moving her lips. So that no one nearby could see or hear her talking. She didn't look at the Sharks.

"What did they say?" Millican asked.

"I was right with her all morning," Calver protested. "There was nothing said. I can guarantee that."

Tamara's temper flared. "You haven't been paying any attention! How would you know?"

"Maybe I should just slam you back in your cell."

"What the—"

Millican nudged Tamara. Not a poke with his baton or anything threatening, just getting her attention.

"Now *you're* losing it," he warned. "You're not paying any attention to the threats. You're just focused on Calver."

Tamara realized instantly it was true and cut her tirade short. She looked quickly around the yard, checking for anyone who had moved or who was paying attention to her and the guards. Several girls looked quickly away. Tamara swore.

"Maybe you should go somewhere else," Calver suggested. "This doesn't seem like a bright place for you to be right now."

Tamara shook her head. She knew that running away would be the worst thing she could do. Glock had trained her mercilessly. If Tamara wanted to have a good rep, she needed to be there, right in the thick of things. She had to confront it straight on, or she would be deemed a coward and they would not leave her alone. Glock would have told her to watch for the first girl to look her in the eye and then smash her teeth in. That was how to get a rep in juvie.

But then, Glock wouldn't have had a personal guard standing there to make sure she didn't get in any trouble, either.

Tamara had to be content with watching for anyone to meet her eyes, and giving them a stare that left no doubt that she was coming after them when she was no longer being so closely guarded. A few Sharks looked in her direction, and quickly looked away from her angry glare. They started to talk among themselves, jostling each other and throwing only fleeting, tentative glances in Tamara's direction.

"What did they say to you?" Millican asked.

Tamara didn't look at him. She barely moved her lips and didn't speak above the buzz of the yard.

"Blood in the water."

FIVE

TAMARA MADE IT THROUGH the day. The next day was visitor day, which meant there was no yard time or other free time when they were allowed to hang out in the common areas or the library or participate in the crafts room. Instead, nearly all of the guards on duty were needed in the visitor rooms and inmates could choose between staying in their rooms or going to classes. Unless, of course, they had a visitor. Since Tamara had never had a visitor, that had never been an option.

She stayed in her room. The door was open so it wouldn't feel so claustrophobic. Inmates were allowed to leave their rooms only to communicate with their assigned unit guards. If, like a two-year-old repeatedly getting up to ask for a glass of water, an inmate took advantage of this liberty, she would be returned to their cell with the door locked, punishing both the offender and the offender's cell mate. So cellies tended to monitor each other to make sure they didn't both end up getting locked up.

Tamara was still on her own, so she didn't have to worry about a chatterbox cellie getting both of their privileges revoked.

She was startled when a shadow fell across her doorway. She

tensed instantly, preparing for an attack. But it wasn't one of the Sharks. It was Kirk.

"French, you've got a visitor."

Tamara just stared at him. She ran the words back in her brain and replayed them. She was sure it couldn't be true. She didn't get visitors. Who would want to visit her? She didn't have a soul in the world.

Was she hallucinating like she had when she was with the Bakers? She was sure that Kirk must have said something different, so she didn't respond, waiting for some indication of what he had really said.

When she had been on the outside after Vernon let her go, after she had taken Amy and was trying to avoid capture, she'd had visual hallucinations. At one point, when she had been yelling at Mr. Baker, telling him that he could never get Amy back again, trying to avoid his grip, he had vanished, leaving her alone in the middle of a busy intersection, holding the baby and screaming at bewildered motorists.

She had told herself then that she was just short on sleep. That happened when a person didn't get the sleep their brain needed. They went crazy. But her feeling of being on the edge of reality didn't go away when she got back into a normal sleep schedule at juvie. It eased a bit, but she could still feel herself on the verge of the precipice, about to take the plunge.

Kirk stood there, looking at her expectantly. Tamara looked back at him, waiting for him to start melting at the edges or fading away into static like a TV with bad reception. Eyebrows up, he raised his hands in a questioning shrug.

"Uh... *what?*" Tamara asked for clarification, hoping she wasn't talking to a ghost.

"You have a visitor." He pronounced it slowly and clearly as if she were deaf or stupid. He still didn't disappear.

"Who?"

He tilted his head. "French. Get your butt out of your bunk and come. I'm not your personal secretary."

Tamara got up slowly. She moved toward him and he stayed solid and substantial even close up. He moved out of the doorway and she followed him down the hall. She kept her eyes out for other guards who might actually be real and would take away her privileges if they found her walking in the hallway, talking to herself.

No one stopped them. Kirk opened the security doors with his code and escorted Tamara to the visitor room. She had to walk through an x-ray machine to prove she wasn't carrying any weapons and then he led her to a small meeting room. Not a wide-open visitor room like Minimum had, and not the little cubicles with bullet-proof glass between them and a telephone to talk to each other on. A small meeting room, where she was patted down, and then sat on the stained chair that looked like it had come from a garage sale or salvage store. She was not hand-cuffed or shackled. The door was shut and she sat there by herself, wondering what was going on. It had to be a dream, a new nightmare that she hadn't experienced before. Pinching herself and biting the inside of her cheek did not help. She didn't wake up from the strange dream.

The door opened again, and Mrs. Henson walked in. Tamara blinked at her. From strange to stranger. Mrs. Henson smiled.

"Tamara! How are you doing?"

Tamara just stared at her. Mrs. Henson didn't seem to know what to do with her hands. Maybe Tamara was supposed to hug her or shake her hand, but she was glued to her seat, unable to fathom what the strange dream meant.

"Uh—hi."

Mrs. Henson moved to the other side of the table and sat down. She leaned her elbows on the table, making herself closer to Tamara.

"It's nice to see you again. How are you getting along?"

"I'm... I dunno." Tamara had no script for the situation. She had no idea what she was supposed to say.

Mrs. Henson smiled. She brush a lock of blond hair back from her face. "I don't mean for this to be awkward. I just thought... I knew you weren't getting any visitors... and I couldn't imagine not ever having anyone from the outside to talk to. So I thought... I could visit you now and then, if you didn't mind."

"Okay... I guess so."

"Are you settling back in? You're looking better than you did. Your face, I mean."

The last time Mrs. Henson had seen Tamara was after Tamara had been beaten by Vernon and Sly. Bruised face, cut up inside and out, having had hardly anything to eat or any sleep. Taking care of the baby that was literally driving her crazy. Not Tamara's finest moment.

"I guess I'm better."

Mrs. Henson studied her for a minute, silent. "But maybe having some trouble settling back in?" she suggested.

"Yeah."

"I can't imagine how difficult it must be. Everything you've gone through over the last few months."

Tamara nodded.

"Do you have friends here?"

"No, no friends."

Mrs. Henson seemed at a loss for words for a moment. "How about classes? What is your favorite class?"

Tamara thought about it. Classes were something that she did to fill the time. Something other than sitting in her cell all day. She didn't have a favorite class or teacher. Most of the work was remedial, so boring that she felt like she was sitting in a kindergarten class. One of the teachers had tried to get her to sign up for some distance-learning college courses, but Tamara had just rolled her eyes and brushed it off. She wasn't advanced enough to be taking college courses. She wasn't even taking high school classes.

"I dunno. Maybe... English."

Mrs. Henson nodded. "I always liked English. Even when we had assigned books we had to read. I really enjoyed that part."

Tamara nodded. She looked around the room for a moment. Just a plain white meeting room, with the furniture and a camera bubble in the ceiling. Were they watching her talking to Mrs. Henson? Listening in? They were allowed to listen to visitor conversations, Tamara knew. Unless she was talking to her lawyer. And there was no reason for her to be talking to a lawyer. She'd never even had one come to see her.

"The girls have been asking after you," Mrs. Henson said. "They were very excited that I was coming to see you. They want to know how you're doing."

"Oh. Yeah. Say 'hi' for me, I guess."

"I will. They both send their love."

There was another lull in conversation. Tamara knew she should be doing better about holding up her end of the conversation. But she couldn't think of anything to say. She hadn't expected anyone to come and see her, and she hadn't prepared any conversation topics. What would she tell Mrs. Henson about? Fights in the showers? Losing track of the schedule that had been engraved into her brain for three years? How she seemed to be gradually falling to pieces?

"Have you heard anything? About... the Bakers? Do you know if... is he still in prison? And Mrs. Baker...?" Tamara took a deep breath, suddenly unable to get enough oxygen. "I just want to know... if they're..."

"I don't really know any details. As far as I know, Mr. Baker is still in prison. He wasn't given bail. Mrs. Baker... there's an investigation, but I don't know if they've made any determination."

"They didn't give Amy back to her, did they?"

Mrs. Henson hesitated. Tamara was afraid she knew the answer.

"I just don't know, Tamara. They wouldn't tell me anything like that. It isn't any of my business."

Tamara nodded. She looked down at the table.

"You know we're proud of you, don't you, Tamara? The way you helped Mr. Collins, back when... you were on parole. And coming to the house with the baby to try to make things right... Those were hard decisions. But you did the right thing. We're proud of you for that."

"Two decisions out of two hundred," Tamara sighed. "Yay, me."

"You can only make one at a time. Just keep moving forward."

"I guess."

"Is there anything... I could do for you? Or get for you?"

Tamara lifted her head. That was a benefit of having visitors that she hadn't thought about.

"You mean like cigarettes?"

Mrs. Henson shook her head. "That's not exactly what I was thinking, no. It's not even legal for me to buy you cigarettes."

Tamara considered this. "Other girls have them."

"I don't know who is buying them, or why the administration would be allowing them to be brought in. There are some very strict laws about supplying tobacco to minors. Even some of the adult prisons aren't allowing tobacco products anymore."

All of a sudden, Tamara was really craving a nicotine fix. Nothing like telling her she couldn't have something to make her want it more.

"Does the administration know the inmates have cigarettes?" Mrs. Henson asked, frowning.

Back when Glock had first gotten Tamara hooked, the inmates had been allowed to carry their own matches and lighters. But, of course, there had been problems with people using them for things other than lighting cigarettes. Then they had been banned and for a week no one could light up. All of the smokers were climbing the walls, many of them experimenting with other ways of getting their fix from the tobacco supplies they had. Glock had been a terror, and Tamara was sure that one reason the new policy had evolved was to get her calmed down. The guards in the yard carrying lighters became the new normal and things settled back down.

Were the senior administrators like Rice aware of the use and traffic of cigarettes within the facility? Tamara didn't see how they could not be. While there were progressively fewer inmates who smoked or had access to cigarettes, those who did couldn't hide the smell. The yard was always littered with cigarettes in spite of the prominent garbage receptacles. Cigarettes might not be available through the commissary, but the administration would have to be blind not to be aware of them.

Mrs. Henson was still looking at Tamara inquiringly. Tamara tried to pick up the thread of the conversation.

"I guess... they look the other way." She shrugged. "It's not like it's crack."

"It is still very detrimental to your health. Do you know how many kids die of oral cancers?"

Tamara shifted in her chair. She looked toward the door to see if Kirk or one of the other guards was nearby. She scratched the back of her neck.

"I could bring you other things," Mrs. Henson suggested. "I'll get a list of what's allowed."

Tamara shrugged. She hadn't had any personal items or allowance in the three years she had been there, so she was used to making do without any of the extras.

"Books?" Mrs. Henson suggested. "Something to help pass the time?"

"Yeah, sure. They only allow paperbacks. No hardcovers."

Mrs. Henson smiled. "Great! I'll pick something up for you, then. What do you like to read?"

"Anything. I've read all of what's in the library."

"I'll bring you something next time, then."

Tamara nodded. Mrs. Henson drummed her fingers on the table. "I'm hoping that we can help you get to a place where you can succeed next time you're paroled."

Tamara vaguely remembered Collins talking to her about the next time she could try for parole. He would talk to the parole board in her support. She had royally screwed up her parole the first time and she was sure the parole board would take into account the fact that she'd been part of a prison-break and kidnapping since then.

"That's nice of you... but I don't think I'm going to be getting out of here anytime soon."

"I know it seems like a long time, but before you know it, you'll be at the year mark and able to apply again."

"They're not going to approve me."

"If you demonstrate good behavior between now and then, show that you're back on the right track, they'll certainly consider it."

Tamara shook her head.

"You've got a good record. You've demonstrated remorse for your crime, you've followed the rules in detention and been a mentor for other inmates. Those are all things in your favor. Not everybody is able to make it the first try, but if we work with you, make sure you're more ready next time..."

*Tamara French has been a model inmate throughout her incarceration.* Had they really said that about her just a few months before? Tamara was quite sure that if she went before the parole board now, they would be presented with a very different point of view.

"Is something wrong, Tamara?"

"Just... don't count on it. Things are different now."

Mrs. Henson's eyes were searching. "What is it? I suppose since you've gotten so much time in the spotlight, maybe some of the others are giving you attitude. Are you being bullied? Is the administration giving you a hard time for what happened?"

Tamara rubbed the space between her eyebrows. "I dunno. Nothing seems... nothing is the same anymore. And I'm not..." She searched for a way to say that she wasn't a model inmate anymore. How many times had she been told that if she followed the rules she would get what she wanted? Obeying didn't mean she got justice. It just meant she was easier for the rule-makers to control. Just like Glock had said. Tamara didn't actually get any benefit out of it. "I'm... not that girl anymore."

She pressed her palms against her aching eyeballs. She had the uncomfortable feeling that she was back on the track she had been on before juvie. A girl who was trapped and could only escape by breaking the rules. By doing something awful.

"Do you want me to talk to someone?" Mrs. Henson suggested. "You sound like you could use some help... maybe some counseling?"

Talk therapy wasn't going to get Tamara anywhere. She had been talking for three years and it hadn't gotten her anything she wanted.

"No. I already do that."

"I'd like to know how I can help you, Tamara. I don't usually work with kids while they're still in juvie, but we've dealt with enough of them over the years that I think I have a lot to offer. I'm not going to be shocked by anything you say."

"I just... I don't need your help. Maybe you shouldn't come back. Just don't worry about me."

"I'm going to come back." Mrs. Henson put her hand over Tamara's on the table. "I'll bring you back some books and we'll talk again. Maybe then you'll be in a better mood."

Tamara shook off her touch.

"It's not just a mood."

SIX

S HE HAD SPENT A good deal of the day thinking about how to handle the threat from the Sharks. She knew that there was no point in relying on security or administration to deal with it. As much as they might think they could keep her from getting hurt, they couldn't watch her twenty-four hours a day. There were too many girls, too many opportunities for someone to get hurt.

Instead, she had to figure out how to address the threat herself. She would have to make the first strike. It would have to be good, because if she screwed it up they would just think she was weak and an even more attractive target. Gone were the days when she could rely on someone else to watch her back for her. She didn't want to be that girl anymore anyway, trading favors to hide behind someone who was bigger and stronger. Being small didn't mean that she was weak. Being one person didn't mean she couldn't stand up to the gang. But she had to be smart about it.

At breakfast, she sat down in one corner, with her piece of toast and roiling, knotted stomach, and watched the girls who sat down at the Sharks' table. She knew who they all were. Some had been there a couple of years. Some only a couple of weeks. None of them were old hands, there for as long as Tamara had been. So she had the advantage of experience over them.

Being an independent, a lone wolf, meant that she could get around without being noticed as easily as the gang girls. They usually had to move in groups. Being in a gang in juvie was supposed to make them stronger, like having a family, but it did put a big target on their backs as far as the guards were concerned. They had to always be aware of which gangs each of the girls was in, to watch for political tensions between them.

Perez said something to Lewis, who turned around to look at Tamara. Tamara easily adjusted her gaze to middle-distance, not focused on anyone in the gang, and in a few moments, Lewis turned back to her gang and continued her breakfast, unconcerned.

Tamara switched her focus to the back of Lewis's head, staring hard at her, transmitting enmity and loathing, seeing if she could make Lewis turn back around again with the intensity of her gaze. Lewis put her hand over the back of her neck as if blocking the stare. She moved her hand up to rub the back of her head. Several of the Sharks were swiveling to look at Tamara. As soon as Lewis's hand started to drop from her head, Tamara turned and looked in the other direction and, in her peripheral vision, was rewarded by the sight of Lewis turning around again to look at her, but finding Tamara was looking away. Let Lewis be paranoid about whether Tamara was watching her or whether her own gang was gaslighting her.

Meanwhile, Tamara was tallying the strengths and weaknesses of each of the Sharks, picking her target and her timing.

* * *

SHE WAS COUNTING on the Sharks waiting two days before coming after her. Just long enough for everyone to be letting down their guard, not long enough for anyone to forget what the retaliation was for. There was no lesson to be learned if the population at large didn't know what behavior Tamara was being punished for.

That meant that Tamara had only one day to plan her own approach.

She picked early afternoon. People had a post-lunch slump early in the afternoon. The sun was high in the sky so no one anticipated danger the same way they did when it started to get dark out or the return-to-cell bell rang. People were lazy and sloppy early in the afternoon.

Tamara watched Waterson break away from the main group of the Sharks and head to the bathroom. It wasn't far, and no one thought there was a need for her to be protected. Tamara left the room and headed in the direction of her own cell. Nobody paid any mind. She circled around and walked back in the direction of the toilets.

There was a blind corner, a little alcove a short distance away from the restroom door. Tamara picked up her speed and jogged along, silent in her worn, prison-issue tennis shoes. When she was almost caught up to Waterson, she slowed back down again, took a deep, calming breath, and called out.

"Hey! Hey, Waterson." She used a little voice, barely above a whisper, a scared girl, not a threat.

Waterson turned around. She looked at Tamara, and Tamara saw all concern fade from her expression. That was good. Lewis hadn't given her any reason to be worried about Tamara. Waterson gave a broad sneer.

"Frenchie. What are you doing here? Did you get lost?"

"Listen. I wanted to talk to you." Tamara looked around, as if she were afraid someone might overhear them. She drew closer to Waterson. Just a jump away from her. Waterson wasn't bothered. If anything, the sneer grew even more scornful.

"Talk to me about what? You're dead meat, don't you realize that, French?"

"No—I—can't I just talk to you? If I could explain, and you could tell Lewis..."

Waterson reached out a long arm and gave Tamara a shove. It wasn't even a hard shove, to show her who was boss. It was a weak, uncaring, unconcerned push, like she couldn't even be bothered.

"Tell Lewis? Why don't you tell Lewis yourself, princess? You think you got everyone here eating out of your hand. Why don't you have one of your pet guards talk to Lewis, if you're too scared?"

Tamara let herself be pushed again toward that alcove. That blind corner.

"It was a misunderstanding," Tamara whined. "It wasn't my fault. I never meant to..."

"You're so full of crap," Waterson exploded. "Maybe you didn't choose to sit there at our table, but you didn't have to do what you did. That was a mistake. A big mistake. And you're going to pay for it."

Waterson gave her another push. She stopped for a moment, as if realizing that she wasn't supposed to be confronting Tamara herself. The Sharks would have a plan of attack, all worked out and scripted. But with Tamara showing up like that, landing in her lap like ripe fruit, Lewis wouldn't expect Waterson to just ignore such a happy chance.

Tamara smiled at the ripe fruit metaphor, seeing Lewis and the others again, breakfasts in their laps, sticky and greasy and soiled.

Waterson saw the smile and there was a split second—a flash when she stopped, thinking that maybe she shouldn't do what she was doing. But Tamara was there. She was right there, isolated, defenseless, in a blind corner, practically begging Waterson to teach her a lesson. Waterson gave Tamara one more hard shove, driving her into that alcove, her back banging into a closed and locked door, cornered and completely at Waterson's mercy.

Waterson wound up, telegraphing her punch, wanting Tamara to suffer in anticipation. But the blow never landed. Tamara moved inside Waterson's reach, getting up close to her and bringing the shiv in home under the bigger girl's ribs.

Waterson looked shocked. She reached for Tamara's hand, instinctively trying to remove the thorn and cover the wound. But it was too late for that. Tamara knew where to strike.

There was blood on her hand, warm and sticky. But there was no spray, like when Zobel had been slashed. All of the damage was deep inside; the blood dripped from the wound, it didn't spurt.

Waterson grasped Tamara's hand with more strength than Tamara would have thought she would have, trying to pull her away. Tamara obliged, pulling the shiv from the wound and watching Waterson fold over, gasping and groaning, trying to hold the life force in and failing miserably. Waterson was on her knees and then on the tile floor, with barely a protest.

Tamara's head spun. It was like she was two different people. The one who knew what she had to do to protect herself and make sure that no one came after her and the one who was horrified and sickened by it. That was what they had driven her to. That was what they had made her into. It was *their* fault.

Tamara waited in the silent hall, weighing her next action.

In the end, she decided to stay there. She would watch and wait and see who came down the hallway next. Another Shark, a guard, or an inmate not associated with the Sharks, and she would react accordingly. Tamara went into the restroom and stood just inside the doorway, holding the door open so that she wasn't visible from farther down the hallway, but would be able to see who was coming.

And just like a higher power was watching over her, the next person along was Tabby. How perfect was that? Tabby was both Waterson's enemy and Tamara's.

Tabby first saw Tamara, standing in the doorway, and then Waterson's form lying in the alcove. The two sights at once were apparently more than she could process, because she got stuck looking from one to the other and back again, her mouth open, voiceless and paralyzed.

"She's faking," Tamara said. Ridiculous, of course, given the amount of blood pooled around Waterson and the shocking blue pallor of her skin, but Tabby wasn't thinking straight. It was just one more wrench thrown into the gears to prevent Tabby from sorting out what was going on in the split-second she had. And she made the wrong choice, turning toward Waterson to make sure that she was really, truly dead or dying, and that she wasn't somehow a threat, just lying in wait for someone to come along and fall into her trap.

The shiv was still in Tamara's hand. She patted Tabby on the back. She buried the shiv as far as it would go, not sure how far she had to drive it in to hit something vital from that position. And in a moment, Tabby's body was over Waterson's.

Tamara moved quickly, patting at Tabby to find the weapon that she knew the girl would be carrying. She wouldn't be a cat without claws. There wasn't time to think through if the scenario would make sense or not, she just pressed both shivs into both girls' hands, contaminating them both with the fingerprints and blood of the other. She pushed the bodies around the best she could, both of them bigger and heavier than she was, so that it would look like they had been fighting each other.

Her heart was pounding hard and fast. Tamara went into the bathroom and washed up at the sink, getting every speck of blood off of her hands and checking her uniform for any telltale spatter. Then she made herself scarce.

SEVEN

TAMARA DIDN'T THINK IT would be very long until the bodies were discovered. She had been lucky not to be caught in the act; it was a well-trafficked hallway with the restroom right there. As she fled the scene, she was expecting the general alarm bell to ring any minute. But it didn't. She was several halls away before she forced herself to slow down, to walk at a normal pace and breathe slowly and evenly as if she weren't running for her life. Waterson and Tabby. A two-for-one. She'd never anticipated being so lucky. And a clean getaway.

If Glock and Vernon could only see her now.

For a minute, that thought sent her into a tailspin of shame and self-disgust. She clenched her fists and ground her teeth, reminding herself that she had done what she had to survive. She had struck first because that was the only way for her to go up against the Sharks. Eliminate one of theirs before they could get on solid footing.

It had worked out even better than she had expected. Throwing suspicion elsewhere. Making the Sharks and the TMJ look at each other instead of at Tamara. No one was going to suspect Tamara of killing both of them.

She paced up and down an empty hallway, waiting for the general alarm to sound, hardly believing that they could take so long to find the two girls.

And then screaming. Distant, but unmistakable—a girl's shriek. Tamara steadied herself, one hand on the wall, trying not to see the bodies again in her mind's eye. She had done what needed to be done. Waterson and Tabby wouldn't haunt her dreams like Corinne and Julie. They weren't innocent. They could just as easily have killed Tamara.

The general alarm came a long time after the scream. Maybe it was only thirty seconds while a guard hurried over to see what she was screaming about and hit his panic button. Then the loud siren whooped and Tamara heard the electromagnets on all of the hallway doors release, and the heavy doors fall together to seal off every section of the wing. It was only a matter of time. The guards would sweep each section to gather up all of the girls and take them all back to their cells. It was a general lockdown and would probably last at least two days while they investigated.

Two more days locked in her cell. Tamara was not looking forward to it, but it was two days that she would be safe. At least she didn't have a cellie to share the air with, both of them going stir crazy.

Tamara paced up and down the hallway between the sealed security doors, unable to stay still. She tried to breathe evenly, but found herself gasping like an asthmatic. Her head spun. She felt sick to her stomach. She shouldn't have eaten lunch before putting her plan into action but, having missed dinner the day before, she couldn't risk being reported for missing another meal within twenty-four hours. Dr. Eastport was nothing to be scared of, but spending time in the infirmary would be seen as weak. It might even be seen as running away from the Sharks, not just weak, but a yellow coward.

It was Gomez who conducted the sweep through the hallway Tamara was stuck in. He punched his code into the keypad to unlock the door and scowled at her. "What are you doing all the way over here?"

Tamara glanced around. He was right. It wasn't close to her cell or the common areas or the classrooms. It wasn't close to any of the areas she should legitimately be in.

"What happened?" she asked, throwing a quaver into her voice. "I heard screaming. I didn't know what was going on. I didn't know where to go. I just wanted... to get away, somewhere safe."

He motioned to her impatiently. "On the wall," he instructed, not deigning to tell her what was going on. Maybe he knew that two girls had been killed and maybe he didn't, but he wasn't giving Tamara any information. Tamara turned her back to him and put her hands on the wall, feet spread apart and back, the movements routine, automatic. She felt calmer as he checked her position and then patted her down. It wasn't just the usual quick once-over, but a thorough search, one that would have turned up any weapon, if Tamara had still been carrying one. Then he pulled her hands behind her, one at a time, with a pause in between, and Tamara could picture him checking her hands for anything unusual. Any cuts. Any smears of blood. Anything that would indicate she had just been in a fight.

"What happened?" Tamara asked again, trying to keep him distracted. "Someone was screaming. Was there a fight?" She forced a little laugh. "Or did someone see a spider?"

Gomez snorted. It was a running joke in the facility since Cammy, former leader of the Sharks, had one day triggered a general alarm when an eight-legged critter had landed on her pillow. Big as a dinner plate, if she were to be believed, but Tamara figured it was probably nothing more than a regular house spider. Cammy had been a big girl, with broad shoulders and prominent muscles. Tamara was pretty sure that she must have had to take steroids to get that cut. When she'd asked Glock about Cammy, Glock had said that Cammy was 'about as tough as she looked.' And she looked plenty tough. But apparently scared of a critter no bigger than a dust ball.

"No spider," Gomez told Tamara. He pulled her away from the wall and started back toward her cell.

"Is it bad, then? Is it something really bad?"

"Just shut up, French. You know I can't tell you anything."

Tamara let him push her along until it looked like he was going to take her right through the crime scene. She resisted.

"Keep going."

"Something is going on," Tamara insisted. She couldn't see it through the window of the next security door, but she pretended she could, because there was no other way to tell him that he was about to make a huge mistake by taking her through there.

Gomez moved past Tamara, still holding on to her arm, and pressed his face up to the window, straining to see whatever it was that Tamara had seen. They couldn't really see anything, but Tamara could hear someone barking orders and a bustle of noise that just wasn't routine for juvie. Gomez clicked the radio on his shoulder, still straining to see through the door. They could see a couple of the security staff farther down the hall, but most of the activity was around the corner.

"Clear me for corridor three-west," Gomez said into his radio. He released the button and waited for a response.

"Negative," the response came back. "Three-west is quarantined."

Gomez swore. "Couldn't tell me that ahead of time, could you?" he muttered. But he didn't say it to the guard in the control room. He looked around and took Tamara back to the last door they had come through, punching in his code again to backtrack and detour around the restricted corridor. Tamara watched his fingers fly over the keypad. Normally, she didn't pay much attention to the security codes that each of the guards used to access locked areas. Normally, she wasn't in an area that was locked, and if a guard had to use his code, it was a quick, one-time affair. But Gomez had to take her through a dozen doors to get her back to her cell. They should have switched to a swipe card or a proximity key. That was what a lot of the prison facilities were doing. But cards and keys could be grabbed by inmates and a memorized numeric code could not.

Eventually, they returned to Tamara's cell and Gomez motioned her in.

"General lockdown," he explained. Not that she needed any explanation. Tamara had been there long enough to know the sound of the alarm and what it meant.

"How long?"

"How do I know that? My job right now is to get everyone back to their rooms. I haven't been told anything else."

"Did somebody get killed?"

She knew it was a mistake before the words left her mouth, but she couldn't stop them. Gomez looked at her, frowning, brows drawn down.

"Did somebody get killed?" he repeated. "Nobody is saying anything about anyone getting killed. Obviously whoever was screaming was alive and well." He gave her another long stare before closing her cell door and checking the handle to make sure that the latch had engaged properly. Tamara looked at the security keypad on the inside of her cell, and lay down on her bunk.

## EIGHT

F RENCH! FRENCH, WAKE UP! Hey!"

Tamara tried to pull away from the insistent shaking. She had slept through reveille bell again. That shouldn't matter, though, because they were on general lockdown and breakfast would be brought to the cells rather than taking it in the canteen. But maybe he was waking her up because he had brought her breakfast.

Tamara tried to rub her eyes, but the guard had a firm grip on her bruised left arm, and Tamara couldn't pull away.

"I'm awake," she groaned. "Just leave it there."

"Wake up!"

Tamara wanted to turn over and go back to sleep again, but she felt like she was floating. She wasn't even lying in her bed. She tried to force her eyes open to get her bearings. They were heavy and sticky with sleep and didn't want to open in the brightness of the room.

Tamara squinted and blinked, trying to clear her vision and get her eyes open wide enough to take in her surroundings.

"What—?" She shook her head. "Where am I?"

He gave her another shake for good measure, squeezing the tender bruise. "You're sleepwalking."

That didn't make any sense.

Eyes still squeezed most of the way shut, Tamara looked around. She was in a corridor. Not in her cell. How could she be sleepwalking in the corridor?

"Where am I?"

"Three-west," the unfamiliar guard growled.

"Three..." Tamara trailed off.

"How the hell did you get here?"

"I... don't know."

"You're not allowed to be here."

She didn't know why he felt the need to tell her that. Obviously, she wasn't supposed to be there. She was supposed to be in her cell, asleep.

"You brought me here," she said.

"I didn't bring you here. You were wandering. Sleepwalking. On your own. Nobody brought you here."

"But I can't..." Tamara shook her head, trying to wake herself up and make sense of the situation. "I can't... the doors are locked."

"Well, that's what I thought. But apparently, you can walk through locked doors. Or jimmy them. I don't know how else to explain it."

She tried again to pull her arm out of his grasp. "Let go. You're hurting me."

He released her, his face twisted into a sneer. Then he saw the black and yellow bruise, and didn't ridicule her for being oversensitive. Tamara used both hands to rub her eyes.

"Can I go back to my room?"

"I'd like to see how you're getting through those doors."

Tamara walked up to the nearest locked door and looked at it. She tried the handle, but it was locked, as it was supposed to be. She pressed random numbers on the keypad.

"I don't know how I got here," she repeated. "You must have brought me."

"I didn't." His voice was a growl.

Tamara looked at her hands and wiped them on her uniform. "This place creeps me out." The bodies and blood had been cleaned up. There was no crime scene tape. Smudges of fingerprint powder were the only evidence there was a crime scene. Still, Tamara didn't want to be there.

She could still see where the girls had been.

Waterson's eyes when she realized she'd been stabbed.

The guard grabbed her by both shoulders. Tamara realized that she had been tipping over, nearly fainting. She righted herself, trying to focus on staying balanced instead of the flashbacks.

"I'm just tired. I need to go back to bed..."

The guard relented. He punched his code into the keypad and the door unlocked. They walked in silence back to Tamara's cell. Tamara watched as he punched the last keypad to open her cell door. She walked in, heading for her bed. She had no clue what had just happened. She just knew she wanted to get back to sleep.

She knew he was still standing there, even after she climbed into bed and pulled the blanket over her head. She could feel him watching her.

He stood there for a long time.

THE SECOND WAKENING was not identical to the first. Rather than a hand on her arm and commands to wake up, she was being pushed into the wall, into position to be frisked. Angry curses.

"What the hell is going on?"

Tamara should have been the one asking, but she was not.

Voices on the radios, but no general alarm. The unit was already under lockdown; there was no benefit to sounding the alarm. More feet and voices. Tamara was being held in position and didn't try to look around. She tried to pry her eyes open to see where she was, but she didn't want to know. Didn't want to hear that she was in three-west again.

The night security was a skeleton staff. Funding cut-backs meant as small a payroll as possible, so after lights-out, they didn't have the forces to handle anything other than routine disturbances. A fight between cellmates, somebody sick with the flu or appendicitis, a greenie crying for her mama.

"What are we supposed to do with her?" one of the guards demanded.

"She's not trying to escape. She's sleepwalking."

"Sleepwalkers can't unlock sealed security doors!"

Someone snickered. "Apparently..."

"She won't stay in her cell. She should be put in the isolation unit."

"What difference is that going to make?"

They talked in circles without coming up with a solution. Tamara tried to shake off the conversation as it buzzed around in her head.

They finally came to some kind of agreement. What it was, Tamara really wasn't awake enough to process. They pulled her away from the wall, handcuffed her, and escorted her through the corridors again.

Not back to her cell, but to the isolation block. Tamara waited at each sealed door for them to punch in the security code and go through. The isolation unit had apparently already been informed of the situation before her arrival.

"She needs to be searched before she's put in a cell," said Enfield, the guard who was in charge of the isolation unit for the night. The only one of the guards on duty that night who was senior enough for Tamara to know his name.

"Already searched her," one of the others said.

"Not a pat-down. A real search."

The younger guard swore, annoyed.

"Did you have somewhere else to be?" Enfield demanded. "Planning a nap, were you?"

"No," the guard who had complained was sullen. "I just don't think there's a need for all that bother."

"Obviously, if you can't keep her in a cell in the quarters, there is."

"She hasn't got a key. She couldn't open these doors with a key."

"She's getting around somehow."

Tamara was rerouted to a small room to be strip-searched, which was incredibly annoying when all she wanted to do was sleep. She was half dead on her feet. They didn't find anything in the search. There was nothing to find. Then she was taken to an observation cell.

Big windows, unlike her cell in the living quarters. It was like being a fish in a tank. The cell was bare, not even a pillow or blanket on the bunk. At least they had given Tamara her clothes back. She lay down on the bunk, her back to the big windows, and closed her eyes, seeking to find sleep one more time.

* * *

THE GENERAL LOCKDOWN continued the next day, as Tamara had been sure that it would. But for her, there was no peace. If she'd had her choice, she would have been sleeping in her usual cell, having a quiet breakfast and lunch brought to her on trays, spending the day sleeping to catch up after all of the disruption of the night before. Instead, she was in a meeting room similar to the one she had talked to Mrs. Henson in. Two chairs, one square table, a camera bubble in the ceiling.

"Why do I have to sit here?" Tamara complained.

"Because you're a security risk," a high-ranking security guard called Buxton snapped. She didn't know him; she gathered he worked with administration and maybe in the control room.

"Why can't I just be in my bunk or iso? This is stupid."

"I have questions for you and we're going to have more questions for you as the day goes by. I want you here where you're secure."

"Why is this more secure than iso?"

He just stared at her, his face as blank as a brick wall. She wasn't getting anything out of him. She had been planning to ask him about the lockdown to see if he would tell her about Waterson and Tabby, but she abandoned that idea. He wasn't going to be the one to leak it.

"How about you tell me how you got out of your cell last night?"

"I don't know. Must have been one of the guards. I don't know the codes to get past the locked doors."

"You're telling me that one of the guards released you from your cell and through each of the doors back to the quarantined corridor."

"I couldn't have done it myself. I don't know the security codes."

"That's ridiculous."

"How else would I get through the locked doors?"

"You tell me."

Tamara folded her arms across her chest. "I was sleeping. I don't know what happened."

"I've got my staff checking the cameras and unlock logs, so I'll have all of the details in a few minutes. Why don't you just tell me?"

"I don't know anything."

"Because you were *sleepwalking*," he sneered.

"I don't know. I guess."

"You've been here for three years, sleepwalking has never been a problem before."

Tamara didn't say anything.

"What would make you start sleepwalking after three years?"

"I dunno. I've been segregated most of a week... maybe my subconscious doesn't like being cooped up."

"How did you get through the locked doors?"

"I don't know."

One of the other guards opened the door of the meeting room and motioned to his boss. Buxton went to him, stepping out into the hall but not closing the door all the way. Tamara saw papers passed from the younger guard to Buxton. Their heads both bent over them, studying the data.

"You have video that matches up?" Buxton demanded.

"Yes. Just getting copies compiled right now."

"And what do they show? Who was keying the codes?"

"She was doing it herself."

"No one with her at any time?"

"Not until she was returned to her room. Like he reported."

"And then..." Buxton glanced over his shoulder at Tamara, then continued the conversation in a lower voice. Exactly what was he afraid that she would hear? If they thought she had done something wrong and somehow pulled something over on security, then she would already know all of the details they were discussing.

When he finished the conversation, Buxton returned to the table. He threw the papers down and looked at her. Tamara knew he was trying to use his height to intimidate her. Even if he hadn't been taller—and he most certainly was—he had the advantage over her. She had to sit and listen to whatever he had to say while he was allowed freedom of movement.

"So, can I go back to my room now?" Tamara demanded.

"You're not going anywhere."

He looked at the papers in front of him. Several columns of numbers, densely written, too far away for her to make any sense of.

"What code were you using to open the security doors last night?"

Tamara shrugged. "I don't remember anything. I don't know what happened."

"What is Gomez's security code?"

Tamara had wondered whether they would have records of which codes were used to open which doors. Apparently, they did.

"I don't know."

"You used it last night."

"I didn't."

"Yes, you did. We have video of you unlocking the doors, synchronized with which code was used to open the door. You used Gomez's security code to unlock the doors last night."

Tamara didn't respond. He hadn't exactly asked her anything. It was best to keep her mouth shut.

"Did Gomez give you his code? Were you supposed to meet him last night?"

"No."

"Was he supposed to be in that hallway? A little assignation at the crime scene? Did that sound exciting to you?"

Tamara shook her head in disgust. She knew there were relationships between guards and inmates. Strictly prohibited by the facility, of course, but they could never completely quash illicit activities. Tamara had never responded to overtures from any of the guards and Gomez had never made any toward her. As far as she knew, he had never been involved with any of the inmates. The guards who got involved didn't usually last long. Juvies had loose lips. They weren't good at keeping secrets. Gossip spread like wildfire.

"I never did anything with Gomez. Or any of the others."

She thought she detected relief in his eyes and a little dip in his shoulders. He didn't want to hear that there was anything inappropriate going on with his staff. Tamara could well be lying, but he was happy to hear the denial.

"Why did he give you his number, then?"

"He never gave me his number."

"No. You just guessed it. Pulled it out of thin air."

"I don't know it."

"Give me a guess."

"No idea."

"And then you got Durham to give you his number."

"Durham?"

"The guard who took you back to your cell the first time. You just turned around and used his number after he was gone."

Tamara shook her head.

"I don't even know him. Why would he give it to me?"

THEY BROUGHT in a video machine and played the footage they had compiled. Tamara watched with fascination. She was surprised to see that her eyes were open. She remembered the heavy-lidded, sticky feeling when Durham had woken her up. She would have sworn that her eyes had been shut.

But on the screen her eyes were open. Squinted like the light bothered her, but open. She approached the keypad at the end of the corridor her room was in and tapped in the numbers without hesitation. The door unlocked and she walked through. The scene jumped to another camera on another door. Tamara stopped for a moment, a guard walked by the other side of the door, and after he was gone, she pressed the buttons and headed in the direction that the guard had come from.

Buxton shook his head at her boldness. "This isn't the first time you were out, was it?"

"If I'd been sleepwalking before, wouldn't you have caught me before? I'm not exactly avoiding the cameras," Tamara pointed out, watching herself on the screen.

He pursed his lips, not disagreeing. She *had* been caught twice in one night. That wasn't exactly covert.

Tamara's anxiety built as she watched herself drawing closer and closer to the quarantined hallway. She was finding it hard to breathe. Even though she knew that everything had been cleaned up—after all, she'd seen it the night before—she was sure that the next camera was going to show a picture of the dead girls, their blood black on the floor.

But then Durham had intervened. He shook her awake. Tamara watched herself blinking drowsily, blank-faced as a zombie. She resisted Durham's grasp, tried to pull away, and spoke little. At least she looked as confused on the screen as she had felt at the time. Anyone could see how muddled she was.

They watched the reverse route, Tamara being taken back to her room and locked in. They watched Durham standing outside Tamara's door, looking in the observation window at her. Then eventually, he withdrew, returning to his patrol.

Tamara looked over at Buxton for his reaction or for a clue as to what was going to happen next. The fact that his eyes remained intent on the screen instead of looking at her for her reaction meant there was still more to come. And really, she already knew that. She hadn't stayed in her bunk, but had eventually ended up in isolation.

They watched the screen. In a few minutes, Tamara's face showed up in the window of her door, looking up and down to see if Durham was still there. Then she reached over to the keypad and punched in a code, letting herself out.

"Now you're using Durham's number," Buxton said.

Tamara shook her head. "I don't know Durham's number."

"You obviously do."

"I don't." Tamara motioned toward the screen. "I didn't talk to him. He didn't give it to me. You would have seen."

Buxton watched the image on the screen without acknowledging the fact. The guards had obviously been put on the alert and Tamara didn't get nearly as far from her cell the second time around. A few corridors away, and she was again caught by a guard. Frisked, other guards brought in to help sort out a plan of action, then a couple of clips of her being marched to the isolation unit, where she was searched and put into the isolation cell. Tamara thought that was the end of the video, but Buxton still didn't look at her. She turned her eyes back to the screen. Through the big observation window, she watched herself get out of bed again and walk up to the number pad. Before she could tap a number in, a guard opened the door, grabbed her by the arm, and took her back to the bunk.

Then the tape ended. Buxton turned his gaze on her. His eyes were cold, no indication that he felt any sympathy for her or the situation she now found herself in.

"You tried to get out of the isolation cell how many times?"

Tamara gestured toward the screen. "Just once."

He shook his head. "Try again."

"Well... I don't know. You only showed me once."

"I don't need to tell you what you did."

"I was asleep."

"You were very active for someone who was asleep."

"I don't know what happened. Just what you showed me on the tape."

"You still tried to get out of the isolation cell another three times."

Tamara rubbed her forehead. "It's no wonder I'm so tired."

"You think this is a joke? You think that's funny?"

"I... I wasn't joking. I was just saying. I'm tired. I feel like I was up all night. And I guess... I was."

"Stop playing games with me!" Buxton shouted, smacking one palm down on the table with a sharp crack.

It made Tamara jump, but it didn't alarm her. How many times had she put up with Glock's flares of temper? How many times had she been sitting there minding her own business when a fight broke out only inches from her? He wasn't going to break her down by abusing the table.

She didn't protest. She just sat there and looked at him. Buxton whirled around and marched toward the door. Then, like he had changed his mind, he turned around to face her again.

"Have you ever sleepwalked before?"

"Uh..." Tamara thought about it. Not as a child. She'd been shifted around between her Gram and various other relatives, but even in all of the upheaval, she hadn't sleepwalked. She'd sometimes woken up disoriented, not sure where she was, but she'd always been in her room. Whatever room that happened to be. Then with the Bakers... Tamara closed her eyes and rubbed her temples, trying to conjure the memories up. It was a time she had tried to forget. She had done the best she could to keep from thinking about the Bakers and remembering how things had been at their house. But in those last few weeks or months... "Maybe... I think... I think when I was with the Bakers I might have. She'd beat me... say it was because I was trying to run away... I couldn't figure out why she kept accusing me of stuff I didn't do."

"How long ago was that?"

"Before I came here. Three years..."

"What did you say when she would accuse you of trying to run away?"

"Nothing... tell her that I didn't. What else was I supposed to do?"

"You didn't think that maybe you'd been sleepwalking?"

"No."

"Do you think you did?"

"I don't know." Tamara shook her head. "Wouldn't I know if I was sleepwalking?"

"What do you think you were doing last night?"

Tamara shook her head, frustrated. "I wasn't awake... so I guess I was sleepwalking... but I wasn't dreaming. Aren't people who are sleepwalking supposed to be dreaming?"

"How would I know? Do I look like a shrink?"

Tamara bit back a smart reply. He could have been a shrink. What did a shrink look like? They didn't all look like Freud or Dr. Sutherland.

"I'm tired. Can't I go to bed now?"

"I don't think you'd better. Stay up today so you'll be extra tired at bedtime. Maybe then you'll sleep through the night."

"I can't stay up all day. I'm too tired. I need to go to sleep."

"You're staying here."

"Why do I have to stay here? Why can't I go sleep where I was last night?"

"Because we want to keep an eye on you."

## NINE

I T WASN'T MORE THAN an hour or so later that the guards were brought into the room. Gomez, Durham, and a sprinkling of other guards Tamara supposed had been involved in her capture the night before. It was a small meeting room and quickly became crowded, the air getting hot and laden with sweat and body odor. Tamara gagged. How fast would they clear the room if she threw up her breakfast? What did Buxton think he was going to accomplish, stuffing them all into the room like sardines in a tin?

Tamara breathed through her mouth, trying to avoid smelling all of the bodies and to prevent herself from being sick. She could barely get enough oxygen in the crowded room.

Buxton called the room to order. He was no orator, snapping at them to all shut up and pay attention. The room went still, all speculation ceasing. There were still questioning glances in Tamara's direction, but no one said anything to her. Buxton operated the buttons on a remote control to bring the TV back to life again and start playing the recording. Guards watched with open mouths as they saw Tamara moving through the hallways, opening doors at will. There were some glances exchanged back and forth, everyone wondering whether they were somehow to blame.

Buxton didn't play the entire recording for them like he had for Tamara. He switched over to another recording, and Tamara saw herself again, this time being escorted by Gomez. Tamara's movements were jerky. Lots of hand movements when she talked. She was clearly anxious or upset. Gomez was calm. There might have just been a double-homicide, but no one would have recognized it by his expression or his actions. Buxton paused the recording and pointed at Gomez tapping his code into the number pad.

"What are you doing there?" he challenged.

Gomez looked at the screen and then looked at Buxton like he was crazy.

"Taking her back to her cell," he said. "It was a general lockdown. It's my job to put them back in their cells."

"You're punching your code into the keypad."

"Yeah."

"She's standing right beside you."

"Yes."

"You're not making any attempt to shield the code from her sight."

Gomez swallowed. He looked around the room. They suddenly all knew why they were there. They were all going to be called on the carpet for their involvement in the breach of security.

"It's never really been an issue," he said. "The codes are six digits. You enter them quickly, no one can really see what the number is..."

"How many locked doors did you go through taking her back to her room?"

"Uh..." Tamara could see Gomez trying to estimate. He was sweating heavily. The whole room was rank with sweat. The smell of fear. "I would guess... maybe... five."

She felt bad for him. But there was nothing she could do to help him. There was no alternative theory she could provide for how she had gotten his number. She couldn't deny that she had seen his number. They had all watched her entering his number as she went through each door.

"You might be closer if you doubled that."

"Okay. Ten, then."

"You gave her a chance to see your number more than ten times."

"I guess. I never really thought about it that way," Gomez admitted.

"And not once did you attempt to shield the number from her."

"No. I guess not," Gomez admitted.

A collective sigh went around the room. Like everyone had been holding their breaths to see if he had some explanation or excuse. But if he said straight out that he hadn't been trying to shield his code from Tamara, then everybody else could admit to being in the same boat. He was a senior guard, experienced. If he had made that mistake, anyone could have.

Buxton wasn't willing to let it go at that. He jumped to the next video. Durham this time. Also escorting Tamara back to her cell. Also punching his security code into the keypad with complete disregard to whether his detainee could see it or not. Tamara appeared to be sleepy and bleary-eyed, but her subconscious had still picked up on it, storing it away for her next chance at escape.

"It never occurred to any of you idiots that you were giving her your security code?" Buxton challenged, his voice rising into a harangue. "Not one person thought that maybe she kept getting out because she knew someone's security code? And that if she knew someone else's, maybe you ought to protect yours?"

Buxton hadn't dared yell at Gomez, a senior guard, but he was going to make sure that everyone else in the room got their due. Durham was red-faced. He looked down, throat working. Gomez raised both of his hands in a calming gesture.

"Look... we get it. We screwed up. This has never happened before. We enter those numbers all day long, and normally there isn't anyone close enough to see what they are. Even if I am escorting someone, I rarely have to go through more than one security lock to get them where I'm going. It's hard to tell with any accuracy what number someone has entered on a PIN pad. Six digits is pretty safe. This was a unique case... a lock down... an inmate that was far from where she should have been at that time." He looked briefly at Tamara, then back at Buxton and the rest of the room. "We'll know better now. We'll be more careful."

"In the meantime, you've facilitated a huge security breach."

Tamara put her elbows on the table and rested her head against her hands. She wished that they would just finish up and leave her alone. There wasn't any reason she had to be part of the dressing-down. They would have been able to speak more freely if she weren't there to listen in.

"There was a security breach. But no harm was done. A sleepwalking inmate got a few hallways away from her room. She probably had no idea she was doing it and no plan to do anything wrong. She happens to be a well-behaved inmate. We have the advantage of learning something from this. So that next time it isn't someone with a score to settle."

"You think you're just off the hook because no one got hurt or escaped?"

There was silence in the room. Gomez shrugged. "I admit I made a mistake. If you need to take disciplinary action..."

"There *will* be consequences," Buxton agreed. He looked around the room. "For everyone who was involved in this debacle. Everyone will be assigned a new security code, and they will be changed regularly. Just how regularly, I'm not sure, but we can't take the chance of inmates being able to have the run of the facility. If this had been an attempt at a prison break or retaliatory action, things would look a lot different this morning. You will shield your number from anyone in the vicinity when you use a keypad. You will report any suspicious activity or suspected breaches to me."

No one objected. Eyes were downcast. Everyone was trying to look remorseful and cooperative. Buxton shook his head, biting off further recriminations.

"There will be consequences," he repeated. "I will be reviewing other security footage. It would appear that this is a wide-spread practice. That changes now."

If a pin had dropped, everyone in the room would have heard it. There was not a whisper of movement. Finally, Buxton nodded his head. "You're dismissed. Those of you who are off duty can go home. You'll be issued your new security code when you return for your next shift. Those of you who are on shift, report to the control room now for your new number. Mr. Gomez, please stay behind."

Everyone filed out of the room, shuffling their feet, coughing behind their hands, exchanging significant glances. Tamara was impressed with how calm and cool Gomez appeared, after being on the hot seat and then kept after like a kid on detention.

"Can I go to my room now?" Tamara whined. "If everyone's codes have been changed, then I can't use them to get out now. Please?"

Buxton ignored her request. He closed the door behind the departing guards and turned to face Gomez.

"I'd like to know some more details about what happened last night when you found Ms. French in that hallway."

Gomez raised his brows. "Okay... what would you like to know?"

"What she was doing there. What direction she was headed. What sort of... mood she was in."

Gomez nodded and scratched the back of his neck. "I'm not sure what direction she was going. The doors had already been locked for some time, so she couldn't go in any direction. Unless she knew someone else's code. She was on the move, but I figured she was just pacing."

Buxton looked at Tamara. She shrugged and nodded. Buxton could check the videos and see that for himself.

"What was she doing there, so far off on her own?"

"I don't know for sure. She's been having some difficulties with the Sharks. Maybe she wanted to get farther away from them."

"Off on her own? Vulnerable to attack?" Buxton was wily; he wasn't buying it. "One of the girls who was killed was a Shark, wasn't she?"

"Waterson was, yes."

"But not the other one."

"Tabitha Smith. No. I guess the two of them ran into each other on the way in or out of the restroom, had words... one thing led to another..."

"You don't think French had anything to do with it."

"No." Gomez looked at Tamara, frowning. Tamara hoped he wasn't twigging to the fact that she had known which hall the incident had taken place in before he had. Such a little thing was hopefully lost in a sea of memories of far more important things that had happened that night. "French...? No." Again, a sort of a hitch in his voice. A hesitation. Tamara had had a beef with the Sharks. She'd had words with Tabby. "I've never known French to be violent that way."

Buxton wasn't buying it. "She's been in fights here."

"Of course. Who hasn't? But she isn't a troublemaker. She wasn't ever looking for a fight."

"She's serving time for murder."

"Yes." Gomez looked at Tamara. They had never talked about her convictions. She'd never had opportunity to tell him what had driven her to kill. It wouldn't likely have helped if she had.

"But she's not violent."

"No, sir. She... hasn't been."

Buxton tilted his head. "Hasn't been?"

"She's never been a problem before."

"Before what? Before this?"

"Her behavior has been... more erratic lately. She has been... more prone to outbursts."

Buxton looked Tamara in the eye, holding her gaze for too long. "Can you tell me why that is, Ms. French?"

Tamara shook her head. "I'm just tired. I just need to get some rest. Can't I go back to my room now?"

Buxton's jaws worked like he was chewing gum or a big wad of tobacco. "What did you have against those girls?"

"They attacked me," Tamara snapped. "It wasn't my fault."

"Yesterday? They attacked you together?"

"They wouldn't do that, they were enemies."

"Then what happened?"

The room started to spin around Tamara. She didn't want to think of the night before. She wanted it to be gone from her mind forever.

"I don't know."

The vertigo was too much for her. Tamara held her head, trying to stop the merry-go-round.

* * *

SHE DIDN'T REMEMBER BEING TAKEN to the infirmary. Everything was a spinning, sticky morass of images in Tamara's head. She didn't want to stay in that meeting room any longer. She didn't want to have to answer questions about what had happened. As much as she wanted to say that she hadn't been anywhere near three-west, they would know differently when they looked at all of the surveillance footage. Maybe they already had. Just like they had made copies of Tamara sleepwalking through the facility in the middle of the night. That would have been a higher priority than figuring out how Tamara was wandering around on her own.

The surveillance footage would put her near the girls at the right time, but they wouldn't be able to tie her to the killings because of the blind spot. They could see that she went to the restroom at the same time as the other girls had been around, but they wouldn't be able to prove that she had anything to do with their deaths. Not if she'd done her job.

"Tamara. Tamara, can you talk to me?"

Tamara hadn't noticed before that Dr. Eastport always called her by her first name. He was the only one. It was nice to hear her name now and then. She shook his fingers from her wrist.

"Just leave me alone."

"How are you feeling, dear? Can you tell me?" he coaxed.

Tamara lay with her eyes closed, not wanting to look at them. "I'm just tired. I want to go to my room."

"You can rest here once I've checked you out. Can you tell me what's going on?"

"She fainted," Buxton said flatly.

"That room was stifling," Gomez contributed. "No air. It's really no wonder."

"Mm-hmm. What room? What happened?"

"She was being questioned about the killings and about her wandering the halls last night."

"You know you have to take care of her physical needs. If she's not well, it's too hot, or she hasn't eaten, it could be a human rights violation. You need to look after your detainees." Eastport's tone was light, not accusing, but Tamara knew it was a serious warning.

"I am tired," she told Eastport. "Hot and tired and I don't feel good. I just want to sleep."

"I know, dear. After I have a chance to examine you."

He put on his stethoscope and listened to her heart and

breathing. He put the blood pressure cuff on her arm and, just like usual, started to pump the bulb to fill it with air. Tamara felt like it was choking her. She grasped at the edge of the cuff with her other hand.

"Ow! Get it off! That hurts."

"Just a bit more," he soothed, still pumping. It was so tight she was sure it was going to leave black bruises, like the baton bruise on her other arm. It was like a snake constricting around her, going to consume her.

Tamara opened her eyes. "Get it off!" she demanded, finding the edge and ripping the Velcro apart to relieve the pressure.

Eastport wrapped the cuff up and put it back in its cage on the wall, frowning at Tamara. "You need to let me examine you, Tamara. You want to feel better, don't you?"

"I don't want you to do anything. I refuse treatment. I can do that, can't I?"

"Well..." Dr. Eastport looked at the two guards as if they could fill him in on the legalities of the matter. "You're a minor. You're in custody, so the facility makes the decisions with regard to your care..."

"I'm not going to die. I just want to sleep."

Dr. Eastport shook his head, bemused. "All right, dear." He shrugged at the guards. "If you think the room was too hot and that was why she fainted, we'll just go with that. If her symptoms worsen, we'll address it then." He rubbed Tamara's shoulder soothingly. "When did you last eat?"

"I don't know..." Tamara tried to put the recent events into a timeline. But as much as she tried to pin it all down in chronological order, her brain refused to function and she was just left with the spinning. A time vortex, like on a TV space drama. It sucked everything into it, and she couldn't even look at it without getting disoriented.

"She had a little at breakfast," Buxton supplied. "Just some toast."

"That's normal," Gomez confirmed, nodding.

How could anything be normal? Tamara's whole life was getting sucked into a vortex.

"Make it stop," Tamara murmured. "I just want to get off." She held on to the sides of the bed, hoping it would help to stop the spinning.

"I recommend sleep," Dr. Eastport advised the two guards. "That's what she says she needs. You can leave her with me. I'll file a report at the end of my shift, letting you know if I see any reason for concern."

Gomez seemed unperturbed, but Buxton didn't like it. "She needs to be in restraints."

"She's not violent. It will restrict her ability to rest. I wouldn't recommend it."

"With what I've seen of her activities over the last twenty-four hours? No. Absolutely not. She must be restrained. She's a security risk."

Dr. Eastport looked at Gomez, one eyebrow up, hoping for some further tidbit of information or for Gomez to support his position.

"We *are* on general lockdown," Gomez pointed out.

"So she's not going to get anywhere. All the doors are locked."

"If there's any possibility she was involved in Waterson's and Tabitha Smith's deaths last night, we can't be too cautious," Gomez said, with a glance at his boss. He looked at Tamara, eyes searching. He wasn't convinced that she'd had anything to do with them.

But he wasn't convinced that she was innocent, either.

## TEN

AFTER SPENDING MOST OF the day sleeping, or at least pretending to sleep and not having to face real life, Tamara was able to pull herself together enough to convince Dr. Eastport that she was just fine and had simply been suffering from lack of sleep and the heat of the room. He released her and Tamara was escorted back to her own room, the general lockdown still in effect.

As they passed the guard station, Tamara saw Zobel. Or she thought she saw him. White, stocky, maybe his late thirties, with a shaved head that probably indicated he had been starting to go bald. The last time she had seen Zobel for sure had been in the common room, when he was lying on the floor in a pool of blood, one of the other guards administering first aid, trying to keep him from bleeding out. She hadn't seen anything of him on her return and hadn't known whether he had died or was out on medical leave.

Tamara wasn't sure she could trust her own vision and be sure that he was there, in the guard room, having a coffee before suiting up for his shift. It might just be wishful thinking. It might be a memory. Or it might be a hallucination. She couldn't ask the guard who was escorting her. If she said she had seen Zobel and he wasn't really there, the guard would turn around and march her right back to the infirmary.

It had only been a glimpse, and Tamara just wasn't sure.

At each set of doors they went through, the young guard put his body between Tamara and the keypad to shield his hands from her sight and quickly punched his new code in. The keys all beeped in the same tone, not like a telephone where each had a different sound that it could be identified by.

When she reached her cell and the big door was shut, Tamara stood there for a moment looking at the keypad. Buxton had said that they were changing all of the security codes, and they'd had all day to do it, so she was sure none of the numbers she had seen before then would still work. Buxton was bound to have eyes on her. There was a camera pointed right at her, recording her every move, watching to see if she would try using the keypad again.

She didn't.

She sat for few minutes on the bunk, thinking.

She hoped that Zobel was back. That he hadn't been killed or permanently injured by Tabby.

Either way, Tabby had deserved what she had gotten.

* * *

TAMARA HAD PREDICTED at least two days of general lock-down and she was apparently right. The time dragged on. She had been dreading being taken her out of her cell for questioning again after they looked at the videos. *What were you doing in that area? What did you see? Why didn't you report whatever was going on?*

But they didn't. They left her in her own cell and she was allowed to sleep, eat, and sleep again.

By the time the lockdown was lifted, everyone was ready to get out. While it was nice not to have to deal with the politics and having to be vigilant around the other inmates, it was mind-numbing to be confined to cells twenty-four hours a day. And for those who had cellmates, which was pretty much everyone except Tamara, it was that much worse. Having to deal with being locked in a tiny cell with nothing to do but listen to your cellmate grind her teeth or pick her toenails or whatever other infuriating personal habits she might have. Tamara had heard a couple of blow-ups during the lockdown. Some of the girls would have to be taken to isolation to keep them apart or sent to the infirmary if they got too physical.

She could hear other voices when the doors were unlocked; high girl voices, excited and impatient to get out of their rooms. There would be a rush for the showers. Much more crowded than usual. Tamara would wait until things had quieted down. Maybe even skip her shower altogether and have one the next day when things were calmer.

There was excited chatter up and down the hall. The inmates were finally able to talk to each other and to try to get details on what had happened the night that the lockdown had been put into place. There would be wild rumors but, considering that two of the girls were now without a cellmate, it wouldn't take long before everyone knew that two girls had been killed, and that was why the lockdown had been imposed.

The guards might fill in a few details. They were in a position of power not just by virtue of the fact that they carried weapons, but because they had knowledge. Everyone was going to want the scoop.

After the noise of the walking and talking inmates passed, Tamara could hear the feet of one of the guards taking a slow walk down the corridor of the housing section. It was Kirk. He looked in at Tamara, raising one eyebrow in surprise at finding her still there.

"Reveille's gone, French. Showers or breakfast. Move along."

"I was just waiting for it to quiet down..."

"It's quiet now. Clear out. We want to do a cell search and clean up."

Tamara had been getting to her feet, but at the mention of a cell search she froze. It wasn't like she had any contraband, but it still gave her pause. Someone else could have gone into her room and put something there without Tamara realizing it. Normally, she did a quick search of her own cell every couple of days. There weren't many places to look, but it was important to stay alert in case anyone had wanted to get contraband out of her own room, or to implicate Tamara in some way.

"Keep going," Kirk growled.

Tamara took a quick glance around her cell. Clothes, hygiene kit, and a clear plastic shoebox that was intended to store any personal possessions. Tamara's was empty, or it should be.

"I just wanted to—"

"You can brush your teeth after breakfast. Out you go."

Tamara reluctantly dragged herself to her feet and went out to the hallway. "I don't have anything." She wasn't sure why she felt the need to explain. "It's just... sometimes things show up in unexpected places."

He chuckled and nudged her toward the canteen. "I'll keep that in mind."

* * *

TAMARA LOOKED AROUND THE CANTEEN. There were small groups of girls chattering, not yet serving themselves or sitting down at tables. It was unusual, as conversation was normally kept to a minimum during meals and the girls were supposed to go down the counter immediately and not cluster together and socialize. Too much could happen in the canteen if the guards couldn't watch the girls closely.

Tamara didn't approach the counter immediately. She wasn't making herself a target by turning her back to them and acting differently from the group. She folded her arms and looked around, trying to decide what to do. She didn't have a circle of friends to swap gossip with. She wasn't part of a gang that would need to update each other and maybe give assignments after having been separated for two days.

Tamara wondered how many of them had been questioned. Surely Buxton would have talked to the leaders of each gang, to anyone the guards identified as being enemies to the dead girls, and to anyone they thought might snitch or offer up some small pearl of information. He had talked to Tamara, but that didn't mean she was a suspect. Certainly not their prime suspect. The girls looked like they had killed each other. A fight between the two of them. Not something to do with a third party.

"Come on, line up and get your meal, or you'll be sent back to your rooms," one of the guards warned, raising his voice over the unusual hubbub.

The inmates started moving toward the serving counter. Still talking to each other, but complying with the instruction to move on. Tamara let a few people line up in front of her and merged herself into the crowd as they lengthened out into a line. A few people gave her speculative looks. Were they remembering Tamara's grudge with Tabby and the Sharks? Did they know she'd been questioned by Buxton? That she'd been in the area when the two girls were killed? Tamara aimed glares at anyone who looked too long in her direction, and remarkably, they all looked back away, not engaging. Maybe she had succeeded. Maybe she had shored up her rep enough that people would leave her alone.

It was when she was at the counter that the crowd shifted and she caught sight of Zobel. Tamara was so startled by his ghostly appearance that she dropped her tray the couple of inches from where she was holding it to the counter in a clatter of dishes and cutlery. Zobel didn't look in her direction, but some of the girls around her jumped and turned toward her, startled and alert for trouble. Tamara pretended to be straightening things on her tray,

There were several choice words tossed in her direction, but no one said anything loudly enough or to her face so that she could identify them. Tamara would have been pissed if someone else had dropped their tray and made her jump, so she couldn't really blame them. She didn't apologize, but when the line started to move again, slid her tray forward, trying to catch another glimpse of Zobel. The crowd was blocking her view. When she got to the end of the counter, she moved to the outer edge of the girls, circling around them and looking for Zobel.

She couldn't see him. Just a ghost, then. Tamara let out her breath, disappointed, and aimed for one of the tables she usually sat at.

The discussion at the table quieted as she approached, as if they had been discussing her. Tamara looked over the faces warily, but no one challenged her, so she sat down and tried to relax. If they chose not to discuss her or anything she might have been involved in when she was at the table, that was good. That was a sign of respect. If they didn't respect her, they would have just gone on discussing it to her face. Then she'd have to do something about it.

Tamara sat down and picked at the unappetizing food. On the TV in the common room she'd seen a news story about how some schools were shifting their cafeteria menus to salad bars and fresh foods, even hiring on-site chefs to manage their menus and cooking. She wished that the prison facilities would take up the challenge as well and start feeding them real food like Tamara used to eat on Gram's farm, instead of reconstituted or over-processed slop.

She shredded the crusts of her toast and opened her juice.

"French!"

Tamara jumped and whirled around at her name. There were a few giggles at her reaction. Perez was talking, gesturing animatedly. She had not been calling Tamara, but had only mentioned her name in the course of her conversation. She saw Tamara's eyes on her and she dropped her spoon. It fell to the floor with a clatter. Lewis was sitting nearby and slow-clapped.

"Smooth, Perez."

"I just..." Perez couldn't explain. She blushed red despite her dark complexion. She bent over to pick up her spoon. Tamara wouldn't have opened herself up for a face-first shove into the floor that way, but Perez was surrounded by the Sharks. They would watch her back rather than take advantage of her. Perez retrieved the spoon and put it back on her tray. She tried to find her place in the conversation but, looking up, saw Tamara's eyes still on her.

Did Perez know something? She and Waterson had been admitted to juvie at the same time. The same day Tamara had returned to the facility after her breach of parole. They had moved into the Sharks together. How much else had they shared? They were always together, like two sisters. But it wasn't like Waterson had known what was going to happen. She couldn't have sensed something, some malevolence from Tamara. It was only chance that she had left the Sharks and gone off on her own when Tamara was watching for her chance. Tamara hadn't felt any particular animosity for her. The Shark she would have preferred to take out was Blacksnake, a girl who had been Tamara's cellie for a few short days before the prison break.

Tamara finally turned back around to face her plate and take a bite of the toast. It was simultaneously dry and greasy and a little sour, like it had been made from bread that had gone off before it was sold to the prison. Prisoners would eat anything; it didn't matter what kind of shape it was in. Administrators were always looking for ways to cut costs.

Tamara waited a while longer, until other inmates started to put their empty trays and dishes on the counter. Then she did the same, dumping the rest of her food in the garbage on the way. None of the guards noticed; or if they did, they didn't say anything.

She waited for others to start leaving the canteen. Eventually, the bell rang so she could get out the door with the group without being noticed.

It was when she walked out the canteen door that she saw Zobel again, stationed with his back against the wall, watching the exiting inmates. Tamara stopped stock-still and stared at him. The inmates exiting behind her shoved her out of the way.

Then Zobel saw her. His eyes widened just a bit and a smile tugged at the corners of his mouth and eyes. Tamara wasn't close enough to talk to him, but she saw his mouth form the words, 'Tamara French' in greeting.

She was afraid to approach him. Afraid he was just a ghost or hallucination and that she would give herself away in front of the other inmates. Once they knew how crazily muddled her head was, there would be no way to protect herself.

She took a couple of steps toward him and Zobel took a tentative one toward her, putting space between himself and the wall he had been standing against. He had a job to do, keeping an eye on the inmates exiting the cafeteria and looking for any weapons or threats, but his attention was on Tamara instead.

"How are you?" he asked, closer. "Are you okay?"

"Yeah," Tamara breathed, worried about raising her voice above the hum of the crowd. "What about you?"

He stood before her, big as life. They were both awkward. Tamara thought maybe she should hug him, or at least shake his hand. Something to show how glad she was that he wasn't dead.

That she had been part of keeping him alive. But touching was prohibited. Tamara wouldn't have shown affection in front of the other juvies even if it weren't.

Zobel turned his arm to show it to her, the long scar that was still healing. It seemed like a lifetime ago that he had been slashed, but it had only been a few weeks earlier. The scar was still pink and bright. "Almost as good as new."

Tamara looked around at the other inmates flowing past her and was glad to see their surreptitious glances toward Zobel, taking in his presence and the scar and his conversation with Tamara. That meant that Zobel was really there. He wasn't just a hallucination. Unless the other girls were actually looking at Tamara because she was talking to thin air.

"I didn't know... if you had made it."

"Thanks to you," Zobel acknowledged, with a little nod. Tamara drank in the sight of him. He was really there. He was really okay. Because of what she had done.

"*You're* looking a little piqued, though," Zobel observed. "You been sick?"

Tamara shrugged. If anyone else had asked her, it would have been a challenge. She would have had to jump at the opportunity to prove that she was just as capable as ever. But with Zobel, it was different. He'd seen her at her worst with Glock. He knew she was tough. And he owed her.

"I'm fine," she said. "Just getting settled in... we've been on lockdown."

"I know."

"And I guess you know..." Tamara trailed off and shrugged.

"About Waterson and Tabitha Smith? Yes, I heard."

"Tabby... did you know that she was the one who..." Tamara nodded to his arm. Zobel looked down at the scar and then back at Tamara.

"No. I couldn't remember any of it. I only know what they

told me. And what I've seen in the video. But it's not clear; there are too many people between the camera and what happened to see who it was that got me."

Tamara nodded. "Yeah. That's what they said. But it was Tabby. She tried once and I stopped her. Then she tried again... but I couldn't..."

"You still helped me. Thank you." He made a movement like he was going to shake her hand or touch her arm, then stopped. Guards were not allowed to have physical contact with the juvies. Not unless they were putting them in handcuffs, escorting them, doing a search, or some other part of their job. Any other contact between guards and inmates was prohibited and the guards who broke the rule were likely to get thrown out, either for abuse or for fraternization, which was another way of saying they couldn't have girlfriends among the juvies.

Zobel and Tamara just looked at each other, uncertain how to proceed. Tamara shrugged. "Yeah. I'm glad... you didn't die."

She stared at the wall behind Zobel, reliving the scene. Zobel's blood spurting across her, warm and sticky. Trying to somehow keep him from bleeding to death before help could arrive. The rest of the guards arriving in riot gear, their faces covered, like some paramilitary operation. Tamara swallowed. *He was okay.* He had wilted in front of her, faded away, but she had done everything she could. Somehow, it had all worked out. She couldn't stop seeing Tabby's knife flash across Zobel's body and the shower of blood that had drenched her.

"French."

Tamara startled and looked at Zobel. She tried to remain focused on him. He was there. He was in the present, not the past. She didn't need to remember what had happened. He had survived and he was back guarding juvie again.

"Yeah."

His hand went out again. Came close to touching her. Sketched a path over the surface of her arm without making contact. He pulled back and put both his hands behind him, clasped behind him in a military 'at ease' stance to keep himself from touching her. "Sorry."

"It's okay."

There was a crash and a yelp as two girls went through the door at once, horsing around and breaking the 'single file' rule. Tamara whirled around to protect herself, fists up to her chest before seeing the two were laughing rather than fighting. Tamara blew out a breath and tried to shake it off, her heart still pounding wildly. She looked at Zobel to say something casual to him, to make fun of herself for overreacting to nothing.

Zobel's face was pale and bloodless, even his lips were almost white. He grasped his handgun with his right hand, though he hadn't cleared the holster. It was clear that he had been prepared to. Tamara gave a wide shrug with her hands, excusing him. No one else seemed to have noticed his overreaction. A few inmates scowled at the girls who were roughhousing, but no one looked at Zobel to see him there with his gun almost out.

"You'd better move on," Zobel said finally. "I want to talk to you more... but this isn't the place."

Tamara wondered if there would ever be a time and place. He wasn't supposed to fraternize with her. She couldn't spend any time paying attention to him without the other juvies noticing and wondering what was going on and starting rumors. She didn't need the reputation of being a cop lover. She had already pushed the envelope on that one, having twice turned herself in instead of running when she had the chance. Most of the girls thought that if they'd been given the chance to run, they would have taken it. They didn't know what it was like to be trying to make it on the outside after living an institutional lifestyle for three years. Making choices, taking responsibility, expected to live like a free person after taking away her ability to make any choices for three years.

Tamara hadn't understood either, when she was on the

inside, how girls could come back to juvie broken and despairing after they had sworn they would make good on the outside. She hadn't understood how hard it would be to be human again, and how all she would want was to be back in the familiar environment with someone else making all of the choices for her.

ELEVEN

TAMARA SAT IN A classroom. She wasn't even sure what subject was being taught. She was thinking about seeing Zobel and what it meant to her. Now they were both back, guard and inmate. He appeared to be in good health, the scar on his arm healing as quickly as could be expected. He'd returned to duty, passing whatever qualifications he had to in order to prove he was once more fit for duty.

Tamara, who hadn't been through the same physical trauma as he had, who'd never been on the edge of losing her life like he had, felt like she was still spiraling downward. She didn't know how deep the vortex would take her or what would happen when she hit bottom. She wanted to be normal again, to pretend that, like Mrs. Henson said, she was working on succeeding the next time she made parole, but that seemed laughable. Her? She already had two strikes against her. Why would they ever consider letting her out again? More likely, she was just going to fall farther and farther, sinking into her own deranged mind, until she didn't even know she wanted to climb out again.

"Tamara French?"

Tamara raised her head. The teacher must have asked her a

question, but Tamara had no idea what. Everyone was looking at her expectantly. A female guard was moving toward her. Interrupting the class to deal with her. Tamara held on to the desktop with both hands, trying to stabilize herself and keep herself present.

"What?"

"Come on. Come with me."

Tamara tried to make herself move before the guard got to her side, but she couldn't. There were snickers around the classroom, whispered comments back and forth, the teacher waiting impatiently at the front of the room.

The guard, a young woman with a plain, angry resting face, took Tamara's arm. "I said come with me. Let's go."

Tamara's body followed without any conscious design. She was halfway to the door before she thought of resisting and pulled back.

The guard just gripped her tighter and kept moving. They were out of the classroom and Tamara was wondering what was going on and what she should do when the woman pulled her handcuffs from her heavy belt and slapped them over Tamara's wrists.

"What? I didn't do anything," Tamara protested. "What's this for? I came with you."

The guard didn't answer. Without the lockdown, it didn't take long to get from one part of the facility to another and in a few minutes they were in the housing wing and Tamara was in the doorway of her own cell, looking in.

"You want to explain where this came from?"

Tamara looked at the guard, then at her bunk. A shiv. Someone had either known that the search was coming and ditched her weapon in Tamara's room to keep from being caught, or someone had been trying to frame Tamara.

"I've never seen that before." Tamara's voice was calm and flat. She was proud of her reaction. It was controlled. It wasn't a crazy, hysterical protest. It wasn't an overdramatized denial. Just nice and straightforward and honest. It wasn't her shiv. She'd never seen it before.

"No, of course not," the woman guard said.

Tamara turned slightly, trying to see her name bar. Winder. A short *i* or a long *i*? Tamara decided on a short *i*, not liking the association with snakes that Winder with a long *i* brought to mind.

"It was hidden in a slit in your mattress. But of course, you've never seen it before."

"I've only been in this cell a few days," Tamara said. "Maybe the girl who was here before me..."

"Cells are checked and are clean before new inmates are assigned. This isn't someone else's weapon, this is yours."

"Did you check for prints?" Tamara demanded. "You're not going to find my prints on it."

"It was in your cell, it's yours, whether you wiped it down or not."

"I've never—"

"Don't try to snow me," Winder snapped. "I wasn't born yesterday."

What an odd thing to say. Tamara pondered this. She wasn't even sure why Winder was questioning her. Wasn't it Kirk who had searched the room? Shouldn't he be the one telling Tamara where he found the weapon and that he knew it was hers? If not Kirk, then why wasn't a senior guard or staff member questioning her? Sitting in a meeting room, not standing in her doorway. A rookie guard asking Tamara about it in the hallway didn't seem right. If Tamara were to be pulled out of class, it should have been for a formal inquiry. Not a hallway conversation.

"You don't know me," Tamara said. "I've never been caught using a weapon. Check my record."

"I don't care if you've never been caught before. You're caught now."

"It's not mine."

"Right. Someone just planted it there." Winder's voice was heavy with sarcasm.

"Yeah."

"Look," Winder pulled Tamara back out of the doorway and shoved her into the wall. "I've had enough of your attitude. You can't pull one over on me. Your cell, your knife. I'm sure you know how serious it is to be caught with a knife here."

*Did Winder?* She seemed to think that Tamara should fear the consequences, but Tamara wasn't worried. The experienced guards would know it wasn't hers. If it had been, Tamara would surely have been carrying it with her in the hallway. With the bad blood between her and the Sharks and two girls already dead in the hallway, no one with any sense would have left a weapon behind in her room to walk around unprotected.

"It's not mine," Tamara repeated. *Broken record,* the juvies called it. Just keep repeating the same thing over and over again. No matter what question was asked, just keep repeating the same thing. Few people could keep an interrogation going when the offender just kept repeating herself without variation.

Winder pushed Tamara into the wall again, harder.

Tamara resisted. "Get off of me!" she growled. "You're not allowed to shove me around."

"I can do whatever I want. You resist, you're going to end up hurt."

"Leave me alone," Tamara raised her voice to a yell, to a level where anyone in the surrounding hallways would be able to hear her. "Quit hitting me!"

Winder tried again with a shove into the wall, getting her face in close to Tamara's, trying to bully her by invading her personal space instead of just using physical force. "Shut up. You are going to confess that shiv is yours or you're going to be sorry."

"I'm not resisting! Quit hitting me!" Tamara yelled again.

Winder's face got red. She pulled Tamara away from the

wall in order to get good momentum, then shoved her back into it with such force that Tamara's head snapped back and hit the wall. Tamara swore. She ignored the pain, focusing instead on riling Winder up. Getting her even madder and more violent. "You think that's hard?" she hissed. "I been beaten up by fourteen-year-olds tougher than you!"

The funny thing was, it was true.

Tamara had played it just right and a couple of other guards came around the corner to see what all of the fuss was about just as Winder sucker-punched Tamara.

Tamara doubled over, coughing and gasping for air. Her hands were still cuffed behind her back; it was obvious that she hadn't been a security threat to Winder.

"Whoa, whoa, whoa!" Kirk raced forward and pulled Winder back a couple of feet. "Let's cool things down here."

Tamara fell to her knees, still trying to pull in a breath.

Kirk put his hand on her back. "You okay, French?"

"She was—" Winder sputtered, "—don't believe anything she tells you! She had a weapon in her cell. She was being defiant. She..."

"You don't sucker punch an inmate in handcuffs. Doesn't matter what you think she's done."

The other guard who had come to see what all the noise was about was Millican. He looked into Tamara's cell and saw the shiv on the bunk.

"Where'd that come from?"

"It was in her mattress," Kirk said. "I found it when I tossed the cells this morning. Told Winder to bring French in for me."

It was Winder with a long *i*, contrary to what Tamara had thought. She took in a couple of deep, gulping breaths, forcing her diaphragm to operate.

"French doesn't use weapons," Millican said.

"Just because she hasn't before, that doesn't mean she can't start. She's feeling the heat. Got trouble with the Sharks. So she gets or makes a shiv," Kirk countered.

"Then she would carry it with her when she left her cell."

"Not if I hustled her out before she had a chance to grab it. She didn't like it when I said I was going to search it this morning."

Millican looked down at Tamara. "This your knife, French?"

"No."

"She's not going to tell the truth," Winder objected, like an exasperated mother trying to explain something to a two-year-old.

"You pat her down?"

"No."

"Aren't you concerned about what she might be carrying?"

Winder looked at Kirk. He obviously hadn't given her any special instructions on how to bring Tamara back to the housing unit. Kirk didn't help Winder out.

"*You* think it was hers?" Millican asked Kirk.

"No." Kirk gave a shrug. "When I said I was searching the room, she looked at her bag and her box. Not a flicker toward the bunk."

"So she's smart," Winder said.

"I don't think it's hers," Kirk reiterated. Winder looked at the makeshift knife and then back at Kirk. He was her superior and a more experienced guard. She might not like the answer or his conclusion, but he was far more likely to be right than she was.

"Why did you tell me to bring her down, then?"

"I wanted to talk to her, get some intel." Kirk looked down at Tamara. "Not likely to happen now."

"She was mouthing off. I didn't—I wasn't—"

"Like I said, doesn't matter what you think she's done. You can't do that. A security officer who can't stay in control isn't any use to us here."

Winder appeared to understand what that meant for her. She swallowed and nodded, mouth a grim line.

"Why don't you head to the break room and have a coffee or two? I'll follow up with you later."

They all watched Winder head off down the hallway. Kirk swore.

Millican sighed. "You said it. Let's get you on your feet, French."

They each put a hand under one of Tamara's arms and lifted her easily to her feet. Tamara's breathing was starting to ease.

"You know whose it is?" Kirk asked, nodding in the direction of the weapon.

"No."

"No idea?"

Tamara shrugged. "Your guess is as good as mine. Anyone." She took another long breath. "Maybe someone with a grudge. Maybe just someone who needed to get rid of it quick."

"Sharks?"

Tamara considered. She shook her head. "Don't think so. Lewis wouldn't want to arm me and she wouldn't want me to get caught. What she wants is to beat the hell out of me."

Kirk suppressed a laugh, snorting. Millican nodded, agreeing with Tamara's assessment.

"You can stay here until class change," Kirk said. "Then if you're feeling okay, you can go on to your next class. Let me just grab that first."

Tamara waited while Kirk went into her cell and picked the shiv up off of the bed. He handled it without gloves and nodded to Millican as he walked by them to properly log it at the guard station.

"You can take off the cuffs and slot her away. I'll take care of this."

Millican waited until Kirk was most of the way back to the guard station before unlocking Tamara's handcuffs. Tamara brought her hands back around in front of her and rubbed her stomach where Winder had hit her. It was going to be sore for days. But it was muscle, not ribs. At least Winder hadn't re-broken Tamara's ribs. Tamara explored the back of her head where it had hit the wall. There was a knot starting to swell up.

"You hit your head?" Millican inquired. He didn't wait for a response, but turned Tamara around by her shoulder and examined her head.

"It's nothing," Tamara said.

"I should take you to the infirmary."

"For this? It's nothing. I've had plenty worse."

And he knew she had. She'd been Glock's cellie for almost two years. But there was a list of injuries that inmates were supposed to be sent to the infirmary for, and blows to the head were on it.

"Just get me ice," Tamara said. "That's all they're going to do. I don't want all the fuss."

Millican prodded the bump for a few more seconds, then withdrew. "Ice it is," he agreed. He didn't want to have to fill out the paperwork any more than Tamara wanted to be seen in the infirmary again. If the other juvies kept seeing her in the infirmary, they were going to label her a victim. She was fighting hard enough for her rep as it was.

* * *

AN ICE PACK on her head for half an hour and Tamara was ready to go back to classes when the change bell rang. She was breathing normally and, though she had bruises, it was all par for the course in juvie and she was ready to get back into the regular routine. Kirk cleared her and she went on to her next class.

For a couple of days, things were as normal as they could be in juvie. Tamara kept a close eye on the Sharks, and they kept a close eye on her. The guards kept a close eye on both of them.

TMJ had been run by Vernon before the prison break. During the time that Tamara had been away, the mantle had been taken up by Brett, but Tamara had a pretty good idea that she wasn't going to be able to retain power. She was a good lackey or lieutenant to Vernon and to Rosie, but she really wasn't gang leadership material. She had stepped in to fill a void and, with the losses and injuries both gangs had suffered during the riot that led up to the prison break, neither gang had been in any position to wield its full power.

Tamara watched Brett across the common room where only weeks before she had acknowledged Vernon as the rightful leader of TMJ. Brett spoke with a couple of the older girls in the gang, her manner covert, head swiveling to make sure nobody was close enough to overhear them. Tamara did the best she could to read lips and body language. Were they just chatting about internal affairs? Were they discussing another fight with the Sharks? Other targets or concerns? Was Tamara herself a topic of conversation? Was she ever anything more than a passing reference or footnote to their conversation?

Lewis and a couple of Sharks entered the common room and Tamara's heart nearly stopped. She looked around at the guards, sure that it was a mirror of the previous riot. The Sharks were there to start a fight for power over the block. They wanted to be the undisputed authority and to run things as they saw fit.

But they entered casually, not like they were heading into a fight. Their gang tats were not on display. They didn't have members strategically positioned throughout the room. No one else around Tamara seemed to notice anything out of the ordinary. Just a normal, routine day. A few bored girls walking into the common room to see if there were anything good on TV.

"Little jumpy there?"

Tamara whirled around at the voice, too close to her ear. Blacksnake. An enemy Tamara had made before the break-out. She was taller than Tamara, heavier, but not more skilled. She might have strength, but she thought just a little too slowly, which made her easier to take advantage of.

Blacksnake laughed at Tamara's overblown reaction. Tamara didn't stop to think things through and come up with the best strategy for dealing with Blacksnake, she just did what she had once before and threw a punch straight into the bigger girl's face, landing square on her nose.

Blacksnake bleated a protest, both of her hands coming up to her face to gauge the damage, leaving her body open. In former days, Tamara would have left it at that, backing off and waiting for the security staff to take over and clean things up. But that was before. There was bad blood between Tamara and the Sharks and Blacksnake was a Shark. And not just any Shark, but one who had a personal grudge against Tamara. If she were going to convince Lewis and the Sharks to just leave her alone, Tamara couldn't stop at a bloody nose.

Tamara followed up with a couple of body blows and when Blacksnake decided that it would be wise to open her eyes and protect her body, Tamara used her lower center of gravity to get in low and sweep Blacksnake. The bigger girl landed hard on her butt. Tamara allowed herself one wince of sympathy. The floors at the facility were tile over concrete, and if Blacksnake had fallen the right way, she was going to be dealing with a broken tailbone. Wouldn't she look tough sitting on a pillow or inflatable donut waiting for it to heal?

By the time Tamara got Blacksnake to the floor, the guards were moving in to break it up, but they weren't in any hurry. If there wasn't a big risk that two isolated inmates having a fist fight were going to permanently injure or kill each other, the guards were happy to just let them blow off some steam before interfering.

Tamara wasn't like Glock. She wasn't fighting just to blow off some steam or to satisfy her bloodlust. She was protecting herself and her rep. Tamara kicked Blacksnake, watching the girl's hands and trying to avoid getting tripped up. She didn't want to be on the floor with Blacksnake on top of her. Her kicks were ineffectual; no reinforced toes, just canvas runners.

Finally, Tamara was pulled back. Once far enough away from Blacksnake that she was safe from any retaliation, Tamara took a glance around the room. The Sharks who had just come into the room, Lewis and a couple of others, stood watching. They didn't have any reason to start a gang fight over the altercation, especially when the combatant was Tamara, not a member of TMJ.

Blacksnake was hauled to her feet by a couple of guards, her nose dripping a steady stream of blood. She cursed angrily. No permanent injuries. Tamara wasn't that dangerous. She could hold her own, but she wasn't out to disable anyone in front of the whole common room.

"What's going on here? What's the problem with you two?" the guard who had jerked her back demanded.

Looking around to make sure there were no further threats, Tamara saw Zobel out the corner of her eye.

The sight of Zobel in the common room and the adrenaline of the fight sent Tamara spinning back to the day of the prison break. She was in the common room, caught between the two opposing forces. Zobel and the other guards were trying to break things up. Tamara tried to protect Zobel from Tabby's attack and then to staunch the spurting fountain of blood.

"No."

She clutched at him. The blood was everywhere. In her face and hair. Pumping with each of Zobel's heartbeats. She gagged and gripped his arm, trying to keep it from all pumping out before help could arrive. But it was going too fast. His face was almost blue. He was unconscious, life draining away from him. Tamara choked, halfway between crying and being sick.

"No, no, no!"

Somewhere behind her was Vernon, and in a few moments

events would take another turn. Another twist that would change her life forever. She should have killed Tabby sooner. Killed her before the gang fight. Before the series of events that had fallen like dominoes, one on top of the other, ending with Zobel lying there inches from death and Tamara about to be taken hostage with the point of a shiv pressed to her jugular.

"Calm down," a voice urged. "Shh. Take a breath, French. Come on, now. Take a deep breath."

She tried, but her heart was beating faster than she could draw in oxygen, and she panted for air, straining hard.

"Focus on me. Everything is fine. Right here."

Tamara tried to follow the voice to its owner. She was looking at Zobel. Not stretched out on the floor, but at her side. Not dead. Not white and still and dead.

"What...?"

"French. Tamara. You're okay. Just look at me. Stay with me."

She tried desperately to do as he said. She stared into his eyes, forcing herself to connect, to stay there. She found herself breathing more easily. The fight started to dissolve from her vision.

"What happened?"

"Take some deep breaths. Think about your body. You're here now. Listen to me. Look at me. Smell. Feel. You're right here."

Tamara's vision was clearing. She took only brief glances away from Zobel's eyes to look around her and gradually assess the situation. It was not the gang fight. It wasn't her kidnapping by Vernon. She had just had a brief fight with Blacksnake. She wasn't hurt. Neither of them was really injured, though because she was bleeding, Blacksnake would be taken to the infirmary. Once the bleeding was staunched, she would be given the choice of staying there or going back to her room. She'd choose to go back to her room.

Tamara felt in front of herself, sure that's where Zobel's body was, that she couldn't let him go until someone was there who could help and administer first aid. But it wasn't there, and there was no sticky blood on her face and arm. There was nothing on the floor in front of her.

"Let's get up," Zobel suggested.

Tamara was crouching, her arms out in front of her where Zobel had been, or where she had thought he had been. Tamara rose to her feet, her head whirling. She wasn't sure what was real and what was not. She was afraid to say anything, for fear that she wasn't really there.

"Okay?" Zobel asked.

Tamara nodded.

"What was all that?" one of the other guards demanded.

Blacksnake was still there, a tissue held over her nose while she complained in a clogged-up voice that she hadn't done anything to warrant the attack, but also to protest that she wasn't actually hurt and didn't have to go to the infirmary.

The other inmates stood around in little clumps, or watched from their comfortable seats in front of the TV, whatever fictional drama was showing on the screen long forgotten. They whispered back and forth to each other, but Tamara noticed that none of them met her eyes, not even Lewis.

"If I'm right, a flashback," Zobel said. He looked at Tamara, his clear blue eyes unchanged. "Am I right?"

A flashback. It sounded so innocuous. Just a small inconvenience. A memory blip. Tamara swallowed and nodded her head. "Yeah," she agreed hoarsely. "Just remembering... it's nothing."

"I'll take her to her room," Zobel suggested.

"She should be in isolation after physically assaulting another inmate," another voice disagreed. Tamara didn't have the energy to identify who was talking and to follow all of the back-and-forth. It was unimportant. All that was important was that she stayed there in the present and didn't make a further fool of herself.

"Isolation is not a punishment," Zobel quoted policy to the objector. "Its purpose is to keep inmates safe. The housing sheet I looked at this morning said she's odd man out. She's not sharing a cell."

"She's odd man," a woman guard confirmed.

"Then the only reason to put her in isolation instead of her own room is if she's a danger to herself."

There was an uncomfortable silence. Tamara rubbed her forehead. All of the tension seemed to be gathering in the middle of her forehead, the pain getting more and more intense.

"She's not on watch," Zobel said. "Does anyone think she should be?"

"Can we just go?" Tamara growled, irritated that her mental status would be discussed in front of all of the other juvies in the common room.

"Maybe she should go to the infirmary."

"Blacksnake is going to the infirmary. You really want them both sent there? We'll need twice the security measures."

"Take me to my room," Tamara said. "I'm not gonna hang myself with the sheets."

There was another silence.

"I don't see a problem," one of them said. "Let's just get this mess cleaned up."

Zobel touched Tamara's shoulder. "Let's go."

She appreciated that he didn't see the need to handcuff her. He escorted her one direction and Blacksnake was escorted toward the infirmary.

"Blacksnake been getting on your case?" Zobel asked, his voice casual, as if nothing out of the ordinary had happened.

"Just now, but... not since I came back. Me and the Sharks, though... aren't exactly on good terms right now."

Zobel nodded slowly. "I read in the logs that you had some kind of an upset with Lewis."

An upset. Tamara couldn't hide the sheepish smile that pulled at her lips. "Uh... yeah. I kinda flipped the whole breakfast table into her lap. Her and the rest of the Sharks sitting with her."

"I can see how that might annoy her."

Tamara glanced at Zobel's face, hearing the amusement in his voice.

"They shouldn't have made me sit at that table."

"You ought to control yourself. No matter what position they put you into, you still have a choice."

The amusement was gone, but his face was still pleasant, not angry or accusing. Tamara could have argued with him, but she supposed it was true. She could have moderated her reaction. She could have chosen not to do something that would humiliate Lewis in front of the entire canteen and make her look like a fool. Something that wouldn't demand retaliation and an escalation of tensions between them. So Tamara kept her mouth shut and didn't take it up with Zobel. They walked on in silence to her cell.

Zobel stood in the doorway and didn't close the door immediately upon Tamara entering. She looked at him.

"You want to talk about it?" Zobel asked.

"What?"

He leaned his shoulder against the doorframe. "That flashback."

Tamara gave a wide shrug. "What about it?"

"Seemed like quite a doozy."

Tamara didn't know what to say. She sat on her bunk and put her back to the wall, watching him. Knees bent in front of her chest, like she needed a shield.

"Have you been having a lot?"

"No."

His eyes were quick and discerning. "But it wasn't the first one, was it?"

"You're not my doctor."

Zobel considered this. "Have you talked to a doctor about it?"

"No. I'm fine. It's not such a big deal."

"Tamara..." He spoke softly, in a voice that wouldn't carry to any of the other cells. "Lots of people deal with PTSD. Lots of cops. Lots of inmates."

Tamara scratched at the fabric of her uniform as if there were something spilled on it and it was important to get it off.

"I don't know anyone who's got that," she challenged. She'd heard of PTSD. That was what soldiers got. She could understand their being traumatized by their wartime experiences. Bombs exploding, planes crashing, women and children in suicide vests, being shot at. That made sense. That was the stuff that nightmares were made of. But living in a country where there was no war, even living in juvie, a person had to be weak-minded to get PTSD from that.

"You don't think anyone else here has PTSD?"

Tamara shifted, pressing herself solidly against the wall. "I don't know."

"Do you know..." Zobel ran his finger down the long pink scar on his arm. "I've been having a lot of trouble since this happened. They put me into counseling. They're helping me deal with it. When I looked at your file, saw all of the trouble you'd been having since you came back here... well, I figured maybe PTSD was the reason."

Tamara shrugged. Was *that* what had been going on in her brain? Was it as simple as that? Maybe there was a pill she could pop, something simple that would make it all just go away and go back to normal. She could have her old brain back. The one that worked instead of the one that kept throwing roadblocks up in her path. Hallucinations, screwed up timelines and memories, overwrought emotions, flashbacks. She could do without all of that.

"Then in the common room..." Zobel went on. "Like I said, that looked like a hell of a flashback."

"It was *you*. I tried to help you, but I thought you were going to die. I was sure of it." Tamara swore. "The blood... it was everywhere."

"I saw the video." He didn't say he had seen how she had been covered in his blood. "I'm... sorry."

Tamara snorted. "Wasn't your fault."

"If I'd followed protocol, maybe things would have turned out differently. Maybe I wouldn't have gotten hurt."

And unspoken, maybe she wouldn't have gotten crazy.

"You had to help. There were other guards down. You couldn't leave them there." She cleared her throat. "Did anyone die? Any of the staff?"

"No. We all made it out of there alive, miraculously. Things could have been a lot different."

"If you didn't help the others, maybe they would have died. You did what you had to."

Zobel's eyes were far away. He ran his fingers over his scalp. Tamara watched him carefully. He didn't look crazy. He wasn't acting erratically like she had. He was just distant. As the minutes ticked by without him saying or doing anything, she wondered how far away he was. If he was having a flashback like she'd had, only quieter, everything enacted inside his brain rather than out where everyone could see it.

She didn't know whether she should call him back, as he had called her, or just to wait until it ended by itself. She bit the skin around her nails, waiting to see what would happen.

Zobel blinked a few times and focused in on Tamara. "What did you say?"

But she too had lost the thread of the conversation. "Nothing. You okay?"

"Sure, I'm fine." Then Zobel frowned and chewed on his lip. "Maybe not fine. But... I'll get through it. The therapy is helping. It would help you."

"I dunno." Tamara hugged her knees close. "Yeah, I was in the middle of that fight, but so what? Everyone who was there doesn't have PTSD. Just you. You were hurt; just about killed. I wasn't."

"And you think I believe that what happened to you wasn't traumatic? Vernon taking you at knifepoint? Her and her ex-con boyfriend holding you hostage for days? That's not just as traumatic as a little knife-wound?" He motioned to his scar as if it were a mere scratch.

"It wasn't that bad. Not like they had me in chains for three days."

Tamara's stomach turned over. She could minimize the experience all she liked, but her body knew she was lying. Tamara held her stomach, waiting for the nausea to pass. Zobel raised an eyebrow, clearly not believing a word she said.

"I don't know what else went on. And I don't know all of what you went through at that foster family." It had been all over the news, so Tamara couldn't be surprised that he knew details of her life that she would rather everyone at juvie didn't know. "But I don't think you can say that you haven't been through any traumatic experiences in your life. Even just being cellmates with Spielman for two years... you dealt with a lot of crap from her, too."

Tamara wound a lock of hair tightly around her finger. Looking down at it, she felt like it was foreign. The dark brown hair gave her a strange feeling of unreality every time she saw it. As if she were living in someone else's body. She wasn't entirely sure that she was the same person she had been before the kidnapping. That girl had been replaced with someone completely foreign.

"I'll set up an appointment for you with Dr. Sutherland,"

Zobel suggested. "You can talk to him about the PTSD. The flashbacks and other symptoms you're having. He can talk about it with you. Help you work through it."

"That's it?" Tamara asked. "No meds? Just talk?"

Zobel pursed his lips and scratched his head. "Well... maybe. He might have suggestions for meds that will help with particular symptoms. To help you sleep, reduce anxiety, treat depression..."

It sounded like Zobel was taking an entire pharmacy. Tamara didn't want to be that inmate. Plenty of them had daily prescriptions they were taking for one thing or another. But there were always one or two girls who were taking so many different pills that they practically rattled when they walked. The girls who were always in and out of the Psych unit, who people avoided having anything to do with because they were so erratic.

"Don't bother," she told him. "I don't want a bunch of pills."

"You should have one appointment with him to discuss it, at least. It doesn't mean he'll put you on a bunch of meds. But if there's something you need; wouldn't you rather feel better?"

Tamara stared into her knees. She rested her forehead on them and shook her head.

## TWELVE

ZOBEL LEFT TAMARA TO her whirling thoughts, needing to get back to his other duties. Tamara watched through the narrow window in the door as he walked away, disappearing from sight. She was finally alone again and could just let loose. She didn't know whether she wanted to cry or to go back to sleep.

As it turned out, she didn't cry or go back to sleep. She rolled off her bunk and barely made it to the stainless steel toilet bowl to throw up.

*Vernon and her ex-con boyfriend.*

Zobel's words echoed in her head, bringing Vernon and Sly's faces into Tamara's mind. The meaningful looks they exchanged, their smiles, the way they had treated her. She didn't want to remember. Her body didn't want to remember. She retched and retched over the toilet like her body could purge the memories.

When her stomach finally stopped trying to turn itself inside-out, Tamara leaned on her arm, braced on the edge of the toilet.

She tried to reconstruct her life without the bad memories. Living with Gram. That had been good. The most stable place she'd ever had to live. She could add in some of the memories of the Hensons and Sybil. She could even include portions of the three years she had spent at juvie. Times when things had been quiet. When she hadn't been so worried about her personal safety. When things had been repetitive and routine and it was almost like being away at camp instead of prison.

If she could just get rid of the bad memories and focus on the good ones, there would be no PTSD. There would be no traumatic events. No flashbacks.

Tamara's stomach heaved again. She coughed and blew her nose, trying to get all of the bile and shreds of dinner out of her mouth and nose. There wasn't anything left in her stomach, so her body should just stop trying. Tamara climbed back into bed and curled up, closing her eyes.

Despite the fact that she had told Zobel not to set up an appointment with Dr. Sutherland, he did. Such a helpful guy. She saved his life and he repaid her by ratting her out to the prison shrink. Of course, it could have been any of the other guards who had witnessed what happened in the common room, but Tamara's money was on Zobel.

Dumas was in Tamara's room first thing in the morning, before Tamara had even had a chance to shower or have breakfast. She sniffed the air, looking around the cell with a frown. Tamara wondered if she could still smell the sour scent of vomit from the night before. Tamara pulled a lock of her hair under her nose to smell it, wondering if her whole body reeked of it. She hadn't been planning on having a shower, avoiding it for as long as she possibly could, but if she were starting to stink, the staff would force the issue, taking her to the showers and physically putting her under the spray if they had to.

"You have an appointment with Sutherland," Dumas informed Tamara, wrinkling her nose but saying nothing about the smell. "I'm supposed to take you straight down."

"I'm still in my pinks. Give me a second."

Dumas just stared at her. Tamara looked down at her clothing and saw that she was in her orange day uniform. She ground her knuckles into her forehead, trying to remember whether she had gone to sleep in her days, or whether she had already changed that morning without remembering. She blinked and looked back at Dumas.

"I mean... I need to comb my hair. Just..."

She grabbed her hygiene kit and ran her comb through her long dark hair a few times to get out the night-time snarls and make herself presentable. She tied it back with an elastic and unbuttoned a couple of buttons on her uniform to smear deodorant into her pits, unsure of whether she had already done that or not.

"Let's go, then," Dumas urged impatiently.

"Yeah... okay. I'm coming."

She was surprised to be seeing Sutherland so early in the day. He must have decided it was the only way he could fit Tamara in without having to bump other appointments he already had scheduled.

Tamara smothered a yawn as she entered Dr. Sutherland's office. A big yawn that she couldn't hold back, the kind that meant she probably still needed another hour or two of sleep. She rubbed her eyes, wiping away the tears that the yawn had brought on, and faced Dr. Sutherland.

"Well, good morning, sleepyhead," Dr. Sutherland greeted with a chuckle.

"Sorry," Tamara said, sliding into the chair and trying to restrain another yawn. "Guess I'm just not awake yet."

"I took the liberty of making coffee," Dr. Sutherland said in a confidential tone, indicating two mugs on his desk. "I know that we're not supposed to be providing coffee to minor inmates under all of the nutritional guidelines, but if a cup happened to go missing from my desk, I'm not sure how I could be blamed for that."

"Oh!" Tamara didn't hesitate, grabbing the one that was closer to her. He had sugar packets and cream powder on his desk, so she doctored it up.

Dr. Sutherland opened a box and took out a honey-glazed donut. The smell of fresh baking wafted through the small office. Dr. Sutherland nodded to it, which Tamara took as an invitation. She opened the box and looked over the variety Dr. Sutherland had provided.

"I can't take you away from your breakfast in the canteen without providing an alternative, can I?"

Tamara's stomach rumbled. Coffee and a real, fresh donut instead of stale toast and room temperature juice. She would take an early-morning appointment with Dr. Sutherland any day without complaint after that.

Finally settling on a chocolate-glazed confection with colorful sprinkles, Tamara settled back in her chair again, taking a long sniff of the coffee and donut before starting in.

"I understand you wanted to talk to me today about some symptoms you've been having," Dr. Sutherland suggested. "You thought that maybe I could help you with some flashbacks...?"

Tamara took a bite of the donut and a sip of the scalding-hot coffee.

"I didn't make the appointment."

"But you are experiencing some troublesome symptoms?"

She eyed him, wondering how much Zobel had told him. Dr. Sutherland was good at pretending he knew far less than he did in order to draw a person out.

"Sort of."

Dr. Sutherland tipped his chair back with a creak. "Maybe you don't want to feel better," he suggested. "If this isn't something that's bothering you..."

Tamara nibbled the icing off the donut. "Like I said, I didn't make the appointment."

"You had a fight in the common room the other day?"

She didn't think another 'sort of' would go over well. She was pretty sure he must know all of the details already. She couldn't very well keep the fact that she'd had a fight with Blacksnake a secret.

"I guess so. Just..." she held her fingers up like she was measuring something, "a little one."

"Ah. Well, I suppose that's better than a big one. Do you want to tell me what happened?"

"Blacksnake was bugging me. I... defended myself."

"What did she do to bug you?"

Tamara thought back. The events that had precipitated the fight were only vague memories. Cloudy and murky.

"She was getting in my space. Trying to start a fight."

"Did she say or do something?"

"She was standing too close to me."

Dr. Sutherland waited. Tamara looked away. "I just didn't want a big gang fight. Then she started harassing me... I wasn't going to let her diss me like that."

"What made you think there was going to be a big gang fight?"

Tamara picked at the donut with her fingers. "I was in the common room... it was like before... I thought... it just looked like there might be a fight. I didn't want to get caught in the middle of it, like last time."

"How did that make you feel?"

Did he want her to say that she was scared? Or that she was angry? Or was there something else that would identify whether her reaction was normal or not?

"I was... anxious. Last time... Zobel got hurt, and..."

A shudder ran through Tamara's body. She tried to stay focused on the donut and the coffee. On the fact that she was just sitting in Dr. Sutherland's office, where she was perfectly safe. She looked to the side to see if Zobel were there. She clenched her hands into fists. She wasn't back there again. She wasn't going to slide back into it again.

"You helped Mr. Zobel when he was hurt."

Tamara put her coffee down on the edge of the desk. She lined up the donut beside it. Her stomach was heaving under her uniform. She tried to keep Dr. Sutherland from seeing how much it upset her to talk about Zobel getting hurt. She knew her reaction was overblown. Other inmates would be happy to talk about saving someone's life. Even if it was a guard or a cop. People liked to brag up their accomplishments.

"Sure. I did."

"After your 'little fight' with Ms. Blacksnake, something triggered a flashback to that."

He did know everything. Or at least, everything that the people who had observed Tamara in the common room knew. She contemplated taking a sip of the coffee to steady herself, but was afraid that she would end up dropping it and spilling it all over if one of the flashbacks or hallucinations became real. It was all she could do to stay focused on Dr. Sutherland, pretending that there was really nothing wrong.

"What was it that triggered that flashback, Tamara? Do you know what it was? Sometimes it is a sight or a smell. Sometimes just a feeling. Do you know what it was that triggered you?"

"I just... I just got distracted for a minute."

"By what?"

"By... Zobel being there. That's where it happened, him getting hurt."

"And is that what you saw? Is that what you flashed back to?"

Tamara swallowed. "I guess so," she said in a firm, calm voice. It was a voice that said she didn't care. It was just a little thing, of no consequence. Hardly worth mentioning.

Even with the long sleeves of the uniform, Tamara was sure Dr. Sutherland could see that she was sweating buckets. The room was warm and close and must have been rank with the smell of her sweat.

"You've heard of PTSD, Tamara?"

"Yes. Everybody has."

"Do you know what it stands for?"

"Post-Traumatic Stress Disorder," Tamara said glibly, the words rolling easily off her tongue.

"So what does the name of the disorder tell you about it?"

"That... it's... a disorder you get... after a trauma."

"Yes," Dr. Sutherland agreed. "Do you think it's traumatic to see someone stabbed right in front of you? Mere feet away? Not even feet, just inches?"

"I guess. It could be."

"It could," Dr. Sutherland agreed. "Even if it was someone you didn't like?"

"I never said I didn't like him!" Tamara protested.

Dr. Sutherland raised an eyebrow. "No," he agreed. "I'm just running through scenarios. Zobel has been here for quite some time. Most of your incarceration, if I'm not mistaken."

"All of it. He's been here the whole time."

"The good ones... you develop a relationship over time. I don't mean an inappropriate relationship. Just that you get to know each other. Get a feel for each other."

"Yeah."

"So maybe you thought of Zobel as a friend."

"Maybe—almost—like that."

"And seeing someone who was almost like a friend stabbed in front of you, that would be pretty scary. That would be something traumatic."

Tamara chewed her thumbnail. She stared intently at her cup of coffee. She didn't know if Dr. Sutherland was trying to trigger another flashback. If so, he was doing a good job. She breathed shallowly and tried to focus on anything but what he was talking about. She'd been momentarily distracted by the offering of fresh coffee and donuts, thinking that she was actually happy to be there. She couldn't let herself be fooled so easily. She had to remain on her guard despite Dr. Sutherland's bribes. He was very good at what he did.

"PTSD can cause a wide range of symptoms," Dr. Sutherland said, shifting his approach. "Not just flashbacks. Anxiety and hypervigilance, anger and other strong emotions, sleeplessness. It can cause physical symptoms like nausea, muscle aches, and loss of appetite. Confusion. Difficulty keeping track of time."

Tamara leaned forward. "All of that?"

"Yes. Maybe some of those symptoms sound familiar?"

"I—how did you know all that?"

"The rate of PTSD is very high in juvenile offenders. It can make people behave in ways that they wouldn't have otherwise. It can contribute to impulsive or violent behavior. You wouldn't be the only person in this facility to suffer from it," Sutherland gave a little smile. "Not by a long shot."

"Zobel said he had it."

"I couldn't comment on Mr. Zobel's specifics," Dr. Sutherland said, "but working daily with violent offenders and being stabbed like he was could certainly lead to PTSD. A lot of police and emergency responders end up with it."

"I don't want any meds," Tamara said flatly.

Dr. Sutherland stroked his goatee, considering that. "The right prescription could really help. You'd feel a lot better."

"I don't want them," Tamara insisted, shaking her head.

"I see. Is there... any particular reason...?"

"I'm not crazy. I don't need it."

"Nobody said you were crazy. Taking a prescription for your mental health does not mean you're crazy."

"I don't want anything."

"Well..." he gave her a slow smile. "Let's not worry about that just now. Why don't you just give me a quick rundown of how you are feeling right now? You have been rather agitated since your return."

Tamara considered her coffee and donut. She took a deep breath and took a glance around the room to make sure once more that Zobel hadn't appeared there and that there was nothing else to trigger a flashback.

"Some of the stuff you said," she admitted. "Having trouble sleeping at night... or waking up in the morning."

He nodded encouragingly.

"I dunno... guess maybe I've been kind of... moody..." She thought about throwing the table over on Lewis and grimaced. "Overreacting... not thinking..."

"Feeling a little bit out of control?" Dr. Sutherland suggested.

Just a little.

That didn't even begin to describe the feeling Tamara had of standing at the top of a precipice, the wind getting stronger and stronger.

She picked up her coffee and took a gulp that burned her throat. The coffee felt like acid in her stomach and she fought to keep it down. As much as she wanted to eat the donut, maybe the first thing that had been appetizing since returning to juvie, she didn't think she was going to be able to manage it.

"My stomach is messed up," she grumbled. "I just... I can't eat."

"I'm sure that's something you would like to improve."

"Doesn't help that the food here is crap."

"I'm afraid that the canteen food is not something I have any control over. You can't eat the donut?"

"Don't know."

"Less anxiety would improve the stomach issues. If you don't want medication, then how about some relaxation and visualization exercises?"

Tamara rolled her eyes. "That stuff doesn't help."

"Meditation can have a very powerful effect on the body and brain. If stress can cause the problems you are experiencing, then de-stressing can help to reverse them."

Tamara had to admit it made sense. She'd never bought into all of the guided relaxation exercises that Dr. Sutherland and the therapist she had seen while she was on parole had recommended. But maybe it was time to reconsider. If they would help to bring her world back into focus...

"Fine," she sighed, "tell me what to do."

THIRTEEN

O N VISITOR DAY, MRS. Henson returned with a
small stack of paperbacks that had been approved by
the administration. Tamara flipped through them,
nodding.

"These look really good. Thanks."

Mrs. Henson nodded. "I hope you enjoy them. Let me know
which you like best and then I know what to get next time."

"Okay." Tamara left them on the table between them. She
ran her thumbnail along a deep cut in the top of the table as if
she were fascinated by it. She didn't want to look at Mrs.
Henson.

"Are you okay?" Mrs. Henson asked. "Are you feeling any
better than you were last time? I know you were a bit down…"

"Yeah, I'm fine."

"That's good." She was smiling brightly when Tamara
glanced up at her face and then looked away again. "Everybody's
entitled to a mood now and then. This has got to be a tough place
for a girl like you to be."

*A girl like her?* Tamara wasn't sure what Mrs. Henson
thought she was like. She'd always seemed to think that Tamara

was better than she was. That if she just put a bit of effort into it, she could be like Nita and Deshawn. Like normal people. Maybe Tamara too had thought that if everybody just gave her a chance, she would show them that she was a good girl. A good girl that bad things had happened to. Things that weren't her fault.

The Hensons took on lots of teen girls. But Tamara didn't know how many came to them from juvie. Harry had been in juvie, she knew that. But he seemed normal. Like he'd recovered from that black mark against his name. Maybe that was why Tamara had thought she could escape the stigma of juvie as well.

"How is everyone?" Tamara asked abruptly, as it occurred to her in a brilliant flash of insight that if she talked about the others, the focus would be off of her. The visit would go by faster, without Tamara feeling like she was under a microscope the whole time, and she could go back to her cell and read a book before bed.

"Things are going fine. Harry got a promotion at work, which is really fantastic. He'll actually earn a living income, so he can start looking at getting a place of his own. Not that we're kicking him out or want him to go. We'll miss having him there. But he'll be so happy to be on his own."

Tamara nodded with interest.

"Jason will miss him terribly, so hopefully we can get another boy to keep him company. Give him someone that he can help out, instead of being so focused on himself."

Tamara didn't remember Jason being particularly self-centered. But then, she didn't remember much about him. He'd been in the background.

"Nita and Deshawn are still joined at the hip. You'd think they were really sisters with how close they are. They send their love, of course. They're still in school. Deshawn is really struggling with the work." Mrs. Henson's brow furrowed. "She has a lot of challenges... we've been able to keep her in school, but I don't know... they're talking about special education if she doesn't show any improvement. She'll drop out before she'll go into a special ed program."

Tamara straightened a little in her chair. "I didn't know Deshawn was..." she couldn't find the politically correct words. Too much time in juvie where words like 'retarded' were thrown around without concern for anyone's feelings. "That she... had... challenges."

"Everybody has their own thing." Mrs. Henson brushed her bangs back. "I don't know much of Deshawn's background you remember..."

They wouldn't have told Tamara anything about Deshawn's past or 'challenges,' would they? Had that been shared with her?

"I... don't think I knew..."

Mrs. Henson raised her eyebrows skeptically. Tamara felt a knot tighten in her stomach. Had she been so focused on herself while at the Hensons' that she hadn't paid any attention to the others and their stories? She remembered Harry had been at juvie. She remembered... Tamara hit a blank wall. Nothing. She didn't remember anything about their backgrounds.

Tamara cleared her throat.

"So she's been having trouble at school...?" She tried to divert Mrs. Henson's attention back to her story.

"Deshawn is very sensitive. It bothers her when other kids think she's stupid or judge her. With her history—alcoholic parents, abuse, poverty—she hasn't had the nurturing, or the opportunity to have her disabilities addressed. She won't accept any accommodations. She doesn't want to look any different from anyone else. It's so important to her to be accepted."

Tamara nodded, trying to read between the lines. "But if she got help...?"

"I don't know how much it would advance her, but *not* getting any help isn't helping her. She's just got it in her head that everyone else is smart and she can't let them see she's stupid."

"But she's not!"

"No. That's her analysis, not mine. That's how she sees herself. And her biggest mission in life is to make sure that nobody else can find out. To look and act just like everyone else."

Tamara had run into girls in juvie who were desperate like that. Always in a gang, because they needed that group behind them, that feeling of belonging. Even if the gang were just as abusive toward them as an enemy would have been. Thinking of Deshawn in that position made her sad.

"Deshawn was always nice to me."

Tamara hadn't always been nice back.

Mrs. Henson nodded. "She's a very sweet girl in spite of being on the receiving end of some very cruel behavior. I just hope we can do something to keep her from dropping out."

"Yeah."

Mrs. Henson sighed and looked up at the ceiling, thinking. "Nita is doing great. If you ever want an example of a kid who has turned her life one-eighty, you look at her. She's a completely different girl than she was when she came to us. I wish you had gotten to know them better when you were with us."

"I guess... I was just too distracted by school and everything. It was... a lot harder than I expected. I thought I'd be able to just... be normal. That everything would be like it was before I went to the Bakers." Tamara tried to breathe through the knot in her stomach. "But it wasn't."

"At least you know that for next time. You'll know what to expect next time."

Tamara pushed herself back from the table slightly, uncomfortable with the direction of the conversation. "I'm not gonna be getting back out. You think I am, but I'm not. You don't know."

"I haven't heard anyone say that you're going to be disqualified from applying again. I think you're the one making assumptions and prejudging the situation."

"It's not your life. I know."

"What have they told you? Has there been some kind of filing made? Some kind of report made against you? Did they tell you that you aren't going to be able to apply for parole again next year?"

"No. I just know. They're never going to put me on parole again. Not after all of that stuff. Not with..." Tamara didn't finish with, "what's been going on lately." Then she would have to explain to Mrs. Henson just what had been going on.

"Tamara..." Mrs. Henson shook her head, smiling a little. "You sound just like you did when they found the marijuana in your locker. You insisted they were going to send you straight back to juvie, no matter what Mr. Collins said."

Tamara looked around her. "They should have. Woulda saved a lot of trouble if they had just put me away."

"They will give you a chance. Even if the parole board doesn't decide for you... they'll still hear you out. They'll still give you a chance to appear and plead your case. And if you're working hard at following the rules here, I don't think they're going to turn you down."

"I'm *not* trying to follow the rules," Tamara insisted, frustrated to have to tell Mrs. Henson again. "I've done that and it got me nothing but trouble. Look at me, I'm right back where I started. Worse than that!"

But Mrs. Henson couldn't see it. She couldn't see inside Tamara's head. She couldn't understand how deeply Tamara was sinking into the quicksand. Tamara wasn't a little girl anymore. She no longer looked like the little twelve-year-old who had been admitted three years before, striped with bruises, abused and pregnant, half out of her mind. But inside, she was still that sad, scared little girl fighting against an unfair and unreasonable world.

"How are you worse off than you were before?"

"You don't get it."

"Then explain it to me."

Tamara shoved the table, her anger swinging in like a wrecking ball. But the table was bolted to the floor, so instead of shoving it into Mrs. Henson, she just pushed herself back.

"I've had enough. Don't bother bringing more books. Don't bother visiting. You're not my family." She got to her feet, ready for the guard to take her back to her room.

"Tamara, it's okay. I'm sorry." Mrs. Henson held up her hands.

Tamara caught a flash of the guard's face in the window.

"Tamara. We can still visit. I'm sorry. I know I'm not in charge of you. I'm so used to being a mom to all of these kids that I just slip into the role without thinking. You're right. You have the right to make your own decisions. I won't push you."

Tears prickled in Tamara's eyes. She took a deep breath, trying to stay in control. It was better if she held on to her anger. It was better to be angry and erratic than vulnerable. Anything was better than being vulnerable.

Mrs. Henson didn't move. She didn't stand up and go after Tamara. She didn't shout at her or threaten her or try to manipulate her. She just sat there, waiting. Tamara lowered herself back into her chair, trying to get the anger back. Mrs. Henson didn't have any right to be pushing her around and dictating what she should do. She shouldn't even be visiting Tamara, who wasn't her foster daughter any longer.

She sat there rigidly, folding her arms across her chest and looking at Mrs. Henson. The guard's face disappeared from the window as he continued on his patrol or to deal with another task.

"I really don't mean to push, Tamara. I'm just trying to help you to get ready, because I know it's going to come around again fast. But you don't have to do anything on my say-so."

Tamara gave a curt nod.

"So... I guess I've updated you on everyone. Jesse and I are just the same. No new developments with us. We do have a new ward and a baby on the way..."

Tamara gasped. Her eyes dropped immediately to Mrs. Henson's belly. A baby on the way wasn't a 'new development?' She pressed her fingers to her mouth, acid rising in the back of her throat. Pregnancy and babies were big, red flags for Tamara. Big, red danger flags.

"No, no!" Mrs. Henson laughed. She put one hand over her slightly round middle-age-spread. "Not me!"

The words took a few minutes to pierce Tamara's consciousness. Not Mrs. Henson. Mrs. Henson wasn't pregnant. She wasn't expecting a new baby. It had been a misunderstanding on Tamara's part.

She drew in a deep breath and tried to force a smile, to put on that she was laughing at herself. But the laughs were sobs, so she kept them in, just giving Mrs. Henson a wide, mad grin.

Mrs. Henson laughed. "Oh, goodness, no," she assured Tamara. "Jesse and I are not having a baby. We have a new foster daughter, Cecelia. She's fifteen, like you, and *she's* expecting. You know that we often help girls out for the first few months, teaching them what they need to know about caring for a baby. Getting them off to a good start. Cecelia will be staying with us until she has her baby and we'll help her with all of those life skills. She has a lot of decisions ahead of her, but she's got a few months to sort things out."

The words were so innocuous. Just Mrs. Henson chattering on about another foster daughter. Of course they had taken on a new girl once Tamara was out of there and they had the space. That space already equipped with a bed and a baby crib just waiting to be used.

Tamara pressed harder over her mouth. "I don't..." She had no idea what she wanted to say.

She was back in that bedroom. Seeing Julie in the crib. Julie had never been in that crib. She'd been long dead by the time Tamara was sent to the Hensons. But the images were all jumbled; her brain was pulling from all different timelines at once like a bad sci-fi movie. Tamara was looking down at Julie in the crib, grey and flaccid, only minutes from death. Jesse opening the door and coming into her room with a cheerful smile on his face, unsuspecting, not realizing the scene that was playing out before Tamara's eyes.

"No."

Tamara put a hand over her own belly.

*"You're pregnant," Dr. Eastport had told her, his sunny face turning serious to deliver the news.*

Tamara wrapped both arms around her stomach, the tears starting, her throat closing up. "No, no, no!"

It wasn't fair. It wasn't fair that they could beat her and use her and put a new life inside her without her consent. She was just a girl and they were adults. The adults held all of the power and Tamara held none. She had no other home or family. No other way to survive. All she had was what they gave her.

The black fog was closing in. Tamara closed her eyes and keened, no longer able to see the baby, Dr. Eastport, or herself.

# FOURTEEN

T AMARA!"

Mrs. Henson was far away. Tamara didn't try to find her or reach her. She was lost inside herself, locked into a prison that had no key and no security code. She sobbed, trying to find her balance.

There would be no more babies. Mr. Baker was locked up and they weren't going to let him go. He wasn't going to be able to get near Mrs. Baker or any other woman. He would be locked in prison for the remainder of his days, or at least most of them, and he would never get the chance to have another baby.

Tamara would not have to take care of them again. Not Corrine, not Julie, and not Amy. Never again. That was over.

"Tamara. What's wrong? Can you talk?"

There was another voice, gruff male, intruding on the space and speaking to Mrs. Henson with a growl. "Move back from the inmate. There's no personal contact allowed in visiting rooms."

"I don't know what happened. She just... collapsed..."

"How? Did she faint?" Already, his hands were on her, feeling her wrist, patting her face briskly. Tamara groaned in protest and tried to move away from him.

More voices, more questions, insistent, drilling into Tamara's skull. She pulled her hands away from her face. "Leave me alone."

"Tamara?" The room was full of people. Mrs. Henson was on the other side of the room, kept back from Tamara. There was relief in her voice. She took a half-step toward Tamara as if she would go back to her side, but the guards prevented her.

"Is she injured?" one of the guards barked. His hands ran over her body, investigating. Tamara tried to squirm away from him.

"Don't touch me!"

"No one is hurting you. Can you tell me what happened?"

Tamara shook her head, her eyes closing, trying to shut out the sensations of his hands on her.

"Let me," a woman's voice said firmly. "We don't need so many people in here. Why don't you take the visitor out? We don't need more than two of us in the room."

The grasping hands withdrew. Tamara could hear Mrs. Henson being taken out, whispering to the guard. The number of bodies in the room was reduced. She no longer felt so closed in.

"Tamara." The woman's voice was close to her. "Can you hear me?"

"Yes." Tamara's voice came out in a tiny whisper, like the cheep of a bird. She had a sudden vision of Sybil's youngest sister, the little one she called Boo, whispering to Sybil.

"Are you hurt somewhere?"

Tamara felt her stomach, which she had been grasping, wondering if she had a stomach-ache or was sick. She blinked, opening her eyes for the barest instant to get the lay of the land. Tamara and two guards, one of them close and one of them at the door.

She rolled onto her side, curved in a fetal position for a few moments. She felt her legs. Mrs. Baker had whipped the hell out of her. Mrs. Baker liked to make her cry and beg for mercy, and then to refuse to give it. But the painful stripes were gone. Her legs, too, were fine.

Tamara slowly sat up. She wasn't sure why she was on the floor of the meeting room. The woman guard didn't tell her to lie back down again. Tamara felt better sitting up, able to see more of what was going on. The vertigo lifted a little.

She felt her throat where it had been cut. While she could still feel the thin lines of scar tissue, it was no longer visible, at least not in the dull metal mirrors of the prison.

"Are you okay?"

Tamara ran her tongue around her mouth. It too was healed. The teeth solidly set and no longer loose.

"I'm fine."

"It's warm in here," the guard at the door observed. "She probably just fainted. Mom's a little hysterical."

"No... she's not my mom."

The woman guard was studying Tamara's face. "How about a drink? You want to get her a glass of water?"

The guard at the door grunted and left the room, shutting the door behind him with a soft snick of the latch. Tamara felt the room temperature immediately rise several degrees. She looked with apprehension at the guard, but the woman made no move toward her, either to secure her or to examine her. The room was claustrophobic. Tamara didn't think there was enough air for them both to breathe for long.

"You'll be okay," the guard assured her. "Just stay calm."

"What happened?"

"I didn't see. Have you ever fainted before?"

"No."

"On any medications?"

"No." She was glad to be able to answer in the negative and not to have to give any details of problems that she might or might not have. "Not on anything."

"Fever today or any time lately?"

"No."

"Are you pregnant?"

"No."

*Never again. Never, ever, ever again.* She could never let any man touch her again.

She next became aware of the plastic cup pressed against her lips. She was still sitting up, though her spine was hunched, like she had fallen asleep sitting in a car.

"Just a sip," the woman encouraged. "You'll feel better."

Tamara parted her lips to let in some of the water, and took a tiny sip. It was cold. She could taste the plastic of the cup and the chlorine of tap water, but it was cold and she hadn't realized how parched she was. She took another swallow and tried to bring her hands up to support the cup herself instead of being fed like an invalid. The guard let Tamara take the cup from her.

"How's that? Little better?"

"Uh-huh."

The woman held the back of her hand out toward Tamara. "I just want to check your temperature. Can I touch you?"

Tamara took a few breaths. She nodded, deciding she could manage that.

The guard's hand was cool. She held it to Tamara's forehead for a moment, then to her cheek, then withdrew.

"Maybe a little warm," she said with a head-shake. "No fever, I don't think."

She crouched there, watching Tamara as she took a few more swallows of water.

"Have you had any new work done?" she asked. "New tats or piercings?"

"No." Tamara touched the teardrop tattoos on her face. "No, nothing since I got back."

"You sure? If you've got an infection, you want the doctor to take care of it right away. They can make a real mess if you let it go too long."

"No. Nothing."

The woman nodded.

When Tamara had finished the cup of water, she handed it back. The guard put it onto the table.

"Ready to get up?"

"I think so."

The guard stood first. She held a hand down to Tamara to assist her. "Hang on to me."

Tamara used the proffered hand to get up, but then let go of her. She stood on her own two feet, getting her balance back again. Feeling like a toddler just learning to walk on shaky, uncertain legs. But in a few minutes she would be okay. The ground would be more solid under her feet. She'd be off and running.

Or walking, anyway.

The guard waited patiently for Tamara to get her bearings back. Tamara walked a little around the room.

"I'll go back to my room," Tamara told her.

The woman looked at her, thinking about it. Whether or not she had to go to the infirmary after a faint was at the guard's discretion. If she made the wrong choice and a girl ended up being really sick, it could be a big deal.

"I'm okay," Tamara said. "Really. Just got too warm, I guess."

"It is warm in here."

Tamara nodded.

Eventually, the woman agreed, giving a tight nod. "Handcuffs for transfer," she advised.

Tamara put her hands behind her back.

"Let's do them in front. If you get dizzy or trip, you can at least catch yourself."

Tamara held her hands in front instead and the guard closed her handcuffs over them.

* * *

TAMARA HAD BEEN BACK in her room for a while before realizing that in all the confusion, she had left her books in the meeting room. The first time that she had gotten a gift from the outside and she had forgotten all about it.

She got up, hoping that pacing would help to clear some of the black fog from her brain. She felt wrung out after the flashback, but couldn't sleep. She wanted to just get her mind right again.

But pacing back and forth across her cell didn't calm her down or clear her brain. The more she paced, the more agitated she got. Irritated, she grabbed the shampoo bottle from her hygiene kit off the dresser, and with a growl, fired it across the room. It bounced back and forth between the walls like a pinball, forcing her to duck and jump out of the way.

Tamara picked the bottle back up. Not even a crack in the plastic.

There was a movement in the doorway and she looked up, tensing, drawing her hand back to fire the indestructible bottle at the threat.

It was Zobel. Tamara lowered her hand again. He looked at her, one eyebrow raised.

"Everything okay in here?"

Tamara let out her breath. "I'm just pissed off."

"About...?"

"Everything. Nothing. At the whole world. At myself."

He gave a laugh and leaned against the doorframe, looking as if he planned to stay for a while.

"I heard you had... an incident in the visitor room."

"Who told you that?" Tamara wondered whether it had already spread all over juvie.

"There was a report in the log." He paused. "It said you fainted because of overheating."

Tamara looked down at her feet, wiggling her toes in her shoes. "Yeah. That's all."

"Uh-huh." He was obviously on to her. Not that she had thought that she could fool him. Not when he'd been the one to figure out in the first place that she was having flashbacks or PTSD, if that was what was going on and she wasn't losing her mind to schizophrenia or some kind of psychosis.

"Mrs. Henson brought me books," Tamara told him. "Then I didn't get to bring them back here, because of... all that. So I don't know where they are. Can you find out?"

Zobel nodded. "Of course. Sure. They were probably just put aside for you. I'll track them down."

"Okay." Tamara let out her breath and tried to relax her stomach muscles. It wasn't all screwed up. She could still get her books back. She didn't know if Mrs. Henson would ever come back after the way Tamara had treated her. But maybe it would be for the better if she didn't. Tamara didn't want to keep fighting her.

"So... how did it go with the doctor?"

"Uh..." Tamara thought quickly. Dr. Sutherland, like the other doctors, always said that anything Tamara told him was completely confidential. He wouldn't share it with anyone else. Even the courts couldn't make him. Unless he had information that led him to believe she was a danger to someone else, he was always very careful to add. That was the one case that he had to tell someone. And Tamara hadn't told him anything like that. "Yeah, it went fine."

Zobel folded his arms across his chest. He studied her closely. "Talking about it helps, huh?"

She swallowed. Why did he have to be so persistent? "I don't know. I just started."

"Is he going to put you on something? I didn't see anything on the med log..."

Tamara opened her mouth to lie. To tell him that Dr. Sutherland didn't want to put her on meds, or it just wasn't on the log yet. Then she changed her mind. "I don't want anything. I told him no."

"Why?"

"I don't... I don't want anything screwing up my brain... and I don't need the others thinking I'm some kind of nut case... if they don't already."

"Having PTSD doesn't mean you're crazy. I think you'd be crazy not to be affected by the things you've been through, don't you?"

Tamara shook her head stubbornly. "You don't know what it's like."

"I told you, I do know. That's how I knew what it was that was happening to you."

"Not that." Tamara shook her head impatiently. "Maybe you have PTSD; that's not what I meant. I meant... you don't know what it's like to be here, a juvie, and have to deal with all that..." she made a motion to encompass the other girls in the unit. "You don't have to survive in here."

His expression changed and Tamara realized she'd said the wrong thing. He didn't have to survive? He almost hadn't. She meant the gang politics and fighting every day for her rep. Protecting herself from immediate physical danger too, but it ran much deeper than that.

"I didn't mean..." Tamara chewed on her lip. She was talking to a wall. He was still looking at her, but he was gone. "Zobel..."

It wasn't a long time. Not like when Tamara fell into one of her flashbacks. He turned his head slightly, his eyes returning to her.

"I'm sorry. I meant... I wasn't talking about..."

"No, it's okay." His voice was not right. He sounded like he was talking underwater. She didn't know if it was because of him or her. "You're right. I carry weapons. I clock out at the end of my shift. I go home." He swallowed. "We're in the same place, but it's not the same."

"I got seven more years." Tamara was desperate for him to understand. "When I'm too old for juvie, they'll move me to the adult prison. You know what it'll be like there? I don't know if I'll ever get out."

He frowned. "You will get out. Parole in a year, or possible release in two. They'd rather have you out of the system than have to transfer you to adult. So they will get you outside, if they can. You're not going to be in prison for the rest of your life. Even if you served your full ten, that's not forever. It might feel like it to you, right now, but it isn't. You will get out."

Tamara shook her head. The hole she was falling down... she would be gone long before her term was up.

"Are you thinking about suicide?"

Tamara brought her hands up to her face and rubbed her eyes, the bridge of her nose, and her temples. Everything hurt. She was so wrung out.

"No." There was no way she was letting them put her on suicide watch. If she wasn't already going crazy, that would do it for sure. Having someone watching her all the time in an observation cell, logging her every fifteen minutes, it was enough to put even a sane person over the edge. "I wouldn't do that. I just... don't see a way out."

Zobel straightened up, no longer leaning on the door frame. "You have a choice," he said. "You don't have to let yourself be blown around by what everyone else does and by every impulse. You can fight this and become a stronger person. I know it isn't easy... trust me, I know that... but you can get better. Things will get better, if you don't give up."

FIFTEEN

TAMARA THOUGHT THAT THEY were taking her to see Dr. Sutherland. Or maybe she was cracking up so obviously that they were going to take her to Psych, despite Tamara's repeated insistence to Zobel that she wasn't going to do anything to hurt herself. It wasn't visitor day, so it wasn't Mrs. Henson with more books. Tamara had told her on each visit that she didn't need to keep coming. Tamara was getting along fine without her and it didn't matter if she didn't have any visitors. Even the books didn't matter, though Tamara had been devouring them faster than Mrs. Henson could bring them.

It was only when she was reading that Tamara felt like she was truly grounded in reality. That was the only time she could escape the dreams, the flashbacks, and the hallucinations. Only when she was living in her mind completely that she no longer felt like she was teetering between reality and insanity.

But she told Mrs. Henson that the books didn't matter. That she didn't need to keep coming to visit and bringing them.

It was hard to keep the flashbacks hidden from Mrs. Henson.

Many days, she called for the guard to end the visit early, knowing she wasn't going to be able to hold it together. Mrs. Henson looked hurt when Tamara wouldn't stay, but she did her best to give Tamara her space. She wasn't, as Tamara continued to remind her, Tamara's mother.

Other people were less likely to notice the flashbacks. Tamara did the guided relaxation exercises with Dr. Sutherland and told him it was helping and she was feeling better. And when she was in a session, she did feel a little better. The relaxation exercises were good for a while. Once she left his office, the benefits fled. By the time she was back to the housing unit, it had all slid away and she was again fighting her demons.

She stayed in her room, away from the common areas, as much as she could, reading and rereading her books, pacing, sleeping, and when she was too exhausted to fight them anymore, lost in wildly distorted flashbacks and imaginings.

She had an uneasy truce with Lewis and the Sharks. Tamara thought by the way Lewis looked at her that she suspected Tamara had something to do with Tabby's and Waterson's deaths. While the security staff knew that Tamara had been in the hallway close to the time of the apparent duel to the death, Tamara said that she had just gone to the john, and the footage didn't prove otherwise. All of the action in the corridor was off-camera. Maybe Lewis knew what the security tapes showed, and maybe she didn't, but it seemed she suspected enough to tell her girls to just leave Tamara alone. She wouldn't want the Sharks getting picked off one at a time whenever Tamara could cut them away from the pack.

"Where am I going?" Tamara demanded, when Kirk didn't take the turn for Dr. Sutherland's office, but instead kept going straight.

"You have a visitor."

"It's not visiting day," Tamara pointed out.

"I'm aware of that."

They walked through a few hallways before Kirk spoke again. "Lawyers don't have to wait for visiting day."

"Lawyers?" Tamara shook her head. "I don't have a lawyer."

"You've been assigned one."

Tamara was slowing down. Kirk reached back to grab her arm and hustle her forward.

"A lawyer for what?" Tamara thought first of Tabby and Waterson. But she hadn't been charged with anything in relation to their deaths. It wasn't anything to do with Corinne's and Julie's deaths, because Tamara had already been convicted of those and was serving out her term. No need for a lawyer.

"I'm not privy to your legal matters," Kirk said dryly.

"But..."

"I'm sure when you get there..." he dragged her forward again, "...he'll tell you what it's all about."

"I don't have a lawyer."

"Go and meet him. If you don't want him to represent you and want to go back to your room, you just say so, and we take you back. But you don't know if you don't meet him in the first place."

"Let go." Tamara yanked irritably on her arm and he released her.

She kept up with his long strides with difficulty. He was probably hurrying because he was irritated with her questions. Tamara's body felt unaccountably slow and clumsy. Maybe coming down with a cold or flu. Tamara went through a final security check to ensure she didn't have a weapon and then was taken into the room where she would meet her lawyer.

It was a few minutes before he was escorted into the room. Tamara studied him. He was about what she expected, a white man in a suit with a shiny black briefcase which had undoubtedly been searched before being allowed in. He was younger than she would have thought, but she supposed they gave the grunt work to the newbies who were still trying to earn their stripes. Let them make their mistakes on the cases that didn't matter.

"Tamara? Hi, I'm Bron Ritter. I've been asked to stand as your counsel in matters coming up on the court calendar in the next few weeks."

He put his hand out. Tamara didn't shake it. "We're not supposed to touch."

"Oh." He dropped his hand to his side, face getting red. "Right." He pulled out the other chair noisily and sat down. He gave her a forced smile, expectant.

"What court cases?" Tamara asked, rubbing the place between her eyebrows where a headache was already starting to pulse.

He raised his eyebrows. "Hasn't anyone talked to you before this?"

"No." Tamara didn't think anyone had mentioned court to her. She would have remembered if someone had told her she was going to court.

"Ah. Well..." Ritter started busying himself with files from his briefcase, not looking at her. He laid the files out and flipped through them, as if he weren't familiar with the details. "The first one is an action against a Mr. Denny Baker for child molestation. You and his wife are the primary witnesses in that case."

He paused to look at her for her reaction. Tamara stared back at him.

"I gotta testify against Mr. Baker?"

"Yes. Yes, that's correct. You are one of the witnesses against him."

Tamara's stomach lurched. She held her arms across it. "What?"

"You are an eyewitness. Aren't you?" He was starting to sound less certain of himself, worried by her reaction.

Tamara wiped her forehead with the back of her arm. "Yeah." Her voice came out in a forced whisper. "Yeah, I'm a witness."

"You gave a statement to the police."

"Did I...?"

He drummed his fingers on the table. "No one has come out to talk to you about it since then?"

"No."

"I'm surprised that neither side has come to depose you, get your full story firsthand."

Tamara shook her head. "Who do *you* act for?" If he were defending Mr. Baker, she was out of there.

Ritter held up his hands in a calming motion. "I don't act for the prosecution or the defense. I have just been appointed to make sure that you have legal advice and someone looking out for your interests."

"Oh." Tamara had never heard of that before. She'd watched plenty of courtroom dramas on TV and thought there were only two sides in a criminal trial.

In her own trial, the public defender had tried hard, but as far as Tamara was concerned, hadn't done anything for her. Not that she helped much in her own defense. Everybody knew she had done it. She never took the stand. She spent most of the trial with her head down on the table, blocking it all out. She didn't talk with her lawyer. She didn't look at anyone in the courtroom or doodle or fidget. She was mentally as far away from there as she could possibly manage.

"Tamara."

Tamara returned her attention to the room, Ritter staring across the table at her, wondering why she had stopped responding to him. Tamara swallowed and cleared her throat.

"I was just thinking."

"About the case?"

"Sort of."

"I need you to say focused here. I don't have a lot of time to spend with you, and I want to make sure we cover all of the main points. We can deal with some details in the next few weeks, but since I don't know how much I'll be able to meet with you, I want to hit the big stuff first."

"Okay."

"From what I understand," his eyes again dropped to his papers instead of looking at Tamara, which was fine with her, "you are here because you were convicted of killing the Bakers' two children."

"Yeah." Tamara's vision blurred. Glock had told her that if she talked about what had happened, Tamara would be able to put it behind her, to stop having the flashbacks and be able to move on in her life. But it hadn't worked that way. It didn't matter if she talked about it or not, she couldn't erase the memories. Not the ones she wanted to. She took deep breaths, trying to focus on her surroundings and not let the flashbacks wash her away.

"At the time you were arrested and tried for the murders, you never said Mr. Baker had done anything to them."

Tamara frowned and looked at him. "Why would I?"

"Well... it might have come up."

"It didn't."

"So you never told anyone three years ago that Mr. Baker had been molesting his children."

"No." Tamara tried to come up with an explanation, but it was difficult for her to understand, let alone explain. "No one listened to anything I had to say. And... I always told myself he wasn't doing anything to them. Only to me."

Ritter picked up a sheaf of pages in his file and tapped the edges on the table to square them.

"I need you to be clear whether you *thought* he *might* be touching them, or whether you *saw* him touching them."

Tamara's stomach rebelled. She sprang up from her chair

and banged her fist on the door, calling for the guard. Ritter sat frozen, unsure what to do.

A guard Tamara didn't know well came to the door.

"The can," Tamara said urgently, gripping his arm. "I gotta go. I gotta go!"

He made a motion to indicate he was going to handcuff her, but Tamara shook her head, looking up and down the hall. "Which way?"

He pointed and started to speak. Tamara ignored whatever he was going to tell her about having to follow security protocols and dashed in the direction he indicated. She didn't look back to see if he followed or was angry, she just ran, scanning for the restroom sign.

Luckily, the door was not locked or alarmed and she made it to the nearest toilet before she lost her lunch, which was a better outcome than she had expected. She hadn't even been sure she'd be able to get out of the meeting room before puking.

She hated her body. Hated her brain. Hated herself for being so weak and so easily upset. At school, she'd always been the kid that would get motion-sickness on the bus when they went on a field trip. As soon as she got a hint of the flu, she'd be throwing up. And at juvie, it seemed that all it took was the right memory, and she was fainting or throwing up. She hated her body for being so weak.

She didn't hear the guard enter, but he was inside the restroom door when she eventually made her way out of the stall.

"I'm sorry," she snapped at him on her way to the sinks. "I couldn't stop. Or I would have puked all over your shoes."

She splashed water on her face, rinsed her mouth, and soaked a folded-up pad of paper towels to put on the back of her neck.

"You wouldn't be the first one," the guard said with good humor.

Tamara looked over her shoulder at him. "Yeah?"

"Yeah."

He didn't rush her through her oblations. Tamara concentrated on what she was going to say. If she had to testify against Mr. Baker, then obviously she was going to have to be able to tell the judge and jury what had happened. If she didn't want to him to be released and go on to molest other girls, they had to be able to put him behind bars.

"You want to go back in?" the guard asked her, when she finally turned off the taps and headed back for the door.

"Yeah. I gotta do it."

"He can come back another day, if you're too sick today. You could go back to your cell and go to sleep."

"No." Tamara sighed. "It doesn't matter when he comes, I'm gonna be sick. May as well get it over with."

"Okay, then. Let's go." He escorted her back to the meeting room, and Tamara reluctantly sat back down in her chair.

Ritter's eyes were wide. "Uh... are you okay?"

Tamara pushed back against his baffled tone. "Would you be okay if some sicko raped you and got away with it, and then you had to go to court to tell them how he messed with his kids too? They're not gonna believe me any more than you do."

"I didn't say I don't believe you." He held his hands out in protest, his voice going up several notes. "I just asked you a simple question. Whether you saw."

"Yeah. I saw," Tamara said stonily, folding her arms across her chest.

"Okay." He took a moment to write a note on his yellow legal pad. "If you saw, why didn't you tell anybody when you became aware of it?"

"Nobody believed anything I said," Tamara insisted. "When I told them other things about Mr. and Mrs. Baker, they didn't believe me. Didn't think they were doing anything wrong. If I told someone he was messing with the kids, they'd have sent me here. Or Mrs. Baker would've beaten me. There wasn't anyone who would listen."

"You don't think that if you reported that he was sexually abusing his little girls that anyone would have investigated it?"

"No. If they did, what would they find? Just touching isn't going to leave any evidence. They were too little to tell. Corrine was three. Julie was just a baby."

"You said you had tried to tell about other things. What do you mean? Did you tell them about Mr. Baker abusing you?"

Tamara shook her head. Her face got hot. Three years ago, she'd only been twelve. Still a baby herself. She remembered trying to work up the courage to talk to her teachers at school, her guidance counselor. They always said their doors were open. If anyone had anything they needed to talk about, they only had to ask. But that wasn't how it had worked. When she skulked around the office, watching for an opportunity to talk to her counselor, the secretarial staff grilled her about what she was doing there. When she said she wanted to see her counselor, they said she had to schedule an appointment, he was too busy. They wanted to know why she wanted to speak to him.

When her math teacher kept her in after school for falling asleep during class, she had tried, one revelation at a time, to explain to him the situation she was stuck in. She didn't get enough sleep because she had to take care of the babies at night. She had to take care of the cooking and the house cleaning. Mrs. Baker was working at night and Tamara had to take over all her duties. But the teacher had just rolled his eyes and told her that she needed to turn off the TV and get to bed in good time so that she'd get enough sleep. He was unsympathetic about her having to do work around the house, to babysit the kids. He'd had a part-time job when he was a teenager. It had been good for him, taught him responsibility. It was good that she was learning to be responsible too.

When she refused to change for gym, the teacher had asked what was wrong. Tamara confessed that she didn't feel well, but not that her body was so bruised and flayed that she couldn't undress or put on shorts. They didn't think she was really sick, insisting on a doctor's note, or at least a parent's note, but Tamara steadfastly refused, choosing instead to serve detentions.

"What's wrong, Tamara?" the gym teacher wheedled, wanting Tamara to change and join in on the volleyball lesson. "Is something wrong? You can tell me what's going on, I won't share it with anyone else."

Maybe she thought Tamara was just on her period or had a skin condition. None of them had considered that it might actually be something serious, something way beyond the scope of being ashamed of her body or having cramps.

"I'm not feeling good," Tamara whispered, holding her stomach. "And I hurt my knee. Mrs. Baker said I should sit out."

"Maybe we should call Mrs. Baker to confirm that."

"No!" Tamara swallowed. "You can't call her. She works nights. She's asleep right now. You can't wake her up or..." she trailed off, not able to name what Mrs. Baker would do to her.

"Then you're not *really* hurt or sick, are you?" the teacher asked with a knowing smile. "If you were really hurt or sick, you would have a note from the doctor or your mother."

"I... I can't play today."

So she had sat on the stage watching the other girls play. Ignoring them when they asked her why she didn't join in, or made comments about her and made up nasty reasons why she couldn't play, all of which were much closer to the truth than anything the teachers had suggested. She'd even fallen asleep once watching the gym class, resting her eyes for just a moment... waking to find an angry boys' basketball coach shaking her awake.

"You're not supposed to be here. You should be in your next class by now. What are you doing sleeping here?"

Tamara knew that her teacher had decided to teach her a lesson. To face the natural consequences of falling asleep, having all of the boys laugh at her and tease her.

When things had gotten really bad, when she was constantly missing morning classes to throw up in the girls' room, failing to hand in any work, in such a fog that she didn't know which class she was supposed to be in when the class change bells rang, then they had hauled her in front of her guidance counselor. Then he suddenly had time to meet with Tamara to give her dire warnings about the direction her life was going. Before she went to the Bakers, she had been getting all A's. By then, her grades had all fallen to F's. Her counselor was sure she was drinking and on drugs and had lectured and cajoled her, trying to get her to admit it.

Why would she have told any of them what Mrs. and Mr. Baker were doing to her? Or to the babies? Why would she humiliate herself like that? She was so beaten down and exhausted, she would have done anything to get out of there.

Anything.

"I told them other things. They never cared. I wasn't going to tell them I let him... do what he did to me. To the girls. I was supposed to take care of them. To protect them. How could I protect them against him?"

"Did Mrs. Baker know? Did you talk to her about it?"

"Talk to her?" Tamara saw Mrs. Baker's bleached blond hair falling tousled around her face, the cruelty in her face, the predatory eyes and sharp lines of her face. The woman had slapped and pinched Tamara as often as she talked to her, punctuating each command or criticism with physical punishment. Such casual cruelty. Which was nothing like when she was truly mad about something and she took Tamara downstairs to where no passersby would be able to hear Tamara's screams. To the cement-floored room Mrs. Baker kept stocked with whatever she might need to teach Tamara the error of her ways and train her to perform her duties in a satisfactory way. The woman was a demon, but they just kept letting her go.

"So Mrs. Baker might *not* have known at that time that Mr. Baker was hurting the children."

"She knew," Tamara said with certainty. "That's why they got me. So that he could get what he wanted and she wouldn't have to worry about him touching the babies."

"Did she say that? Did either of them say that?"

"No."

"So that's only conjecture."

"I know what happened. He was on to me the first day I got there. He didn't wait one day before he started moving in." She opened her mouth to say more, but the words were strangled in her throat. She cleared her throat a couple of times and looked around for a drink, but no cup or bottle of water had been provided.

Ritter waited for more, then shrugged, deciding she was done.

"I'm sorry for what you went through with them, Tamara. No one should have to put up with being treated like that."

She appreciated that he at least attempted to apologize to her. Few other adults had shown her any sympathy for what she had gone through. And rightly so, as she had gone from being the prey to being the predator. No one had sympathy for a predator.

"They never had to serve any time," Tamara told him. "Not one single day for what they did to me."

"That's not right."

Tamara nodded.

"When did you become aware that he was interfering with the little children as well?"

Tamara wished there were a window to look out. She would have given anything to be able to look outside and just watch the cars drive by or the birds flying in the sky. Anything but having to see Mr. Baker standing before her. She shifted in her chair, wishing she could throw up again. Wishing there were some escape for her. She got up and paced across the room, her guts tied too tightly in knots to sit any longer.

"It wasn't all at once... and it wasn't real obvious. You had to be paying attention. But if you did..." Tamara gulped. She put her hands on the wall to brace herself. Leaned her forehead against it. "When he got Corrine ready for bed... bathed her, cuddled with her while he told her stories... if you watched his hands..." Her voice cracked. "Or when he was changing Julie. Wiping her. Putting cream on her..." Tamara clutched her stomach and turned around so that her back was against the wall, leaning on it to hold herself up. She breathed heavily. "At first I thought... I was just imagining. But I wasn't. Every chance he got, he was touching them. Even if I was in the room, or Mrs. Baker was. He just... pretended he was taking care of them like a good daddy. And they loved him. They weren't scared of him, didn't ask for someone else to give them baths or put them to bed instead of him. They didn't cry."

"Did you ever confront him? Accuse him?"

"No!" Tamara wiped at the corners of her eyes. "I was *twelve years old!*"

Surely he could understand the position she was in. She'd had no other home or family. Mr. Baker using her and Mrs. Baker beating her at the slightest hint of laziness or opposition. Their threats about what would happen if she had to leave there. Where she would end up if she told her social worker. She had been tired and sick and scared and frantic to find some way out. Any way to escape.

"And Mrs. Baker? Did she ever say anything to him about it? Tell him to stop?"

"Mostly, she would just look at him, and he'd give her this smirk like it was all a big joke... sometimes she'd tell him to cut it out, and then he'd complain about how she was neglecting him, how she never showed any interest in him. She'd tell him to get me to help him out..." Tamara swore. She rubbed her aching head. "I didn't get it then... I was such a baby, so naive, I missed all of the stuff they weren't saying... but when I look back at it now..." She shook her head. "They were so sick. So, so twisted."

Ritter nodded his agreement. His face, rather than being sympathetic like before, was blank. He didn't get red and embarrassed like he had at first. He didn't try to apologize to her. He just looked... sickened. Tamara put her face in her hands. She didn't cry, but she just couldn't look Ritter in the face.

"You realize, don't you, that the jury is going to have a hard time believing you. The fact that you never suggested this to anyone until after going back and kidnapping Amy..."

"I recorded him. When I went back and they had Amy. I recorded them on the baby monitor, her telling him not to touch her. I gave it to the police."

"But they can't see what's happening. It's only your interpretation of what was happening."

"I saw him do it before! And Mrs. Baker was there. She's testifying."

"She's cut a deal for that testimony. And you've cut a deal for the kidnapping charges. You can see how it might look to the jury like the prosecutor is railroading him, bribing the two of you to testify against him."

"That's not true!"

"That's how they're going to see it."

"What am I supposed to do, then? What am I supposed to say?" She was glad to have anger displacing the horror of those memories. It was better to be angry than to be a victim. She was justified in the rage that boiled up in her. After all that had been done to her, she was right to be angry.

"All you can do is tell them the truth, like you're telling me.

I'm just warning you what you're going to face. You have a lot of strikes against you as a witness. The defense is going to try to pull your testimony apart. They're going to try to make it sound like you're responsible for letting it happen."

Tamara glared at him, letting the anger simmer, but he held her gaze, eyes steady. Tamara let her breath out slowly and nodded.

"Okay."

"Don't try to dress it up. Don't try to justify yourself or embellish what he did. Just keep your testimony true and straightforward."

Tamara nodded again. She looked toward the door, anxious to get back to her bunk and to bury it all away again the best she could.

"We're not done," Ritter warned, understanding the look.

"What else?" Tamara snapped.

"The other case."

"Oh." He had told her that there were a couple of cases, but it hadn't really sunk in. "Is it Mrs. Baker? Am I supposed to be testifying against her too?"

"No. The other case is unrelated."

"What is it, then?"

Again, the show of shuffling papers and looking at his file as though he couldn't quite remember the details of the case.

"You are subpoenaed as a witness in the case of assault against Mr. Quentin McClure."

Tamara stepped toward Ritter and leaned on the back of her chair. "Coach McClure? Did he... survive? It's not murder, just assault?"

Ritter nodded, his eyes curious.

"Is he... is he okay? I mean... is he in hospital still? Is he... better?"

She was hopeful and dreading his answer at the same time.

She didn't want to have been involved in a murder or in leaving Coach McClure in a coma or disabled, but at the same time, she didn't want him preying on anyone else.

She shuddered, remembering Glock's words after the attack.

"You were worried about that scum molesting Lotta or other girls? I took care of it. He's never gonna do that again. You don't have to worry."

"You killed him!" Tamara protested.

"Maybe I did. Maybe I didn't. Won't know until we hear the news tomorrow. But either way, he's not going to be hurting anyone else again anytime soon."

Tamara had been sure at the time that Glock had killed McClure. The scene had been horrific. She was sure that no one could have survived the bludgeoning that McClure had taken and survive.

But Dr. Eastport had once chattered cheerfully to Tamara about how hard human skulls were, after examining Tamara's head injury to make sure he didn't have to have her sent to the hospital after an incident.

"You never know, from one person to the next, how sturdy or fragile their skull is. You can't tell by looking at a person and the size or shape of their head how thick and solid it is. Some skulls will fracture like an eggshell. Others... I once examined a fellow who was hit in the head with an I-beam on a construction site. The blow threw him twenty feet and put him out cold. But he was conscious by the time the ambulance got there and, other than a bruise and a headache, there was no appreciable damage. Not even a hairline crack." Dr. Eastport lifted the ice pack to examine the swelling knot on Tamara's own head. "You, my dear, may be thankful that you do not have an eggshell. Your head is at least as hard as the average skull, if not harder."

"Great."

"*Tamara.*"

Tamara closed her eyes, trying to stay in the moment, with Dr. Eastport in the infirmary, having a lighthearted conversation while he treated her. But Ritter pulled her back to the present.

"Tamara, did you hear me?"

She rubbed her head. "Yes! No, what did you say?"

"Please pay attention." He looked at his watch. "I don't know how much more time I'll have."

"Sorry."

"McClure is out of hospital. On disability. He's doing therapy, but they don't know how much function he'll recover."

"So..." she tried to unwind his words. "He's okay? He's getting better?"

"He's well enough to be out of the hospital," Ritter's voice was sharp. "I don't think there's any likelihood that he will go back to his old job again."

"I hope not! He should be behind bars, not at home!"

"I know there are rumors going around—"

"Rumors?" Tamara's voice rose. "Those weren't rumors! He got one of the girls on the volleyball team pregnant! And he was messing around with another one of them. Who knows how many years he'd been doing it. How many girls' lives he ruined!"

"Unless he was inappropriate toward you, I don't think we can assume his guilt. He hasn't been tried—"

"I saw with my own eyes. It's not just a rumor."

Ritter pressed his lips together. "Tamara, I don't know all of the details of this assault, but it's my understanding that you are not being charged with being an accessory. If you start saying things like that on the stand... you're just asking for them to lay charges against you too."

"I'm not saying anything that isn't true," Tamara growled.

"That's not the point. My point is, if you get up on the stand and spout about how he deserved what he got, you can expect retaliation. You don't have a deal on this one. There's nothing to stop them from charging you at any time. So you'd better be careful what you say when you get up on the stand."

"Fine." Tamara slid into her chair, her knees wobbly. She didn't want him to see how weak she was. "I'll keep my big mouth shut."

"You still need to talk. You still need to testify as to what happened. I'm just warning you, keep it calm and don't start throwing around accusations, or you're going to end up in front of a judge as well."

"I got it." Tamara bit off each word.

He sat there, looking at her without speaking. Tamara hunched her shoulders over and rubbed her head. She just wanted so much for it to be over, so she could go back to her room, close her eyes, and pretend it had never happened.

"So... this isn't Coach McClure's trial," she said, slowly understanding what Ritter was saying. "This is about Glock."

"Uh—Kayla Spielman," Ritter said, looking at his papers.

Tamara knew that Spielman was Glock's last name. That was what the guards had called her, rarely acknowledging the nickname she preferred. Tamara had never actually heard her first name before. Kayla. It was foreign, something that didn't belong to her. Even Collins and the TV news hadn't called her Kayla, but referred to her as Glock Spielman.

"Yeah... Glock is what she goes by."

"Is testifying against her a problem?"

It was obvious from the tone of his voice that he thought it would be. They had gone to see McClure together. Tamara had associated with Glock even though she was out on parole and not supposed to have anything to do with felons.

"The two of you were friends?" Ritter pressed.

"No... she was... she was my cellie here for two years. My cellmate. For two years." Tamara knew she was repeating herself, but no other words would come to her. Glock wasn't her friend. That wasn't how it worked. Tamara was guilty of taking Glock to the school to talk to McClure, but she hadn't had a clue what Glock had really had in mind.

"I assume since you weren't charged, that the prosecution had reason to believe you either weren't involved or would testify against Spielman in court."

Tamara's mind was racing. Was she up to testifying against Glock? They were no longer in the same facility, so Glock couldn't retaliate. She would be in prison a long time for what she had done to Coach McClure. And for threatening to kill Tamara's parole officer. Could Tamara be sure that Glock wouldn't be able to reach out to her through other inmates in the system?

"I never hit Coach McClure," she told Ritter. "I only went there to talk to him, to get him to confess to what he did to Lotta and Holly. Glock said if I could get a recording of him admitting it... we could put him away. That's why I was there. Not to hurt him." She shook her head and closed her eyes, as if that would stop the images from coming back to her. She had been paralyzed, unable to do anything to stop Glock. Even if she tried, she knew Glock was bigger, stronger, and crueler than Tamara could ever be. She could just as easily bludgeon Tamara as McClure. Tamara wouldn't have stood a chance. Not without guards there to stop Glock.

She had screamed and screamed at Glock, but that was all she could do. Helpless and hopeless. She couldn't believe that was what Glock had been planning from the beginning. And she couldn't believe that she hadn't seen it coming. Of course Glock had been planning to hurt McClure. Glock wasn't the type who talked things over. Tamara had been an idiot not to have seen it.

"No..." Tamara shook her head, unable to stop the beating playing out in front of her eyes again and again. "No..."

"No, what?" Ritter asked.

Tamara got farther away from the scene, until she couldn't really see it anymore. She could just hear the blows falling, over and over again, the dull thuds of the heavy trophy landing against McClure's skull. Glock's grunts of effort. Tamara realized that her hand was hitting the table, punctuating the memory. Hitting it for every time Glock hit McClure. She caught her fist in her other hand and held it still.

"No, what?" Ritter repeated.

"No... I never hit him. I never intended to hit him. That was all Glock."

"And you'll testify in court. You'll tell them what she said and did. How she planned it herself and that you didn't take part."

Tamara nodded. "Yeah."

"It might be hard for people to believe. That you didn't know what you were getting into, I mean. That you didn't hit McClure as well, the two of you together."

"But I recorded it," Tamara said. "I recorded the whole thing. They'll play it. They'll hear me yelling at her to stop."

Ritter raised his brows.

"If they have that kind of evidence, why is this going to trial? Why doesn't Spielman just take a plea? Save the taxpayers the expense of a trial."

Tamara snorted. "Glock never did anything for anyone else's good. She only does what she wants."

"You think she wants to take this to trial?"

"Probably."

"Why? Why would she want that?"

Tamara looked down at her feet, considering. "Maybe she wants the attention. I don't know. She wants people to look at her and know what she did. She wants to get out of prison on a day trip. How do I know?"

"Do you think maybe she wants to throw some of the blame back on you? Say that it was all your idea? Maybe that you wimped out in the end, but it was all your plan."

Tamara lifted her hands in a helpless shrug. "I don't know what's in her head."

"Put yourself in her head. You said you shared a cell for two years. You must have gotten some insight into her thought processes."

"Yeah... enough to know that her brain isn't somewhere I want to be."

# SIXTEEN

TAMARA HAD A COUPLE more visits with her lawyer over the ensuing weeks, occasional blips in the otherwise mind-numbing routine of juvie. Tamara knew that she should be happy that things weren't interesting or exciting. She'd had enough excitement, she didn't need any more. Lewis and the Sharks seemed to have forgotten about her, letting her fade back into the woodwork. Though things weren't quite the same as they had been; Tamara had been quiet and unobtrusive before, which had made her easy to ignore. That had changed.

Tamara was sitting in math class when she heard it.

At first it seemed quiet and far away, like a squeak in the ventilation. Something that was just at the edge of her ability to hear. She looked around covertly at the others, seeing if anyone gave any sign of having heard it as well.

Everyone sat casually, bored attitudes, slumped to one side or leaning on an elbow, head thrown back in algebra overload or nodding to their chests. No one seemed the least bit interested in the lesson or the noise.

Tamara cocked her head, listening for it, trying to catch it again.

It seemed a little closer. A little more clear. A bird call or a small animal. But there were no outside windows in the room. No way they could hear anything from the outside. Unlikely there would be any kind of animal on the inside. Not even rats.

Tamara tried to tune it out and focus on the lesson. The teacher had noticed her distraction and was trying to catch her eye. Tamara stared at the board and tried to work out the next step to solve the problem.

It was closer. Clearer still. Not an animal. A voice.

Quavering high notes. A throbbing sob. More wails, followed by chugs. Tamara looked around her.

"What *is* that?"

Girls' heads snapped up. They looked at Tamara.

"What?"

Eyes grew wider and heads cocked as others tried to identify what Tamara was talking about. But it wasn't hard to hear. They shouldn't have had to strain to hear it or question what it was Tamara was talking about. It was as clear as a bell.

"*That.* That crying. Is it a baby?" Tamara looked around at the faces, all turned in her direction. They all seemed baffled. Tamara listened. It was. It was a baby. But who would bring a baby to juvie? It wasn't even visiting day. Some of the girls were pregnant; it was a fact of life, a foregone conclusion that some of the girls would, like Tamara, enter juvie pregnant. They were allowed the option of carrying a pregnancy to term if they really wanted to, though few did. What was the point when the baby would just be apprehended when it was born, given to some foster family DFS chose at random? Who would want to go through all of the trouble and risk of a pregnancy, just to have a baby in juvie and give it away?

Some of the girls figured they'd be able to get their babies back once they got out, if they only had a short time before release. Someone with a sentence like Tamara's would be crazy to think they could carry a baby to term and have a chance of parenting it someday.

But there was a baby. Tamara could hear it.

Maybe one of the girls who had been pregnant had delivered. It could happen unexpectedly. Too early or too fast to get a girl to hospital in time. Tamara couldn't think of anyone in the unit who was that close, but that didn't mean anything. Some girls hid their pregnancies well, and it was a possibility that someone who hadn't even been identified as being pregnant had made it to delivery without being discovered.

"A baby?" echoed Perez, eyeing Tamara. "What are you talking about? There's no baby."

"Are you deaf?" Tamara challenged. "I can hear it as clear as day. You don't hear *anything?*"

"No."

Tamara frowned at her, wondering if Perez were trying to gaslight her or just being funny. Perez didn't crack a grin. If she were baiting Tamara, she was a pro. There were no tells. No facial expression indicating she was lying.

One of the other girls swore. "You're flippin' crazy, French. There's no baby here. No one is crying."

Tamara looked around at their faces, trying to find a crack in their armor. They couldn't all pull it off. One of them would look away. One would be unable to hide a smile.

For a minute, it was quiet. The crying ceased and Tamara could hear nothing but restless feet under desks, papers shuffling, whispered comments.

"It... I guess it stopped," Tamara said, her face getting warm. She hadn't been making it up. It had been there.

The other students turned away from her, the teacher resuming the interrupted lesson. A few seconds went by and then the crying started again.

"There it is!" Tamara exclaimed. "You can hear that, can't you?"

She wasn't talking to anyone in particular, but she desperately wanted someone else to agree that yes, they heard a baby crying too. But they all just looked at her.

"Do you want to be excused, French?"

Mrs. Hawkins was one of the older teachers. Crusty, but fair, and a good teacher. Good at explaining concepts to girls at all different levels and with all sorts of challenges. She was the kind of teacher who could actually tell them when they were going to need to know a particular skill in their lives. Going grocery shopping. Balancing a check book. Budgeting. Maybe going to college to upgrade their skills and have a chance at a better life and a bigger paycheck.

Did she think that Tamara was just looking for an excuse to get out of class? Tamara didn't need an excuse. She'd been there long enough to know that all she had to do if she didn't want to stay was to walk out. She could go back to her bunk if she wanted to. She could put her head under her pillow and see and hear nothing and pretend that math class didn't even exist.

"*You* can hear that, can't you?"

Mrs. Hawkins raised her brows, cocked her head to the side and appeared to be paying attention.

"No. I'm sorry. Old ears. Listened to too much heavy metal." Mrs. Hawkins gave a little laugh and waited for everyone else to do the same.

Tamara swore and slammed her hand down hard on the top of her desk. "This isn't funny! Don't laugh at me! I can hear it. You can all hear it. Quit messing around with me!"

The good-humored smile on Mrs. Hawkins' face disappeared. "No, Miss French. I'm not making fun of you. Maybe... maybe your ears are ringing. You have a cold? Coming down with the flu?"

Tamara shook her head impatiently. She knew the difference

between ringing ears and a baby crying. It was closer now. She knew it had to be very close by. She stood up. She inadvertently knocked several books to the floor, but she didn't try to retrieve them. She just headed for the door. It was ridiculous for them to keep telling her they couldn't hear something that was so plain. Tamara didn't understand the point.

She pulled open the classroom door and looked around, expecting to see the baby in the hallway. Someone would be holding it. A guard who had been unable to find child care for their sick baby before coming to work. A couple of paramedics with a gurney, taking out an inmate who had just delivered a premature baby. Somebody playing a sound effect from a digital recorder.

But the hallway was nearly empty. Tamara looked at the guard she had startled by opening the door. He looked at her as she looked up and down the silent, still hallway. "Something wrong, French?"

"Shut up," Tamara snapped. She looked back and forth. Which way had the baby gone? Around the corner one way or the other. There were only two possibilities. She moved to the right. Chances were, she'd run right into them. If the baby started crying and it was coming from the other direction, Tamara could reverse direction and find it.

As she moved, the guard shadowed her. Tamara wanted to tell him to get lost, but she was too busy trying to find the baby to spend any time arguing with him. She had to prove to herself that there was a baby. She hadn't just been hearing things. Who knew why the class had been trying to fool her? She'd sort that out later.

Tamara rounded the corner at the end of the hall and again faced an empty hall.

"Where did they go?" she demanded. Not that there was anyone to ask but the guard trailing behind her. Tamara hurried on. They had to be close by. She hesitated about which direction to go, and then heard it again. A chugging sob. Close by. Very close by. She went to the end of the hall and looked around. Nothing.

Nothing and no one.

Were they broadcasting it on the speakers? Through the PA system? Maybe it was some kind of feedback loop? Or were they running an experiment, seeing if they could actually drive her crazy, or at least make her think that she was?

"Stop it!" she shouted. "Just cut it out!"

Silence. And then the low throb of a baby's cry. Farther away. They were trying to take it away. Erase the evidence. Make everyone think that Tamara had just been hearing things.

There was a hand on her arm. Grabbing her and pulling her back. Tamara threw back an elbow into her attacker and whirled around to face him. One of the guards. His hands still reached out, threatening.

"Just chill, French. You want to tell me what this is all about? What's going on?"

"You know what is going on," Tamara accused. "You know as well as anyone here what is going on. Whatever this is, it isn't going to work. You hear me?" Tamara looked up and yelled at the surveillance cameras. "You hear me?"

"I'm not sure what's bothering you, but I think you need to take a deep breath and relax." The guard took a deep breath himself to demonstrate. "Just a nice, deep breath. Can you do that?"

"Go to hell!" She didn't need anyone giving her relaxation exercises. She wasn't cracking up. She was the only sane one there. She took a step toward him, and he took a step back, keeping a cushion of space in between them, even though he had been the one pursuing Tamara.

"It's okay. Just take it easy. Why don't you fill me it? Tell me what it is that has upset you."

"Like you don't already know?" She swore at him. "Get out of here. Just leave me alone."

She was allowed to walk around without an escort. She wasn't on any restrictions.

"I can't leave you alone when you're so agitated."

"I'm not agitated. I'm going for a walk. Back to my bunk. So just leave me be and I'll get there just fine."

He stood there, not arguing with her, but Tamara knew very well that as soon as she started walking again, he was going to be with her. She looked down the hallway, listening for the sound of the baby. Had they taken the baby away? Had it ever been in the hallway, or just in the PA system? Or transmitted directly to her brain? She was sure they had the technology. It wouldn't be so hard to do.

"What are you looking for?" the guard prompted.

"I want to know how they did that. Made me hear that when no one else could. Was it a trick?"

"I don't know. Maybe we should go see someone, find out."

"Go see who? No one is going to admit it."

"But maybe we should get you checked out. Just make sure everything is okay."

"Where, the infirmary? There's nothing wrong with me."

"I'm not saying there is," he soothed. "I just think it would be better at this point if we checked in, made sure there was nothing to be concerned about."

"Do you think I'm stupid?"

"No. I just think you're confused. You're acting confused."

Then the baby started crying again. Tamara's head went up as if she'd received an electric shock. It was close. Very close. She glanced at the nearest speaker, just to make sure the noise wasn't coming out of the system, and then dashed down the hall, determined this time to be fast enough to catch them and prove what was going on.

"I hear you! I know you're there!"

But it wasn't in the next hall, or the next, and Tamara's legs were starting to shake like she'd run a marathon instead of a few hallways. What kind of shape was she going to be in at the end of ten years, if after three she couldn't even run down a couple of corridors?

Tamara stopped, bracing herself with a hand on the wall. She took a few long breaths.

"It was here," she told the guard who approached her. "I swear, it was."

He nodded. "Okay."

"It's not the flu. I don't have a fever." Tamara felt her own forehead. That never worked.

"We should probably check, just to be sure," the guard suggested. "The doc, he's got one of those electronic ear-temperature testers. It's so quick…"

"I don't want to go to the doctor," Tamara groaned. "I'm not sick."

"It will only take a few minutes and then you can go back to your bunk."

Tamara started walking with him. The halls seemed long, like marching in a desert. Maybe she was coming down with something. Maybe she did have a temperature. It was possible.

"I was just fooling around," she told the guard. "I didn't really hear anything. I was just joking."

"Okay."

They walked a little farther. "What was it that you didn't hear?"

"A baby. I heard—I didn't hear—a baby crying. It wasn't. I just made it up. Having a little fun with you."

"Funny girl."

"It doesn't mean anything. It was just a silly thing. A whim. A dare."

"Okay."

"Why would there be a baby here?" Tamara gave a little

laugh. "There's no babies around here. If I was going to hear something, it should at least be something that I could actually have heard. Something that made sense."

"Oh, I don't know. Everybody else does logical, why follow the crowd?"

Tamara turned her head to look at him. He was familiar to her, but she couldn't match a name to the face. The turnover of guards at juvie was getting worse and worse. It seemed like there were new faces every week. The old ones went on to do something else, and new ones were brought in. It must have been hell trying to train them all. Constantly trying to teach the policies and procedures to brand new faces.

"You're okay?" he asked.

Tamara nodded. She looked at his name bar. Durham. She thought she had seen that name before. The name and the face; he must not have been brand new. She'd seen him and talked to him before.

Tamara shook her head. She turned a corner to head back to her room.

"This way," Durham corrected, motioning.

Tamara looked at the direction he motioned. "Uh... no. My room is this way."

"We're going to stop at the infirmary first. Remember?"

"No. I'm just going to my bunk."

"French. It will only take a few minutes. Just long enough to make sure everything is hunky-dory."

"I've had enough of doctors."

"Since when? Have you been seeing a lot of doctors lately?" he challenged, a grin on his face and teasing note in his voice.

"I've... no, I just want to... I don't want to see Dr. Sutherland. I just want to go read a book."

"Not Dr. Sutherland," he coaxed. "Just a quick visit with Dr. Eastport. He'll want to see you."

Tamara hesitated. He put his hand on her arm. For the

moment, she was free of handcuffs, but if she fought him, if she pushed it too hard, he would stop being so patient and chain her. She didn't really have the choice whether to go to the infirmary or not. He acted like she had the choice, but she recognized that she really didn't. She had only one choice, whether to go on her own, or whether to be forced.

"I'm just fine," she insisted. "He'll tell you."

"I'm sure he will," Durham agreed. "Let's just go see."

* * *

"IT WAS A JOKE," Tamara repeated, looking up at the ceiling steadily. "I was just messing around with everyone."

Dr. Sutherland had been informed of Tamara's latest episode, and was trying to cajole the truth out of her and to persuade her that it was time to cooperate with him to get some proper testing done.

"Why would you do that?"

"It was the middle of algebra," Tamara informed him. "It was boring!"

"It was boring. So you thought, 'let's stir things up a little by pretending to hear a baby crying.'"

"Exactly. And it worked! No more boring algebra."

"Tamara..."

"I'm fine. F-I-N-E. Fine." She was being deliberately obnoxious. If she riled Dr. Sutherland up enough, maybe he would give up. He would call the guard back in to take her away, making a point of not giving her a candy at the end of the session, and she could go back to normal. Whatever normal was. Whatever it had become.

So she stared up at the ceiling and swung her feet over the arm of the chair, kicking.

"I don't think you're telling me the truth. I don't think you're okay at all, and I believe you know it. I've been getting a lot of reports and concerns about you since you returned here a few months ago, Tamara. You know that. I want you to trust me. Have I ever done anything to make you think you can't trust me?"

*Yup.*

Tamara nearly answered him aloud, the word coming to her lips. She clamped down her teeth and pressed her finger over her lips to make sure they stayed shut.

Did he really think that she would trust him? She knew that he lied to her. He didn't care what the truth was, just that she and the other inmates stayed quiet and didn't cause the administration any trouble.

"You're not alone, Tamara," Dr. Sutherland said, in a voice that was supposed to calm and soothe her. Inviting her trust and her confidence.

But instead, it made Tamara look around, suppressing a shudder. *You are not alone.* She looked for a ghost. For the baby. For a guard sneaking at the corner of her vision, like they insisted on doing.

*You are not alone.*

There was no flitting ghost this time. Of course not. Dr. Sutherland hadn't meant that at all. He had meant himself. She wasn't alone, she was with him. And she could trust him and tell him everything that was going on in her broken brain.

Only she couldn't. Because as broken as her brain was, she still knew that she couldn't trust him. She couldn't trust anyone. They would lock her up and throw away the key if they knew how wrecked she was. Tamara closed her eyes.

There had been a sci-fi movie on in the common room the night before. One in which, in an eerie parallel to Tamara's life, the main character thought he was going crazy, only to find out that he was the only sane one, and everyone around him was being replaced by aliens. She could believe that. It would make perfect sense in her life. Or that she had been infected by an alien life form and it was gradually eating away at her consciousness and replacing hers with its own. Either way, the protagonist did not reveal his situation to anyone else. Because that would be informing the aliens that he was aware of them. It would make him a threat to them.

"Tamara."

"Yes, Dr. Sutherland?" Tamara replied in a sweet, compliant tone.

He'd thought that he'd caught her in a flashback again.

"What are you thinking about?"

"Watching a movie."

"You're watching a movie now?"

"No, I'm thinking about watching a movie. About a movie I watched. In the commons yesterday."

"Ah." A little too normal for Dr. Sutherland. He was expecting something interesting and unusual. More hallucinations. More flashbacks of people bleeding out.

"Do you believe in intelligent life in the universe?" Tamara asked him.

"Do I...? Sure. I don't believe we're alone in the universe. It's too vast. It wouldn't make sense to me that we were the only sentient life forms."

"So not just bacteria. You think there are other beings on other planets who are advanced like we are. Aware of ourselves and each other. Maybe even interested in exploring space."

"It's possible. I'd go so far as to say probable. I think if this one little planet could provide just the right conditions for life and evolution, it would be the height of arrogance to believe that it could never happen anywhere else. It probably does happen all over the universe all the time. Like bubbles in water that is heating up and starting to boil."

Tamara could see it in her mind. The boiling, seething pot of the universe, little bubbles breaking the surface and popping every time a new planet produce the right conditions, and presto! Another sentient life form.

"Do you think they're like we are? Their bodies? Or do you think they would be like other animals? Or plants? Or something totally different than on our planet?"

"I don't know. I'm willing to entertain any of those possibilities."

Tamara nodded at this. Made sense to her. He kept an open mind. They could be anywhere. They could be like anything. Like them, different from them. Something they'd never even dreamed of.

"I think we're getting away from the topic at hand, though," Dr. Sutherland tried to rein her back in. "I'd like to prescribe you, something, Tamara. Just to calm you down a little. And see where that goes. If it helps, maybe you will consider the next step."

"What?"

"I'd like to prescribe—"

"No. What next step? What do you mean by that?"

"The next step in figuring out what is going on with you and how to address it. At this point, I can't tell you for sure what that step would be. But right now, you are so anxious, you are resistant to anything that will allow me to get closer to a solution."

"No. You're not drugging me out. I've seen what happens to those girls. They're like zombies. They don't think for themselves, they just float from one place to another. You're not doing that to me."

"I'm not doing anything to you. I'm suggesting that you might want to try something that makes you feel less anxious. Don't you want to feel better?"

"I want to feel. Not to be a zombie."

"If you feel like a zombie, then the dosage is wrong. We're not looking for something that changes who you are or takes away your enjoyment of life. Just something to take away some of these negative symptoms that are bothering you. Wouldn't you like to—"

"No. Enjoyment of life? You think I enjoy it here? Or that I want to?"

"Tamara—"

"The only way I'm going to enjoy this is if you fill me up with alcohol and something that gives me a really good buzz. Then I'll have the time of my life. But I don't think you care about me enjoying my stay here. It's not the bloody Marriott."

She glared at him, but was disconcerted by the twitch of his lips at her comment.

"No," he agreed, suppressing the smile. "It isn't the Marriott, and I wouldn't expect you to act like it was. But I don't think your quality of life is improved by untreated mental illness, either."

"You can't force me to take drugs."

"This is getting to be pretty serious. We're not just talking about working through a period of depression. We can take it before the court, get an order to treat you without your consent."

Tamara shook her head again. "You can't."

"The courts definitely lean in favor of letting the patient decide whether to accept or reject a course of treatment, even in the case of incarcerated minors. But they can be swayed."

Tamara watched Dr. Sutherland out of the corner of her eye while he picked up a tablet computer and poked and swiped it a few times, eventually propping it up on the desk facing her.

She turned to face the desk square on and looked down at the little screen, intrigued despite herself.

Dr. Sutherland had started a video playing. There was either no sound or it was turned down. The pictures were black and white surveillance video, a little grainy, but clear enough to recognize herself sitting at her desk in class. As Tamara watched, she saw her own head go up suddenly. Everyone else's faces turned toward her. Tamara swallowed. The videos were edited together to follow her progress as she bolted from the classroom and ran willy-nilly down empty hallways. There was no baby being whisked away just ahead of her steps. There was no one else in the hallway but her and the security staff. Tamara's eyes were wide. It was obvious that she was yelling. Her face was contorted in fear or rage.

Tamara shook her head and turned away from the images. "There's no sound," she pointed out. "If there was sound, you would have been able to hear the baby crying."

"I thought you just told me it was all a joke. That there was no baby crying. You just did it to get attention because you were bored in algebra."

Tamara bit the inside of her cheek. Why couldn't she at least think well enough to keep her lies straight? It was overwhelming trying to keep up the appearance of normality under Dr. Sutherland's scrutiny.

"There's nothing wrong with me." She gestured at the tablet. "That's just me having fun. You don't give someone medication for playing a prank. Ground me to my cell for being naughty."

Dr. Sutherland gave her a long, steady look. Tamara looked up at the ceiling again, waiting for him to move on.

"How have your other symptoms been?" Dr. Sutherland asked finally. "Are the relaxation exercises helping with your PTSD? Are you experiencing fewer flashbacks?"

"Yeah. They really help."

"Have you even done any of the exercises?"

She met his eyes. "Well... I've done those ones with you."

"I appreciate the thought, but I don't believe that doing a guided relaxation exercise with me once every week or two is enough to have an impact on your PTSD. I think you need to be doing more than that."

"It's getting better. Maybe it just goes away by itself."

She had, after all, been able to go several months without any major traumatic events in her life. So maybe her brain was healing. Or she was getting better at anticipating and hiding the flashbacks from the people who would report them to Dr. Sutherland.

He let the silence draw out, something he did in hopes that she would feel the need to fill the awkward silence. But Tamara didn't. She just closed her eyes and enjoyed the brief reprieve from his questions.

## SEVENTEEN

TAMARA PACED BACK AND forth across her cell, waiting for reveille. Her back hurt. Her head hurt. Her heart was pounding in her chest like it was trying to get out. It was a relief when the bell finally rang and she could hear the noises of others stirring around her.

Within a few minutes of the bell, there was a quick knock on the door and it opened a crack.

"You decent?"

"Yeah."

Zobel poked his head in, peeking at her as if he weren't sure if she was telling the truth, then opened the door the rest of the way.

"You remember you have court today? You need to get yourself ready quickly to get on the bus. Especially if you want something to eat first. You don't eat breakfast here, you'll miss it. They won't have anything for you at the courthouse."

"I remember. I know all the rules."

"Good." He held a bundle of clothes toward her. "Civvies for court."

"Oh, thanks." Tamara stepped forward and took them from

him, grateful she wouldn't have to appear in court in her orange prison uniform.

He nodded. "Be quick."

Zobel stepped back into the hallway and let the door shut behind him. Tamara quickly stripped off her nighttime pinks and pulled on the pants and blouse that had been provided. Probably by Mrs. Henson. She was the one who thought of that sort of thing.

Everything felt tight and strange against her skin after her uniform. Tamara buttoned up and straightened the shirt a couple of times. The style didn't really suit her. Or maybe it was just because she wasn't used to wearing anything but the one-piece coveralls of the facility.

It seemed like Zobel was a long time in getting back to her. Tamara was starting to feel anxious about missing the bus. If she missed the bus to court, what would they do? Reschedule the case? Go on without her?

The door opened and Zobel looked at her. "There you are. I said to be quick. It's getting too late to eat now."

"I'm not eating. I'm just waiting for you."

He rolled his eyes. "Let's get you on your way, then." He motioned her forward impatiently. Tamara walked with him to the guard station, where Zobel and one of the other guards wrapped her in the full chains and shackles required for transport. Tamara stood still while they locked everything up and each checked the chains independently.

"Do I have to wear these for court?" Nobody was going to believe anything she had to say if she looked like that up on the stand.

"No. When you're at the courthouse, they'll take them off. They come off before you go into the courtroom, and then go back on once you're out. Nobody sees you walk in in chains."

Tamara nodded and swallowed. "Good. Thanks."

He gave her a reassuring smile. "You'll be okay?"

"Yeah. Sure."

"You're all prepared for this. You've met with your lawyer. It will all go like you planned."

She must have looked just as scared and small as she felt. Tamara made an effort to blank her face and straighten her posture. She needed to look confident and capable. She had a job to do. It was her chance to help ensure that Mr. Baker went away for a long time. For the maximum, whatever that was. She was going to make sure he couldn't get access to any more children, no matter how old or young.

Zobel nodded his approval. "Better. Be strong. You can do this."

She wondered how much he and the other guards knew about the court case, why she was going and what she was there to testify about. They knew she was going as a witness, not the accused. But she didn't know if he knew any details.

"I'm strong," she repeated. She needed to feel it. She needed to hear it out loud. She had always felt small and bullied before Mr. Baker. But she was taking control. She was in a position of power over him. He should fear her, because she was the one who had the power to affect the rest of his life. She would stand up and describe everything he had done, and the jury and the judge would make sure he paid for it. She wasn't just speaking for herself and all of the babysitters and other young women that Mr. Baker might have had contact with, but for the babies, who couldn't speak for themselves.

The thought of the babies and of Mrs. Baker also being there made Tamara dizzy for a moment, sliding back toward the past. Zobel held her arm and steadied her.

"You can do this," he repeated. "Just stay focused on the present. What you're going to do today."

"Okay." Tamara nodded and pulled her arm away from him. "Yeah."

He looked her over once more to be sure she was ready, then

escorted her to the transfer point. Tamara and a couple of other girls got onto the bus. One was a Shark, and one a girl Tamara didn't recognize, who must have only been there short-term while waiting for a hearing. Neither one of them paid any attention to her, and Tamara did the same, pretending she was the only one on the bus.

* * *

BEING in the courthouse made her sweat. The only time she had ever been there was when she was in trouble, facing prison time or more prison time. As soon as she got there, sweat was running down her back like she was standing under a shower. Tamara went where she was told to go and stood and waited when she was told to wait, and eventually Zobel escorted her to a room that adjoined the courtroom and contained a couple of tiny open-bar cells and courtroom security guards in brown uniforms who looked hot and bored and irritated. Their name tags read Blau and Lynch. Zobel introduced Tamara to them and they referred to the paperwork that they had to confirm that she was on the witness list for that day.

"You can put her in a cell and take off the chains. We'll escort her in when they call for her." Blau looked at Tamara and gave a shrug. "Doesn't look like *she's* going to give us any trouble."

Zobel cleared his throat and gave Tamara an apologetic look before answering.

"I'm required to inform you that she is a violent offender. She has two murder convictions and has been involved in a prison break. There have been a number of incidents at juvenile detention the last little while when she has not complied with the security staff. You are to take every precaution."

Blau gave Tamara another look and shook his head slowly. "Every precaution except keeping her in chains."

"Yes," Zobel agreed. "She's a witness, not the accused, so the prosecutor does not want her appearing in chains. It's a calculated risk, but we don't believe she will attempt anything in the courtroom. If she does, you have deterrents."

Like the guards at juvie, the courthouse guards wore an arsenal on their belts, with tasers, pepper spray, and firearms close at hand. Blau hitched his heavy belt up, nodding. He'd have a story to tell when he went home to his wife and kids. How he'd protected everyone from a dangerous murderer. A girl who looked like a sweet farm girl, but had murdered two people at the tender age of twelve.

Tamara knew that Zobel was only giving them the warning because he was required to, preventing the prison from being sued or shut down if Tamara walked away from the courthouse because they hadn't explained to anyone how dangerous she was and how closely she needed to be watched. But she still felt betrayed by his words. He knew that she wasn't that kind of person. That she wasn't a danger to the security staff or innocent bystanders. She followed the rules and cooperated with the security and administration.

Or, she had. Before.

He'd been friendly with her. He was the one who told her to keep her chin up and be strong for the trial. She'd saved his life. Twice. But none of that stopped him from giving the caution like she was some axe murderer.

"Put her in the cell," Blau said, motioning to one of the open doors.

Tamara didn't wait for Zobel to tell her to go. She walked into the little cell, heart pounding still harder.

"Stand watch," Zobel instructed as he stepped into the cage behind Tamara. The cell was almost too small for the two of them to stand together. Zobel unlocked the shackles and gave Tamara quiet instructions as he reached around her to remove the chains. They were both sweating. Tamara could see his brow glistening and could feel the heat of his body as he stood close to her.

Finally, he finished. Taking the hardware with him, he stepped outside the cell and swung the barred door shut. It latched. Zobel pulled back on the door to confirm it was properly locked. He nodded to Blau.

"Check to make sure it is secure."

The man rolled his eyes, but he did as he was asked, stepping forward and giving the door a good yank. It didn't budge. He shook it hard so that it made a racket. Lynch, who had been largely ignoring the proceedings looked up from his paperwork and scowled.

"Do you have to do that?"

"Have to make sure it's secure," Blau sneered.

Zobel nodded. "She's all yours until the end of the day, then. Try to get her to eat some lunch; she didn't have any breakfast."

Blau shook his head. "I'm not her mother. She'll be provided with lunch. That's all I do."

Zobel gave a nod in Tamara's direction. He didn't tell her again to be strong or anything else that might make it look like they had a relationship. Then he walked back out of the room. Tamara wanted to call after him for one more reassurance, but she didn't. He was the only person she knew there, and she felt strangely abandoned, even though she knew all of the reasons he had done it and that he would be back to get her at the end of the day. She took a deep breath and sat down on the hard wooden bench inside the cell to wait.

* * *

THE MORNING DRAGGED ON INTERMINABLY. The room got still hotter. Lynch turned on a desk fan, but it didn't blow anywhere near Tamara and he didn't turn it toward her. By noon, she was parched and, while she wasn't hungry, she slurped down her red jello and the fruit drink they provided her. There were also drying-out sandwiches and some potato chips that glistened with oil. Tamara didn't touch them.

She tried not to drink too much, aware that although there was a toilet in the cell, there was no privacy and, if she filled her bladder, she would have to pee in front of the guards. While it certainly wouldn't be her first time peeing in front of strangers, she wanted to avoid it if she possibly could.

But the liquids were meager and Tamara had been sweating all morning. They didn't even come close to replenishing her lost fluids.

The guards talked with each other occasionally, but neither said anything to Tamara. As the room became stifling hot early in the afternoon, Tamara asked if they knew what time she would be called.

Blau looked at her, and then pointedly did not answer. Tamara looked at Lynch to see if he would be more accommodating. He didn't even acknowledge that Tamara had spoken.

So that was how it was going to be.

Mid-afternoon, another man in a uniform stepped into the room from the courtroom side. He didn't have a utility belt full of deterrents, but he looked imposing anyway.

"She's going to be called next," he warned. "Probably about twenty minutes."

If anything, the next twenty minutes crawled by even slower than the rest of the day. Tamara licked her sandpaper lips and tried to prepare herself. Her stomach was queasy and her head started to spin. She was both glad and irritated that she hadn't had anything solid to eat all day. She wasn't sure she'd be able to keep it down, but she was starting to feel lightheaded. It was probably just the heat. She watched drops of sweat trickle down Blau's temple. And he was sitting by the fan. Tamara was no longer sweating, but her clothes hung on her damp and limp. She probably looked like something the cat dragged in instead of fresh and neat like she had when she'd first put on the clothes that morning.

The courtroom door opened again, and the man called in a voice that was intended for the entire courtroom to hear, "Tamara French is called to the stand."

Tamara waited, jittery and anxious. Blau used a key to open the cell, took her by the arm, and escorted her across the room to the courtroom. He walked with her right to the witness stand.

Tamara sat down, only to be told to stand up again so she could be sworn in. She took a nervous glance around the courtroom as she sat down again. Ritter was not sitting at one of the lawyer tables, but in the first row of seats behind them, like he was just part of the audience. Mr. Baker sat at one of the tables with his lawyer. He looked pale and like he'd lost some weight. It made her glad, because it was a good indicator that he was still in prison and not out on bail. She wanted him to suffer for what he had done.

He had been leaning forward on his elbows whispering with his lawyer, but after Tamara was sworn in and sat down, he and his lawyer both sat back. Mr. Baker leaned way back in his chair, looking at her with an attitude that was both challenging and dismissive. Tamara swallowed and stared into middle distance, not meeting his eyes. She could give him attitude too. She was there to make sure he stayed behind bars. She was strong and confident and she was going to be sure he never got out of prison again.

Mrs. Baker was there too. Sitting in the row behind the other table. Perfectly bleached and coiffed hair. Clothes that were almost business wear, but showed too much cleavage and skin to make it all the way to conservative. Her lipstick was blood red. She too studied Tamara, evaluating her.

It was then, even before the first question was put to Tamara, that she started to fall back into the past.

Mrs. Baker's eyes were bottomless as ocean depths. Tamara

held on to the arms of the chair, keeping herself steady. She looked at the lawyer who sat in front of Mrs. Baker. He was the one who would question her, Ritter had told her. Then the lawyer by Mr. Baker would try to attack Tamara's testimony and discredit her.

The lawyer stood up and took a couple of steps toward her, buttoning up a couple of buttons on his suit jacket with one hand. The courtroom was air-conditioned, the air conditioning blowing icy air down Tamara's back, making her damp clothes clammy against her skin.

"Tamara, you were a foster child with the Bakers for a year or so, is that correct?"

Tamara rubbed her goose-bumped arms. "Yeah."

"Speak into the mic, please."

The guard standing nearby stepped in to adjust the microphone that pointed toward Tamara's mouth. Tamara nodded and repeated her answer.

"How did you feel about joining their family?"

Tamara tried to swallow. She tried to lick her lips and moisten her mouth. But her tongue stuck to everything, dry and tacky. The inside of her mouth was all cleaving together and she couldn't find her voice.

The lawyer waited. The judge and the jury and the whole courtroom waited. Tamara tried again to lick her lips. On the first row of the audience, Ritter half-stood. "If we could get the witness a glass of water, your Honor?"

The judge looked sharply at Ritter. He frowned at Ritter's dark suit and snazzy blue tie and briefcase. "And you are...?"

"Bron Ritter, your Honor. Advocate for the witness."

"You don't talk out in my courtroom."

"No, your Honor. I apologize."

Ritter looked like he was going to sit down, lowering himself toward his seat, but still looking at the judge, waiting for his response.

"Glass of water," the judge muttered to the clerk standing nearby.

In a minute, Tamara was handed a glass of cold water, condensation collecting on the outside. She took a sip, worked it around her mouth, then took a couple of bigger gulps, trying to slake the desert inside her mouth, to little avail.

"How did you feel about becoming a member of the Baker family?" the prosecutor repeated.

"I... I was excited. Thought it would be cool... to be part of a real family." Tamara wiped her forehead with her arm. She was coated with cold sweat. "A mom and dad and two little girls. I thought it would be fun." Tamara stopped, then continued before she realized he was starting to ask another question. "But it wasn't."

"Pardon?" the lawyer stopped and asked her to repeat herself.

"It wasn't. Fun. Like I thought."

"And why is that?"

"He... Mr. Baker..." Tamara took a quick glance at Mr. Baker. Trying to make it too fast for her brain to actually process his face and bring back the memories. "He was trying to get to me right that first day—"

The other lawyer bellowed out an objection that made Tamara jump. She looked toward the lawyer to see what he was upset about, but her eyes landed on Mr. Baker. He looked at her through lowered lids and licked his lips, a movement that was only meant to be seen by her. Not because his mouth and lips were dry and cracked like hers, but intended to invite her and mock her at the same time. Even in the position he was in, facing the prospect of years in prison, he was still making advances toward her.

Tamara plunged into the memories like falling into a frigid, bottomless lake. No way to stop or slow herself. She was suddenly in his arms, under his control, forced to do whatever he wanted. She felt herself smothering, gasping for breath, sickened by his demands. Her body hurting from his abuse.

"Stop," she begged out loud. She sobbed and swore. "Please, stop, please...!"

She was aware that she was two places. In the courtroom, silent and still, and back there with him, eleven or twelve, powerless against him.

"Do you need a moment, Ms. French?"

She couldn't answer. She was again powerless and voiceless. There was whispering around her. She tried to focus on her body in the courtroom, like Zobel had prompted her, and to leave the memories behind, but she couldn't escape. He was right there in front of her, smirking at her, superior and powerful and bound to get whatever he wanted.

"Your Honor...?" Ritter tentatively addressed the judge.

"Go ahead."

Ritter was right there in front of her, nudging her glass of water toward her lips and encouraging her to take a drink, murmuring to her in a low voice, his other hand smothering the microphone.

"You can do this, Tamara," he said in a calm, matter-of-fact voice. "Just like we talked about. Just like we went over when we met. You just need to stay calm and focused, and tell them what you saw. Corrine and Julie, remember? This is about them, not you."

Tamara sipped the water. She tried to focus on the coldness, to ground herself in the sensations.

"What he did to me..." she squeaked out.

"No. What he did to Corinne and Julie. He's already served his sentence for what he did to you. The more the prosecutor tries to bring that up, the more the defense is going to object. You aren't going to tell *your* story here. You're going to tell them about Corinne and Julie. Just what you saw. Just like you told me."

Tamara took another sip of water and gave a little nod. She blinked and watched Ritter as he returned to the seat he had previously occupied. There was silence in the courtroom as Tamara collected herself and looked at the prosecuting attorney, waiting for him to ask her the next question.

"You didn't enjoy living with the Bakers?"

"No," Tamara agreed in a low voice, leaning close to the mic.

She tried to keep a narrow focus on the lawyer. She could ignore Mr. and Mrs. Baker; she wasn't there to talk to them. She was only there to answer the lawyer's questions.

"When you lived with them, the Bakers had two children. Can you tell me about them?"

"Corrine, she was three. And Julie, just a baby, not a year old yet. I was supposed to help to take care of them."

"Like a good big sister."

Tamara looked at the lawyer, then looked at Ritter. He hadn't really asked anything, so Tamara didn't respond. She didn't know what to say to that. She hadn't been like a good big sister to the girls. She'd been like a slave. As much as she tried to love and care for them, she also hated them. Every time one of them cried, she was terrified of Mr. and Mrs. Baker's reactions. If either of them thought she was neglecting or hurting her charges, there would be consequences. Tamara stared at the lawyer, trying to shut out everything else, but she could see Mrs. Baker behind him. Mrs. Baker, who was like a wild animal when enraged. She wasn't a delicate little woman. She could easily take Mr. Baker down. A skinny little twelve-year-old didn't stand a chance against her attacks.

"Tamara."

Tamara cleared her throat.

"Yeah?" she whispered.

"You spent a lot of time helping take care of your foster sisters."

"Yes. Whenever I wasn't in school."

Her sisters. Tamara had never thought of them as her sisters. She knew that the lawyer was playing with words. Her 'sisters.' 'Helping take care of' them instead of being forced to take on more responsibility than she could manage. As if she had been that 'good big sister' that he had mentioned. He was trying to paint a picture for the jury. One that he and Tamara knew very well was not accurate—but he wanted the jury to see her as a helpful big sister for a reason.

"Did you ever see either of the Bakers hit their little girls?"

Tamara shivered with cold. "No."

"Did they appear to love their children?"

Tamara gripped hard to the arms of the chair. After giving her a minute to think about her answer, the lawyer prompted her again.

"Did the Bakers give the appearance of loving and caring for their children?"

Tamara looked at Ritter for the answer. He hadn't told her how to answer that question. He gave her no signal, waiting, like the courtroom, for Tamara's response. Tamara looked at the judge, leaning forward over his desk to watch her. He raised an interrogating eyebrow.

"Ms. French. Please answer my question."

"I—I don't know."

There was a murmur in the audience watching the trial.

"Did they... ensure that they were fed, and clean, and dressed appropriately for the weather?"

"Yes."

"So the children were not physically neglected or beaten."

"No."

"Did they yell at the children or use verbally abusive language?"

Tamara shifted her position and rubbed her cold arms. "Um... sometimes..."

The prosecutor raised an eyebrow, obviously surprised at her response, but he continued smoothly, not drawing attention to the fact.

"Did they spend time playing with or reading to the children?"

Tamara's guts were tied in knots as she saw Mr. Baker in bed with Corrine, cuddled up close under the covers with her while he read her bedtime stories. She nodded, tears flooding her eyes.

"You need to answer out loud."

Tamara nodded again, swallowed, and tried to clear her voice so she could produce a sound. "Yes." It came out in barely a whisper, but he didn't censure her.

"And did you become aware at some point that there was something wrong with Mr. Baker's relationship and care for his daughters?"

There was an immediate objection from Mr. Baker's lawyer and some legal argument back and forth that Tamara didn't try to follow. In spite of the chill of the courtroom, she was suddenly sweating again and all of the water that was sitting in her stomach threatened to come back up. Tamara stood, looking for some escape. Back to the anteroom or to a restroom. Somewhere, anywhere other than stuck in that room with Mr. and Mrs. Baker looking at her, having to describe what Mr. Baker had done. Blau stepped closer, gesturing for her to sit down.

"I don't feel good," Tamara objected. "I have to go!"

When she tried to push by him to get into the other room, he grabbed her arm and wrenched her back. "Sit down!" he insisted, pointing to the chair. "You're not done."

"I can't!"

"Sit."

The courtroom was loud with people all talking at once. The judge was banging his gavel down over and over again, shouting for order. When the spectators settled down, the judge turned his steely gaze to Tamara.

"Young lady. You are not finished your testimony and you have not been cross-examined. Take your seat."

Tamara hugged her stomach. "I'm sick, I can't," she moaned.

"You can and you will."

Blau grabbed Tamara's shoulder and shoved her in the direction of the seat. Tamara wiped at tears and sweat on her face.

"Please..."

"Mr. Ritter," the judge looked for the lawyer in the audience. "Can you please direct your client."

Ritter emerged from the spectator seats and approached Tamara, his eyes wide and uncertain. Dealing with a freaking-out client was apparently not part of his usual job description. He stood in front of Tamara, arms held away from his body like he was either holding back the audience or preparing to catch her as she darted past like a spooked horse. He blocked her vision of both Bakers, looking steadily into Tamara's face.

"Tamara. It's okay. We talked about this. Just like when you and I met, you need to talk about what you saw. Don't worry about the objections. The prosecutor will ask you a question you can answer and you just tell them what you told me."

"I'm sick. I don't feel good. I have to get out of here."

He was remembering, she was sure, how she had fled the interview at juvie to throw up. He looked at the judge uncertainly, weighing his options.

"Would it be possible to get a recess, your Honor, so that Miss French could have a minute...?"

"No, it would not. Let's get to this."

"Sit down," Ritter urged. "You'll feel better once it's done. Don't draw it out any longer than necessary."

"I can't," Tamara moaned again, but she sat down in the witness box again. She sat with both arms over her stomach, breathing shallowly, trying to keep her body under control.

Ritter and the guard both hovered close by, making sure she wasn't going to flee. After a few moments of silence, Ritter went back to his chair, giving Tamara what he obviously intended to be a reassuring smile.

The prosecutor was speaking again. Tamara's eyes glazed and she couldn't hear what he was asking. She didn't look in his direction, not wanting to look at Mrs. Baker again. Mrs. Baker was going to be mad if Tamara told about Mr. Baker. She would whip Tamara within an inch of her life and then they would turn her back to social services, and Tamara would have nowhere to live. No family, no home, no one wanted her anymore. Tears streamed down Tamara's face. She put her face in her arm, resting it on the edge of the witness box.

The lawyer got closer, centering himself in front of Tamara, standing uncomfortably close and repeating his questions. But it was like he was underwater. Tamara couldn't hear them clearly. She was in the past, not the present; what he said and did didn't matter. Only what Tamara did. If she did what she was told and kept her stupid mouth shut.

The prosecutor was complaining to the judge that he couldn't get any more out of her. The defense attorney jumped up and started yelling that nothing Tamara had said before or during the trial could be used and that all of the evidence was tainted. Then even Mrs. Baker was on her feet, her voice rising like a siren.

"If the brat's not testifying and none of the evidence can be used then I'm sure as hell not testifying!"

The courtroom was in chaos. Ritter stood to try to talk to Tamara again, but there were more guards in the room than there had been and they prevented him from approaching.

"Everybody take your seats!" the judge barked.

One of the guards approached Mrs. Baker to sit her down and she got right in his face, screaming and threatening. Tamara wanted to curl up into a ball for protection and just dissolve away. She couldn't face her foster mother. When they got home, Mrs. Baker was going to hurt her bad.

Eventually, Mrs. Baker sat back down and the lawyers were each instructed to sit down, even though the prosecutor was supposed to be on his feet when conducting the questioning. The murmur in the courtroom fell off into silence as the judge looked around at them all, waiting, his expression thunderous.

"We are going to try this one last time," he warned. "If Ms. French cannot give testimony today and be properly cross-examined, then her testimony is out. As is her prior statement to the police. The recording stands as both parties on the tape are here to be questioned on its interpretation." He leveled a glare at Mrs. Baker. "If you do not testify here today, whatever deal you have made to avoid prosecution for your complicity in these charges will be null and void. Keep that in mind."

Mrs. Baker didn't look at him, but at Tamara, a laser-beam stare. Tamara buried her face in her arm again. There was silence again in the courtroom, but the voices in Tamara's head were still shouting, cursing and swearing at her and beating her down.

"Have another drink of water, Ms. French, and pull yourself together," the judge instructed. "You have made allegations that need to be supported today with live testimony. We are waiting for you to tell your side of the story."

Tamara tried to get more water down, but it was impossible. She looked at Ritter, trying to draw strength from him. But then her eyes focused again on Mr. Baker.

He smirked at her. He knew she couldn't do it. He still had power over her, no matter how strong she thought she had become. He folded his arms across his chest and gave a little lift with his chin. *Bring it.*

It should have made her angry enough to say all the words that were stuck in her throat, but it didn't. She saw his attitude and she heard his mocking voice.

*You're just a little girl.*

*Who's going to believe you?*

*If you don't do what I say, you're going to be out on the street. You think you won't have to put out then?*

*You can't do anything.*

Tamara stood up, too nauseated to stay there any longer. Blau moved to again put her back in her seat, but Tamara moved quickly to avoid him.

"No! Didn't you hear what he said?" she demanded. "I'm not doing it."

"He didn't say anything. Now sit down and—"

When he grabbed for her, Tamara swung. She'd been in juvie for over three years. She might not be the biggest or the strongest, but she had learned to fight. She went straight for his nose, and then to scratch his eyes. When his hands were up and his eyes were closed, she drove a shoulder into his midriff and bowled him over to the floor. If she'd been smart about it, she could have grabbed his sidearm and threatened her way out of the courthouse before any tactical team could get there to talk her down, but she didn't. She left him on the floor and made a dash for the anteroom door. The extra guards who had been called to deal with the outbursts in the courtroom tripped over each other, all with different ideas about what to do about her bolting. Tamara reached the door and found, to her relief, that it was not locked.

She darted into the sweltering room and went straight for the cell she had been sitting in earlier. A couple of the guards were right behind her. Tamara pulled on the cell door, slamming it shut with a bang. It tried to bounce back open, but she pulled it firmly toward her. It clicked into place as the guards reached her.

"No! Leave me alone! Just leave me alone, I'm done!"

They stood there, looking stupidly through the bars at her. Blau strode into the room and went straight up to the cell. Tamara shrank back from him, but kept her hands wrapped around the bars of the cell door, determined to prevent him from opening it and dragging her out again.

The guard put his key into the lock, furious.

"May as well just leave her there," one of the others said. "She might not go back in so easily next time." He snickered. "And she throws a mean right."

Blau turned part way around. "What did you say?"

"She's not testifying, so she's right where we want her to be. There's no point in taking her out just to put her back again, especially if she gets ideas."

Tamara's breath rasped loudly in her chest. She didn't know whether he was going to listen to the other guards or take her out and give her a beating for messing with him. She'd hit him in front of his coworkers, in front of the judge. In front of everyone else in the courtroom. His reputation would be forever marred, remembered as the man who let himself be beaten by a girl.

Blau stared at her balefully through the bars. "You are crazy, you know that?" he demanded. "I've never seen such a display in a courtroom. I have no idea why they ever thought you could come in here and be a witness. You couldn't have made a much bigger mess of it than you did."

Tamara swallowed. Everything he said was true. She couldn't argue with it.

"You don't know what it's like," she told him in a whisper. "You don't know what kind of monsters they are."

"Then I would think you would want to convict him, instead of whatever balls-up that was. They shouldn't have even sent you."

Tamara pried her fingers loose from the bars and retreated to sit on the bench. He didn't unlock the door.

"You'd better hope that his wife doesn't change her mind about testifying against him. Or *accidentally* say something to throw the case and get him off. You'd better hope that she puts him away, or he's going to be back out there again and you'll know it's your fault."

Tamara put her face in her hands, covering her eyes. She just wanted to sleep and pretend that nothing had happened. Pretend that the day hadn't even come. The little group of guards eventually decided that she wasn't a danger and wasn't going to do anything else interesting, and eventually disbanded. Lynch remained at the desk with the fan blowing on himself, shuffling papers and tapping at his phone.

EIGHTEEN

A T THE END OF the day, it was Zobel who was there to pick her up again and take her home. Tamara didn't stir when he entered the airless room. He took off his cap and wiped his forehead.

"Little warm in here!"

Blau had replaced Lynch at the desk. He turned his head to look sourly at Zobel.

"Your girl screwed up royally today."

"Uh-oh." Zobel looked over at Tamara. "Is she all right?"

"Other than being a complete psycho? Yes, she's fine."

Zobel couldn't fail to miss the anger and sarcasm in Blau's voice. Tamara breathed, trying to keep her consciousness suspended somewhere in the center of the room, where she didn't have to think of the past or the future or who was angry with her or not. She could just keep floating there and not think about the consequences.

"What happened?" Zobel asked cautiously.

"She freaked out. Wouldn't testify against him after all. Wouldn't stay to answer questions and give her testimony." He pointed to his swollen nose and scratched face. "Gave me this."

Zobel cleared his throat and threw a look in Tamara's direction. In a voice that was much flatter than his usual timbre, he said, "I did warn you that she was violent."

That didn't go over well with Blau. But Zobel was right, he had been warned.

"I'll just be happy to have her off of my hands." Blau pushed himself up from his chair with a grunt and went over to Tamara's cage. This time when he inserted his key in the lock, Tamara didn't try to stop him. She watched him through barely-cracked lids. "Your babysitter is here for you," Blau sneered. "Come on out." He swung the door open.

"Uh, we've got protocols for transfer," Zobel said. "She stays in the cell until she's shackled and chained." He picked up the hardware he'd previously left in the guard room and entered the cell. Blau started to turn to go back to his desk work and Zobel turned his head to look at him. "Stand watch," he said. "This is a two-person job."

"You look more than capable of doing it yourself."

"I can chain her, but I need a second person ready in case something was to go wrong. Most custody breaches happen during transfer."

Blau made a huffing noise and stood where he was to supervise.

"Let's go, French," Zobel said.

Tamara didn't move. Zobel waited for a few seconds and then approached her. "French. On your feet, please."

When she still didn't stir, he put a hand on her arm, nudging her into action. "Come on. Time to get out of here."

Tamara didn't have the energy to get to her feet. She wasn't sure what Zobel was going to do about it, but she knew that she just wasn't going to be able to do anything by herself.

Zobel's hand moved to Tamara's face, touching the back of his fingers to her hot, dry skin. He swore. "How long has she been sitting in here like this?"

Blau looked at Tamara. "Since she left the courtroom. Sat down there and hasn't been a bother. Good thing, after all of the trouble she caused in there."

Zobel felt Tamara's pulse. "We might need an ambulance." He shook his head, swearing. "Ambulance transfer is not secure."

Blau was starting to get an inkling that there was a problem. "Ambulance? Ambulance for what?"

"She's hot and dry with a fast, weak pulse. What does that tell you?"

"Of course she's hot. It's like an oven in here. Maybe she's faking sick... like you said, breaches of custody happen during transfers, she wants to escape..."

"She should be sweating. You're sweating, aren't you?" Zobel wiped his own dripping temples.

"Yes."

"Has she had anything to eat or drink?"

"No. She had water in the courtroom."

"Get me a water bottle. We'll see if she can take any fluids."

Blau hesitated. "I thought I wasn't supposed to leave you alone with her."

"Shut the gate."

Blau did, pushing the cell door shut until it clicked into place. As an afterthought, he gave it a shake to make sure it was properly engaged. Then he walked away to get a water bottle.

Zobel patted Tamara's cheeks. "Tamara. Can you hear me?"

Tamara wished he would just leave her alone. She turned her head slightly, trying to avoid the slaps on her cheeks.

"I need you to stay with me. Talk to me. Tell me if you're okay."

"Mmm," Tamara groaned. She couldn't form words. She didn't want to leave the comfortable space her consciousness was suspended in and be forced to move her body, which was heavy and weak and sore.

"That's right," Zobel murmured. "Stay with me. Remember

when I got cut? Remember how you held on to me? Didn't let me bleed out? Well, I'm going to do the same for you."

Tamara had never thought she would regret saving Zobel's life.

Blau returned with a water bottle. He handed it through the bars to Zobel. Zobel cracked the cap and held the bottle to Tamara's mouth. Most of the first splash went down her front, but some of it got into her mouth and made Tamara choke, spitting it back out again. She turned her head away from him, coughing weakly and wishing he would just leave her alone. Zobel put his hand under her chin to hold her steady, and again tipped the bottle into her mouth. The water was surprisingly good and Tamara took a couple of weak swallows to slake her dry throat.

"Good girl." Zobel gave Tamara a break to breathe, then tipped the bottle up again.

After a few minutes, Tamara lifted her hand to steady the bottle. She opened her eyes and looked at Zobel.

"Hey," he greeted. "Are you okay?"

Tamara made a noise that wasn't actually speech, but was an acknowledgment.

"Hear you had a fun day in court."

Tamara couldn't manage a laugh or a protest.

"More." Zobel held the bottle up to her mouth. "We've got to get as much into you as possible."

Tamara took a few swallows, then pulled away. Her stomach was hurting, sloshing with the water. She couldn't handle any more.

Zobel's fingers found her pulse again. He gazed into her face. "You think you can make it to the bus?" he asked. "And back home?"

All Tamara wanted was to be back in her own bunk again, but she couldn't summon the massive energy that would be required to get back to the juvie transport bus and then from the bus to her cell. She closed her eyes.

"French. Come on. Don't pass out on me. Can you stand up? We'll get you back into your gear?"

"No."

"We've progressed to words! Maybe with a little more water, you'll be able to get back on your feet."

"Mmm-mmn"

Tamara's eyes were open just the barest slit. She saw Zobel look at his watch. He shook his head in frustration and pulled out his phone. Tamara drifted again while he made phone calls to make arrangements to send the other juvies back home and get Tamara medical attention. He shook or nudged her a couple of times to keep her conscious, but Tamara made no effort to stay awake. It was just too hard.

# NINETEEN

EVENTUALLY, THEY HAD NO choice but to get an ambulance for Tamara. There was just no way she was getting back to the transport bus under her own steam. When the paramedics arrived, they looked curiously into the cell at Tamara and Zobel.

"What seems to be the problem?" asked the woman paramedic, short and sturdy with her black hair in a bun.

"I'm guessing heat stroke," Zobel offered.

He had ordered that the hallway and courtroom doors be opened to provide some airflow into the room and commandeered the fan, which he had pointed directly at Tamara. But even with these measures, the room was still uncomfortably hot.

"We're going to need to get in to examine and treat her."

"I need to ensure she is secure at all times."

"So what do you want to do?"

Zobel looked around uncertainly, though he had surely been considering the problem the whole time he was waiting for them.

"At the very least, I'll need to put her in handcuffs and leg shackles. We'd better shut both doors again. I'll put her on the gurney... you can strap her in... and then you can examine her."

"You've got to be kidding me," the woman laughed. "How about I just come in there and check her out?"

"I can't leave you alone in here with her and there's not room for all three of us."

"What is she, Harry Houdini? Jack the Ripper? Maybe both rolled into one? It doesn't look to me like she's going anywhere."

Tamara would have seconded that opinion, but it would have taken more energy than she had. She wanted to tell Zobel that there was no need to go to such lengths to make sure she didn't escape. But she couldn't. Even if she did, he'd still have to follow the best security protocols he could. Too many times, convicts escaped because of stupid mistakes and wrong assumptions. Zobel had to assume that she was perfectly capable of escape and act accordingly.

"Let's shut and lock both doors," Zobel said to Blau.

"How long is this going to take? I'm supposed to be off now."

"You'll need to stay until she's out of here."

Blau grumbled as he went to each of the doors and shut and locked them with a key. "No one can get out of here now except for me."

"Or someone who gets your keys. I'm going to shackle her now."

Zobel did so without any resistance or protest from Tamara. Zobel checked each cuff and chain. Blau unlocked and opened the cell. Zobel scooped Tamara up in his arms and took her the few steps to the waiting gurney. Tamara opened her eyes briefly to take in the new perspective. With Zobel watching, the paramedics strapped Tamara in. Zobel checked each strap and pulled on Tamara's limbs to see whether she could move and slip out of the restraints. He frowned.

"I guess that will do."

He removed the shackles then stepped back and watched like a hawk while the paramedics gave Tamara a cursory examination.

"You're probably right," the male medic, who had remained quiet up until then, confirmed. "Classic symptoms. Any nausea or vomiting?"

Zobel looked at Blau, who nodded. "She was complaining in the courtroom that she was sick. Came back in here and refused to testify. Some dry heaves, but I figured she was just putting it on."

The paramedic looked at Blau. "How long has she been sick?"

"That was a few hours ago."

"Someone should have called us a lot earlier."

Tamara wanted them to stop poking and prodding and talking about her. She moved restlessly, trying to get comfortable with the way her arms and legs were being restrained. Zobel rested a hand on her shoulder. She tried to stay still.

"I gave her some water. What else do we need to do?"

"She needs more fluids, but we probably can't get enough in her orally. We're going to need to get her on IV. Hopefully, there hasn't been any organ damage and she'll be released tomorrow."

* * *

TAMARA DIDN'T REMEMBER MUCH between the arrival of the paramedics and waking up the next morning with a killer headache. She was in a hospital bed with wrist and ankle restraints, as well as a set of handcuffs from her wrist to the rail on the side of the bed.

She closed her eyes and tried to go back to sleep, but her body didn't cooperate. She lay there and stared up at the IV bag hanging above her. She no longer felt so tired and parched, so it must have done its job.

Once back in juvie, Tamara was transferred to Psych for observation, which she didn't think was really fair when she had been hospitalized for dehydration. But word of her meltdown on the witness stand had gotten back to the administration and Dr. Sutherland recommended that she be watched, just in case she was having a nervous breakdown or was a danger to herself.

Tamara hated the rooms with the bright lights and big observation windows, feeling like a fish in an aquarium. It was enough to make even a stable person break down. Dr. Sutherland made the trip to see her there instead of having her brought to his office.

"Mind if I come in?"

Tamara shifted uncomfortably. "Did you tell them they can't listen in?" she demanded, nodding to the window. "This is doctor-patient, so they can't be listening in. Tell them to take a break. Get lost."

Sutherland moved into the room, despite her less-than-welcoming response. There was nowhere for him to sit down other than on the bunk, so he leaned against the wall opposite the observation window, giving a reassuring smile.

"Actually, I can't tell them to go away. You're right, they can't listen in on a consultation between doctor and patient, but they still need to be watching. For your own protection."

"My protection? What are you going to do in here?"

He just smiled and didn't bother to answer.

"So... how are you feeling today?"

Tamara was sitting on the bunk, back to the wall, knees bent to her chest. She sighed. "Fine. So can I go back to my own room?"

"I think I'm going to actually need a little more information than that. Just a little."

"The hospital said I'm good as new. No permanent damage."

"That's good. Maybe you'd like to talk to me about what happened. It sounds like it was a pretty rough day."

"It wasn't the best."

"We could start with that. I thought you were ready for your court appearance."

"Yeah. That's what Ritter said. I was all ready, and I just had to tell everybody what I knew…"

"So what happened?"

Tamara shook her head. "I dunno. I kind of freaked out. I wasn't feeling good…"

"It was physical, you think?"

"What else would it be?" Tamara snapped.

"I think we've talked about your anxiety before. Anxiety can show up in a lot of ways. Maybe you weren't quite as prepared as you had hoped."

"I was just sick. It was too hot in the room where I had to wait."

"And that's why you were unable to testify."

"Yeah. I was sick. Ask Zobel. He's the one who had to take me to hospital."

"Yes. I've already heard from him. He also got as much information as he could about what happened during the trial."

"So you know. I was sick. I couldn't stay in there. I had to go sit down."

"In the room that was too hot. And you didn't ask for any water or medical care."

"Do you think they would have given it to me? They wouldn't even point the fan at me. That guard had it in for me."

"I see."

"Maybe I could go back," Tamara offered, knowing full well that it was too late to fix what she had so royally screwed up. The judge had made it clear that if she didn't testify, that was it. She wasn't getting another chance.

"No, I don't think that's going to happen."

Tamara gave a shrug like she didn't care. She wondered what would happen to Mr. Baker. Would the recording and Mrs. Baker's testimony be enough to convict him? Had Mrs. Baker decided not to testify or had she gone ahead?

"How do you feel today?" Dr. Sutherland asked.

"I know I screwed up." Tamara stared off into space, not looking at Dr. Sutherland. "So, I feel pretty crappy, if you want to know the truth."

He nodded. "That's understandable. I wouldn't expect you to be feeling too good about the way it turned out."

"Thanks," she snarled.

"Would it be better if I tried to cheer you up?"

Tamara shook her head. "No."

"I didn't think so. Then I won't do that."

Tamara tightened her grip around her knees and pressed her face into them. "I screwed up so bad. I was gonna go in there and tell everyone what a sick creep he was and make sure that he couldn't ever hurt anyone again. I thought I could do it." Tamara looked at Dr. Sutherland, shaking her head. "I couldn't even tell my lawyer without freaking out, so how did I think I was going to tell the whole courtroom? With him sitting right there in front of me?"

"Your intentions were good. And I was hoping that with the progress we were making with your relaxation exercises..."

Tamara knew very well that they had made no progress. Sutherland was seeing what he wanted to or she was getting better at hiding the flashbacks and other crazy stuff. Or he was testing her to see if she'd admit that it wasn't getting any better.

She didn't.

"I really thought I'd be able to do it."

"Well... water under the bridge, now. We need to live in the present, not in the past. Where do we go from here?"

Tamara closed her eyes. "Nowhere."

"Nowhere? What do you mean by that?"

"I'm not going anywhere. I'm stuck here until I serve out my sentence. I'm here until I age, and then transferred to the women's prison."

"That doesn't mean you can't improve yourself. It doesn't mean you can't go forward in other ways. People earn degrees in prison, learn new things, make new friends. You don't have to stagnate."

"None of that is going to happen to me."

"It doesn't just happen to you. It's something that you make happen. Because you decide that you don't want to just stay here and stagnate, but to move forward and improve yourself. You can't just wait for things to happen to you."

Tamara opened her eyes again and looked at him. "Not me. I give up."

Dr. Sutherland lowered his head, studying her carefully. "Are you thinking of harming yourself, Tamara?"

"No."

"That's not what you mean when you say you've given up?"

"No. I just mean... I'm not trying anymore. I just fail. I just end up worse off than where I started. So I give up. That's it. I'm not trying anymore."

"I think you'll change your mind after a while."

"No. I won't. Why would you think that?"

"I just don't think you're the kind of person who can stand to sit in one place and not do anything for a long period of time. I think you're the type who can't stand to be still and gets an itch. And after a while, the itch becomes uncontrollable. You have to act on it. You can't just sit and not do anything."

"Huh." Tamara rested her head back against the wall. "Shows how much you know."

Dr. Sutherland pulled a small notebook out of his pocket. Tamara watched curiously as he opened it up and flipped through a couple of pages.

"What's that?"

"Just some notes I made. Things I might want to talk to you about."

"Like what?"

Sutherland rubbed his chin. "Things like whether you were having hallucinations in the courtroom."

"Oh." Tamara bit her lip. "No."

"Don't lie to me, Tamara. I can't help you if you lie to me."

"I was... confused. I don't know. Lots was going on."

"A couple of people said that you seemed to be talking to someone who wasn't there, and that you said, 'Did you hear what he said?' when no one had said anything."

"That doesn't mean I was seeing things."

"How about hearing things?" Dr. Sutherland asked shrewdly.

"I... what does it matter if I was hearing things or seeing things or just freaked out? It's all the same. What difference does it make?"

"It might."

"It's just like you told me before. It doesn't make any difference if I was seeing or hearing things. You said it didn't matter if I was having hallucinations when I... did what I did... when I killed Corrine and Julie."

"That's not exactly what I said. Why don't you answer my question? Were you having hallucinations in the courtroom? Were you seeing things, or hearing things, or having some other kind of hallucination?"

"I was sick," Tamara said. "I was overheated when I went in there. That could make you confused, could make you see or hear things..."

"Yes. And did you?"

Tamara still didn't want to answer in the affirmative. Even though he'd given her an out, agreed that it might have just been her heatstroke and dehydration, she couldn't bring herself to say that she had been hallucinating. Especially since she knew what the next question would be after that.

"Tamara. Tell me the truth now. Were you?"

Tamara dug her fingernails into her palms and clenched her teeth. "Yes."

"Thank you." Dr. Sutherland nodded. "Is that the first time you've had hallucinations?"

"Before. When I was pregnant. When I... did what I did."

"And any time in between? Any time... recently?"

Tamara scratched the heavy fabric of her uniform. She chewed on a nail.

"Tamara. I need you to be honest."

"Why does it matter? It doesn't matter!"

"If it doesn't matter to you then why are you having such a hard time answering the question? If it didn't matter to you, you would just answer me without thinking about it or trying to lie to me."

Tamara blew out her breath impatiently. "Sometimes, okay?" She looked at the window, feeling the eyes of the observers on her. "Sometimes maybe I do. But it doesn't matter. It doesn't make any difference. I'm still guilty of murder, right? I still didn't testify against Mr. Baker, after everything he did to me and the little girls. It doesn't make any difference whether I was having... weird crap happening to me when I did."

"Sometimes. I said before I would like to try out some meds to see if we can help you. If you're having these hallucinations, and not just flashbacks from PTSD, then relaxation exercises are not going to cut it. We need to try some antipsychotics. See if we can... even you out again. It's been several months now and I think we need to step up your treatment."

"I don't want pills. Pills are for losers who can't control themselves."

Dr. Sutherland just stood there looking at her. Tamara's face heated. She grew angry and embarrassed.

"I'm not a loser!"

"I didn't say you were, Tamara. But I want you to think about your behavior, both in court, and over the last few months. Have you been able to keep yourself under control? Or do you need help? I think things are... slipping. That's not your fault.

You can't decide to control your brain simply by willpower. If you have psychosis, we need to treat it."

Tamara clamped her mouth closed and refused to engage with him. If she didn't answer him, he didn't have anyone to argue with. She had told him before that she wasn't going to take any meds and he couldn't force her to. He'd just have to deal with it.

"I know you don't want to. But you haven't tried. You don't know what kind of a difference it will make for you. I promise that if it gives you side effects, we'll do our best to deal with them. There are a lot of different options out there. There's no reason to think that they won't work."

She still didn't answer. Sutherland sighed and looked down at the notes in his little notepad again.

"Maybe we could try this. I want you to tell me about Corrine and Julie. I want you to describe in detail what happened and what symptoms you were having at the time. Hallucinations, intrusive thoughts, disordered thinking... I'd like you to go through all of it."

Tamara examined his request from several angles. She had already been convicted of Corrine's and Julie's deaths. So it didn't matter what she said about them now. Nothing could get any worse. Dr. Sutherland knew that she had been pregnant at the time and had said that her pregnancy had triggered the psychosis. Since she wasn't pregnant again, there was no need for him to suggest that she was having psychosis again. He knew she hadn't been treated for it, and it had just gone away naturally.

"What do you want me to tell you?"

"You told me that you were expected to take care of the children all the time, other than when you were at school."

"Yeah. All the time."

"What felt like all the time, anyway. Obviously, if you saw

Mr. Baker taking care of them, there were times that you weren't."

Tamara frowned at this suggestion, but shrugged. "Okay. Most of the time." Sometimes he liked to take one of them off of her hands. He'd say it was to give her a break, or because he wanted to spend some time with his daughters. But now she realized those had just been lies.

"I'm sorry. I don't mean to interrupt. So you were taking care of them most of the time. And it was too much. You were feeling... tired...?"

"Exhausted," Tamara agreed. "I couldn't get any sleep. They were always waking me up, and when I got them down to sleep, my brain... kept going. I couldn't shut it off. It wouldn't let me sleep. So I'd fall asleep at my desk at school or when I was supposed to be taking care of the girls. Mrs. Baker woke me up once when I was supposed to be giving them their baths. I fell asleep while Corrine was playing in the tub. I hadn't bathed Julie yet. But when I went to bed... nothing. I couldn't get my body comfortable. I couldn't tell my brain it was time to sleep. I was walking around like a zombie all the time."

"That must have been very difficult. Falling asleep when Corrine was in the bath... was that what... made you think about drowning her, when you felt so overwhelmed?"

Tamara nodded. It was such a clear and overpowering memory. Mrs. Baker waking her up as she sat beside the tub, Julie in her arms and Corrine in the tub, screaming that Corrine was going to drown because Tamara had closed her eyes for a few minutes. Corrine splashed happily in the water beside her, completely unharmed, and Mrs. Baker acted like Tamara had killed her. She could remember the idea starting to form in her head, like a black fog curling around her brain.

How would Mrs. Baker feel if Corrine really did drown? What would she think then? Maybe then she wouldn't be so nasty. People didn't hit when they were sad, only when they were angry. And if they were both dead, then the Bakers wouldn't want Tamara anymore. She could get away from them. She could be free. And if the children were dead, Mr. Baker couldn't hurt them anymore either. They would be safe from his abuse.

"Tamara."

"They would be safe," Tamara said softly. "I could get them away from him for good."

"Is that what you thought?"

She nodded. But she was still back there, not in the same timeline as Dr. Sutherland. "I didn't want to hurt them. I just wanted to stop it. To stop them from hurting me. And from hurting the babies."

"But you planned to run away, too. You didn't just stay there, thinking the Bakers would be nicer to you if the other children were out of the way."

"I could run away. But Corrine and Julie couldn't. I couldn't take them with me. They wouldn't be able to get away from him, not for years."

"You could have called the police. Reported them."

Tamara had been so tired and confused. Every time she had tried to tell someone, to reach out to someone, it had backfired, and each punishment had been worse than the last.

"What did you see and hear? Do you remember? You told me you had wild dreams, but that they weren't always sleeping dreams. Sometimes you were awake."

"I'd hear her coming when she wasn't even home... see a car and be sure it was him. And sometimes... bugs or snakes or other scary stuff..."

"Funny how when we hallucinate, it is never fluffy bunnies or puppies," Dr. Sutherland said.

"I was going crazy. I didn't know what to do. I wanted it all to stop."

"That must have been very scary. You must have felt very alone."

"No one cared."

"Did you hear voices telling you to do things?"

"Sometimes... her voice, or his voice..." Tamara hesitated, trying to explain. "Not just... random voices, or Satan..."

"And what did their voices say?"

"What to do... all the chores... taking care of the babies... or him, whispering disgusting things... filling my brain..."

"And have you been hearing those voices again? The Bakers'? Or other voices, ones that are more recent, people who are here at the prison?"

"It was him. His voice at the trial."

"And other times when you were here and were hearing things?"

"I hear... babies crying... Things that happened to me here. Glock... Vernon..."

"You have been through some very traumatic things. Do you hear voices telling you to do things?"

"No." Tamara frowned, listening. "I don't know."

"Are you hearing voices right now, Tamara?"

"I hear you."

Dr. Sutherland chuckled. "But I'm here," he said. "I mean any other voices?"

He didn't seem to understand that he wasn't there with her, where she was. He was in a different time and place, and she was with the Bakers, slogging through the mud in her brain, trying to make sense of it.

"No. Just the Bakers. Mr. Baker..." His voice seemed vague and changeable, like it was in a dream, where reality was always shifting and changing. She wasn't sure where he was or what he was saying. And she really didn't want to find out.

"He's the one you heard at the trial. Why are you hearing him now, do you think?"

"He still wants me. He kept... looking at me... talking to me."

"And you're afraid? You don't want him to talk to you?"

"No."

"Wouldn't you like to shut his voice off? So you didn't have to listen to him talking to you anymore?"

"I can just..." Tamara's voice faded away into nothing.

For a while, neither of them said anything.

"You drowned Corrine," Dr. Sutherland said. "But not Julie. Why was that?"

Tamara's throat tightened. She was fully immersed in the memory, alert and aware of every detail. She could feel the luke-warm water, Corrine's slippery, smooth skin, the strong muscles that she had to fight against, using all her strength to keep Corrine under the water. "She fought so hard. I thought... drowning was peaceful. I thought she would just breathe in the water, and slide away... she wouldn't even know... it would be calm and peaceful."

"But that's not what happened?"

"I could hardly hold her. She was so strong and tried so hard to get back up." Tears streamed down Tamara's face. She tried to swallow the big, hot lump in her throat. "I couldn't do it again. I couldn't do that to Julie too. So... I stopped. I didn't know what to do. I knew when they got back from work, they'd find Corrine, and then... if both the babies were dead, I wouldn't have to stay there. But if Julie was still alive... I didn't know what would happen."

"You knew better than to shake her."

"No. I... Sometimes she would start to cry, and if I gave her a shake, she would stop. Like, she was startled, and it would stop her... for just long enough to find her soother, or think of some-thing else... I couldn't let her cry, because Mister or Missus..."

"Tell me how it happened."

"I don't know... I don't even know. She was screaming after Corrine... drowned... because I had to put her down, and nobody was holding her or looking after her. I shook her... but she wouldn't stop. Mrs. Baker was screaming at me. I couldn't think of what to do to make Julie stop... and then she did, for a few seconds. And I got her a bottle, and fed her... and I thought she was okay, but she kept fussing and spitting up... She was acting really tired, but she wouldn't go to sleep. Kept throwing up and then... she was just..."

"Mrs. Baker was home?"

"No. She was out at work. Mr. Baker was out... he finished work, but he liked to go do other things. Leave me with the kids so he could go... do whatever."

"But you said Mrs. Baker was screaming at you when you were trying to calm Julie."

"She always screamed at me when they cried."

"Even when she wasn't there?"

Tamara shook her spinning head. He didn't understand. It didn't work the way he thought.

"She doesn't like the babies to cry. So she screams at me to keep them quiet. Or if I can't get them quiet, or I did something really bad, then she takes me... and whips me."

"It was wrong of her to do that and it makes me angry that she would treat you like that. It must have made you upset too."

"She just... hates me when I let the babies cry... she wants to hurt me..."

"Before Corrine died? Or after? Which are you talking about, Tamara? Do you mean now?"

"She's not here now."

"No."

"She hates me. She says she does. And it hurts so bad..."

"What hurts? Her words? Does it hurt your feelings when she talks that way?"

Tamara rubbed her burning legs. "It hurts. She hurt me so bad. But it didn't matter. I still had to work. Go to school. She didn't care."

"She shouldn't have done that."

There was quiet for a few minutes. Tamara tried to pull herself out of the whirlpool and think in a straight line, like Dr. Sutherland and everyone else. If she could just think straight, she could keep them all from hurting her.

"Tamara, wouldn't you like it if you didn't have to hear them anymore? Wouldn't it be better if we took the voices away?"

"I can't," Tamara despaired. "I already tried when I was at the Bakers and it didn't work."

TWENTY

I T WAS A RELIEF to get back to her own cell. Tamara
was so glad to get away from the eyes of the observers
behind the windows. And she was glad to get away from
Dr. Sutherland's questions.

She was sure that he had triggered the flashbacks on purpose.
He wanted to get her wound up and feeling worse so that she
would agree to take the pills he prescribed. And she had almost
agreed. But in the end, she had managed to hold out and pretend
to be normal long enough for them to move her back to her own
cell.

But there had been several new transfers in, and she
returned to her cell to find that it was occupied by another
inmate.

"This is my room!" Tamara growled, immediately territorial.
She stepped out of the room to make sure that she had, in fact,
entered her cell and not someone else's by mistake. It was her
cell. She looked back at the guard who had escorted her back to
make sure that she was right about the room, and that she hadn't
returned to her old cell by mistake. The guard looked at her and
nodded.

"You have a roommate."

"But I was…"

Tamara knew very well how it worked. She only got a cell to herself for a short time, and then a new transfer would be assigned to her. They had let her stay odd man out for a few months, choosing instead to fill Tabby's and Waterson's places and to shuffle others around. Tamara had gotten accustomed to being by herself and thought that being an old-timer, she had earned the right to her own cell.

"Sorry, but we're full up. Can't put her anywhere else. You're going to have to adjust."

Tamara turned her eyes back to her new cellie, not pleased.

"Bottom is mine," she snapped, even though the fact was obvious, and the new girl hadn't staked a claim.

"Yeah, okay." The girl's eyes were wary, scoping Tamara out and trying to get her measure. "Top is fine with me."

Tamara spun around, looking over the rest of the cell, making sure that the girl hadn't touched or moved anything. A second hygiene kit was on the top of the dresser, but it hadn't been touched yet, and Tamara's seemed to be where she had left it before going to court. She turned back to face her new cellmate.

"I'm French. Who are you?"

The girl's head twitched to the side and back again. "Becky Chase. Aren't you the one…"

"You don't know me, so don't act like you do," Tamara cut her off. "Just stay out of my way and we'll be fine."

"Okay." The girl's voice was small. It grated on Tamara's nerves. Chase wasn't going to get anywhere by using that tiny, little girl voice. She'd get beaten up, or eaten up by the Sharks. She'd be recruited in two minutes by one of the gangs and that wasn't a recipe for staying safe from harm, no matter what the gangs told her.

"Toughen up," Tamara grumbled. She knew she was echoing the lessons that Glock had given her. Glock had been right; she had known what she was talking about. "You gotta be strong and assertive, don't be a little girl."

Chase frowned, not understanding.

"You listen to me because I'm your cellie," Tamara said. "But if you let everybody push you around, you're going to get hurt. You need to stand up for yourself. Got it?"

"Uh..." Chase processed this, comical in her attempt to come up with the correct response to the conflicting advice. "I will. Yeah." She straightened her posture, trying to look more confident.

Tamara had to shake her head. Had she ever been as green and uncertain as that? She remembered the way that Glock used to ride her, telling her to stop acting like a naive little princess and not to let anyone walk over her. It hadn't been an easy path.

"You need to make your bed," Tamara told Chase, indicating the sheets and blanket piled on it. "There might not be time later on and you don't want to catch trouble because it's not ready at lights out."

Chase looked over at the bare bunk. "I'll do it later," she said, trying out her assertiveness.

Tamara shrugged. "Makes no difference to me."

There were footsteps in the hall. Tamara looked up when they stopped at her door. Zobel looked in.

"You're back. I see you met your new cellie."

"Yeah."

"You let me know if you have any problems."

Tamara rolled her eyes. "You think I'm gonna have trouble with one like this? She's not going to bother me."

Zobel gave her a smile. "Maybe I was talking to her." He turned his attention to the greenie. "I'm Zobel," he informed her. "And yeah, French here gives you any trouble, you talk to me or one of the other security staff."

Chase's eyes widened. She looked back at Tamara. Zobel laughed. "She isn't likely to cause you any trouble. That's why you were put in here. Just give us a heads-up if you do have any trouble with anyone. Right, French?"

Tamara scowled. The security staff knew very well that snitching on a cellie or filing a complaint about another juvie was likely to lead to more problems, not less. But what was he supposed to tell her? Keep quiet about any abuse? Don't come to us if there's a problem? They had to say that they were there to help and that they would take care of any problems. Chase would have to learn for herself just how far to take the advice.

Zobel raised his eyebrow, giving Tamara a look that she interpreted as meaning he wanted a private word with her. Kicking her greenie out to fend for herself while Tamara talked with him was probably not the right thing to do, so Tamara headed to the door.

"Catch you later, Chase. Stay out of trouble."

Zobel stepped back from the doorway and they both walked down the hall in the same direction.

"Good advice," Zobel said. "How about you? Are you staying out of trouble?"

"You know me better than that."

Zobel chuckled. "Unfortunately, that's been true too much lately. I gather everybody has cleared you? Back to normal?"

"Hospital cleared me. Sutherland and Psych cleared me. So, yeah. All back to normal."

"Are you... feeling up to it? You're okay?"

Tamara stared at the end of the hallway, not looking at him. "What other choice do I have? Here or where? Stay in Psych? What else am I going to do?"

"Well, if you weren't up to it... stay there a little longer or get moved to Forensic. See if they could help you get straightened out."

"I'm done with shrinks."

"Okay. It's just... I know things didn't go well in court."

"Don't want to talk about it."

"What about when you go back? What's going to happen then?"

"I'm not going back," Tamara said flatly. "That's it. I only had one chance to testify against him."

"No, I meant... your other trial. You've got another court date, don't you?"

Tamara's heart sank when she realized he was right.

Next she had to testify at Glock's trial.

* * *

TAMARA HAD BEEN PRETTY calm when she got out of Psych, happy to be back out on her own recognizance and away from the mental poking and prodding. But Zobel's remarks didn't serve to make her happier. She walked back to her cell, bubbling with impotent fury. She wasn't mad at him for reminding her about her second court date. But her anxiety over the second trial going over like the first made her want to throw something. Or hit someone.

"Hey," Chase greeted, when she walked in, opening her mouth to ask Tamara something. She saw Tamara's face and closed her mouth, going pale.

Tamara picked up her current read from the top of the dresser and threw it across the cell. She didn't throw it at Chase and, seeing as it was only a paperback, it didn't do anything more than hit the wall and then the floor with a soft thud with some new bent corners. Chase flinched away anyway, raising her hands in a half-placating, half-defensive gesture.

"What's wrong? What happened?"

Tamara threw herself down on her bunk and covered her face with her hands.

"Nothing wrong," she growled. "Leave it alone."

Chase stood there looking at her. "Okay..."

"Don't need you staring at me, either."

Chase shifted. "Do you want me to go, then?"

It was obvious from her voice that she wasn't ready to face the rest of the unit yet. She wanted to just shelter in her room and not have to go to the common room and face the gangs and the rest of the girls. She was smart to be nervous about it.

Tamara wondered briefly who Chase's senior mentor was. Someone should have been assigned to her to help make the transition easier. But whoever it was, it would appear she had dropped Chase off in her cell and abandoned her there.

"You don't gotta go. Just give me my space." Not that she had any space, now that she had a cellie. "Read a book or have a nap."

Chase was silent. Tamara spread her fingers so she could see Chase through the cracks. The girl was considering Tamara's suggestions.

"This book...?" She indicated the one that Tamara had thrown.

"No, I'm reading that one. There's some in the dresser."

The dresser had open shelves rather than drawers, so that nothing could be hidden from sight. Maybe that made it a cupboard rather than a dresser. But Chase knew what Tamara was talking about and didn't have any trouble finding the small stack of books piled on one shelf. She took them out to look through.

"My—I got a visitor who brings them to me," Tamara said. "If you like something particular, I can have her bring it."

"These are great, thanks." Chase made her selection and climbed up into her bunk, moving carefully and keeping an eye on Tamara.

* * *

TIME DRAGGED ON. Tamara was annoyed every time Chase turned a page in the book or put it down with a bored sigh. One of the hardest things to adjust to in juvie was getting used to doing nothing, a skill that Tamara couldn't seem to re-learn and that Chase didn't yet have a clue about. At least Chase hadn't tried to initiate a conversation with Tamara, getting all chummy and asking her about her past. That was the last thing Tamara needed.

The dinner bell rang, and they could hear feet and voices all through the block as people left their cells or other activities and headed toward the canteen.

"Supper," Tamara announced, getting up. "I'll show you where it is."

Chase could have followed her nose or the other girls, all of whom were headed in the same direction, but it wasn't just her navigation skills Tamara was offering. Chase was the junior cellie, and it was Tamara's responsibility to help her get settled and learn appropriate behavior. Maybe it was the administration's newest ploy to get Tamara to behave herself. Have her teach someone else the rules.

"Finally," Chase groaned. She jumped down from the bunk beside Tamara.

Tamara looked at her, then looked at the bunk.

"You can't leave anything on your bunk. You have to put the book back."

Chase rolled her eyes. "I'm just going to come back after dinner and read some more."

Tamara shrugged. She wasn't going to nursemaid the newbie and force her to follow the rules. If she didn't want to listen to Tamara's warnings, she'd suffer the consequences. She headed to the canteen, Chase stuck close to her side. Tamara gave her a glare.

"Give me some space."

"Oh." Chase adjusted, putting a few more inches between them. "Sorry."

Tamara moved a bit farther from her and Chase maintained the distance. Tamara didn't say anything else on the way to the canteen, keeping a sharp eye out for any trouble. If she had a newbie to babysit, she had to be twice as alert as usual, and she didn't know what kind of damage her rep might have suffered as a result of landing in Psych. No one challenged her on the way there. Tamara noticed that Chase's pace picked up as they neared the canteen; she headed eagerly for the serving counter when they entered. Unless she was malnourished—and she didn't look it—she wasn't likely to be too excited about what she found there.

"Slow down, Chase."

Chase looked back over her shoulder. "Why?" She slowed her pace slightly.

"Look around and be aware." Tamara drew closer so she could lower her voice. "Watch for problems. Who's around you. If you cut in front of someone important, you're going to be in trouble."

Her brow furrowed, Chase waited for Tamara to catch up again. Tamara was scanning the canteen to see who was already there, both seated and in line.

"This is stupid," Chase complained. "How am I supposed to know who's important and who's not?" Her mouth twisted into a sneer. It was obvious she figured she should have some standing. She might be a newbie, but she had an attitude.

"Right now, you're lowest man on the totem pole. Everyone else is ahead of you. You're new. You're green. You're unaffiliated. I don't know what you're in for, but being bad on the outside doesn't make you something in here. This is high security. You don't get in here for shoplifting candy bars."

Chase folded her arms over her chest. "So what do I do?"

"Get in behind me."

The other girl's nostrils flared as Tamara passed her in order to get into the line. "So all of that was just so you could get into line ahead of me?"

Tamara didn't bother to answer. She scanned around before

she actually slid into place in the line, making sure, as she had told Chase, that she wasn't cutting ahead of anyone important.

Brett, the girl ahead of Tamara, looked up and down the line as she stood sideways, facing the warming trays. She twitched an inch farther from Tamara, sneering. "What are you doing here?"

Tamara struggled to keep her response low-key. She wanted to pop Brett right there. Just out of hospital and Psych, she needed to reassert her hierarchical position and ensure she didn't backslide. But with a newbie to look after, at least until Chase made a decision about joining one of the gangs, Tamara had to be cautious.

"Same old, same old," she murmured. "Where else would I be?"

Brett, stiff and ready for an overblown reaction from Tamara, blinked in surprise. "They put you on meds, or what?"

Brett had better hope so, because Tamara wasn't going to forget Brett goading her. Once she was free of her responsibilities...

"I got eyes on me or you'd be on the floor right now."

Brett was a good fighter. Tamara probably wouldn't have been able to get her down when Brett was the one initiating a fight. She'd have to catch Brett off guard for that. Maybe one day soon, she would do just that.

Brett continued to proceed up the counter, keeping pace with the rest of the line. She took a quick scan around the canteen to see who was watching them. She frowned.

"I don't see your pet bull. Guess maybe he stepped out for a smoke break. Or maybe he's making time with another honey."

A wave of cold went over Tamara. She had thought that she and Zobel had been careful about their relationship—which wasn't romantic—but apparently, others had still noticed the friendship.

Tamara didn't say anything in response to Brett's comments,

but she strode forward in time with Brett, stepping on the heel of her shoe.

Brett wheeled around, throwing down her tray with a crash. Tamara had not picked hers up from the counter in the first place, keeping her hands free in case the situation developed. She clawed for Brett's eyes, going for distraction rather than brute force. Brett reacted as expected, shielding her face with one hand and reaching out with the other. But Tamara hadn't been lying about having eyes on her; she and Brett barely had time to try to get ahold of each other before a couple of the guards were there breaking them up. Tamara let Millican pull her back. One of the junior guards grappled with Brett, having a more difficult time getting her under control even though one of her shoes was flopping loose and tripping her up.

"Back of the line," Millican growled in Tamara's ear, holding her arms behind her back, "and no more nonsense from you."

Tamara didn't argue or try to pull away from him, but she turned her head slightly toward Chase. Millican looked at Chase and swore.

"What are you doing starting fights when you've got a greenie to look after?"

"I didn't start it."

"Sure, you didn't."

The younger guard finally managed to get Brett under control, handcuffing her hands behind her back. "What do you want me to do with this one?"

"Better take her to iso. Let her cool off." Millican glared at Brett. "Happy with yourself? Now you're going to miss dinner."

"Who wants to eat this crap day after day?" Brett growled.

But Tamara knew that, like Glock, Brett had an appetite and didn't really care about the quality of what she put in her mouth. Glock had always cleaned Tamara's plate as well as her own. While Tamara wouldn't have cared one way or the other about losing her supper, Brett *would* be upset about it, and that made

Tamara smile. If Brett were going to pick fights, she had better do it at a time other than mealtimes.

Brett was taken out of the canteen, still struggling and growling at the guard escorting her. Still tripping over her loose shoe and trying to get it back on. Millican released his hold on Tamara and let her take her own place in line.

"No more trouble out of you."

"I didn't do anything." Tamara smiled sweetly. "Why would I do that when I've got a greenie to babysit?"

Millican shook his head. He looked at Chase.

"I'm Millican." He tapped his name bar. "Saw your name come up on the briefing this morning. You're Chase?"

Chase nodded. She looked over at Tamara to make sure she wasn't doing anything wrong in talking to one of the security guards. Tamara slid her tray along the counter to collect the rest of her dinner.

"You keep your nose clean and let me or one of the others know if you have any problems," Millican advised.

"Yeah. Thanks."

Millican drifted away, returning to his post. Chase blew out her breath and looked at Tamara. "Should I have said *sir*? Is he going to have it out for me now?"

"Nah. If you're in trouble, or talking to Rice or someone in admin, then 'sir' them for all you're worth. But just casual conversation... no, most of them don't care. If they do, they'll let you know."

"He seemed okay."

Tamara resisted looking back toward Millican, looking down at her tray and then taking another look around to make sure that no one else was going to pick up where Brett had left off. "Yeah. He's been here a long time. He's pretty good."

Chase nodded. She was looking at what appeared to be a tray full of slop, her nose wrinkled. "What's that?"

"That's dinner." Tamara examined what was on her tray. "I think it's supposed to be beef stew today."

"Looks like someone threw up in there."

Tamara snorted. "Sometimes it tastes like it too." She picked up a sad little half-cup of gelatin at the end of the counter and added it to Chase's tray. "There. Now you got dessert."

Chase studied it. "Is that what it's supposed to be?"

Tamara picked up her plate and looked around. Chase stood beside her and motioned to a couple of empty chairs. "Couple over there."

"No. Not there."

"Why not? They saving for someone else?"

"TMJ."

"TMJ?"

"Gang. Only the gang sits there. And over there," she nodded to another of the tables without meeting anyone's eyes. "Sharks. Control of the block usually goes to one of them. Don't let anyone in any smaller gang tell you that they're going to take over because they all got together into a coalition. Ain't gonna happen."

"So I should join one of the others. Sharks or... whatsit."

"TMJ. Yeah, if you want to join up, go with one of them."

"The girl you were fighting with. She's...?"

"TMJ. They used to have control, but lately, it's the Sharks."

"That one?" Chase pointed to the Sharks' table.

Tamara swore and grabbed Chase's hand, pulling it down. Too late; Lewis and a couple of her girls had already seen Chase's pointing finger and stood up.

"What?" Chase yanked her hand way from Tamara. "Keep your hands off me!"

Lewis strode over quickly, her two goons flanking her, then moving outward to get in behind Tamara and Chase, to pincer them from both sides.

"You oughta listen to your cellie," Lewis sneered at Chase.

"You gonna point at someone, you'd better be ready to fight. That finger better be a gun, or you're gonna get your face stomped in."

Chase was sheet-white, her eyes going from Lewis to the goons and back again. She gulped and balled her free hand up in a fist, held uncertainly, ready to defend herself but not sure if she was going to have to or if she was just challenging Lewis further by assuming an aggressive posture.

Lewis reached out and shoved Chase in the middle of the chest, forcing her to take a couple of steps back. "You're stupid. They send you here for being an idiot? Too stupid to be allowed to walk around loose on the outside?"

Chase's lips moved, but nothing came out. Which Tamara was glad for, because it wasn't the time for a smart-aleck reply. If they could draw the confrontation out for long enough, the guards would break it up before it became physical. Tamara didn't think she could defend both herself and Chase against three attackers without a weapon, and the only things she had were her tray and her plate. She'd used both before, but they weren't very effective.

"She's almost as stupid as you, French!" Lewis sneered.

Tamara tilted her tray and shoved it forward into Lewis's chest as hard as she could, forcing the bigger girl back with the force of it. Chase was lagging behind, not sure what to do with herself. Tamara turned to her right, where she knew one of the goons was coming up on her flank, and kicked into her assailant's knee as hard as she could manage. She came in at a bad angle, and the girl, Cinco, had seen her use that move often enough to expect it. She grabbed Tamara's leg and used it as leverage to flip Tamara, sending her crashing to the floor. Tamara saw red. The rest of the canteen dissolved around her and she aimed her rage at Cinco, sweeping her legs to bring her down to where Tamara could get in close to her.

She pummeled Cinco, only getting in a good blow with one

out of every five she threw, but moving fast enough, she managed to get several in before the guards could sound the alarm and get in to stop them.

The alarm whooped in her ears. Crouched low, Tamara looked around, trying to locate Chase to see if she needed protection. Tamara had not disabled Lewis and there had been a third girl somewhere behind them and to the left.

"Get your hands up! Drop your weapons! All of you!"

Tamara wasn't about to be the first to obey. Not if there were weapons involved, which she hadn't even seen. She wrenched her neck looking for Chase and found her in a clinch with the other goon. Rafferty. And Rafferty was the one with a knife.

Tamara didn't wait for the security staff to follow their protocols and de-escalate Rafferty. Tamara's cellie wasn't even a day old and Tamara had already let her get herself into a fight against a shiv. Tamara launched herself at Rafferty, hitting her low in the back and side to knock her away from Chase and to the floor. As she tried to wrestle the shiv from Rafferty or at least get her into a position where the guards could get control of her, she kicked at Chase, who had also fallen. "Get out of here!"

Chase was moving like a dazed calf, eyes all big and hardly able to get her wobbly legs underneath her. But she got to her feet and Tamara hadn't seen any blood, so Tamara turned her attention back to Rafferty and trying to get the knife away from her or pinned beneath her.

"French, back!" one of the guard's voices boomed.

Tamara squeezed her eyes shut and threw herself to the side, rolling away from Rafferty. She held her breath and heard the hiss of the pepper spray. Rafferty shouted, which meant she took in an even bigger breath of the spray. She coughed and sputtered as they disarmed her.

"On your belly! Get down on your belly!"

Tamara turned her head and opened her eyes a crack to make sure it was safe. None of the guards were threatening to spray Rafferty again, so Tamara opened her eyes the rest of the way. Rafferty had her hands up to her eyes, face dyed a bright red, and she coughed and spasmed uncontrollably. Millican forced Rafferty onto her stomach, shouting and smacking her with his baton and eventually kneeling on her back while she writhed and shouted. With the help of the other guards, he managed to pull her hands away from her face and twist them around behind her to cuff them. Rafferty's coughing was interspersed with protests and swearing. Two of them hauled her up to her feet to take her to the infirmary, leaving Millican behind. Tamara didn't envy Rafferty the sore eyes and throat she was going to have, even after they were properly washed out.

Tamara looked around to see where everyone else was. Cinco and Lewis were both on the floor, hands secured behind their backs. Chase was still on her feet, looking around at the scene with wide eyes.

"Belly down, French."

Tamara obeyed Kirk's instruction, rolling over onto her stomach and putting her hands behind her head. Kirk gave her a cursory pat-down, probably figuring that Tamara would have pulled any weapon she was carrying during the fight instead of going after Rafferty bare-handed. He zip-tied her wrists and helped her to her feet.

"You injured?" His eyes flicked over her.

"No."

"Catch any of the pepper spray?"

"No."

His hands were red with the back-spray from the pepper spray, so he was the one who had sprayed Rafferty. Tamara blinked, her eyes burning a little at his suggestion.

"You," Kirk motioned to Chase, "hands behind your head."

Chase looked at him, frowning.

"Come on," Kirk encouraged, motioning to her. "Hands."

"I didn't do anything," Chase protested.

"You were involved. Everyone involved gets checked."

"But I didn't..."

"Chase," Tamara growled, "just shut up and do it."

Chase moved slowly, bringing her hands up to her head as she had been told. She still looked confused. Kirk left Tamara standing where she was and went over to Chase, patting her down and restraining her.

"I didn't do anything," Chase repeated.

Kirk paid no attention to her protest. He looked down at his hands. "Are you hurt?"

"No."

Kirk rubbed his fingers together, smeared red not just with the bright pepper spray dye, but also with darker red blood. He patted Chase's torso down again, then looked at her hands.

"You are hurt. Rafferty get you?"

"No, I don't think so."

Kirk cut the zip tie he'd just put on to free up Chase's arms, pushed her uniform sleeves up, and found a cut on one arm. "She did get you."

Chase looked down at the cut and swore in surprise. "Didn't even feel it."

Tamara studied the tattoos Kirk had revealed on Chase's arms. Mostly gang ink. Tamara wondered where she was from. For being in a gang, she wasn't a very good fighter. Or maybe she was when it was a planned fight, but she didn't know what to do when surprised.

It wasn't a bad cut, not arterial like when Zobel was slashed. But it was more than a surface cut. Blood dripping steadily down Chase's arm.

Tamara was hot, but shivered like she was cold. She tried to force herself to breathe slowly and deeply. "Not here."

Kirk's eyes flicked over to her. "What?"

"Not here," Tamara repeated, even though she hadn't been

talking to him and he wouldn't understand. She said the words aloud for herself, trying to keep herself calm and present.

She heard screaming. Shouting and swearing all around her. She felt the warm spray of Zobel's blood against her face. She could taste it, coppery, on her tongue.

"It was Tabby," Tamara whispered. "She had a shiv."

"Tabby is dead," Kirk said, his voice gruff. "It was Rafferty. We all saw."

"It was Tabby."

"No. Pull it together, French." He shook her arm. "French. Come on."

She swallowed and blinked her eyes, trying to focus and shift herself back to the present. Chase was looking at her, eyes so wide that Tamara could see the whites all the way around her dark irises.

"What's wrong with her?" Chase asked.

Kirk gave Tamara another shake. "No more nonsense, French. Pay attention."

"You should put pressure on it," Tamara said. "Slow the bleeding down."

Kirk nodded. He let go of Tamara's arm and fumbled with fat fingers with the pouches in his belt to find gloves and gauze. He pressed the gauze over the cut in Chase's arm, making her wince. Chase turned her attention from Tamara to her arm.

"Does it need stitches?" she demanded. "How bad is it?"

"Not bad," Kirk assured her. "We'll see what Doc Eastport says. He can stitch it if it needs to be."

Millican, who had been talking with the other guards and seeing Cinco and Lewis off, walked over. "We got an injury?" he demanded.

"Just a nick," Kirk said. "Not serious."

Millican shook his head. He looked at Tamara. "What do I gotta do to keep you out of trouble?"

"It wasn't me. I was minding my own business."

"What happened, then? Lewis was already settled. Why was she back over here mixing it up with you again?"

Tamara glanced sideways at Chase. She wasn't going to blame the greenie for breaching the unwritten rules at juvie. Coming from a gang, Chase should have known that pointing to the Sharks might cause problems, but the rules on the inside weren't always the same as the rules on the outside.

"They just wanted fresh meat," Tamara said, shrugging. "Wanted to recruit Chase, I guess."

"You don't recruit someone by cutting them!" Chase objected, her voice rising. Now that the danger was over, she was left with her system filled with adrenaline and nothing to do with it. Her muscles were probably all shaking, her brain revved up. Just two steps from hysteria.

"Sometimes they do," Kirk admitted.

One cut to persuade you to join up. A worse one if you said no.

Millican shook his head. "What a mess. I'll need to hear everyone's stories." He sighed. A mountain of paperwork was required with a gang-initiated fight, especially one with injuries or where pepper spray or tasers had to be deployed. "You've got Chase, so why don't you take her down to the infirmary? I'll return French to her room."

Tamara gave a shrug. Chase resisted Kirk's pull on her arm and he attempted to escort her out of the canteen.

"Wait a minute," she protested, "I haven't had anything to eat!"

Tamara and Millican just looked at each other and laughed.

## TWENTY-ONE

I T SEEMED LIKE IT was only a day or two before Tamara was again being shackled and chained for her court appearance, though a number of weeks had passed.

"Don't know why we're bothering," Durham complained, as he checked each of the locks. "It's just going to be another catastrophe."

Tamara bit the inside of her cheek. She did not want to go through with it, but she had to try to redeem herself. Prove to everyone else that she wasn't a total screw-up. She could testify in court. It wasn't going to be like facing Mr. and Mrs. Baker. She wouldn't be sick. She could face Glock and confirm what everyone was going to hear on the recording. That it was Glock who had attacked McClure, not Tamara. That was all she had to do.

"It's not going to be like that again," Tamara insisted.

Durham looked at her face and shook his head. "You're already freaking out. By the time we get there you're going to be a complete mess."

Tamara breathed slowly. She welcomed the surge of anger at his words. She'd rather be mad at him than dreading what was to come. She wasn't freaking out. She was perfectly calm. She could face Glock in the courtroom. She could face McClure. All she had to do was to sit down and confirm what had happened. It was a no-brainer.

"I'm fine," she insisted.

She was sweating and her heart was beating hard and fast. But that didn't mean she was going to have a meltdown. She wasn't going to be sick this time. She wasn't going to be facing her abusers.

Living with Glock as her cellie hadn't been all unicorns and rainbows, but Glock had protected her from the worst elements at juvie until Tamara was strong enough and skilled enough to look after herself. That had meant putting up with Glock's bad moods and bloodlust, but those hadn't been nonstop. Glock could easily be mellow for a week or two when everything was going the right way.

Exchanging favors for Glock's protection hadn't been the same as putting up with Mr. Baker's abuse. It was Tamara's choice and she was getting a benefit in return.

*What're you going to give me in exchange for protection?*

Tamara dragged her hand up to her face to wipe away a bead of sweat. Her stomach was starting to shake inside, but she wasn't going to tell Durham that she was sick and couldn't go. She had just finished telling him she was fine.

Durham looked at her sharply at the noise of her wrist chains clinking, but didn't say anything. He checked the ankle shackles and stepped back. Gomez was the second guard there to verify that Tamara was secure for transport. He stepped forward and checked the locks and the chains with easy familiarity.

"You're gonna be fine," he told Tamara. "You've got nothing to worry about."

Tamara nodded without speaking.

*No one's gonna bother you if you're my girl. Whether you're with me or not, you'll be safe. But that comes with a price tag.*

She had made a choice. She hadn't had to pair up with Glock. She could have chosen one of the gangs. She could have tried to go it on her own, even if she was a naive greenie who had never even been in a fight before. Smaller than anyone else, a mere twelve years old.

How else was she supposed to survive? She needed someone to shelter her, to teach her the unwritten protocols and politics of the block. She needed someone to show her how to hold herself, to talk, to fight when she had to. Tamara didn't know the simplest things about eye contact, how to talk to the others when they approached her, how to deal with the constant jockeying for position in the social hierarchy at juvie. Under Glock's protection, she'd had the time to learn all of those things.

*There are safer people to make friends with.* Zobel had been the one to warn Tamara right from the start. He'd seen the bruises on her and knew where they came from. But being with Glock hadn't been about friendship. It had been about safety. And Tamara couldn't exactly back out of it once she understood what she'd gotten herself into.

Being with Glock had been a choice. Tamara's choice. Not like with Mr. Baker, where she was trapped and had no other options.

"French."

Tamara startled away from the touch on her arm and looked around. She had walked all the way to the prison bus without even realizing it. Durham motioned impatiently for her to enter ahead of him. Tamara went up the stairs and he let her select her own seat, anchoring her in as usual and then going up to the front of the bus to sit where he could watch her and the other juvies headed over to the courthouse.

Tamara stared out the window, taking deep breaths to try to ground herself in the moment. What point was there in going over the past? The choices she had made as a twelve-year-old newbie couldn't be undone. She'd lived with the consequences.

It hadn't turned out so badly. She'd toughened up, learned to fight, learned how to stand up for herself and her rep. She never would have been able to stay out of the gangs on her own before.

She felt sick. Gomez hadn't let her get away with not eating before her court appearance. Not after what had happened the last time. And he forced her to drink as much water as she could, ignoring Tamara's protests that she was going to spend all morning peeing.

"Better than ending up in the hospital with dehydration again," he said unsympathetically.

*He* didn't have to pee in front of strangers, locked in an open-barred cell.

Her breakfast and all of that water was just sitting in her stomach, sloshing around when she moved. The transfer bus didn't exactly have world-class suspension, and would bounce her around all the way to the courthouse. She was sweating, even though the morning air outside was cool.

Tamara shifted, trying to get comfortable in the hard, beaten-up bench seat. Her chains rattled and Durham's eyes focused on her, waiting for her to settle back in. Tamara rolled her shoulders and tried to regulate her breathing. A couple more girls were escorted onto the bus and anchored in place. The other guards left, but Durham remained watching them.

Gomez poked his head in the door. "That's it."

Durham looked at the list on his clipboard. "What about Perez?"

"Sick. Not coming on."

Durham nodded. He stood up and walked down the aisle, checking each of their chains again to ensure they were anchored securely. Tamara flinched away from his touch, her stomach tight.

"Calm down, French."

Because she had pulled away from him, he checked each individual chain and lock to make sure she hadn't been trying to hide something. He couldn't do a proper pat-down with her sitting down chained, but he did a quick check anyway, even making her take her shoes off so he could make sure she didn't have a shiv or tool hidden there. He straightened up, looking her over once more.

"You gonna cause me problems?" he demanded.

If he thought she might be a security risk, he could delay the bus, take her off, have her thoroughly searched and x-rayed.

"No, sir."

"What are you so jumpy about?"

Tamara swallowed. She shrugged. "Court didn't go so good last time. And seeing Glock."

"Ah." Even though he hadn't been there when Glock was, he had heard about her. Everybody knew about Glock and Tamara from what had happened when she was out on parole. "Not so sure about seeing your old cellie?"

Tamara's skin itched. She wanted to shower. She wanted to get up and move around and just shake it off. But the more she moved around, the more she attracted Durham's attention and made him nervous about security.

"Not just seeing her," Tamara said. "Testifying..." She couldn't finish the sentence and say she was testifying against Glock. She wasn't doing anything against Glock, wasn't trying to hurt or accuse her. Tamara was just confirming what the police already knew, that it had been Glock who had attacked McClure and Tamara was just a witness. She wasn't there to accuse Glock, just to defend herself.

She swallowed. She wasn't going there to testify against Glock.

Durham gave her one long, considering stare.

"Can we just get going?" one of the other juvies demanded.

Durham shrugged and turned around to walk back up to the front of the bus. He sat down and nodded to Eli that he could get under way. Eli closed the door, put the bus into gear, and they were on their way.

The bouncing of the bus increased Tamara's nausea and gave her a headache. She closed her eyes, but that didn't help. She just kept seeing Glock. Her cellie. Her protector.

Her tormentor.

Tamara opened her eyes. She leaned her head against the window and watched the traffic go by outside the bus. A lot of people stared at the bus, goggling at the dangerous convicts on their way to the courthouse.

Tamara was relieved when they reached the courthouse and she could finally rest from the vibrations and bouncing of the bus. She already had to use the toilet, thanks to Gomez. She waited for Durham to complete the disembark procedures to get them on their way. The other two juvies were off the bus ahead of Tamara. She sat, growing more and more uncomfortable, as they were seen to their courtrooms or waiting areas.

Durham returned to the bus and looked at Tamara, but he didn't immediately walk up to her to unlock her anchor.

"Even when you're not causing trouble, you're causing trouble," he complained.

"What? I'm not doing anything!"

"They're not too happy about having you back here. Say we should have notified them ahead of time because you require an increased security presence. They don't want you off the bus."

Tamara rolled her eyes. "I can't exactly testify from here. I've got court!"

"Well, as it turns out... you might not."

Tamara lifted up and dropped her hands in frustration, making the chains ring out. "You gotta get me going one direction or the other, I have to use the facilities!"

He shook his head unsympathetically. "You're going to have to wait."

"I've *been* waiting."

"You're going to have to wait longer. Cross your legs. I can't get you off of this bus without clearance and we can't drive you back to juvie without clearing it on that end."

Tamara swore. She stared out her window at the inside of the building's garage and loading dock. Durham got off the bus, talked to men on the loading dock, waited, talked to some more, and again waited.

Tamara muttered to herself, in growing pain from having to wait. She'd go right there, but she would be the one who suffered, having to sit in wet clothes all day, or at least until she got back to juvie.

Durham returned to the bus. "Okay, looks like we got permission."

"Hallelujah."

He bent down to unlock her anchor. Tamara was eager to get up, but she held herself back, waiting until he had stepped back again and was ready. Standing up right in his face and trying to push past him would only end up with her getting sprayed or tased.

It hurt to move. Tamara hunched over a little, protecting her sore bladder, trying not to bump or stretch it any more.

"Get me to the nearest restroom," she told Durham.

He looked at her. "You think I can just walk you into a public toilet? You're going to have to wait until we've got you settled."

Tamara hunched over, pressing her hands to her thighs and trying to ease the pain and pressure. "Seriously," she breathed, "I can't wait."

"Then you'd better get moving."

Tamara walked with him, her steps slow and painful, knowing that if she walked too fast or relaxed her muscles, she was going to lose control. She swore steadily under her breath. Durham ignored the stream of invectives, leading her off of the bus to where three armed guards were waiting on the loading dock. Apparently, Tamara was dangerous enough to need four guards to protect the public. When all she had done when called on to testify was run away. She hadn't exactly put anyone in the public at risk. Just one guard who happened to get in the way of her retreat.

Walking slowly, the little entourage made their way through the dark back hallways and elevators until they reached the courtroom level. The room they entered wasn't the same one as Tamara had waited in before, but its mirror. Tamara wondered whether it led into the same courtroom, but from the other side. She had no idea how many of the small holding areas they had in the building.

She was shaking when they finally got her into the small cell, and the three guards plus the two who were already working in the room stood and watched as Durham unlocked Tamara's chains and then shut the door. He checked that the barred door was latched properly and then had one of the other guards check.

"All right, paperwork," Durham announced, and they proceeded to exchange the various bits of documentation required to transfer her into their custody.

"I gotta pee," Tamara announced, hoping that at least a couple of them could leave the room. But none of them made any move to do so.

"Go ahead," Durham said, without looking up from his clipboard.

Groaning to herself, Tamara did. If they all wanted a show, they were welcome to it. She wasn't going to wait until her bladder burst like a balloon.

* * *

TAMARA PREPARED TO WAIT. She sat on the hard bench in the cell, leaned back against the wall, and mentally drifted.

She had no book, no TV, nothing to keep her occupied. The memories of Glock and Tamara's early days in juvie pressed in on her. Those first few days after she was released into General Population had been cruel. She'd felt like a hunted animal, in danger at every turn. No matter where she went or what she did, she was under constant threat.

"You want some advice?" Nadine had asked, that first day when she was so raw she didn't even know how to avoid challenging someone with a look that was half a second too long.

"I dunno." Tamara had a feeling the girl was going to give it, whether she wanted it or not.

"You got three choices. You join a gang or you get a friend who will protect you."

"That's two," Tamara pointed out.

"Third is getting used to being beat up."

"Oh."

"You need protection if you want to survive around here."

Nadine's counsel was good. Of course, one of Nadine's functions in TMJ was to recruit new members. Her first approach was the soft touch. Feeling Tamara out and encouraging her to join up. Her subsequent attempts were not nearly so civil.

She caught Tamara in the restroom, somewhere Tamara avoided going unless she really had no other choice.

"Frenchie," Nadine snapped sharply as Tamara headed for the door.

Tamara froze and tried to figure out an avenue of escape, while remaining a healthy distance from Nadine.

"Yeah?"

"You made your decision yet about joining TMJ?"

TMJ and Sharks had both made offers, both stepping up the pressure as several days passed without Tamara picking one.

"No..." Tamara said tentatively.

Nadine stepped forward and shoved her hard into the wall.

"You a moron, Frenchie? Don't you understand that I'm

trying to protect you? I told you if you wanna stay safe around here, you gotta join one of the gangs. You don't believe me, or what?" Every few words she emphasized her point with another shove, Tamara's back, neck, and head growing sore from the abuse.

"I understand," she protested.

"Then you dissing me?" Nadine slapped her across the face. "You think you're better than me or something?"

"No." The slap stung. Tamara's face throbbed.

Nadine slapped her again. "You're joining TMJ."

Tamara was ready to give in. The door opened and another girl walked in. Glock; one of the biggest, meanest girls on the block. Tamara's heart sank. It was two-to-one. She tensed even more, feeling sick. But it was Nadine who reacted. She backed up, turned, and walked out.

Tamara sagged against the wall, relief washing over her. She just stood there breathing, trying to calm the pounding of her heart.

When Glock walked back out of the stall, Tamara realized that she was not out of danger. One danger had just been substituted for another. She froze where she was, measuring the distance to the door.

"You shouldn't be hanging around here," Glock said flatly, washing her hands.

Tamara tried to nod.

"Don't you think you'd better go?" Glock demanded.

Tamara wanted to move. But her body was not cooperating. Frozen in place like a rabbit, hoping the predator would just miss her. Glock turned off the water and wiped her hands on her uniform, moving towards Tamara.

"You okay?"

Tamara nodded unsteadily. "Thanks."

"I didn't do anything."

"You scared her off."

"She's yellow. I got nothing to do with that."

"If you hadn't come in..."

"I had to take a leak. You can't rely on dumb luck to save your butt. You gotta be smart and take care of yourself."

"I'm not strong enough to protect myself."

Glock shrugged and started to move away.

"Are you in one of the gangs?" Tamara questioned.

Glock shook her head. Tamara followed her, sticking close.

"I'm a loner," Glock said. "I don't hang with gangs."

The conversation was obviously over. But Tamara wasn't ready to be left behind. She tagged along with Glock. The bigger girl turned to her in irritation.

"Back off, will you? I'm not looking for a lost puppy."

Tamara hung back a little, but still followed her.

And that was how it had all started. One chance encounter, fortuitous timing, and Tamara had attached to Glock as her new protector. Before long, she'd been transferred to Glock's cell.

*What're you going to give me in exchange for protection?*

Tamara shuddered. She had done what she had to in juvie to survive. Every choice was aimed at surviving one more day. Or sometimes, just one more hour. Just like at the Bakers', it was all about survival.

"French, you're up,"

Tamara was brought out of her reverie by one of the courtroom guards. She was glad that it wasn't Blau again. At least one thing was in her favor.

Lunch hadn't been offered, so it was still morning, and the room was not as hot and still as its twin had been. She'd eaten breakfast and drunk lots of water, so she would be just fine for the trial. No fainting, no freaking out. She would be able to give her testimony clearly and succinctly, sit through the cross-examination, and be on her way back to juvie at the end of the day, satisfied that she had done her duty.

She stood up and the guard motioned her to the access hole

in the door to handcuff her. Tamara stood looking at him, not offering her hands. His brass name tag said Snipes.

"Let's go," Snipes ordered, with an impatient huff and another motion. "Hands."

"I'm just going in there," Tamara nodded to the door to the courtroom. "I don't need to be handcuffed."

"I don't care how far it is. You're not leaving that cell without being cuffed."

"I'm supposed to be able to testify without handcuffs or shackles."

"After attacking a guard last time you were in this courthouse? I don't think so."

"I didn't attack him. He just... got in my way when I was trying to get back to the holding cell."

"Doesn't matter why. You're not getting out of there without handcuffs."

"Where's my lawyer? I'm supposed to be able to testify without handcuffs. Otherwise, people will think of me as a criminal."

"You *are* a criminal."

"But they'll make judgments. They won't believe what I say. Where's Ritter? I want my lawyer."

She was pretty sure he had to produce her lawyer if she asked for him. Ritter was just sitting in the next room. He could smooth it over. He could get them to let Tamara testify without handcuffs. She had to be able to walk in there under her own power, with no restraints, so that the jury wouldn't be prejudiced against her.

"Just get them on," the guard argued. "If they decide in there they want to take them off..."

"No! I'm not going in there in handcuffs. My lawyer is in there. Ask him. That's how it's supposed to be."

"There are extra security measures in place because of your previous incident. We have to protect the public."

"Go ask him!"

"I'm not in the habit of asking lawyers what I can do as part of my job. He's not my boss."

"I can't go in there chained. I'll give my testimony. But not in chains."

Snipes scowled. He looked at the other guards to see what their thoughts were.

"Talk to her lawyer and the judge," one of them, a white-haired man, suggested. Tamara hoped that his venerable appearance meant that Snipes would listen to him.

There was silence.

"What's it going to hurt to ask? Chances are, they're on the side of public safety over one witness's reputation, and they tell you to take her in handcuffs."

Snipes threw his hands up in disgust, and walked up to the door to the courtroom. He talked through the crack to someone inside the courtroom, and then waited while, presumably, that man then spoke to the lawyer, or the judge, or someone else who passed the message along. Eventually, like a game of telephone, the answer would come back to Tamara.

After a minute, Snipes went into the courtroom. The minutes ticked by. Tamara shifted. It was good that the judge hadn't made a snap decision. The fact that he was taking time to consider the issue was a good sign. She hoped.

Eventually, Snipes returned to the holding room. He shook his head and blew out his breath. "Judge says forego the hand-cuffs. But if you cause me any trouble..." he patted the gear on his belt, "I will use whatever measures I deem necessary to protect the public from a threat."

Tamara nodded and kept her eyes down, trying to convey to him how cooperative and non-threatening she was. She might be a convicted killer, but she wasn't someone who just went around attacking people for no reason.

It wasn't the same judge as had heard the other trial. Tamara didn't imagine that *he* would have allowed her into his courtroom again without handcuffs. Tamara was escorted to the witness box and she looked at the two tables as she was sworn in.

McClure at one table. He was recognizable, but not the same man as she had known at school when she was out on bail. Then he'd been an adult with authority over her. Coaching her, telling her how to train, yelling when she screwed up. He'd seemed a lot bigger than he did sitting at that table, hunched over, his grey hair very short, so that Tamara could see red scars snaking over his scalp. His face, too, was scarred, and one eye bulged like it was going to pop out of its socket. He looked at her on the stand, and his expression was inscrutable. Did he hate her for her part in the attack? For being the one to expose his secret? Or did he forgive her because she wasn't the one who had hurt him and had tried to stop the attack?

Maybe his brain was damaged and he didn't even know what was going on.

He had a woman lawyer. Tamara supposed that made sense. Show that he wasn't a predator. That she supported him and wasn't afraid of him.

Tamara's eyes drifted to the other table.

Glock.

They had done their best to make her over. They had dressed her in conservative street clothes like Tamara, rather than her prison jumpsuit. Clothes that covered up most of her ink so she didn't look as scary to the jury. Her hair had been trimmed.

But she was still Glock. They hadn't given her any makeup, so she still had some tats showing and her features were hard, the lines not softened with expert colors and brushes. Her eyes were bloodshot and red rimmed.

Tamara swallowed and tried to keep the thumping of her heart under control. She thought that everybody in the court-room must be able to hear it. Must be able to read her face when she looked at McClure and Glock. Everyone's eyes were on her, curious about her and what she had to say.

"You may be seated."

Tamara didn't move.

"Miss French. Please take your seat."

Tamara wished that she could remain standing. She was stronger on her feet. It put her above the people seated at the two tables, giving her an advantage over them. She obeyed and sat down. Snipes relaxed visibly. Other guards discreetly stationed themselves around the courtroom.

"You're here today to tell us about what happened the day that Quentin McClure was assaulted," the lawyer said.

Tamara nodded and wet her lips. "Yeah."

"Tell me why you went to the school that day."

"I wanted to talk to Coach McClure. To... get him to talk about what—" Ritter caught Tamara's eye and she remembered what he had told her repeatedly. Don't try to throw the blame back on McClure. Don't try to make him look like the bad guy. No accusations. No hint that he'd been molesting the girls in his care. "Yeah. To talk to him."

"You were angry with him?"

"No. I just wanted to ask him about something."

"Something school related? You were on his volleyball team, weren't you?"

"I was... but it wasn't about that. It was just... something personal."

"I see. And did you go alone?"

"No. I went with Glock." Tamara nodded to Glock.

"And by Glock, you mean the defendant, Kayla Spielman."

"Yeah. Spielman." Tamara could call her Spielman. She'd never been Kayla as long as Tamara had known her.

"Why did she go with you?"

Tamara tried to construct an answer that was true, but didn't reflect badly on her or make it sound like she was accusing Coach McClure of something.

"She was there... for moral support. She said she'd come along to watch my back. Make sure everything was okay."

"Why would you need someone along to watch your back to talk to your volleyball coach?"

"I was scared..." Tamara inadvertently looked over at Glock, who had one corner of her lip curled up in a sneer. She flashed back to that day. Approaching the coach, thinking that all she had to do was ask him questions and he would conveniently answer on tape, implicating himself. "I just needed someone with me..."

Glock towered over her, wielding the big trophy as a weapon, bringing it down on McClure's head again and again, the corners and edges slicing into his skin, cast-off blood spattering everywhere, the thuds coming over and over again. McClure fought long after he should have been beaten senseless. Tamara's own pleas rang in her ears again.

"No, no, no..."

"Miss French."

"Stop. Stop!" Glock's eyes were pools of black, swallowing Tamara up. "No! Stop it, please!"

Both corners of Glock's mouth curled up. She smiled at Tamara, lips parting to reveal her uneven teeth, like a shark.

"You have to stop her!"

Several seconds of silence passed. The screams faded away. Tamara was again looking at Coach McClure, head scarred, as he stared back at her. Tamara gulped the air.

"We are trying to stop her," the prosecutor agreed. "If you could just focus on answering my questions..."

"She tricked me."

The other lawyer jumped up, objecting at Tamara's words. Tamara just kept going.

"She told me she wanted to help me, that it would fix everything if I could just get him on tape. But that's not what she wanted. She wanted me to get her in there so she could beat him, kill him. That was what she wanted. That's why she wanted to be there."

The judge was sustaining the objections, motioning for Tamara to stop. He ordered her testimony stricken from the record. But the jury would remember. They wouldn't be able to disregard what she had said that easily.

"Miss French, why did Kayla Spielman *say* she wanted to go with you."

"Glock said she'd help me." Tamara deliberately used her name. The name that reminded the jury just how dangerous she was. "She said she'd protect me."

"And is that what she did?"

"No, she—"

"Coach McClure never attacked you, did he? He never hurt you or threatened you?"

"No. Glock just came in. She just started hitting him."

"I didn't protect you?" Glock demanded from the other table. Her lawyer tried to silence her. Snipes took a couple of steps closer to Glock, preparing to deal with her if she got violent or needed to be removed. "I made sure that perv would never touch you, didn't I? I did exactly what you wanted me to. Exactly what we were there for."

"No," Tamara said faintly, shaking her head.

There were objections from both sides, orders from the judge, excited chatter among the jury and the spectators. Tamara couldn't take her eyes off of Glock.

"I was there to protect you, just like I always protected you!" Glock stood up at the table. Her lawyer tried to get her to sit down. Several of the guards moved toward her.

Tamara's mind flooded with memories of how Glock had protected her. Painful bruises, broken nose, broken ribs, sprains and strains she had reported to Dr. Eastport as accidents, when he and the guards had no doubt where they were actually from. Other insults to her body that she kept quiet about, suffered through silently.

Yes, Glock had protected her from the gangs and the other juvies. But always for a price.

"You didn't come to protect me," Tamara snapped. "You tricked me. You were there because you wanted to hurt someone. McClure was just a good target!"

"Be glad it wasn't you!" Glock shot back, her face suffused with blood.

*Not that time.*

Tamara's blood was boiling with rage at how she'd been treated by Glock for two years. Over how Glock had talked her into going to see McClure that day, promising Tamara it was her one chance for redemption.

Glock's lawyer and Snipes finally succeeded in making Glock sit back down. The judge was banging his gavel, no one taking any note of it. The sleeve of his robe caught on an expensive-looking silver pen, sending it spinning across his desk toward Tamara.

"I will have order in this courtroom!" the judge demanded. "Everybody will stay seated, or I will have you removed!" He glared at Glock. "This is not a forum for you to express yourself!"

Glock leaned back in her chair, smirking. She folded her arms across her chest and stared directly at Tamara. "I didn't have to trick you. You would have gone if I told you to. Just like you always did what I told you to."

A swell of hate surged through Tamara, blinding her to everything else. She grabbed the pen from the judge's desk and jumped out of the witness box all in one movement. Before the guards could process what was happening, Tamara vaulted the defense table and launched herself at Glock. Glock saw her coming and was faster to react than anyone else in the courtroom, trying to get to her feet before Tamara landed on her.

Tamara stabbed down into Glock's throat with the pen, but ran into too much gristle and bone. Shifting her grip as she and Glock fell together to the floor, Tamara tried again, stabbing the pen up into the soft of Glock's belly.

"Is this doing what I'm told?" Tamara asked through gritted teeth. *"Kayla?"*

Glock grunted as the pen went in. She wrapped her arms around Tamara in a bear hug, as if the pen were only an annoyance. She clinched Tamara to herself so she was unable to move.

"Look at the little hellcat I raised." She chuckled in Tamara's ear. "How ya been, Princess?"

Tamara attempted to free herself, even though she knew better, knew that it would only make Glock tighten her grip. She twisted the pen, tried to dig it deeper.

One of the guards deployed a taser, which attached to Tamara and made her convulse in Glock's arms, but it failed to affect Glock. Glock was on the floor on her back with her face presenting to the guards, so one of them sprayed her. Glock howled as the capsaicin hit her eyes. She released her hold on Tamara to clap her hands to her eyes.

Tamara was hauled back by her shirt. They threw her to the floor of the courtroom and wrenched her hands behind her. Someone stripped the sticky pen from her grip. They were not gentle about securing her. Tamara could hear Snipes's bass voice yelling over a phone or radio for assistance.

"We need medical! Weapon in courtroom three! All parties secure, but we have injuries."

Tamara's brain was still surging with adrenaline. She didn't fight back against the guard pinning her down, but her skin was crawling and her heart was pounding. She wanted to get up and fight, to put Glock down for good. She turned her head, trying to see Glock, trying to see the rest of the courtroom, which appeared to be in the midst of being evacuated. Glock had been secured and was lying on her back, hands cuffed beneath her.

Her shirt, stained with blood, was pulled up away from the wound for examination.

Tamara flashed back to Zobel, his blood everywhere. To Tabby and Waterson, their bloody bodies tangled together. To Glock's assault on McClure, bludgeoning him over and over, his blood spreading and spattering.

"You have to stop her," Tamara insisted, stuck in the wrong timeline. "She's killing him! You've got to stop her!"

"Shut up."

Tamara squirmed. "She'll kill him! She's going to kill him!"

"Can't you shut her up?"

"There's going to be hell to pay over this!"

One of them gripped the back of Tamara's head and pressed her face hard nose-down into the floor so she couldn't see Glock. "Shut your mouth. Understand? Shut your face!"

Tamara's teeth cut into her lips and she grimaced, trying to pull them away. She tasted blood.

"I have to stop her!" Tamara insisted, barely able to form the words. "If you don't let me go, she's gonna kill Coach McClure!"

"She's off her head," one of the guards said.

"Get her into the holding room."

Two of them levered her up to her feet.

"She's going to kill Coach McClure," Tamara insisted, hearing the dreadful sound of the trophy crashing into McClure's skull over and over.

"McClure isn't even in the room, you moron!"

"No point trying to reason with a lunatic."

"I have to stop her," Tamara repeated. "Just let me go, I'm the only one who can talk to her."

Snipes, holding on to her right arm, snorted. "Well, you know how to speak her language, all right! I haven't seen her turn a hair before now."

"I can stop her."

"You'll need more than a pen for that."

She should have gone for one of Glock's eyes. That was the only way she could have gotten a fatal blow with her improvised weapon. If she could just try again, rewind and go for Glock's eye instead of her gut...

"Let me... let me go back..."

"Not on your life."

They pushed her through the door into the holding room.

"Do we take off the cuffs?"

"No way. We're going to have to treat her face. I say we shackle her feet too. I don't want to take a chance of that one coming at me."

"Not you," Tamara moaned. "I just want to kill *her*. It's the only way."

"You're probably right," a young guard agreed. "Did you read in the paper about Spielman's record?" he asked his colleagues conversationally. "Talk about a sicko. The only way to stop a psychopath like that is to put her in the ground."

Together, they grabbed Tamara and laid her on the tile floor, moving in concert like synchronized swimmers. She squirmed uncomfortably, but didn't try to kick them as they held down her legs and shackled her ankles. They shuffled her into the cell, lying on her side.

"Where's Zobel?" Tamara demanded, looking around the holding room. "Where's McClure?"

"McClure's not coming in here and I don't have a clue who Zobel is." Snipes pulled on a pair of blue gloves and held Tamara's face still, looking at her lip. "Well, you're not going to bleed out from that. You're lucky that's all you got, going after someone with a weapon in the courtroom. Lucky you got tased instead of shot."

"Zobel got stabbed," Tamara told him urgently. "He's bleeding real bad. If someone doesn't get to him, he's going to die!"

"A lot of people are apparently going to die in your little

world. How about you just lie here and cool down. Maybe if you decide to be a good girl and stop trying to kill everyone, we'll have a nice doctor bandage that up for you."

Tamara rested her head on the tile, exasperated. "I want to sit up."

"I think you're better off resting. Just stay there and we won't have to use any further measures." Snipes patted his taser, but he could have meant any of the ordnance on his belt.

"You gotta let me kill her," Tamara entreated one last time.

"No." He put his hand on her shoulder for a moment. "Now just calm down and stay put."

## TWENTY-TWO

TAMARA THOUGHT THINGS WOULD happen quickly. The police would come and take her to jail or Eli would bring the juvie bus to take her back home. But time moved slowly, with no one talking to Tamara or removing her from the cell. The panic and chaos that had ruled in the courtroom had only lasted a few minutes. The judge sent the jurors their lunch. After they had eaten, the trial reconvened without Tamara. Tamara didn't know if Glock was back in there, treated for a superficial stab wound and released. Tamara doubted she'd been lucky enough to hit anything vital. She could only hope she had punctured a major blood vessel or nicked the liver. Something that would cause Glock to bleed internally for a long time before they realized she was seriously hurt.

The guards came and went, mostly talking in lowered voices and throwing glances in her direction to make sure she wasn't listening in on their conversations. A few of them mocked her or threw insults in her direction. Tamara didn't care. It wasn't like they were inmates at juvie and she had to defend her reputation.

She recovered enough to know that Zobel wasn't injured. Not again. Glock hadn't had anything to do with Zobel getting hurt. That had been Tabby. Tamara had already taken care of Tabby. Zobel was okay.

So she talked to him.

Tamara didn't know why Zobel wasn't there to help her to sort out what had happened and what she should do or think once it was all over. He wasn't there to tell her to relax or that everything was going to be okay. She didn't know why he wasn't there, so she made him there. She pictured him in her mind, heard him talking to her.

"You really screwed things up this time, French."

"I had to," Tamara murmured to him, trying to keep her voice low enough that the courthouse guards wouldn't be able to tell what she was saying. "You get that, don't you? She wasn't going to stop. She was just going to keep killing."

"But it wasn't your place to act. You were supposed to be testifying, putting her behind bars for as long as you could. *That* was your job."

"You weren't there or you would understand." Had he been there? He should have been. Maybe he was. Maybe he was one of the other guards she hadn't looked closely at. Security staff turnover was brutal. There were always new guards and it didn't make sense to try to get to know them all when most would last only a few days.

"Ground yourself," Zobel advised, noting her disconnected thinking. "Feel what's going on in this time and place. You keep slipping."

"I am here. I'm here with you now, in a holding cell at the courthouse."

"That's right."

"Floor, bars, lights," Tamara listed off the things she could see. The things that she was sure were there in front of her. "Guards, doors. Sandwiches." She couldn't see the sandwiches, but she could smell them. She hadn't been offered anything when lunch had been brought around. Not even water. Luckily, it wasn't as hot as the other day. She wouldn't get heat stroke again. Slightly dehydrated and low blood sugar, maybe, but not enough to kill her. She listed things she could hear. "People talking. Air vents." She wasn't in the courtroom anymore. She wasn't at juvie. She wasn't in that little basement office with Glock beating Coach McClure senseless. "In the holding cell. In the holding cell at the courthouse."

"That's right," Zobel encouraged. "Just stay focused. You can do this. You have to hold it together so you can testify against Glock Spielman. And Denny Baker."

Tamara shook her head, confused. "No... I can't... I can't do that anymore."

"Pull yourself together. You have to. You have to do the right thing."

"No. It's too late, I can't do anything."

"Why do you think you're still waiting here? You still have something to do."

Tamara blinked, looking around. What was left for her to do? She was done testifying. They wouldn't call her in again. So what else was she supposed to do? Why was she still there?

There was a knock at the door and, after checking to see who it was, the guard let Durham in. Tamara stared at him. Why was he there when Zobel was already there to do the job? It didn't make sense for both of them to be there.

Durham looked down at Tamara, still lying on the floor where the guards had left her.

"Didn't I tell you not to cause any more trouble, French?"

"I had my orders," Tamara told him.

His brows and the corners of his mouth drew down in a deep frown. "What the hell does that mean?"

"Don't expect her to make sense," Snipes said. "She's been babbling all afternoon, completely off her nut."

"What happened?"

"She and the defendant got into a shouting match. Then she attacked Spielman with a weapon."

"A weapon?" Durham looked baffled. "I searched her for a weapon myself. Twice. She was secure. How did she get a weapon?"

At that, Snipes shifted uncomfortably, aware that that shortcoming was to his account. He and the other guards had been distracted by the verbal exchange between Glock and Tamara and had not been standing close enough to Tamara. They hadn't seen the danger of the judge's sharply pointed, silver-plated pen. They had zeroed in on Glock when she had stood up, forgetting that Tamara had already been identified as a security risk.

"She, uh, got her hands on a pen."

"She attacked Spielman with a pen."

It shouldn't have been a shock to Durham. He'd been supervising juvie long enough to know that virtually any object could be made into a weapon, given enough motivation and creativity on the part of the wielder.

"Yeah. Stabbed her twice."

"Any damage?"

Tamara raised her head slightly to look at the guard, wanting to hear the details.

"Haven't had word back. They took her to the hospital."

Durham tilted his head toward the courtroom. "Doesn't sound like they adjourned the trial."

"Judge's decision. I think he'd like to get as much done as possible while Spielman is out of the way. She's been... disruptive."

Durham looked back at Tamara. "I can't understand it. From what I hear, they always got along in juvie. If there were ever any problems, it was always French on the receiving end."

"Maybe she got tired of it."

"Has she been seen by a doctor?" Durham stared down at Tamara. "She's a mess."

The guard rolled his eyes. "One of the paramedics came in. But she wouldn't calm down enough for him to examine and treat her. She doesn't have any serious injuries. Just a lacerated lip. It will heal on its own. Your doc can put a couple of stitches in it."

Durham hooked his thumbs in his belt, looking Tamara over. "Transport time," he snapped. "Up on your feet."

Tamara moved stiffly. She'd obeyed the guard's instructions to stay put and not try to sit up, and her whole body ached from lying for so long on the floor without a reprieve. She managed to get up into a sitting position, then used her feet to propel herself, sliding on her butt, over to the bars of the cage. She sat there for a moment, getting her bearings.

"Are you here now?" she asked Durham.

"What?" He scowled down at her.

Tamara looked around for Zobel. He was the one who had been with her all afternoon. He was the one she expected to take her back to the bus. But then she remembered. "He got slashed. Tabby got him. I tried to stop her..."

Durham looked at Snipes, who shook his head. Durham shook his in response, expressing some unspoken agreement.

Tamara used her feet to push her back against the bars and then to slide herself up, getting to her feet. Durham studied her for a minute, then nodded at Snipes. "Okay. Let's get her chains on. You unlock the cage and stand watch." His head turned back toward Tamara. "You're not going to cause me any trouble, are you?"

"You're talking to someone who's been having discussions with invisible people all afternoon," Snipes said. "You can't trust any answer you get from her. Expect anything."

"She's been searched? She doesn't have any other weapons?"

"She only had the one," Snipes growled. "Obviously, we took that away from her."

"And searched her?"

There was a silence of several seconds. "No."

Durham swore under his breath. "Get the gate unlocked. French, turn around. Back to me."

Tamara obeyed, turning to face the back wall while the guard unlocked the door and Durham approached her. Blue gloves on, he gave her a thorough pat-down and made her kick off her shoes. He put the belly chain on her and ran the other chains from hand to foot. Normally, they transported juvies with their hands cuffed in front, but Durham made no move to unlock Tamara's wrists and re-cuff them in front of her. Tamara rolled her stiff shoulders. After checking her shoes, Durham allowed her to slide them back onto her feet, but she couldn't get her heels in without her hands, so they flopped on her feet like sandals.

"Exactly what possessed you to attack Spielman?" Durham asked as he pointed her toward the door of the cell.

"*Someone* has to kill her," Tamara informed him.

Durham gave a short bark of laughter. "Okay, then."

* * *

WHEN THE BUS REACHED JUVIE, Tamara expected to be offloaded immediately. She was still bleeding and should have been the priority. But the other girls were removed first. Then Durham got back onto the bus, Eli closed the door, and the bus started moving again. Tamara sat up, alarmed.

"Wait! What's going on? Where are you going? You have to let me off."

"You're being transferred, French."

"Transferred? Where? I'm... supposed to be... where else would you take me?" Her thoughts jumped to the other state facilities. The juvenile prison upstate where Glock had been transferred. The women's prison Vernon had been transferred to. Tamara couldn't go either of those places. They had to know that they couldn't put her into either of those facilities. How could they transfer her that quickly? Transfers usually took several days, with lots of paperwork to be filled out and arrangements to be made.

"Just chill."

"But, I'm not..."

Tamara couldn't find the words to protest the move. She knew she'd been causing a lot of extra trouble over the previous months, but a transfer was completely unexpected.

The bus didn't pick up speed and didn't exit the grounds. Instead, it went around the long loop of sprawling buildings that were unfamiliar to Tamara from the outside. The bus stopped in front of an attractive brick building that looked more like a school or community center than the bigger buildings.

"What's this?" Tamara's heart was in her throat, pounding so hard she could hardly breathe. Nothing was making sense to her.

"Forensic unit," Durham said, getting to his feet and walking toward Tamara. "Just stay calm. Everything is all right."

"What's a forensic unit?" Tamara demanded, but she had a feeling she already knew. And she didn't like it.

"This is where they're going to try to help you. Figure out what's going on with you and get you treatment."

"Psych? This isn't Psych."

"Psychiatric is short-term," Durham explained. "Somewhere to hold you for a day or two for suicide watch or evaluation. Forensic is... housing quarters. A treatment unit."

"No..." Tamara pulled back when Durham reached down to free her from the anchor. "No, take me back to my room."

He shook his head. "Your new room is over here. They'll help figure out what's wrong—what's going on with you."

"You can't do that. You can't just move me to a different unit..."

"Actually, we can. It's not me, I'm just the grunt. If it *was* my decision... you would have been here a couple of months ago."

Tamara tried to jerk away from him when he stood her up, but he hung on.

"I'm not crazy!"

"French... you need help. Everybody knows it. So they're finally moving you to where you can get the help you need."

"This is because I attacked Glock? You're punishing me for attacking her in the courthouse?"

"You're not rational. If you were, you never would have gone after her. You would have just given your testimony and been done with it. Like a normal person. Going after her was..." Tamara knew he was thinking 'crazy,' but he caught himself before saying it. "It wasn't smart, French. No one who was thinking about what they were doing would have done that."

"It was an impulse."

"Uh-huh."

"I just... I just did it. I got mad..."

"Sure you did. Anyone would have gotten mad. But not just anyone would have grabbed the judge's pen and tried to stab her to death with it."

Tamara wasn't sure what part of that was not rational. After all that Glock had done to Tamara, to Coach McClure, and to everyone else, it seemed more rational to kill her than to put on the charade of a trial. Pretending that they might find her not guilty and let her go free, that was crazy. Pretending that they weren't trying to put her in prison for the rest of her life was crazy. Pretending they wouldn't all feel safer with her in the ground was crazy.

Tamara didn't tell Durham that. She allowed him to escort her, not telling him what she was thinking, while she tried to come up with a reasonable argument for returning her to her own cell.

There were several levels of security measures to go through. Locked doors, body search, and x-ray, like she would have had going back to her own unit. They removed her chains and shackles for the search and didn't put them back on. She thought there were more cameras than in General Population. More double-secure doors, like an air lock, where they had to get through the first set of doors, wait until the doors closed tight and a green light indicated it was okay to go, and then went through the second set of doors.

"I want to go back to my room," she complained again.

"Just chill. This will be good for you."

"Never liked broccoli," Tamara muttered.

Durham smiled tightly, acknowledging the comparison.

They got through the last set of double-secure doors and entered a lobby area that looked like the nursing station or reception area at a hospital. Tamara didn't have long to look around. Dr. Sutherland turned around and saw her. He smiled and reached out a comforting hand.

"Tamara. I'm glad you made it."

"Get me back to my own room!"

"I'm afraid this is going to be your home for the next little while."

"I was stupid at the courthouse. I know. I shouldn't have done that. You can't put me here."

"I've been resisting putting you here for some time. All of my arguments and reasons not to have been exhausted. This isn't just because of what happened at the courthouse, Tamara. You've been heading here for some time."

"No!" Tears sprang to Tamara's eyes. It was just because of her low blood sugar. She would have been able to stay in control of her emotions otherwise. "No, I just want to go to my room."

"I know. But here you are. It's not a bad place. This isn't a punishment. You need help, and we're more equipped to give it to you here. We'll be able to monitor your behavior. Figure out what's going on with you. Find a treatment plan."

"No." Tamara swore between sobs. "I'm not crazy. I don't need this."

"You do. And I think deep down, you know you do. You've been crying out for help. We're listening." He touched her arm. "Come on. I'll show you your new room."

The unit was too quiet. Tamara was used to a buzz of activity in all but the quietest halls. People coming and going, chatting with each other, the TV blasting loud enough for everyone to hear it, classes and crafts and living skills. The Forensic unit was too quiet. She expected to hear screams at any moment. Insane people. Electroshock. Uncontrollable hallucinations.

Some of the rooms they walked by were occupied. Apparently, only one person to a cell. No cellmates. At least she'd be able to have some semblance of privacy and not have to worry about taking care of her newbie. The people she saw didn't look insane. They didn't have wild hair and eyes and spout off Shakespeare or poetry. They didn't growl like dogs or threaten her as she walked by their cells.

It was too quiet. And she knew why. They were medicated. Zombies. Unable to fight back because they were being controlled with drugs.

Dr. Sutherland motioned to one of the rooms. "Here you go. Home, sweet home."

Tamara walked into it. The bunk was made. There was a hygiene kit on the small shelf in the tiny cupboard, obviously brand new and untouched. Not her kit from her own room. There was no sign of her personal possessions. Her books, brought to her by Mrs. Henson.

"Where's all my stuff?"

Dr. Sutherland raised an eyebrow at her. "All your stuff?" He looked around the bare cell. "I'm sure they'll transfer any possessions over tomorrow. Sometimes these things take a day or two."

"I need my stuff. You can't take away my personal property!"

"Nobody is taking anything away from you. It will come. Just be patient."

"It's not fair. You can't just move me like this. Doesn't there need to be a hearing? Don't I get any say?"

"No. We've already gone through all of the formalities."

"This is because I screwed up in court!"

"No. That didn't help, but it just expedited the process that was already in place. Made us push things ahead a little more quickly. Like I said, your possessions will be brought over. Don't you worry about that."

"You can't do this."

"Why don't you sit down and relax? I understand you've had a very trying day. A nurse will be around later to bandage up your lip. In the meantime, are you hungry? It's suppertime."

Tamara could smell the institutional food. Just like in her own unit, the slop had a distinctive, nauseating smell. But even so, Tamara's stomach rumbled and she felt like the sides of her stomach were rubbing together, she was so hungry. She wanted to punish Dr. Sutherland by saying no. She wouldn't eat his food. She'd have a hunger strike. She'd force him to put her back in General Population by refusing to eat. But she couldn't. She wasn't strong enough.

"Yes," she admitted in a small voice. "I'm hungry."

"I'll make sure they bring you a tray."

"Don't I just go to canteen?"

"No. Different here. Here you take your meals in your room."

"Is it segregation?" Tamara had seen that everyone wasn't locked in their cells, but she couldn't think of any other reason they would have meals served to them in their rooms.

"No. You can still socialize. There is a common room and group sessions. You won't be segregated. But your food will be served in your room."

"Why?"

"Different protocols than in General Pop," Dr. Sutherland dismissed. "Don't get concerned about it. Is there anything else I can do for you? Do you want to talk about what happened in court today?"

"I just tried to kill Glock." Tamara could be dismissive too. "Nothing to be concerned about."

Dr. Sutherland gave her a small smile. "We'll talk about it later, then. I expect you'll want to stay in your cell the rest of the day. If you want to, you can shut the door. Someone will come take care of your injury and bring your dinner."

"Fine."

Tamara went to the bunk and sat down. Dr. Sutherland watched her for a minute, then smiled, nodded, and left the room.

Tamara remained sitting on the bunk, examining her surroundings. It wasn't much different from her usual cell. Just built for one person instead of two. At least there wasn't a big observation window like in Psych. There were probably a few cells like that in the Forensic unit as well. There was a security camera in the corner, inconspicuous, which appeared to take in the whole room. No dresser, but a small cupboard or closet for her things. No plastic shoebox. Everything would have to be out on the shelf, fully visible.

She didn't want to be there, but it was quiet and she was exhausted after her adrenaline-fueled fight, the hallucinations and flashbacks, and lying on the cold, hard floor for hours with her hands chained behind her back. Her shoulders were stiff and her fingers still tingling as full circulation was restored. Tamara tentatively felt her cut, swollen lip. It was tender and still bleeding but, like the guard at the courthouse had said, it wasn't going to kill her.

Tamara wondered how Glock was doing. They probably hadn't kept her at the hospital. No one liked to keep a psychotic convict like she was in the hospital instead of the prison where she could be properly secured. As long as Glock were able to walk around, they'd have her back in her own facility. Was she in General Population, or had she been singled out because of what she was? She had proudly admitted to being a psychopathic sadist. Was that something they put a person in the Forensic unit for? Was Tamara going to be surrounded by people like Glock, free of conscience, who enjoyed hurting others?

She didn't want to be there. She didn't want to be surrounded by crazy people. She wanted to be back in her own room.

## TWENTY-THREE

K NOCK, KNOCK?" A PLEASANT voice chimed, startling Tamara out of her state of half-sleep.

Tamara sat up, rubbing her eyes and looking at the woman who hovered in the doorway. She was dressed in a nurse's smock and had glasses, reddish hair in a bun, and a pleasant smile. Seeing that Tamara was up, she entered, carrying a meal tray, which she set on the floor.

"Hi, Tamara. I brought your dinner. But before you start on that, why don't we have a look at your mouth, huh?"

Tamara fingered it.

"There now, don't touch it. Let me have a quick look."

The nurse pulled on gloves. She tilted Tamara's head back to look at it.

"Ouch. Bit it, huh?" She turned Tamara's head back and forth. "I actually don't think it's going to need any stitches. Facial injuries always bleed like the dickens. Lots of blood vessels near the surface."

She had materials in the pockets of her smock and efficiently cleaned up the cut and bandaged it.

"I'll get you some ice, which will help to take down the

swelling. That will feel a lot better. I'll wait until after you have had a chance to eat, though."

Tamara wiggled her lips, stiff and awkward with the bandage. "Thanks."

"I'm Mary Anne," the nurse said, tapping the name bar over her pocket. "It's nice to meet you, Tamara. You make sure you let me know if there is anything you need."

"Dr. Sutherland said they'd get me my stuff." At Mary Anne's blank look, Tamara clarified. "From my room... in General Pop. My personal property."

"Oh. Of course. I'll make a note of it and if no one ships them over, we'll follow up."

Tamara nodded, feeling more reassured. She didn't trust Dr. Sutherland to look after something so menial himself and she didn't trust the prison administration to do it. More than likely, her books would just be turned over to the library without Tamara having a chance to read them first and her hygiene kit wouldn't matter to anyone but her.

"How are you feeling?"

Tamara looked at her. "I dunno. Fine."

"You had a hard time at court today, I understand. The guard who brought you back reported that you were talking to yourself and not entirely coherent."

Tamara avoided her eyes.

"And you attacked someone today. Sounds to me like you might need some help."

Tamara folded her arms over her chest. "Guess that's why I'm here."

"Tell me about it, then. We need to know what's going on to know how best to treat you."

Tamara shrugged.

"Who did you attack?"

"Glock. She... used to be here. Not in this unit, I mean."

Tamara felt her face flushing. "She was my cellie for a couple of years."

"And why did you attack her?"

"Because..." Calmer now, Tamara wasn't sure she wanted to tell Mary Anne 'because she needed killing.' She didn't think she could explain her thought processes to the nurse. Tamara scratched her ear, thinking about it. "She hurts people. She's dangerous. I wanted... to stop her."

"I see." The nurse nodded. "I guess you caused quite a scene. And talking to yourself?"

"I can talk to myself."

"Of course you can. But it can be a symptom that we need to consider. *Why* were you talking to yourself?"

"Nobody else to talk to."

"And were you experiencing confusion? Having trouble communicating with those around you?"

Tamara weighed her answer. "Dr. Sutherland thinks I have PTSD."

Mary Anne nodded encouragingly. "Yes. That wouldn't be surprising. A lot of the girls here have been through serious trauma."

Mary Anne waited for details, but Tamara didn't offer any. "We'll be getting your meds sorted out. See what we can do to help you."

"I'm not on meds."

"We'll find a combination that will make you feel better."

"I don't want meds," Tamara insisted, letting her voice get louder. Making sure not to let it go higher, making her sound girlish or uncertain. She wanted Mary Anne and the others to understand. She wasn't there to be put on drugs.

"Patients are often resistant to medication at first. But when you find out how much it helps, you'll change your attitude."

"You can't put me on anything against my wishes."

"There are exceptions," Mary Anne said placidly. Tamara

was ready to argue every one one of them, but the nurse didn't offer anything further.

"You can't put me on anything!" Tamara repeated, raising her voice so that it bounced off the walls. There was stillness around her. The quiet ward was listening to her. Judging her.

"No need to get yourself worked up. Here is your supper," Mary Anne picked up the dinner tray and set it on the bunk beside Tamara. "And you tell me if you need anything else. Do you need something to help you sleep tonight?"

Tamara's sleep in her own unit had been disrupted ever since she had gotten back from the prison break. She sometimes went all night without sleeping a wink, restless, uncomfortable, and hypervigilant the whole night long.

"No."

She wasn't going to ask for a sleeping pill when she had just said she didn't need any meds. Mary Anne gazed at her, seeming to be able to read her thoughts.

"Okay. But if you change your mind, all you have to do is ask. A good sleep is vital to mental health."

Tamara rolled her eyes. She picked up the dinner tray, looking the bland meal over. She would have told Mary Anne how disgusting it was, except that she hadn't eaten since breakfast and was starving. The institutional food might not be good, but it would fill the hollow space inside her.

"All right, Tamara. I'll talk to you later. Let us know if you need anything."

Mary Anne gave her a smile and headed back out. Tamara caught a glimpse of a guard in the hallway. Someone who had been standing by and keeping an eye on things in case the nurse needed any assistance. What was Tamara going to do? Attack the nurse for bringing her dinner and bandaging her lip? For no reason at all?

Tamara didn't just go around attacking people.

* * *

THE NIGHT PASSED SLOWLY. Tamara fell asleep right away, but she kept waking up, terrified, disoriented, unable to separate out the images of what had happened during the day from what had been in the more distant past, and what had just been part of her dreams. It seemed like every time she got to sleep, she just woke up again ten minutes later. The sleeping pill that Mary Anne had offered would have been a welcome relief, but Tamara wasn't going to bend to ask for one. They had to understand that she didn't need their medications. She could do just fine without them.

Morning brought with it a bustle of activity throughout the unit. Tamara listened, ears pricked for any trouble. While the reveille bell rang at the same time as Tamara was used to, there was no obvious rush for the showers or canteen. There was no canteen. All meals would be brought to her in her room. Tamara was uneasy about that change. It sounded good, because it meant avoiding the confrontations that inevitably occurred whenever a group of juvies were jammed together in one place. But after being habituated to the schedule and procedures in the General Population, any kind of change made her anxious.

She got out of bed and ran her fingers through her hair to untangle it, leaving the hygiene kit untouched. She paced, waiting for the breakfast they had promised to bring. It wasn't long before she heard the rattle of wheels in the corridor. Pushing her door open a few inches, she saw a multi-shelved cart filled with meal trays being pushed from one room to the next. Tamara ducked back into her room and paced, waiting for it.

There was a cursory knock on the door and then it was opened all the way, snapping into the magnet that held it open during the day. A nurse—not Mary Anne, but a new one—came into the room with Tamara's breakfast tray.

"How are you this morning, Tamara?" she asked in a loud,

intrusive tone people used for old, sick, or crazy people. Expecting a positive answer, if any answer was given. But not really expecting even that. "I've got your breakfast for you."

Tamara's body was tense. She didn't like the habit of the nurses to just barge into the room whenever they pleased. She was used to the protocol, written or unwritten, in the General Population. No one entered a cell without the resident's permission, other than for security reasons. When someone wanted to talk to her, they waited outside the cell or in the doorway until she invited them in or she exited the cell. If a guard wanted to search her cell or take her to an appointment, they asked her out and did not come in unless she refused to cooperate.

She took the tray from the nurse without comment, scowling. It was the usual full breakfast and Tamara didn't usually have more than a piece of toast and juice. Not since her return.

"I don't eat that much. Can I just say... just bring me toast?"

"Sorry, no special orders except for allergies and dietary needs."

"It's just a waste."

She nodded. "We throw a lot out," she admitted, "but processing different orders for everyone would be a huge administrative time suck. Just eat what you want to. Leave the rest."

Tamara rolled her eyes.

The nurse handed Tamara a small cup with three pills in the bottom. "There's your meds."

Tamara didn't take them from her. "I don't take meds."

The nurse set them back down to pull out a clipboard of orders and flip through it. "I see they are a new prescription," she agreed, "but they are correct." She held the little cup out to Tamara again. "Down the hatch."

"I don't want anything. You can't make me take them."

She gave a sigh. "Honey, you can swallow the pills, or I can come back with some help and three needles. Do you really want forcible restraints and three jabs instead of one simple swallow?"

"You wouldn't do that. You can't. I have rights!"

"You're in treatment. You're a minor. You're in custody. Do I need to explain what each of those means?"

"I don't want..." Tamara stared down at the pills in the cup, a lump in her throat.

"Why don't you put a little trust in Dr. Sutherland and give them a try?"

Tamara stared at them mutely.

"There's juice on your tray."

Tamara picked up the sealed cup of orange juice. Was she really going to let the nurse bully her into taking the pills that she had said over and over again she wouldn't take?

If they were going to physically force her anyway, what was the point in fighting?

Tamara peeled off the tinfoil top.

"Down they go," the nurse prompted.

"I don't want them."

"Noted."

Tamara sighed and swallowed the three pills down. Her throat ached.

"Good girl. You want to start feeling better, don't you? That's why you're here."

Tamara turned her face away, refusing to answer. The nurse departed, going out to the hall to her cart and pushing it down to the next cell door.

Tamara just sat there for a long time, staring at her breakfast tray and wondering how long it would take the pills to kick in. Would she be able to tell when they were working? Would her brain suddenly just start working again, like it used to? Would they make her sick? Dopey?

Her stomach started growling, teased by the taste of orange juice and expecting the rest of her meal. Tamara picked up a piece of toast by the corner and examined it. She didn't know whether the pills would make things look or taste different. She nibbled at the toast. It was just as stale and greasy as the toast she normally got in the canteen, which made her feel a bit better. Not everything was different in Forensic.

She was able to linger over her breakfast, something she never would have done in General, but eventually didn't want any more and put her tray to the side. She was restless and wanted to get the lay of the land.

She peeked out her door and looked up and down the hall. All was quiet. The nurse who had brought the breakfast trays around was gone. Tamara turned to the right, the opposite direction from the reception area she remembered coming to her room from. She hadn't seen the common room the previous evening, so it was logical that it must be the other way.

Tamara allowed herself only brief glances into the other rooms that she passed. She didn't want to get in trouble for looking or staring at someone, but she was curious about the other girls in the unit and what issues they had.

At the end of the hallway, she found a small common area. There were a couple of girls there already, staring at the TV playing some morning show. Tamara took a careful look around, alert for any threats.

Only two girls in the common room, and no sign of a gang banding together. Had she actually escaped the gangs by being transferred to Forensic? Maybe she should have been trying to get there a lot sooner. One of the girls watching the TV was spread out sideways over an easy chair, legs over the arm. She looked away from the TV to examine Tamara.

"Sit down if you're gonna stay. Don't hover."

Tamara selected a chair that wasn't too close to either girl, watching for any changes in their body language. No one stopped her, so she sat down.

"You're new."

"Yeah."

"Welcome to the loony bin."

Tamara laughed shortly. "Yeah. Thanks."

They both watched the TV, not saying anything. Tamara kept an eye on the girl out the corner of her eye. The second girl hadn't said anything or given any indication that she even knew there was someone else in the room with her. Neither of them looked at Tamara or got up or said anything to indicate that they saw her as a threat. Both were average size, bigger than Tamara, but not huge. She could take either of them on in a fight. Tamara breathed out, trying to calm her pounding heart.

The morning show broke for commercials and the girl turned slightly to look at Tamara.

"Sarah Brinkley," she introduced herself.

"Uh... Tamara French."

If Brinkley recognized Tamara's name from the news or prison grapevine, she didn't give any indication.

"And what's *your* problem?"

"I don't have a problem."

"Yeah, you do, actually, or you wouldn't be here." Brinkley looked back at the TV and watched part of a cat food commercial. "I'm schizoaffective. What about you?"

Tamara shifted. "I... uh... I don't think they know yet."

"Yeah?" Brinkley kicked a foot. She didn't seem to think there was anything unusual or concerning about this.

"Dr. Sutherland thought maybe PTSD."

Another look at the television screen. Another kick of Brinkley's foot. "People don't usually come here for just PTSD," Brinkley observed. "Not saying it doesn't happen, but they can usually manage that in General."

"What does schizoaffective mean?"

"Like a combo of schizophrenia and mood disorder," Brinkley said, her voice just as casual as if she was announcing the day's weather forecast.

"Oh."

"Lots of fun," Brinkley said. "Like a box full of kittens."

"Uh..."

"Just shut up," the other girl in the room snapped. "It's back on and no one wants to hear your stupid crap."

Brinkley looked back at the TV and Tamara followed suit. But she wanted to learn more about the unit, so she wasn't really watching the show, but watching the two girls and trying to glean what she could from their spare surroundings. There was a video camera bubble in the corner of the room which presumably gave remote observers a full view of the common room and recorded everything that happened there for playback later. There wasn't a lot of furniture. Some easy chairs, a stained couch, and a few ugly orange-upholstered stacking chairs like a hotel would use at a banquet or lecture. The unit wasn't very big, or not very many people ventured out to use the common room. There was one guard, leaning casually on the couch, his eyes on the TV instead of the inmates.

"We can talk if you want," Brinkley said. "Alyssa isn't anyone's boss."

Tamara took a glance in the direction of the other girl. "Alyssa...?"

"I don't remember more than that."

Alyssa didn't jump in with her last name. Tamara watched her covertly under half-closed lids. Alyssa might have fallen asleep watching the TV. She wasn't moving and paid no attention to the conversation, even though she had told Brinkley to shut up.

Tamara swallowed and nodded. Brinkley seemed happy to chat, so she continued. "How long have you been here?"

"Here in juvie or in Forensic?"

"Either. Both."

"In juvie... a year and a half, I guess. Forensic... six months... eight... maybe half... I kind of lose track of time."

Tamara nodded. Things varied little one day to the next in juvie; it was easy for the days to run together and to lose track of how long she had been drifting along. Until something happened to remind her just how long it had been.

"I'm not crazy or stupid," Alyssa said suddenly, "or deaf. Don't talk about me."

"No one's talking about you, fruit loop," Brinkley shot back. "Pay attention."

"Don't call me names," Alyssa's voice took on a petulant whine. "I'm not calling you anything."

Tamara waited. Neither of them moved from their seats. It was like they were glued in place. Tamara was regretting the decision to sit so close to the two of them. It would have made more sense to put space between her and them. A distant point on the triangle, instead of the three of them in a line. But if she got up at that point, they would both be alerted to the fact that she was worried about them and avoiding confrontation.

"Alyssa is just bipolar," Brinkley said. "She's not here all the time. Usually she's in General, but she ends up back here when she destabilizes." She shot a look toward Alyssa, making sure that Alyssa knew that Brinkley was talking about her, was explaining to Tamara just how crazy she was.

"Who decides? I mean, when someone should be in Forensic instead of General?"

"There's a whole process. Takes a couple weeks to a few months to get all of the approvals from everyone and get someone moved. Sometimes there are emergency transfers, where they rush things through," Brinkley looked briefly at Tamara, then away again, "but usually they don't hurry through anything. They don't like having to transfer inmates back and forth too much."

Tamara tried to analyze that brief look. Did Brinkley mean Tamara had been an emergency transfer? She guessed she probably was, that they had made the decision while she was at the courthouse or sitting on the bus waiting to go back to her room. The guards complained that they couldn't handle her, or the courthouse threatened to make a complaint to the police. Something had made them decide she wasn't safe to go back to her room, even for one night.

"Sutherland's been trying to get me to take meds for a while," she said. "I guess... this was the only way to force me."

"Yeah." Brinkley nodded, eyes fastened on the TV. "Probably."

"Where is everybody?"

"Sleeping, mostly. People like to nap after breakfast. And lunch. Matter of fact, that's probably how most of them spend their days. Eating and napping."

"And therapy," Alyssa chimed in.

"Ugh." Brinkley wrinkled her nose. "Yes. Spend half our lives going to therapy."

"Private therapy. Group therapy. Play therapy. Occupational therapy."

Tamara yawned. The talk of naps and sitting in the warm room with the TV going and no obvious threats was making her tired. The thought of going to therapy, having to talk to Dr. Sutherland, to talk in front of a group of inmates, or to do stupid, meaningless crafts or chores seemed insurmountable. She didn't have the energy for any of it.

"It's so dry in here," Tamara complained. "I'm dying of thirst."

"It's the meds. Go to the nurses. They'll give you water."

Tamara thought about getting up to go back to the reception area or lobby, the nursing station she had seen the night before. But it was so far away, and she didn't really have the energy to get up and track someone down.

"What about the guard?" she suggested. "Can't they get water?"

Brinkley raised her eyebrows.

"Hey, Bruno," Tamara called to the guard who was watching the TV with them. "How about some drinks?"

After a minute, he seemed to realize she was addressing him, and turned his gaze to her.

"What did you say?"

"Drinks. Water. You could get me water, couldn't you? All of us. We all want water, right?"

Brinkley and Alyssa didn't seem impressed by Tamara's brilliant suggestion.

"You want a drink, you go talk to a nurse," the guard said.

Tamara rolled her eyes. "Come on," she wheedled. "You're just sitting there doing nothing. You're being paid to watch us. Why not get us a drink?"

He stared at her. "What's your name?"

"French."

"Well, French, I'm not your babysitter or your nursemaid. If you're going to cause trouble, I'll get you confined to quarters. How about that?"

That didn't sound like where Tamara wanted to end up. The little common room with TV and no competition for seats or threat of gang riot was quite attractive. She didn't feel like sitting in her room with nothing to do, not even a book to read. Like the other inmates, she'd have to just nap her time away. She yawned again, the skin at the corners of her mouth cracking.

"I just wanted a drink," she muttered.

"I should have known you were going to be trouble." The guard pulled out a notepad and wrote something down.

Tamara looked at Brinkley, raising her eyebrows. Brinkley turned away, pretending not to have seen. It was bad, then, the guard writing down her name, and whatever other details he needed to make an incident report on her.

"Why don't you either get back to your room or go find that nurse?" the guard suggested, moving away from the couch and taking a couple of steps toward Tamara.

"I'm sorry. I'll just watch TV."

"I don't think so," he disagreed. "You need to leave now."

If she'd been feeling more like herself, she would have just gotten up and gone out. There was no point in arguing with the guards and getting on their bad side. But Tamara was feeling heavy and tired and really didn't want to move from her spot.

"I'll behave. I'm sorry. I won't talk to you."

"How about you just get back to your room?"

"No."

Telling him 'no' was all it seemed to take. She was being insubordinate. Not just difficult, but defiant, and he was perfectly justified in taking action against her. He took a couple more steps to close in on her and grabbed her arm.

"Let's go."

Tamara stayed limp in the chair. She knew how difficult it was to manage a dead weight, even a small girl like she was, and she didn't have the energy she needed to get back to her cell. If he were going to force the issue, he was going to have to make good on his threats.

He yanked again. Tamara still refused to get up and go under her own power. The guard was either going to have to decide it wasn't worth it and give up, or pick her up and take her against her will. His name, according to his name bar, was Burgess.

The guard wasn't afraid to get physical. He braced himself and jerked up on both of her arms, dragging her to her feet. Tamara didn't try to stand or walk. She didn't resist him, but she didn't cooperate, either. Burgess muttered under his breath and pulled one of her arms around his neck, squeezed her against his side, and walked her out of the room.

It probably would have been easier for him to pick her up like a child or throw her over his shoulder in a fireman's carry, but he didn't do either one, giving the illusion that he was helping her along, that she was moving under her own power and he was just providing the support she needed to get there. It would have been funny, if his taser and pepper spray hadn't been digging painfully into Tamara's side. It would almost be worth it to go with him under her own power. If she had the energy to do it.

One of the nurses was on the prowl when they got closer to Tamara's room.

"Is everything all right? What happened?"

"Nothing happened. She was being disruptive, so I'm taking her back to her room."

The nurse seemed very professional. "Disruptive? Let's have a look, she doesn't seem to be combative..."

"No, just... an irritant."

"Why don't you let her walk on her own? Let me see how she is."

He attempted to set Tamara on her feet and let her go, but Tamara still didn't feel like cooperating. Her knees bent and her legs flopped and there was no way for him to put her on her feet if she didn't straighten her legs and take her weight.

"She's just putting it on," the guard said.

"I don't know about that," the nurse said, looking at Tamara and her floppy spaghetti limbs. "I'd like to have a look at her in her room, if you'd finish taking her there."

He rolled his eyes and grumbled something under his breath that the nurse couldn't hear but that Tamara, her ear against his chest, could hear clearly. It wasn't very complimentary. She let Burgess continue to drag her along, feet trailing on the floor, face pressed against him, stomach against his equipment. It wasn't much farther to her room. He dumped her on the bed. Tamara's teeth clacked together and she bit her tongue. She didn't complain, but sucked on it, tasting blood and wishing she'd been more prepared.

The guard moved out of the way and the nurse moved in. "It's her first day on meds. She could be experiencing some side effects. How was she behaving? What was she doing?"

Burgess was, at that point, wanting badly to get out of the

room. He didn't want to make a report and he didn't want to explain what had gotten him riled up so quickly.

"Nothing. She was just being mouthy. Wouldn't shut up when she was told to. Wouldn't come back to her room. So... I brought her back."

The nurse looked at Tamara's eyes and touched her face. "How are you feeling, dear?" she finally addressed Tamara directly.

"Just thirsty," Tamara said. "And... so tired."

"That's not unusual." She put her hand in Tamara's. "Can you squeeze for me?"

Tamara gave a weak squeeze. She remembered how Dr. Sutherland had told her that the medications wouldn't make her into a zombie. They wouldn't affect her physically. That had obviously been a crock. If Tamara had still been in the General Population, she would have been beaten up and left for dead in some isolated corner. There would have been no way for her to defend herself in the tired, weakened state she found herself in.

"And can you stand up for me? Just walk across the room?"

Tamara could barely contemplate the amount of effort that would take. "Too tired."

"Might have to dial back her dosage," the nurse said, to no one in particular. Tamara wondered whether she had always talked to herself or whether she had picked up the habit on the job, listening to inmates talking to their imaginations all day long. "All right," she told Burgess. "Thank you for bringing her back. I'll look after her. You want some water, Tamara?"

Tamara tried a nod, but that took too much effort. She blinked instead. "Yeah. Please."

Her mouth felt as dry as it had that day in court, dehydrated, trying to work up the will to testify against Mr. Baker. She had hardly been able to unstick her tongue from the inside of her mouth to form the words. It was like a nightmare that kept repeating and wouldn't go away.

"I can't," she said, trying to explain why she couldn't testify against Mr. Baker. "I'm just too tired."

"Yes, I'll get it for you. You just stay here," the nurse agreed.

Tamara was too exhausted to explain any further. The nurse would get her a drink, and then she'd get to sleep for a little bit. Just a nap to clear her head and get a bit of energy back again.

* * *

SHE HAD BEEN asleep by the time the nurse got back with a drink of water. The nurses had woken her several times throughout the day to talk to her, give her more water, and try to persuade her to get up and do something.

It took several of these wake-up calls before Tamara was able to prop herself slightly on one elbow to show that she was awake and could move around. Then she fell back asleep. Eventually, she was able to sit up, though she still hadn't the energy to even tackle her supper.

She was partially awake when Brinkley stood in her doorway and knocked on the open door. Tamara thought it must be nearly lights-out. If she'd been in that condition in General, they would have had to lock her door to ensure no one bothered her.

"Hi," Tamara said.

"You mind company?"

"Come in."

Brinkley entered. She stood a couple of feet away from the bunk. "Feeling any better?"

"I guess. Waking up, I mean. I don't know about... anything else."

"They must have put you on a pretty heavy dose. They don't usually start that high. That, or maybe you're extra sensitive."

"Great."

"They'll adjust it. Or try you on something different.

They're okay with it making you want to sleep. But not this," Brinkley made a little gesture to indicate Tamara's condition.

Tamara drew in a long breath. Even that seemed to take too much energy. Her lids were still heavy and she wanted to close her eyes to go back to sleep.

"What've they got you on?"

Tamara tried to force her eyes wider. She shifted to sit up straighter, but ended up slumping farther down. "I don't know. Not like they told me."

"You can ask. You got the right to know what they're giving you. What did it look like?"

Tamara concentrated and tried to remember the three pills that had been in the little cup that morning. It seemed like a long, long time ago and she wasn't sure why it was important. She described them to Brinkley.

The other girl nodded. "Shoulda known."

Tamara forced her eyes open at Brinkley's tone. "What?"

"Experimental protocol. They've got you on the latest and greatest."

Tamara's stomach tightened, uneasy. "What does that mean?"

Brinkley took a step forward. She lowered her voice. "It means drug companies can't always find good populations to test their drugs on. They gotta go through testing, and who wants to try out a brand new antipsychotic? Prisons are a good captive audience." Brinkley laughed softly at her pun. "A place like this is gold, if you can get it. Uniform sex and age, under constant observation, similar backgrounds and history, controlled diet. It's a pharmaceutical company's dream."

Tamara tried to raise a little outrage over this idea, but her feelings were flat, and other than the stirrings of anxiety starting to bubble in her stomach, she couldn't find it in herself to feel anything about this. The spark that had been so quick to light over the past months seemed to have gone out completely.

"I didn't agree to any experiments."

"Yeah," Brinkley agreed. "Being a minor and all that. Our society has a long history of experimenting on convicts without their consent. They've got rules now that they have to give their consent, and pharm companies sweeten the deal by offering payment for participation. But minors and patients who can't make decisions for themselves... they're a different story."

Brinkley looked out into the hallway at the sound of distant footsteps, but they turned into another room. She looked back at Tamara. "Man, they've really got you dosed up. You must be super sensitive."

"Help me... sit up."

Tamara was already in a sitting position, leaning back against her pillow and the wall, but she was slumping and sliding and couldn't raise the energy to push herself up again. Brinkley glanced at the door again, then moved in close. She slid her hands into Tamara's armpits, and tried to lift her up, while encouraging Tamara to put some effort into it as well.

"Come on, help me out here! You're a little thing, but you're no featherweight!"

Tamara tried to straighten up. There was the noise of approaching feet again. Hard-soled shoes slapping against tile; a couple of guards rather than a nurse. Brinkley gave Tamara another heave and turned her head to look into the hallway just as the guards arrived.

"Get back from her, Brinkley!"

"I'm just helping her out!" Brinkley protested, stepping back and putting her hands up to her shoulder to show compliance.

"She doesn't need your kind of help!" One of them took two long strides into the room and grabbed Brinkley by the upper arm, jerking her still farther away. He swung her around and shoved her toward his partner in the doorway. Rather than just sending her on her way or putting a pair of handcuffs on her, the second guard threw her to the floor.

Tamara heard Brinkley grunt and swear as she hit the tiles, and then she was out of Tamara's line of sight. It was too difficult to move to see any more. Tamara looked at the guard who had entered her room.

"You okay?" he asked her.

"Yeah. She wasn't hurting me... just helping me try to..." Tamara lost her train of thought, unable to concentrate on her words and what had happened and what was happening with Brinkley in the hallway with the other guard.

"That one switches from sweet and helpful to violent delusions in an instant. Don't put yourself too close to her, if you want my advice."

"Oh."

"People are unpredictable," he warned, "and here... more unpredictable than other places."

"Yeah..." Which made sense, of course. Tamara had been lulled by the apparent lack of danger in the unit. But convicted criminals in a forensic unit were probably not the best people to trust, even if they seemed harmless on the surface. "But... isn't she... treated?"

"Everybody in this unit is being treated," the guard pointed out, "but we still have cameras and armed security staff."

"Oh..." Tamara nodded. "Yeah."

He drew back from her, looking toward his partner who, from the sound of it, had Brinkley properly secured. He pulled Tamara's door shut as he walked out, and she heard the lock engage.

TWENTY-FOUR

TAMARA AWOKE GROGGILY TO her arm being shaken. She forced her eyes open, trying to figure out who was waking her up in the middle of the night. Had Brinkley gotten past her locked door, planning a midnight escape? It didn't make much sense, but it was the first thing that came to Tamara's mind. She had been involved in a previous prison-break, though it certainly hadn't been by choice.

"What is it?"

"Time to rise and shine. Up and at 'em."

Tamara blinked, struggling to bring everything into focus. "What...?"

"Reveille bell has gone, and I happen to know they didn't let you sleep in over in General."

"No." Tamara stared blearily at the nurse. She rolled onto her side and tried to push herself up, but it was still a massive effort. "I'm sick. Those meds. Can't get up."

"You took your last meds twenty-four hours ago. Now you're just milking it." The nurse helped her to get propped up into a sitting position. It was easier than it had been the previous day, but still an effort.

Tamara rubbed her eyes. The nurse brought over a breakfast tray and set it on the bed beside Tamara.

"Make sure you eat. I don't want you taking pills on an empty stomach. That's probably why you reacted so strongly yesterday."

"I ate yesterday."

"Not enough, obviously. Your breakfast had barely been touched and you didn't eat anything the rest of the day."

Tamara closed her eyes to rest her heavy lids. "Couldn't. I was too tired."

"Keep your eyes open. Come on." The nurse snapped her fingers in front of Tamara's eyes, making her jump and tense to protect herself, eyelids flying wide open. "That's better. You have something to eat, and get up and move around. That will help. And a shower."

Tamara didn't know where the showers were, but she was pretty sure they were too far away. Anything out of her room was going to be too far away, and she wasn't going to stick her head in the toilet bowl to wake herself up.

"Eat." The nurse pointed at her tray.

Tamara looked up, frowning. "I will."

"I want to see you eating now. Something in your stomach before the meds."

"I can't take them today."

"You can and you will."

"I'm still sick from yesterday," Tamara whined. She didn't care that she sounded like a six-year-old. Dr. Sutherland had promised her that they would find something that wouldn't make her feel like a zombie. He said they would take care of it if there were any problem with the meds. "I can't take them again today."

"They've been adjusted today. Not the same as yesterday. Sometimes it takes a little while to figure out what will work. But I think yesterday was a pretty fair indicator that we didn't get it right the first time. Have some toast. Some of those lovely eggs. I want you to have something in your stomach."

Tamara gazed dubiously at the gray eggs. She somehow doubted that was what the nurse had eaten for breakfast. But the nicknames that the inmates had for the reconstituted eggs and other slop they were fed would probably not go over well with her.

She moved her thick, heavy arm and picked up a slice of toast. Her fingers tingled, and she dropped it like she'd been shocked.

The nurse frowned and looked at Tamara's face. "What was that? You didn't burn yourself." She would have known very well that food was not served hot. Too much of a risk it would be used as a weapon. They were lucky if it was anything more than luke-warm when they got it.

"I slipped."

"You slipped." The nurse picked up the piece of toast and handed it back to Tamara. The rough texture still felt foreign against her skin but, braced for a shock, she didn't jump the second time. Tamara smiled reassuringly at the nurse and lifted the toast to her mouth.

She was worried at what would happen when she took a bite, but her fears were unwarranted. It was just toast. Just the same as it always was, and she didn't need any special intervention. Tamara took three bites of the toast but, after the third, couldn't stomach any more. She laid it down on the plate, her nose wrinkling and mouth twisting itself into a grimace of disgust, even when she was trying her best to keep her expression blank.

"What's wrong?"

"It's... bad..." Tamara shook her head. "It has a bad taste."

"It's just the same as always." The nurse looked down at the piece of toast, studying it and then picking it up. She held it to her nose, but Tamara noted that she did not take a bite to make sure it was okay and didn't taste bad. "Nothing wrong with it. Do you want something on it? Jam? Peanut butter? Most of the girls just put the eggs on the toast, but if you don't like them..."

Tamara shook her head. "The eggs are disgusting even when I'm feeling well."

The nurse didn't argue with this evaluation. She had probably never tasted the reconstituted eggs. She'd probably never been tempted. Despite her calling them 'lovely,' she didn't seem to believe that they actually were.

"You need to eat something more," she encouraged.

There were some sausage patties that Tamara never touched, a second piece of toast, and the juice. Tamara wrinkled her nose. "Just the juice."

"No, you need more. Some of the sausage and eggs? A full piece of toast?"

"I can't. I'll puke."

"I'm sure you didn't get any special treatment over in General. You eat what you get, just like you're used to."

"Didn't really eat breakfast in General either."

"What about oatmeal? Mostly, we don't bother putting it on the trays because no one eats it."

Tamara shook her head.

"More of the toast, then," the nurse insisted. "I'll put some jam on it for you."

Tamara didn't say anything. The nurse picked the untouched piece of toast up, and went back out to her cart full of trays to get a package of jam, which she scooped out and spread over the toast with a plastic spoon.

Tamara did her best, but after a few bites of the toast, she was gagging and couldn't get any more down.

The nurse eyed the two pieces of partially eaten toast and sighed. She handed Tamara a cup with pills in it and removed the top from her juice for her.

"What is it this time?" Tamara asked, looking down at the pills.

"Just swallow them, and hopefully, they won't bother you like the others. But you should get up and walk around. Shake off the cobwebs."

"I can't."

"You're quite the entitled little princess, aren't you?"

Tamara was shocked. She stared at the nurse, mouth open, unable to think of what to say.

"You think we should just cater to you? You should get to eat what you want, lie around all day?"

"No... I just don't feel good. I didn't want the stupid meds and they made me sick."

"You need to do what we tell you to do. This is treatment, and you're not going to get better if you don't follow through on what you're told."

"I can't get up."

The nurse eyed her. "You certainly can."

Tamara glared back. If the nurse felt like physically forcing Tamara to walk, she was welcome to try. Like Burgess the day before, she was likely to get more than she bargained for. Finally, the nurse shook her head and retreated to the hall, where she pushed her cart down to the doorway of the next room.

Tamara breathed out. She closed her eyes and let herself drift back off to sleep.

* * *

THE ADJUSTED MEDS WERE AN IMPROVEMENT, so that Tamara recovered over the next few days to the point that she was able to get up and walk across the room or to the other end of the unit. Her food continued to taste bad, not just the toast, but everything she ate. Dr. Sutherland visited her a couple of times, reassuring her several times that they weren't going to keep Tamara on drugs that made her sick, though it might take some time to find just the right cocktail.

He didn't bring Tamara her books. Nobody did. But on the new meds, Tamara didn't have the motivation to read a book anyway. She found she didn't have any interest in leaving her room most of the time. It took one of the nurses bullying her or Brinkley begging her before she would get up off of her bunk to make the trip down to the common room to watch TV or to go to one of her scheduled group therapy sessions. She didn't see any difference between sitting in her room staring at the wall and sitting in the common room zoning out to the TV or daydreaming in group. While it wasn't as dangerous in Forensic as in General, there was an added layer of challenge caused by the meds and the different procedures.

"French, you've got group," Burgess barked, entering the common room to find her.

Tamara didn't move. Any movement would just take extra energy, and she wanted to conserve as much as she could.

"Don't have group until tomorrow," she murmured.

"You have group today."

"No, Friday."

"Today is Friday."

Tamara thought about that. Had she missed a day? Miscounted? Had she spent an extra day sleeping without even realizing it?

"Group," Burgess snapped again. "Come on. Let's go."

Tamara got her feet under her and rose slowly. She glanced around for Brinkley, but the other girl wasn't around. They didn't share a group therapy session, so she must be somewhere else. Burgess grabbed her arm impatiently, trying to hustle her forward. Tamara got her feet tangled up and nearly fell, only saved by Burgess's hold on her arm.

"Slow down," Tamara urged.

"How about you speed up?"

"I *can't*."

She shuffled along and he was forced to go at Tamara's pace, a fact that obviously galled him, so Tamara slowed down a little more, just to rub it in. By the time they got to the therapy room, Burgess's face was red, his irritation obvious to everyone around him.

"Well, glad you could make it, Tamara."

Tamara ignored Worth, the group therapy leader, and stared at the wall.

"Maybe you could contribute something today. Why don't you tell us how you're feeling?"

Tamara gave no response, waiting for him to move on. Worth stared at her, waiting for her to fill the silence. But Tamara was on to him. She didn't care how long he sat staring at her. That was just less time she had to listen to him and the rest of the group fill the air with their meaningless chatter.

"Maybe you could tell us about what happened when you were last in court," Worth suggested. "When you were supposed to be testifying against your old friend, Spielman."

Tamara looked at him. She hadn't expected that he would actually look at her file or any of her history. He seemed to operate the group session just by drifting from one person's comments to another, trying to get everyone talking around the same topics. Things didn't get personal, unless people wanted them to be that way. Unless they brought something up themselves.

Worth smirked at her, obviously having scored a point by knowing something personal about her and mentioning it before the whole group. Tamara swallowed and looked away from him again.

"Spielman was your cellmate for a long time, wasn't she?" Worth prodded. "The two of you were very close."

Tamara clenched her teeth. She tried to keep her mouth shut and not say anything, but it festered. People always assumed that she was friends with Glock, because they had shared a cell and because that was the way Glock behaved. But they weren't friends. They never had been. That had never been part of the package.

"So what happened? What made you turn on her?"

"I didn't turn on her," Tamara snapped.

"That's not what I hear. From what I understand, you stabbed her and said more than once that you wanted to kill her."

The other inmates were turning to look at Tamara, interested in her story for the first time. Usually, no one paid any attention to anyone else. They just talked about themselves and their challenges. Or stared off into space, pretending they weren't there.

"I shoulda killed her," Tamara asserted. She ignored the dramatically surprised expressions of the other inmates. "Should have killed her the first time she laid hands on me."

Worth's expression was comical. His pencil hovered over his notepad, but he couldn't seem to decide what to write.

"What do you mean? What did she do?"

Despite the heavy oppression of the meds, his words unlocked a flood of memories. Tamara clutched at the sides of her seat, trying to stabilize herself.

She saw herself with Glock. Saw everything she had suffered through, like it was a high-speed movie on the wall in front of her. At the same time, she saw and heard Glock in the courtroom. Her mocking laugh, the smirk as she looked at Tamara sitting there, trying to testify against her.

*You would have gone if I told you to. Just like you always did what I told you to.*

She had listened to Glock, just like she had tried to obey the Bakers and do what she was told. Trying to survive. Trying desperately just to make it from one day to the next.

"Why don't you tell us about it?" Worth's sympathetic voice urged. "I'm sure that the others will relate to what you have gone through…"

"I did what she said," Tamara whispered. "Why do I always do what they say when it just gets me hurt anyway?"

"That doesn't seem very fair, does it?"

"Doesn't seem very fair?" Tamara echoed. "When you do what you're told, it's all supposed to work out. That's what they say. Do what you're told. Toe the line. You'll be rewarded. Take this pill. Go to that therapy!" Tamara's voice rose to a shout. She knew Worth wouldn't like it. Worth wanted her to talk about feelings and coping skills and healing from trauma. He didn't want to hear the truth. The way it really was in juvie and everywhere else.

"Tamara, I think we can all agree that life isn't fair sometimes. Sometimes we make the right choice, and something bad still happens as a result. Does anyone want to share an experience—"

"I'm sharing," Tamara cut across him. "Why should I take meds and come to therapy, just because you say? You and Dr. Sutherland and all of his lackeys? I'm not sick, except from the stupid drugs. It's the drugs that are making me sick."

There were affirmations from some of the other participants. Tamara wasn't the only one who didn't want to be on the prescribed protocols.

Worth put up both of his hands to stop her and motion for her to be calm. "Tamara, I'm going to stop you there. Let's not blame your treatment for—"

"Put your hands down," Tamara hissed.

Worth was so surprised, he froze, staring at her with wide eyes.

"Just put them down and don't threaten me."

Worth's hands lowered slightly as he became aware of his body language. "It wasn't meant to be a threat, Tamara, I just wanted to stop you and say—"

"You wanted me to share. So I'm *sharing*."

"I was hoping you would tell me about Glock—"

So he did know Glock's preferred name, and probably more about her relationship with Tamara than he would have her believe. He'd just been waiting for the opportunity to ask her about it, to dig down deeper and find out all of the tantalizing details.

"You want me to tell you about her?"

He raised an eyebrow and leaned forward in his chair. "Yes, certainly."

There was silence in the room, everyone waiting with baited breath. Tamara jerked her head slightly, motioning for Worth to come closer. He hesitated, then stood up from his place in the circle and walked close to her, leaning on a desk to look casual and open rather than standing over her. Tamara leaned slightly forward in her seat. He mirrored the movement, leaning toward her.

With a flash of insight, Tamara understood why he was asking about Glock. As he stood there in front of her, she saw that he *was* Glock. All of the time he'd been trying to draw her out in group and get her to talk about herself, it was because he was Glock. Trying to reconnect to her. Trying to get close again so that he could manipulate her and make her do whatever he wanted her to. Tamara couldn't understand why she hadn't seen it sooner.

He wore dark slacks and a blue dress shirt with a white lab coat over top to make him look professional and trustworthy, even though Tamara was pretty sure he wasn't really any kind of a doctor, just some college student they had hired to run the group sessions. They had apparently warned him not to carry pens in his pocket while on the unit, and the pencil he gripped awkwardly was short and stubby, like a golf pencil, without much of a point on the end.

But he was wearing an expensive-looking silk tie.

Tamara grabbed the tie as he leaned toward her, whipped the long end once around his throat and pulled both ends tight. She didn't have the energy to walk across the room to confront him, but he had solved that problem by walking to her. All she had to do was pull the tie tight and keep it that way.

The room erupted into screams and shouts. Worth's eyes bugged out. He grabbed Tamara's wrists, trying to force her back away, but she kept a hold on the ends of the tie, so attempting to force her hands away just tightened the noose around his neck.

*Just like you always did what I told you to.*

"Yeah? Did you tell me to do this?" Tamara whispered fiercely. And she heard Glock's chuckle and her reply.

*Look at the little hellcat I raised. How ya been, Princess?*

"How *you* been, Glock?" she hissed at Worth.

His eyes were glazing. She'd cut off the flow of his carotid. His brain would starve of oxygen before the rest of his body.

Hands hauled Tamara back. Big, powerful hands, too strong for her to fight back against, especially in her weakened state. Several guards, and none of them had pens or ties. Tamara didn't have time to figure out how to react or what to do. There was a jab of pain in her thigh, and all ability to fight or think or do anything else drained from Tamara's brain.

They waited several minutes, much longer than they needed to, to be sure that the injection had taken and Tamara couldn't fight back or form a thought. A couple of the guards continued to hold her and watch her closely, while others tended to Worth.

Group session was over. All of the participants were dismissed to go back to their rooms. Worth remained where he was to await proper medical care. The guards holding Tamara picked her up and carried her back to her room.

"I told you that whole zombie shuffle was an act," Burgess said, dropping Tamara onto her bunk from much higher than he needed to.

"How do you medicate someone who does something like that when they're so doped up?" the other guard mused. "Any more, and she's unconscious."

"It takes time to find the right medication and the right

dosage," recited the nurse who had followed them into the room. It was crowded with all three of them packed in there with Tamara. "This might not be the right cocktail, but you can't tell after just a few days. Some of these drugs take weeks or months to reach full efficacy. Until then, we have to just keep experimenting and keep a closer eye on her..."

Burgess turned and looked at her, scowling. "We couldn't keep a much closer watch on her without actually holding her in our laps. Who told the idiot to wear a tie to the forensic unit, anyway?"

The nurses made a noise of acknowledgement that was almost a laugh. "It was a beautiful tie, though." Followed by a noise that definitely was a laugh.

The guards shook their heads. The nurse checked Tamara's pulse and her eyes and nodded. "She'll be down for a few hours. There won't be any more incidents."

* * *

TAMARA WAS PRETTY lucid when Dr. Sutherland came in for a visit. He solved the problem of there not being any place to sit in her cell other than the bunk or the toilet by bringing his own folding chair, which he set against the wall. He sat down and gave her a concerned smile.

"Well, Tamara. Sounds like you had some difficulty today."

"It's the drugs," Tamara muttered, staring at her feet and refusing to look toward him. "I told you I didn't want you messing me up on all of these prescriptions."

"We still need to work some more on your protocol. But I believe this was in spite of, rather than because of the meds."

"Bull."

Dr. Sutherland shook his head. "Why don't you tell me about what happened? The side effects you have been complaining about are lack of energy and motivation, dry mouth, and a bad taste. I don't think this was related to those symptoms."

"I did it... because he was Glock."

"What do you mean by that? You thought that Mr. Worth was Glock Spielman?"

"I didn't think he was. I... knew he was. He *was* Glock."

"That doesn't really make sense, though, does it? How could he be someone who is several hours away from here in another facility? Did you hallucinate that he looked like her? Did he say something that reminded you of her? What exactly triggered this delusion?"

Tamara pulled her gaze away from her feet to look at him. "It's not a delusion," she insisted.

"Do you truly think Mr. Worth and Glock Spielman are the same person?"

"Yes."

"That really doesn't make sense. Do you know that?"

"Yes."

"Okay... well, we're still working on it, Tamara. Sometimes these things take a while to get right."

Tamara looked at the wall behind him. "Do you always get them right? Sooner or later?"

Sutherland took a long time to reply.

"Not to my satisfaction, no. Not always."

* * *

SHE LAY STILL, staring at the wall for a long time after Dr. Sutherland had left. Not just because she didn't have enough energy to do anything else. She had thought at first that she could overcome the problems with her brain by force of will. Or at least hide them and keep everyone from noticing. When she was forced to transfer to the Forensic unit and be treated, she had reluctantly bought into the idea that if they worked hard enough and long enough on the problem, they would be able to cure her. A handful of pills taken faithfully on a prescribed schedule, and she would be fine. She would be back to normal and could live a perfectly normal life, should she ever get out of prison.

But Dr. Sutherland had admitted that it didn't always work that way. They couldn't always find the magic combination needed to stabilize a patient. And even once stabilized on the appropriate cocktail, things weren't static. The body changed, drugs lost their effectiveness over time, life stressors became too great, and the patient would have another psychotic break even while on the correct protocol.

It meant that she was going to be like that for the rest of her life. Never able to separate reality from what her brain constructed. Always fighting her own nature and her own thoughts. Maybe becoming violent with those around her for no reason.

Was that why she had killed Corrine and Julie in the first place? Dr. Sutherland knew that she had been having hallucinations at the time. Were her reasons for harming those poor babies based on delusions? Tricks that her brain was playing on her?

She lay there for a long time before finally falling asleep, fully comprehending for the first time that her brain was her enemy instead of her ally. And there wasn't anything she could do about it.

## TWENTY-FIVE

TAMARA SAT IN A meeting room with Mrs. Henson. It wasn't quite the same as when they met in General. The meeting room was right inside Forensic and she didn't have to go through a big security check before going in. No search or x-ray. But unlike when they had met in General, there was a guard right in the room with them. Tamara scowled at this. She didn't need someone right there listening to her private conversations.

Not that she'd be sharing anything secret with Mrs. Henson; but she still would have liked to have been able to talk to Mrs. Henson without other listening ears.

Jensen, the guard hovering nearby, pretended that he wasn't listening, but Tamara knew otherwise. His eyes were on her the whole time, just waiting for her to make some move to hurt Mrs. Henson.

"I'm not going to do anything," she growled at him.

Jensen's brows went up, but he didn't make any comment. Mrs. Henson patted at her hair before sitting down and gave Tamara reassuring smile. "I'm sure he knows that. It's just their procedure."

Tamara slumped into her seat and put her hands up on the table, clasped together, where Jensen could see them.

"They think I'm going to attack you."

"*I* know you're not going to."

Tamara shook her head. "No, you don't. I could."

Mrs. Henson pressed her lips together, considering this. "Are you upset with me about something?"

"No. But that doesn't matter. If my brain told me you were a threat..."

"Do you think I'm a threat?"

Tamara looked Mrs. Henson over, but she wasn't getting any alarm bells. No little niggling suspicions that might turn into something else.

"No... not yet."

Mrs. Henson smiled. "Then I'm not worried."

Tamara swiveled her head to look at Jensen. "But I might think he's a threat. Why does he have to stay?"

"I think I can defend myself against you," Jensen said. "Don't you worry about that."

Tamara just scowled at him, looking for a way to have him removed or to persuade him to leave her alone with Mrs. Henson.

"You don't have anything to use as a weapon, do you?" Jensen pointed out confidently. "You're not big enough to overcome me."

Tamara cataloged her person and the room. No pens, no ties. Nothing that could obviously be used as a weapon. Mrs. Henson hadn't been able to bring her personal items into the room. She had either been warned ahead against wearing jewelry or they'd had her remove it when she got there. Nothing that could be used to choke or stab a person. Jensen was probably right. Even if she did decide he was a danger to her, there wasn't much she could do that he wouldn't be able to handle. She tried to relax her muscles and unclench her jaw.

She looked back at Mrs. Henson.

"I'm glad that you're here, Tamara," Mrs. Henson confided. "I've been quite worried about you lately. I think this is for the best. So you can get the treatment you need."

Tamara shrugged. "Not like it's helping."

"It takes time. You need to be patient and see how it works out. You can't judge from just a few days."

Tamara sighed and stared at the wall. Same old argument. Everybody had the same argument. Wait. It could take weeks, months, even years to figure out what would work. Or maybe she would be one of those people nothing would help. They'd never be able to take away the delusions and the intrusive thoughts and flashbacks. She'd have to live with it for the rest of her life.

"I can see a difference already," Mrs. Henson offered. "You're a lot more calm today than you have been the last few times I've come to see you. That's good, isn't it? A move in the right direction."

"It's just a side effect. It makes me tired, takes away all my energy."

"But if it calms you down, that's good."

"It doesn't."

Mrs. Henson looked for a way to argue this. Then she shook her head, letting it be. "Well, I'm sorry to hear that. I hope they can find something that will help you soon. It must be very frustrating for you."

Tamara just clenched her teeth. Her jaw ached with the pressure.

"I brought you some more books," Mrs. Henson offered, nodding at the small stack of paperbacks she had been allowed to bring into the meeting room. No hard covers, so they couldn't be used as weapons.

Tamara nodded apathetically.

"The family all says 'hi.' Everybody sends their love and wants to hear how you're doing."

"Yeah, say 'hi' back."

Mrs. Henson nodded, pleased. "I sure will."

Tamara tried to remember what Mrs. Henson might have told her on her last visit. "So, Harry's looking for his own place?"

There was an infinitesimal pause before Mrs. Henson responded. A lightning-quick instant of surprise and evaluation before answering.

"No, he's got a place now. He comes over for Sunday dinner, calls to talk sometimes, but he's really doing well on his own. We're all so proud of him for being able to make a life for himself. He's a great success story."

Unlike Tamara.

"Yeah, that's great," Tamara agreed. "I... forgot he'd gotten his own place... already."

She watched Mrs. Henson's eyes, trying to gauge her reaction to Tamara's words. There was relief and approval there. The right response. She had told Tamara before that Harry had his own place. The news that he had a promotion and might be looking for his own apartment had been months ago, and sometime in the visits since then, Mrs. Henson had told her that he'd found a place and moved out. Tamara had no recollection of it.

"It's hard for you," Mrs. Henson allowed. "You're not home with us and you have a lot of other things on your mind. It must be hard to keep track of everything."

They both knew it was just an excuse. The problem wasn't that Tamara was away from the family, but that her brain was falling apart. She couldn't retain anything. The details she could remember were all jumbled and without order. It took a huge effort to recall what had really happened and what Tamara had only imagined, and in what order. She had to struggle to recreate a timeline every single time.

"And... the girls...?"

"Nita is doing pretty well. Stressed about exams, but she's studying hard and she knows her stuff. She'll pull through just fine. Deshawn is struggling with the new program. We're doing our best to support her. She's become a little withdrawn... hardly even talking to Nita..." Mrs. Henson gave a helpless shrug. "They're so close, it's been hard on Nita to be shut out like that. I'm hoping that maybe some antidepressants will make a difference. For Deshawn. She has an appointment next week."

Tamara tried to sort through the convoluted thoughts. Mrs. Henson assumed that everything she'd previously told Tamara had been retained, but she desperately needed the background to work out what all of the words meant.

"She doesn't like... the new program?" Tamara tried.

"I think it's the best thing for her. But she feels like she's failed. That she should have been able to just complete her education in a mainstream school and program."

Tamara nodded. She remembered that Deshawn had 'challenges.' That was how Mrs. Henson had termed it. The new program had to be a school program. Some kind of alternative stream. She would never go to special ed, Tamara remembered that part. Tamara looked briefly at Mrs. Henson, pretending that it all made sense and had connected.

"And..." Mrs. Henson considered, "then there is Cecelia and her little one." She looked at Tamara expectantly.

Tamara swallowed. She couldn't remember what she was supposed to know about the new girl. "She... had her baby...?"

"Yes. I can't believe he's a month old already. He's such a sweetie. Just enchants everyone who meets him. Such fat cheeks and always smiling. Very social. Hitting all of his milestones, in spite of how hard the pregnancy was."

Tamara tried to imagine the fat, cute, baby boy. Not a girl like Julie or Amy. What would have happened if the Bakers had had boys instead of girls? How different would Tamara's life have been? Or would it have been exactly the same? The world wobbled. Tamara had been keeping her hands on top of the table so they would be within Jensen's sight, but she removed them to steady herself, holding on to the sides of the table, which felt a bit unstable, then to the sides of her chair, trying to ground herself.

"Just breathe."

At first, she looked at Mrs. Henson, thinking the words had come from her, but then realized that she herself had spoken them. Mrs. Henson leaned forward, concerned, but didn't reach out to Tamara. There was no touching in the visitor room in General. Tamara could only assume the same rule applied in Forensic.

"How about..." Tamara tried to remember the other boy's name. She didn't want to talk about Cecelia and her baby. Tamara couldn't help seeing a baby in the crib at Mrs. Henson's house, instantly morphing into Julie. As if the baby boy were Julie, the same way that Worth was Glock. But Dr. Sutherland said that was a delusion. Not a truth. "Um... Jeffrey... no... Jace. Jason?"

"Jason," Mrs. Henson agreed with a laugh. "I'm glad someone else has trouble with names. I live with them and still can't get the names right all the time. I use the excuse that I've had so many boys and girls through there... but I'm afraid that it's just my faulty brain..."

Tamara stared at her. Mrs. Henson's eyes slid away, her face turning pink.

"Jason is fine. He and Dirk are still bumping heads." She rolled her eyes. "Boys are so competitive. Jason has been spoiled before, having Harry there. A mentor for him, confidante, big brother. Now having someone closer to his age, expecting him to be the mature one..."

Tamara nodded. Dirk was new since she had left. Since Harry had left. He'd been there, at most, a few months, and hadn't worked out all of the personal relationships yet.

"It's a full house!" Mrs. Henson said with a little laugh. "Three girls. Two and a half boys. There's always something happening."

"Sounds... busy."

"That's the way we like it. I don't think I would know what to do with a quiet house."

Tamara's stomach twisted and turned. She pressed one hand against it, trying to quiet it, still using the other to hang on to the chair and support herself. Mrs. Henson cocked her head.

"Are you okay?"

"Yeah. Just... cramps." Tamara pressed down, wincing, and waited for it to subside.

When she looked at Mrs. Henson again, the woman had a frown on her face, staring at Tamara's hand over her stomach. She didn't look away when Tamara glared at her.

"Are you having a lot of stomach problems?"

"Probably just the meds," Tamara said.

"You've put on weight."

"The nurses say everyone does. The antipsychotics... they affect your ability to tell when you're full."

Mrs. Henson pushed herself back from the table a little, looking around it at Tamara's midriff. Tamara shifted uncomfortably, putting herself at an angle to her foster mother, not liking the scrutiny.

"Tamara... are you pregnant?"

## TWENTY-SIX

TAMARA LET GO OF her belly and gripped the chair with both hands. The room spun and her stomach again twisted and turned.

"No!"

Tamara held her arm across her stomach and pushed hard. Mrs. Henson's eyes were bright and sharp, looking at Tamara as if she had x-ray vision to see through her orange, voluminous jumpsuit.

"Are you sure?"

"I'm not. I haven't been with anyone; how could I be?"

Mrs. Henson shifted her chair around the table slightly. She looked at the guard and lowered her voice to a murmur he wouldn't be able to hear.

"A lot of the staff are male. Has someone been... abusing you?"

"No!"

"Or maybe there is someone you're... sweet on...?"

Tamara's mind immediately jumped to Zobel. To Brett referring to him as Tamara's pet, implying they were lovers. Such things happened, but Tamara knew her relationship with Zobel had only been friendly.

Unless she was forgetting things. She couldn't have forgotten that.

Could she?

"No," she told Mrs. Henson sharply. Guard-inmate relationships were usually discovered and sorted out pretty quickly. There weren't a lot of places where any kind of assignation could take place outside of camera range. Not only that, but people noticed nonverbal signals and body language that were out of place. There was little privacy in juvie.

Mrs. Henson looked at Jensen, her eyes still suspicious, wondering.

"No, you don't know what you're talking about," Tamara insisted.

"These cramps you're having, is it your period? Are you menstruating?"

Tamara's face got hot. Without looking at Jensen, she could feel his eyes on her. Mrs. Henson's voice was still low, but he could hear if he listened carefully. Tamara raised her hands to her face, covering her flushed cheeks.

"No. It's just crap food and the meds. A stomach-ache. Anyone here could tell you how bad the food is."

"When was your last period?"

"I don't know. I'm not regular. Just let it go. I'm not. I would never *never* get pregnant. Never again."

Mrs. Henson looked at the guard, looked at Tamara, and bit her lip. "It wasn't exactly your choice last time, was it?"

Tamara fought back against the rush of memories. She wasn't going to think about Mr. Baker. She wasn't going to think about what he had done or about Corrine or Julie or Amy. She breathed hard, pushing back against the images.

"Do you feel like you did when you were pregnant before?" Mrs. Henson prodded gently.

"No. I was throwing up all the time. I was..." Tamara tried to remember all of the differences between the blackness, hopelessness, and hallucinations she had had during the month or two before she was arrested and what she had been experiencing since her return to juvie. She remembered how she felt back then before Dr. Eastport told her she was pregnant and she agreed to termination.

The fogginess and crazy thoughts had lifted after the abortion and Tamara had been relieved to find herself comfortable in her own brain again. The psychosis had disappeared, leaving her clear-headed again. For three years. Until it came back.

Tamara looked at Mrs. Henson. "I haven't been with anyone," she insisted, "so I couldn't be."

"For how long?"

"What?"

"When were you last active? What about when you were with us? Did Coach McClure...? Or anyone...? Did you have a boyfriend we didn't know about?"

"No." Parts of the timeline were missing, particularly when Glock and Sybil had gotten her drunk, but Tamara was pretty sure that nothing had happened then. She would have known. Glock would never have let anyone mess with her, Tamara was sure of that. She shook her head again. "I told you, I'm not!"

"What about after the prison break? Is it possible...?"

Panic set in. Tamara jumped to her feet, upsetting the chair and sending it crashing to the floor. There was nowhere to go. She couldn't leave the room or escape the suggestion. She didn't have the energy to run, even if there were somewhere to go.

Jensen was at Tamara's side in an instant, his taser pressed against her shoulder. "Sit back down."

Tamara didn't even look at him. She stared at Mrs. Henson in horror. "No!"

"It's okay. Sit down," Mrs. Henson said, her voice calm and

soothing. "We can talk it through. You don't want to upset..." She indicated Jensen with a tilt of her head.

Tamara looked down, but the chair was on its side, several feet away, and she couldn't reach it. Jensen wasn't going to like it if she moved away from him to get it, and Tamara's head was whirling so fast she wasn't sure she could bend over to pick it up even if it were within reach.

"I can't."

They each considered the situation, calculating the distance and angles. "I can get it," Mrs. Henson offered. "Would that be okay?"

Jensen shook his head. While it wasn't likely that a visitor would attack him with the chair, it wasn't outside the realm of possibility. Tamara was an inmate who had, relying on someone else, escaped before. He had no way of knowing Mrs. Henson's history or risk factors. They all stayed there in tableau, like a kids' game of *Freeze*. Eventually, Jensen pulled back from Tamara, the taser breaking contact with her shoulder as he side-stepped to where the chair had landed. Tasers had good range, he didn't need to be right against Tamara to deploy it. He kept it pointed right at Tamara, ready if she tried anything. He kicked the chair back to Tamara. But she would still have to bend down to pick it up and Tamara wasn't confident she could.

When it became obvious that she wasn't going to move, Jensen stepped back to his original position. He hooked his foot through the back hole of the chair and lifted it back to standing.

"Now sit," he snapped.

Tamara sank back into the chair, her knees and thighs shaking.

"What happened?" Mrs. Henson asked her.

"I took pills. Pills to keep me from getting pregnant," Tamara explained. She shook her head, unable to go on any further.

"Birth control pills? Progesterone?"

"No... not that. Another thing. For... after."

"Morning after pills?"

Tamara nodded. "They said they'd keep me from getting pregnant."

"Well... they can. But like any other method of birth control, there is a failure rate."

"Uh-uh." Tamara swallowed. "No. No." She put her face in her hands. "No, no, no!"

"Running away from it won't make it not true. We need to get you checked out. Maybe I'm wrong... but I don't think so."

"I would know. If I was... that... I would know."

"Did you know last time?"

"I would know!"

"Shh." Mrs. Henson tried to calm her. "It's not the end of the world. It's just something that we need to deal with."

"We?" Tamara challenged. She pulled her face out of her hands to glare at Mrs. Henson. "It's got nothing to do with you!"

Mrs. Henson's lip trembled and Tamara knew she was hurt. But it was the truth. Mrs. Henson had been Tamara's foster mother for a few weeks. She was an occasional visitor at juvie. But she had no legal standing and no place in Tamara's life. She couldn't make decisions for Tamara.

Mrs. Henson swallowed and licked her lips. "I would like to help you. I want to make sure that you're being properly taken care of and have the support and medical treatment you need. I've dealt a lot with teen moms. I know how high-risk teen pregnancy can be. This won't go away just because you ignore it."

"I took the pills. So I wouldn't get pregnant. I took them all, just like the nurse said to."

"I believe you. But sometimes they don't work."

"They have to!"

"I know you're scared."

"You *don't* know!"

"You're scared, you feel alone, and you don't think you can handle this on your own."

Tamara rubbed her eyes. "It's not fair."

"No. It's not."

"You can't tell them."

Mrs. Henson blinked at her and furrowed her brows. "You don't want me to tell the prison authorities? We need to tell them, Tamara. You need specialized care. I need to tell them."

"You don't know anything."

"I'll tell them my suspicions."

Tamara's guts twisted, and she wrapped her arms around her stomach again. She would know if she were pregnant. Mrs. Henson had to be wrong.

* * *

MRS. HENSON WANTED Jensen to take Tamara directly to the infirmary, but he stoically shook his head and informed her that he needed to follow the proper procedures, and if he didn't see any blood or any indication that she was in medical distress, he had to take her back to her room. He couldn't just make a decision like that on his own. It would have to go through channels.

Tamara was relieved to be taken back to her room. Mrs. Henson would find it much more difficult to deal with the juvenile authorities than she thought. She would probably give up, and they would leave Tamara alone and forget that Mrs. Henson had ever accused Tamara of anything.

Jensen walked her back to her room, with no comment on her slow, shuffling pace. She was exhausted when she finally got to her bunk, and lay down and closed her eyes.

It seemed like she had just barely dropped off to sleep when one of the nurses was shaking her awake. Her mouth was a thin line and her eyes beady and sharp. It seemed almost as if she were angry with Tamara for something.

"You need to get up. We have some tests to do. Come on. Wake up."

Tamara pressed her palms into her eyes. "Can't it wait?"

"I would say not."

Tamara got up slowly and sat on the edge of her bed. The nurse thrust a plastic jar with an orange lid into her hands.

"I'm going to go out and I need you to provide me with a urine sample. Think you can manage that?"

Tamara stared down at it. She'd had other medical tests done at juvie. Usually in the infirmary, but she had noticed that Forensic, with nurses on the unit, was able to get by without using the infirmary in many cases. Which was just fine with Tamara. She blinked a few times to try to clear her vision and stay awake, then nodded.

"Yeah."

"All right. I'll be back in five."

She left Tamara's room, shutting the door behind her. Tamara heard the lock engage. With a tired sigh, she plodded over to her toilet to take care of the task at hand.

In another ten minutes, the nurse was making arrangements for a visit to the infirmary. She hadn't told Tamara the results of her test and Tamara did her best not to think about it.

"Can't go to the infirmary," she told the nurse. "Too tired."

"Oh, you're going to the infirmary."

"Already had a visitor today. I don't have the energy."

Apparently, wheelchairs were invented for just that eventuality and, before long, Tamara found herself unceremoniously plonked into one and wheeled briskly to the infirmary. Due to the fact that the Forensic unit was in its own stand-alone building, that meant she got thirty seconds of fresh air between two buildings and had to go through an incredible amount of security, which was ridiculous considering she could barely even stand up on her own.

Dr. Eastport greeted her, wreathed in smiles as always. He sat down on his stool so that he was level with her.

"So, Forensic has some concerns?" He took the clipboard the guard handed him, and his eyebrows climbed up his forehead. "I see. Seems you've had a positive pregnancy test."

"No. I'm not pregnant. I *can't* be pregnant."

"Well, first we need to do a physical exam to verify. No point in jumping to conclusions. Tests can be wrong, or read wrong. It happens." He opened a drawer and handed her a paper robe. "You put that on for me and we'll have a little look, okay?"

Tamara let the cover-up fall into her lap. She vaguely remembered the first exam he had given her when she had been admitted to juvie, beaten black and blue and not knowing that she was pregnant. Dr. Eastport was always gentle and cheerful with even the most oppositional patient.

He left her alone in the examining room to change, her guard also outside the door.

When Dr. Eastport returned, he found Tamara still sitting there in the wheelchair with the paper robe in her lap. He raised his brows. "I need you to change for the exam, Tamara. We need to do this, even if you think the test is wrong."

Tamara looked down at the robe. "I just can't." Even the thought of all of the effort that would be required for her to change was exhausting. She looked at his examining table. If he would help her up there, she could just close her eyes and go to sleep. They could do the exam another time.

Dr. Eastport sat back down in front of her. "Why not?"

"Too tired. These meds..."

"Oh, I think you could manage it. Just a quick strip-down. It will only take a minute."

Tamara closed her eyes.

"Okay, how about we get you up here, at least?"

Tamara opened her eyes again. She nodded. "You have to help, though."

"All right. Let's do this."

He helped her out of the wheelchair and boosted her up onto the table. He grunted with the effort, apparently finding her heavier than he'd expected. Tamara lay flat on her back and closed her eyes again. It was more comfortable than her bunk, in spite of the crinkly paper cover.

"I'll just get a nurse in here to assist, then."

Tamara was nearly asleep when he returned and didn't want to wake up to deal with the exam. Eastport spoke to her as he unbuttoned her day uniform and got the nurse to help him remove it, then draped the cover-up over her. Tamara pushed it all out of her mind as he began the exam, not wanting to hear or feel it. It was easier just to sleep and pretend that nothing was happening.

## TWENTY-SEVEN

WHEN SHE AWOKE, SHE knew that a number of hours had passed. She stretched and rubbed her eyes and looked around. She was not in her bunk, but in an infirmary bed. One handcuffed wrist ensured that she couldn't wander. Not that she would anyway on the meds. She lay there, staring up at the ceiling. She didn't fall back asleep, but had no desire to do anything else.

Eventually, Dr. Eastport came in. Tamara thought that it was nighttime, though there was no window in the room. She wondered if he ever went home. It seemed like whenever she was admitted to the infirmary, he was always there.

"Hello, my dear. Feeling better after your nap?"

Tamara nodded. She stared past him, seeing herself with him three and a half years earlier. How he had come to tell her what she didn't want to hear. And she knew why he was there again.

"I'm not," she insisted. "Tell me I'm not."

"This is all a little too familiar, isn't it?" Dr. Eastport said. He sat down on a wheeled stool. "It seems like just yesterday when you first came here in need of my services. Such a little girl."

"I'm not. I couldn't be. I took that pill after. They said I couldn't get pregnant if I took the pill."

"Who did? You know that not everyone tells the truth all the time."

"It was a nurse. She told me it would stop me from getting pregnant."

"There are many factors involved. It may have been too late, or it may just have failed. Unfortunately, the morning after pill does have a fifteen percent failure rate. Which means that three times out of every twenty..."

"Then why did she tell me it would work?" Tamara put her hands over her face. "I don't want this. You have to get rid of it, just like the last time. I don't want this!"

He scratched behind his ear, looking grave. "Last time, you were in the early stages of pregnancy. The first trimester. You probably remember symptoms like being tired and throwing up a lot."

"I'm tired now too," Tamara reminded him. "You can fix it. You can make all of this go away." She made a motion like he could see all of the problems that had been plaguing her. The voices, the flashbacks, the hallucinations. He could end all of those for her, and maybe she could go back to being herself again. Maybe she didn't have to live with the psychosis forever.

"You are much further along this time. You've probably noticed the weight gain, the baby moving, your body developing in other ways."

Tamara rubbed at her stomach. It was just cramps. He was wrong. "The nurse said everyone gains weight. In Forensic. The nurse said it's because of the meds."

"Antipsychotics often have that effect," Dr. Eastport agreed. "As does pregnancy."

"You just take care of it. Then everything will go back to normal."

"I don't think you're hearing me, Tamara. I will need to

consult with administration and with the hospital... but it's not an easy fix, like last time. You're too far along. I suspect... that they will probably make the decision for you to carry the pregnancy to term. Then the baby can be relinquished."

Tamara stared at him, horrified. "No. I can't handle it any longer. And there can't be any baby. I can't have a baby!"

Her breaths were coming in fast, short bursts, and she couldn't get the oxygen she needed. Dr. Eastport patted her on the shoulder.

"We'll take care of you. We'll make it as easy for you as possible. It won't be that much longer."

"You're supposed to take care of it. You said you'd take care of it. You promised."

"No, Tamara. It's not the same as last time. We're going to have to see what the administration decides."

* * *

TAMARA HAD RARELY BEEN INVOLVED in any kind of meeting with the administration. As a senior mentor, there had been a few information or feedback sessions she and the other mentors had attended. And there had been her Parole Board hearing. She felt awkward and uncomfortable sitting around the table with Rice, Dr. Sutherland, Dr. Eastport, Mrs. Henson, and Kaplan, one of the nurses from the Forensic unit. The meeting being held in the main building, the guard who was standing by to monitor Tamara was Buxton, the one who had interrogated her after the sleepwalking incident.

Rice looked over the people assembled there. His eyes lingered for a few seconds longer on Mrs. Henson. Tamara didn't know what Mrs. Henson was even doing there. She wasn't Tamara's parent or guardian. She didn't have any standing.

"Glad everyone could make it here," he said, opening the meeting. "As you are aware, this is an emergency meeting to discuss the discovery that inmate Tamara French is pregnant." He looked at Mrs. Henson. "Miss French certainly isn't the first pregnant inmate we've had. It is, in fact, fairly routine."

"It hasn't been routine for Tamara. And I don't see how the decision of how to proceed could be routine. This is a pretty unique case."

Rice gave a shrug. He didn't disagree, but he had a mulish expression that clearly indicated he didn't concede the point, either.

"Normally, we are aware of such things on admission. French's pregnancy was a bit more of a surprise..."

"I don't understand why it wasn't discovered earlier." Mrs. Henson's voice was perfectly even and polite, but Tamara watched Rice's face carefully for signs of anger. He wasn't used to having his or the facility's judgment questioned. And Mrs. Henson wasn't exactly an authority. He didn't answer to her. "Why was I the first one to suspect the truth?"

"Physically, French has hidden the signs well. Even though she is small, the pregnancy isn't obvious even at this advanced stage."

"And other signs? There were none?"

There was silence around the table as the facility staff looked at each other, each weighing their responses. It was Dr. Sutherland who broke the silence.

"Tamara told me some time ago that she experienced hallucinations and disordered thinking when she was pregnant before. I perhaps should have twigged to that when she began having... episodes... on her return to the facility after the prison breaking. But the connection is very unusual. Pregnancy triggering psychosis is not something you hear about every day. There are other, more common triggers like stress and trauma."

Mrs. Henson raised her eyebrows, but didn't say anything.

"Pregnancy tests are not something that we do routinely," Rice said, his words clipped. "If an inmate requests one or suggests that she might be pregnant, then of course we would follow up. But Tamara never said anything."

Tamara pressed her lips together and stared at the opposite wall, feeling their eyes on her.

"Tamara is in denial," Mrs. Henson said. "This is very traumatic for her."

"I'm sure it is." Rice's tone indicated he couldn't care less about Tamara's feelings, "and on that note, perhaps we could move forward instead of harping on the fact that none of us—" he looked at Mrs. Henson and repeated it, "*none* of us saw the signs any earlier. Now that we know about Miss French's condition, we need to make some decisions."

"I want you to get rid of it," Tamara said. "Why is that so hard? Why can't you get just rid of it, like last time?"

"This late in the pregnancy, it is not recommended. Physically and emotionally, it is much more difficult."

"I don't care," Tamara insisted. "You think it's harder on me to get rid of it than it is to walk around with it inside me messing with my brain?" Tamara saw the fetus coiled in her brain instead of her belly. That was how it felt. Like the alien being was growing in her brain, taking over her thoughts. She clenched her fingers around handfuls of hair, pulling on it violently like she could rip the foreign creature out of her head with the roots of her hair. It hurt, but she didn't care. "I want it out of me!"

"It won't be much longer," Dr. Eastport repeated what he had told her in the infirmary. "We're talking a matter of weeks at this point. It is an ethical gray area. I, for one, would not be comfortable with terminating such an advanced pregnancy."

"It's my choice! It should be my choice!"

"It's not that cut and dried with a minor in custody," Rice said. "We have to determine what is best for you."

"I know what's best for me! You just don't want to do it!" Tamara looked at Mrs. Henson fiercely, waiting for her to speak up and defend Tamara's rights. But she didn't. She looked pensively at the table in front of her and said nothing. She, too, thought it was a bad idea. Tamara should have expected it. Mrs. Henson fostered teen moms. She was used to helping teens who wanted to keep their babies. She didn't understand how different it was for Tamara.

"I have concerns about Tamara's treatment here," Mrs. Henson said. Everyone turned their heads to look at her, frowns and puzzled expressions. "The issue isn't just the failure to detect her pregnancy or deciding on the best course of action."

"What are you talking about, then?" Rice asked. "Surely you don't think Miss French has been maltreated."

"I'm talking about her medical treatment plan. The meds... are not right. Sometimes she can barely hold a conversation. You've got her so drugged up she can barely walk by herself. Does she do anything during the day other than lie in bed?"

Rice looked at Dr. Sutherland for his response.

"Tamara is being treated with powerful antipsychotics in an effort to control her delusions and violent behavior. Unfortunately, they do have a sedating effect."

"Are they working?"

Dr. Sutherland's eyes slid over to Tamara. "It's hard to judge," he temporized. "She has had several incidents, even on the protocol. I would increase the dosage, but obviously we can't do that. Right now it's a waiting game. Wait a few weeks to see if she will stabilize. Switch meds and try something else. There are no quick solutions."

"So if they're not working and may take weeks or months to figure out, why even bother? Once she has the baby, the psychosis will disappear on its own, won't it?"

"There's no guarantee of that. It could be a temporary effect of the pregnancy, or it could have triggered a permanent shift in her brain chemistry. I'd rather not lose the time in treating her."

"What about the effect of the medication on the fetus?"

"Most antipsychotics are considered safe during pregnancy.

And if not... that ship has sailed. The fetus is far more susceptible during the early stages of pregnancy. Stopping medications now would not make any difference to its development."

"But to be safe... don't you think it would make more sense to discontinue them until she's no longer pregnant?" Mrs. Henson looked at Rice. "Especially since they're not working."

Rice tapped his fingertips together. "While she is still having some... delusions, there has been a noticeable reduction in the frequency of her violent and oppositional behavior. I wouldn't want to lose the progress that has been made."

"Do you think she's had fewer incidents because it is working or because of the sedation effect?"

Rice looked at Sutherland, then over at Eastport. Neither of them jumped in to help him. "It could be in part due to the sedating effect. Impossible for us to know until we've had more time to tweak it."

Tamara shifted restlessly. She had cramps and she had to pee. But a trip out to the bathroom and back would sap all of her energy and she'd miss whatever they wanted to say behind her back. It was bad enough to have them talking about her like she wasn't even in the room. She tried to ignore the discomfort and stay focused on the conversation.

"So you know she's still having mental problems, but you're going to keep her on a protocol that isn't working because it keeps her quiet. Does that about sum it up?" Mrs. Henson challenged.

"That's an oversimplification," Sutherland interjected. "The sedating effect of the antipsychotics might have some benefit in this case, but we are looking for something that is going to help her long-term. Until we can find the right combination of drugs, that's the best we can do."

"So you're using them as chemical restraints."

"That's inflammatory," Rice growled. "We are helping Miss French the best we can. Are you thinking about what damage could be done to her or the baby if she gets into an altercation in this condition? I remind you we've had plenty of experience with pregnant inmates, and the results of a physical fight can be very disturbing."

Mrs. Henson sat back, thinking about this. Tamara shifted again, putting a hand under her abdomen and trying to relieve the pressure.

"The solution is easy," she said. "Just end it. Then you don't have to worry about me getting hurt and I can go back to normal and not need the meds. I won't get into fights because this stupid brain will behave itself." Tamara ground her knuckles into her temple, as if she could force it to reset by sheer will.

If only she could.

"Our decision is final," Rice said. "You will not be getting a late-term abortion."

Tamara's fists clenched. She glared at him and tried to judge whether she'd have enough time and energy to get across the table to either get her hands around his neck or punch him in the face. He sat there looking smug, his eyes cold as ice.

"Stand down, French," Buxton warned, moving closer.

Tamara threw a look at him. His jaw was clenched. He was ready to jump the instant she moved. She unclenched her fists and slouched back in her seat. Buxton relaxed noticeably, but he didn't go back to his previous position. He hovered close by, watching for any wrong move.

* * *

BACK IN HER ROOM, Tamara just floated for a few days. They brought her her meals and her meds and she mostly lay in bed, with no motivation or energy to do anything else.

Brinkley couldn't talk her into coming out of her room. The nurses encouraged her to get out and walk, but she had no desire to. Everything was so screwed up.

But she wasn't finished. They hadn't defeated her. Tamara still had some control over her own life.

She started cheeking her pills. Since she had been taking them for weeks without any problems, the nurses didn't suspect anything and never checked to see if she had swallowed them. They didn't search her room and find her little stash.

In a few days, she started to get back some energy, and that made staying in her room and pretending she was still taking her pills an exquisite torture. Lying in bed, feeling like she was going to jump out of her skin with restlessness and anxiety every time anyone walked by her room. She picked up one of the paperbacks that Mrs. Henson had left for her, but she was finished that within a few hours. She read each of the books she had available, and read them all again, and again.

She didn't have a fully-formed plan. The first part had just been to get off of the pills. She couldn't think straight until she did that.

But the longer she lay there, hand over the baby bulge, thinking of the thing growing inside her, the angrier she got. She hadn't chosen to get pregnant. She had done everything within her power to stop it. Juvie was preventing her from getting rid of it. They wanted that thing to grow inside her.

She didn't know why they wanted her to have the baby. Maybe that had been the plot right from the start. That was why Vernon and Sly had taken her. They had colluded with juvie administration to let Vernon escape and to take Tamara with them. To get her pregnant. The nurse must have been in on it too, giving Tamara something other than the real morning-after pills to make sure she got pregnant. And juvie made sure she didn't discover the pregnancy until too late. Now they were letting it grow inside her, forcing her to carry it to term.

She didn't know why. She didn't know what they wanted with the baby. Did they want to do something to it? Or was it supposed to do something to her? Or maybe they wanted to watch her with the baby, make her take care of it, and see what she would do. See if she would be a good mom or if she would do something terrible. Maybe they wanted to set her up so they could keep her in prison for the rest of her life.

However long that was.

But she could outwit them. She could wreck their plans.

She just had to decide on the best way. She had the pile of pills. She didn't know if there were enough to do the trick. If one dose was enough to sideline her, to make it so that she didn't have the energy to do anything but lie in her bed, would two doses put her in a coma? Would there be enough to kill her? She had more than that, but she worried that it just wouldn't be enough. Would she go to sleep, only to wake up with a headache, maybe in the hospital? She knew of other girls who had tried taking pills. Tried and failed.

There were other ways. Without the antipsychotic drugs in her system, she was able to think and she had more motivation and energy to act.

## TWENTY-EIGHT

S HE DIDN'T COUNT ON the fact that other methods might be just as capricious as an overdose. She had seen other hangings in juvie and they had all been successful. She thought she had done everything right. She had carefully tied and retied the knots, testing them to make sure they were tight and wouldn't slip. She timed it carefully.

But not carefully enough.

She blacked out, thinking that she had been successful and everything was going to go as planned. But the shout of the nurse who had entered her room unexpectedly rang in her ears and she only swam in the mists of darkness for a short interval before she started to resurface.

"French. French!"

She tried to keep her eyes closed, to fall further into that welcome darkness, but someone kept slapping her cheeks, calling her insistently. She had to open her eyes. She had to rejoin the real world.

"Oooh..."

"Come on," the guard shook her shoulder. "Wake up."

"Nooo..."

The nurse and the guard hovered over her, scowling and concerned. Tamara fingered her bruised throat.

"Why?" she whispered.

"Why did we cut you down? What do you think?"

"No... why did you come in?"

The nurse shook her head. "Coming to check your blood pressure. Why would you do something like that? How could you be so stupid?"

Tamara groaned. Her whole body hurt. Her neck and throat hurt from the makeshift noose, but the rest of her body did too. Like she had been battered and stretched and thrown to the side of the road. Her head pounded and she could feel her pulse throbbing inside her throat.

The nurse unbuttoned Tamara's uniform. She put her stethoscope on Tamara's chest and listened to her heartbeat and her breathing. She moved it down to Tamara's belly and held it still for a long time.

"Is it dead?" Tamara asked. But she knew it wasn't. She would know if it were dead.

The nurse looked at the guard as if needing permission to answer Tamara. He gave a shrug.

"Good, strong heartbeat," she advised. "Is that why? You wanted to kill the baby? You didn't care that you would kill yourself too?"

Tamara nodded.

The nurse *tsked* and went on examining Tamara. Tamara closed her eyes. Maybe she should have tried the pills. But even if she had... the nurse would surely have known there was something wrong when she came in to take Tamara's blood pressure anyway. It wouldn't matter which method she chose, it wouldn't have been successful. There *were* other ways. She had lived in juvie for three years. She could be creative.

The squeak of wheels signaled the arrival of a gurney. Tamara looked at it through barely-cracked lids.

"Don't want to go."

"Too bad. You try to hang yourself, you get a trip to the infirmary. You get put on watch. You get extra sessions with Dr. Sutherland. You already made your choice."

Tamara grunted.

"You want to get on under your own power or do we need to lift you?"

Tamara slid off of her bunk. With the nurse steadying her, she walked over to the gurney and got on. She rubbed her throat.

"It hurts."

The nurse and other staff were unsympathetic. Tamara closed her eyes as they pushed the gurney back to the infirmary.

* * *

DR. EASTPORT clucked and fussed over Tamara like a mother hen. "Oh, my dear," he murmured. "Why would you do this to yourself?"

Tamara held the ice pack he had given her in place over her bruised throat, even though it made her shiver. Dr. Eastport said if her throat swelled up too much, they would have to put a tube down her throat to help her breathe and she didn't want to have to go through that.

"I'm not going to let it grow inside me," Tamara said. "This *thing*."

"It's not a thing, Tamara," he pushed a stray lock of hair away from her face. "It's a baby. I know you don't want it, and once you deliver, you never have to see it again, but you're going to have to hang on a little bit longer."

"No."

One of the infirmary staff wheeled a machine into the room.

Tamara eyed it. "What's that?" She turned the ice pack to get a colder section onto her neck. Were they already getting a respirator set up? A crash cart? In spite of her brief period of unconsciousness and the soreness of her body, she was feeling okay. Not like she was going to suddenly stop breathing.

Dr. Eastport didn't answer. He just busied himself with the new equipment. In a few minutes, he turned back to her, and she watched as he pulled back her robe to squirt cold jelly onto her lower abdomen. She had a sneaking suspicion she knew what he was going to do. Dr. Eastport put the transponder to her stomach and moved it around, his movements probing, watching the screen on the machine rather than what he was doing. Tamara watched him searching through the blobs of light and darkness. That was *in* her. All of that darkness. It was no wonder the pregnancy clouded her mind.

Dr. Eastport held the transponder still, pressed into Tamara's abdomen, and pointed at the monitor. "There he is. There's the baby, Tamara."

She didn't want to look, but was drawn toward the shifting pixels. She could make out the little form curled up inside her like a cat in a basket.

"And listen to this." Dr. Eastport turned up a volume dial and Tamara could hear the rapid beating of the little heart.

She put her hand over her slick belly, beside the transponder, feeling the mass under the skin. She dug in her fingers, imagining herself reaching in through her stomach to tear the intruder out. The invader who had taken over her body and her brain. Dr. Eastport abruptly pulled the transponder away and put it on the side of the cart. He pulled Tamara's grasping fingers away from her body.

"No, Tamara. Don't. Don't hurt yourself. It's going to be okay. Don't try to hurt yourself."

Tamara pulled back, but he didn't release his grip.

"I want it out," Tamara insisted. "I'll take it out myself!"

"No. I'm sorry. I thought seeing him would help you. It's okay. Calm down."

She again tried to pull out of his grip.

"I'll let you go," he said, "but you have to promise me not to hurt yourself. And not to try to hurt the baby. Otherwise, I'll have to put you in restraints."

"Okay. I won't. Just let me go!"

Dr. Eastport released her hands, watching her for any sign that she was going to try something. Tamara folded her hands over her chest and waited for him to make the next move. Dr. Eastport pulled her robe back over her belly and pulled the sheet up over her.

"We're here to help you, Tamara. Do you think you can trust me, just a little longer?"

"Will you go back to Rice and tell him they need to get rid of it?"

He gazed at her for a long minute, then nodded. "Yes, I'll tell Mr. Rice they should reconsider, for your safety."

Tamara nodded and relaxed her head back against the pillow. "You tell them to get this monster out of me. Then I'll trust you."

* * *

TAMARA WAITED until Dr. Eastport left her alone, a guard posted outside the door, before making another attempt. Though they had left her with the sheets on her bed, she didn't try hanging again. She had a feeling that they wouldn't leave her unsupervised for long enough to set herself up again.

But she had fixated on the idea of getting the fetus out. If the doctors wouldn't do it, then she would do it herself. She would foil their plans and free her brain from the poisonous influence of the thing growing inside her. It was the only way.

She surreptitiously went through the treatment room, opening and closing drawers as quietly as possible to keep from attracting the attention of the guard outside the door. There was, of course, nothing sharp stored there. Dr. Eastport and his staff were careful.

Tamara feigned sleep, waiting for the next security check. She heard the door snick open and knew the guard was standing there looking in at her. She stayed still and took long, deep, even breaths. Eventually, she heard the door shut again.

She immediately went into action, digging her fingers into the soft flesh of her abdomen, trying to cut and tear at the elastic skin with her nails, shutting out the waves of pain and nausea. It was the only way. The only way to get rid of the alien presence and clear her brain once more. She could feel it moving under her fingers, as if it sensed what she was trying to do and was fighting back against her.

She wasn't aware that she had started shouting. The guard came back through the door with a look of irritation. His face rapidly lost all color and he started yelling for help. He didn't think to hit his panic button, but dove at Tamara, grabbing both her arms and trying to pin them back. Tamara writhed and nearly freed herself from his grip. She kicked, trying to knee him and drive him back. He turned his face away, leaning into her so that his sturdy shoulder was the only target, and Tamara was unable to force him back. She screamed in frustration. Rage boiled inside her and she bucked her body, trying to escape his grasp.

The medical staff hurried in to see what the problem was. They tied back her feet and then her bloody hands. Tamara was left to fight futilely against the restraints, unable to free herself. One of the nurses tried to examine Tamara as another went to get Dr. Eastport.

His face turned almost as pale as the guard's when he saw her bloodied body and hands. He bent over her abdomen to examine the damage, and she thought she saw tears in his eyes.

"You promised me you wouldn't hurt yourself or the baby," he reproached.

Tamara tried to buck her body, but her ankles and wrists were stretched too far to allow her any body movement. Dr. Eastport felt her straining and looked at her face.

"I have to get it out," Tamara insisted. "It's evil!"

"It's not evil." He prodded her torn flesh, examining the damage. "You're confused. You're not thinking right."

"It's not a delusion."

"It is. These thoughts and feelings are being caused by your illness."

"If it's making me sick, then get it out!" She again tried to move, desperate. But even though she wasn't on the antipsychotics anymore, her energy was flagging.

"I'm going to give you a sedative, Tamara. That will help you to calm down. Okay?"

"No, no drugs."

"I can't treat you in this condition and it could be... traumatic for you. So let's just give you something to quiet your mind. You want to relax and have a rest, don't you?"

Tamara blinked slowly, her eyes wanting to close the rest of the way and stay shut.

"Yeah."

"Just give me a minute, then."

He left the room to go get the sedative and returned to give her an injection. There was a brief needle of pain in her thigh muscle, and almost immediately, a warm feeling started to spread through Tamara. In spite of not wanting the medication, she couldn't help welcoming the calm and rest that it brought.

## TWENTY-NINE

WHEN SHE WOKE UP, there was a band around her middle, tight and uncomfortable. She couldn't see the stitches or the bandage under her blankets and uniform, but she knew they were there. It took a while to shake the effects of the sedation. She wondered if they had put her back onto her antipsychotics or decided to try a different protocol to see if something else worked better.

She was still in the infirmary. They hadn't transferred her to the hospital; or if they had, she had already been transferred back again. There was talking outside her door. She watched to see who was there. Eventually, the door opened and a guard walked in, assigned to look after her to make sure she wasn't able to try anything else.

It was Zobel. He gave her a sad smile and walked up to the side of her bed. She was glad to see him, in spite of her condition.

"Hey, French. How are you feeling?"

Tamara wasn't sure how to answer that. She wasn't sure how she felt or what she wanted to tell him.

"I dunno."

His eyes were drawn to her middle. With the baby bulge and

the bulky bandages, the sheets rose in a gentle hill. "So, you've had some setbacks."

She looked at him, then away again. Talk about an understatement.

"Things... haven't been so good."

"You've had a lot of challenges. I heard you melted down at the courthouse again, that they were transferring you to Forensic, and then..." He nodded awkwardly toward her belly, not putting it into words. Not saying the word 'pregnant,' in case it might set her off again. "Now... suicide, self-harming... what's going on?"

"They won't take it out," Tamara griped. "I don't understand why they won't just do it. Why can't they just... fix it? It's their fault it's there in me to start with!"

Zobel's brows drew down. "What?" He looked toward the door, as if someone might be listening in. Maybe they were. "It's whose fault? Did someone here...?"

Tamara nodded. "It's their fault. They made sure I got pregnant, they switched the pills, and then they won't let me get rid of it. They want me to go crazy. Or they want me to kill it. I don't know which."

"You're not making any sense, French."

"It's true!" Tamara insisted. "It's all part of their plan."

"I just assumed that... you got pregnant when you were out. On parole or after that prison breaking. That's what made the most sense."

"They set all of that up," Tamara agreed with a vigorous nod. "They were the ones who arranged for the break-out. You think Vernon was smart enough to get out on her own? Or Sly? They said they were the ones who planned it, but it never made any sense. How could Sly get past all of the cameras without any of them recording his face? Why didn't they stop them before they left the grounds? They just let them through the gates. They didn't stop anyone from doing anything."

Something changed in Zobel's face. He nodded in agreement, but there was a reservation that hadn't been there before. As if he had just figured out why she was telling him her theory. A cold wave of realization rolled over Tamara.

"You already know. You're part of it."

"There is no conspiracy, French. Really. It's just your... your brain is telling you things that aren't true."

"Because of the baby," Tamara told him. She turned her head back and forth, trying to hold it together. "It's growing inside my brain. It's making everything seem wrong. It takes over my thoughts."

"Well... you know that your thinking isn't right, anyway," Zobel conceded. "I think... that's a step."

"A step to what? You want me to go crazy, don't you? You want to see if I'll hurt it." She couldn't point to her stomach, so she jerked her head at it instead. "That monster. That thing growing in there. I tried, you know. I would if I could."

"I know you tried. I... heard all about it." Zobel grimaced and shook his head. "Do you realize how sick you are?"

"You're making me sick. All of you. I don't know why you're experimenting on me like this. I don't know why you had to do this."

He folded his arms and leaned on the wall, looking down on her. Tamara wished that there were a chair for him to sit on, so he didn't have to tower over her.

"You know I'd do anything to make you better," he said. "I don't want you to be sick. I want to help you."

"You're not."

Zobel's lips pressed together, making them stretch out in a thin, elongated line. He shook his head.

"I'm sorry. I really do wish there was something I could do to help."

Tamara looked into his face. He did look sorry. Maybe he wasn't in on it personally. Maybe they hadn't told him the plan, because they knew that Zobel had a soft spot for her. Maybe that was why Tabby had knifed Zobel, because he wouldn't cooperate with the plan. Maybe Tamara wasn't supposed to have saved him. Or maybe Tamara was supposed to have saved him, and that was how they had pulled her in and gotten her off guard. Or maybe Tamara was supposed to die, and Zobel had gotten himself in the way, and all of the rest of the elaborate plot was just to lead Tamara off in the other direction, to be able to catch her off her guard later.

"Did they hurt you?" she asked Zobel. "Was that all part of the plan too?"

He frowned, brows drawing down in consternation. "Hurt me?" he repeated. "Nobody hurt me."

Had it all been a trick? A set-up? He wasn't hurt? Wasn't ever in danger?

But she remembered the sticky blood. Remembered the smell and the taste of it. She had to wash the clotted mats out of her hair. It couldn't have been a trick. Tamara turned her head and tried to see the scar on Zobel's arm. But the way he was standing with his arms folded, he was hiding the scar from her. Or hiding the fact that he didn't have a scar. Maybe he wasn't really Zobel, but a double. He hadn't been hurt; that had been the real Zobel. This one had been sent in to fool her and get information from her.

"You're not really here," she accused.

The frown lines between his brows deepened. "Should I get someone?" he asked. "Maybe I should call the doctor."

"I don't *need* any more doctors!" Tamara growled. "They're the ones who started this. They're the ones who put it in me and got me sick. They just want to make me more sick. They want me to be crazy, to forget everything. They don't want anyone to listen to me."

She remembered how her court cases had gone. How everything had fallen apart and she had broken down on the stand, unable to testify against Mr. Baker or Glock. That had been their goal right from the very start. To discredit her and keep her from being able to testify. Even if she did manage to tell what Mr. Baker and Glock had done to her, no one would believe it. Everyone would think she was just a raving lunatic.

"You should try to calm down," Zobel suggested. "Maybe... take deep breaths, and try to ground yourself. Try to use all of your senses to ground yourself. What you see and hear, taste and smell..."

Tamara didn't plan on following his suggestion, but as soon as he said it, she felt a rush of sensations. The noises outside the room were muted, but she could hear people walking and talking, someone yelling farther down the hall. And in the room, she could hear the air vents, Zobel's breathing, and her own. She could hear her heartbeat and feel the creature moving inside her. She remembered hearing its heartbeat on the ultrasound. Had it been a trick, or did the monster really have a heart just like hers?

The air was heavy with hospital smells. Cleaners and antiseptics and other people. She could smell Zobel beside her, the warm smell of the aftershave that he wore coming off of him with his sweat. Did that mean he was the real Zobel? Or did all of them wear the same aftershave as a way of fooling her? Tamara breathed in the smell and held it in her lungs, thinking about it.

"Is it you?" she asked. "Or not?"

"It's me," Zobel agreed. "I'm right here."

"Yeah? It's you?"

He nodded.

"Why did they do this to me?" Tamara asked. "Do you know? Did they tell you why?"

"No." Zobel gave a little shrug of his folded arms. "I don't know why this happened to you. But it isn't a conspiracy. It wasn't a plan or a plot. It's just... you have a mental illness. Something happened in your brain."

"My head..." Tamara tried to feel her head, but her arms were still in restraints. Not high over her head anymore, like they had been when Dr. Eastport was trying to examine her, but down at her sides. Tamara pulled on them in irritation.

"Can you get these off? I can't move."

"Sorry, no. I'm not allowed to touch them."

"I want to move. I need to... my head hurts. I have something growing in my brain."

"No. Nothing is growing in your brain. That's not real. Stay with me. You can do this."

"I can't," Tamara snapped. "I can't control it."

"I know you can't control it. But if you listen to me, I'll tell you what's true and what's not. I'll help you."

"It's all true," Tamara insisted. "All of it."

"No. Listen to me. I'll tell you."

Tamara breathed and considered what he said. She concentrated on the room around her, trying to use her senses, like he had suggested. She wasn't sure she could tell what was real and what was a delusion. But Zobel could tell her. If he really was Zobel. If he really knew and wasn't just trying to fool her.

"Listen," Zobel said, his voice low and gentle. "Even with what you're going through... you still have choices. You know that it's not right to harm that baby inside you. You know it's not right to kill yourself or him. No matter how confused you are, you still know those things, right?"

"Why? Why is it wrong?"

Zobel opened his mouth, shaking his head. "I... you just know it's wrong. Killing or hurting someone else is wrong. Just like when Tabby tried to kill me. You remember that?"

Tamara nodded. "I remember."

"You didn't want her to kill me. Why not?"

"I... don't know. I can't remember."

"You knew it was wrong. I wasn't doing anything to hurt you or Tabby. I was helping people who were hurt. I was trying to shut down a fight so that no one else would get hurt. You knew that. You knew it would be wrong for her to kill me just because the gangs wanted to have a rumble."

Tamara nodded. That all sounded right. She was pretty sure he was telling the truth about that.

"Yeah."

"Killing people is wrong."

She nodded again, understanding.

"And that includes killing yourself or your baby."

"Does it?" Tamara pursed her lips. "I don't think so."

Zobel laughed. "Yes, French. I'm telling you the truth, remember? I'm telling you the truth so you know what is real and what is just in your brain."

"Yeah."

"Killing yourself or your baby is wrong."

Tamara rested her head back, considering his words. It was wrong. Killing was always wrong, even if it was herself or the thing growing inside her. But Tamara knew that wasn't always true. She had killed before, out of necessity. That was different.

Tamara moved her head back and forth.

"My head hurts," she complained. "My brain itches. I want to scratch it."

"I don't like the sound of that!"

Tamara glowered at him. "Come and take the restraints off. Even just one of them. I can't do anything with just one hand free."

"Heh." Zobel shook his head. "Like I believe that. You can cause trouble no matter how many limbs you have restrained. I was warned not to even touch the restraints. Not to loosen them, not to release one wrist. Not giving you a bit more slack to move around. Nothing."

Tamara swore under her breath. Stupid Rice and his flunkies. Out ahead of her, trying to keep her from getting comfortable.

Zobel just grinned like Tamara had played a trick and he was in on the secret.

* * *

IT WAS some time before they let her out of restraints and released her from the infirmary. Even then, she was watched closely and wasn't allowed to stay in her room for more than ten minutes at a time before they were checking in again to make sure she was all right.

Tamara knew from the colors and shapes of the tablets that they had changed her medications, but she didn't know what they were giving her. The nurses checked carefully after every dose to make sure she had actually swallowed them and wasn't saving them up to overdose.

Gradually, security was reduced. She did as Zobel had suggested, trying to ground herself in the present. But despite the new medications and her best attempts to head off the delusions, she wasn't able to make sense of everything and avoid being tricked by her brain.

Zobel had said that she could still make choices, even if her brain wasn't working right. She still had the ability to choose whether to hurt herself or not. Even being locked up in the Forensic unit, she still had a few choices of her own.

Nurse Shriner looked up from her desk at Tamara's approach, raising an eyebrow and looking a little nervous that Tamara was approaching her. She pasted on a determined smile.

"What can I do for you, Tamara?"

Tamara stopped on the other side of the desk. She bounced on her heels, anxiety bubbling up from her middle.

"I need help."

"What do you need?"

Tamara tried to shut off the competing voices. She only needed to talk to one. Nurse Shriner. She was right there in front of Tamara and Tamara didn't have to guess at whether she was real or not.

"My head is messed up," Tamara said. She held it for a moment on both sides. "None of this crap is helping."

"I'm sorry to hear that. You want a med review? Want to talk to Dr. Sutherland about what is working and what isn't?"

"Nothing is working."

"Are you having more issues today?" Shriner walked around the desk to put herself in front of Tamara. "What's going on?"

"I don't know. I want... to do something to make it stop."

"What is it that's happening?"

"They want me to do things. And I want... I don't want to have this." Tamara put her hands around her more prominent baby bulge. "Can't they take it now? Why do they have to wait longer?"

"We have to make sure the baby's lungs are developed. You're almost there, honey, but not quite. The best place for him right now is right where he is, growing and developing until he's big enough to be born."

Tamara squeezed the round basketball and then let go.

"Zobel said... it's wrong to harm anyone. Even it."

"You know that's true," Shriner agreed. She motioned to someone behind Tamara. "Are you having thoughts about hurting him again?"

Tamara nodded. She rocked back and forth, trying to stay connected. Anchored. Focus on all five senses...

"What's up?"

Tamara jumped at Burgess's voice in her ear. She swung toward him, hands up defensively.

"Easy," Burgess warned. "Just be cool."

"Don't sneak up on me like that," Tamara snapped. She backed up slightly so that she could see both Burgess and Shriner at the same time.

"Tamara is having thoughts about harming the baby,"

Shriner told Burgess. "I think we should get her into an observation room or the infirmary. Call Dr. Sutherland and see what he wants to do about it."

Burgess nodded his agreement. His eyes were intense as he stared at Tamara. She wanted to tell him to stop looking at her and go away, but he needed to watch her. Somebody needed to watch her to make sure she wasn't going to hurt herself. Zobel said it was wrong. Zobel said she could choose whether to do the right thing or not.

"Let's get you into a watch room, then," Burgess said, "and we'll give Sutherland a call."

Tamara ground her teeth. The last thing she wanted was to be shut in one of the fish tanks, exposed to view, unable to find privacy anywhere, even behind a sheet. It was the worst feeling of exposure, having to sit there without anything to do, without being able to make a move that wasn't scrutinized.

Burgess held his hand out to either motion her forward or take her by the arm. Tamara took a deep breath in, let it out, and headed in the direction of the observation rooms. Burgess trailed just behind her, keeping his hands to himself and letting her take it at her own pace. The new meds didn't sedate her quite as much as the previous cocktail had, but everything was harder than it had been when she was unmedicated.

When they got to the observation rooms, Burgess talked to the staff and got her into one. Tamara sat on the bunk with no blankets and stared at herself in the mirrored glass. She hadn't seen her own image for a long time. Seeing herself after so long, the changes were startling.

Her brown-dyed hair had grown out, with only the very ends of her hair dark, and the rest her natural blond. Her belly wasn't the only part of her body that had matured and for the first time she had a real figure. But even with the changes to her body, it was her face that she found herself staring at. In spite of the weight that she had put on, her face seemed narrower and more worn. It was the face of an older woman. In the course of just a few years, she had gone from child to teenager to grown woman, and her experiences had worn their way into her face.

Tamara stared at the teardrop tattoos beside her eye. The prison ink wasn't high quality and the amateur tattooing process left a lot to be desired.

The woman in the mirror was a stranger to Tamara.

THIRTY

TAMARA WAS PACING UP and down the corridor when Mrs. Henson got there. Dr. Sutherland had once again adjusted her meds, hoping to shut down Tamara's thoughts about harming the baby, and still, hopefully to help get rid of her delusions.

Rather than being too tired, the new med, or its combination with one of the others Tamara was on, made her anxious and restless. She couldn't sit down on her bunk or read. She paced up and down the hall, to the nurses' complaints that she was going to wear a hole in the tile.

"Need to meet with your visitor in one of the meeting rooms," Sardis, one of the older guards told her.

"I can't sit still. This is better. You can still see me."

"Needs to be in a meeting room. Controlled environment. Out here, anything could happen." He gestured to his surroundings as if perhaps there were medieval weapons hanging on the walls or a stash of firearms behind glass. *Break glass in case of emergency.* Tamara rolled her eyes at him, but didn't share the images.

"I can walk in the meeting room?"

Sardis considered. It was technically against the rules, but he knew how restive Tamara had been since her last med change.

"You can pace in the meeting room," he agreed. "Unless I think you're losing control. Then you're either going to have to sit down or go back to your room."

Tamara nodded her agreement. It was the best offer she was going to get. The three of them went to the biggest meeting room and Sardis removed the extra chairs so that Mrs. Henson was sitting down and Tamara had room to walk.

Mrs. Henson looked uncomfortable sitting down while everyone else was standing or walking. She shifted in her seat a couple of times. Tamara breathed out heavily and paced the short distance up and down the room.

"I'm glad you asked to see me," Mrs. Henson offered tentatively. She didn't speak the rest of the thought. That Tamara had never asked for her to come before. She'd never asked for anyone.

"Yeah." Tamara nodded. "Thanks for coming."

She tried to get into a rhythm pacing back and forth, but the room was too short and she couldn't move quickly in the narrow space between the table and the wall.

"How have you been?"

"Not so good. Doctor's changed meds around again."

"Did it help? Is it any better?"

"Don't know. Maybe. I'm trying..." Tamara stopped pacing and put one hand on top of her rounded tummy. "I'm trying to do the right thing, but it's hard to know what that is."

Mrs. Henson nodded slowly. "You're in a very challenging situation," she said. "Like a lot of the girls that I get."

"At least they can decide what they want. They won't let me do what I want."

"I know. But a lot of the girls I deal with feel the same way, even if they do have more freedom to choose than you do. A lot of them feel trapped, whether because their parents have told them that they only have one option, or because social services is pushing them in a particular direction, or maybe they can't do what they want to because they don't think they have the skills or the education. They end up losing jobs, dropping out of school, kicked out of families, dumped by their boyfriends... I don't think it's ever easy."

Tamara resumed her pacing, arching her back slightly to try to ease the ache caused by the extra weight in front. She didn't feel like she was ever going to be rid of the baby and be herself again.

"I'm just trying not to harm," she told Mrs. Henson. "The nurses say just a few more weeks... I just have to hold on... that long."

"It probably seems like forever," Mrs. Henson sympathized. Tamara heard the unspoken words in her mind. *But it's not. It's just a little longer.*

For Tamara, the time stretched out in front of her as far ahead as she could see. She kept telling herself that everything would be okay and go back to normal once she had the baby out of her. But she was afraid of what Dr. Sutherland had said. Maybe the pregnancy had triggered a permanent shift in her condition. There was no guarantee that once she was through the pregnancy, she would feel better.

"I don't know what to do."

Mrs. Henson shook her head slowly. "There's not much you can do at this point. Just hang in there like you've been doing. The real question is what you are going to do afterward."

Tamara looked at her. "After? Nothing... just... go on."

"What do you want to happen to the baby after? Do you want to keep him? Do you have someone you want to raise him? Surely you've thought about this."

Tamara shook her head, frowning at the suggestion. "I can't keep it. There's no babies in juvie."

"Maybe not, but you're coming up on your anniversary before too long. If you get out on parole, you could take custody. You would just need someone to look after him for the period between your delivery and getting out on parole."

"They won't let me be near children. That was one of my parole terms. No children under the age of five."

"They can't apply that to your own child."

Just like they hadn't been able to keep Mr. and Mrs. Baker from having another child. They hadn't taken Amy away from them when she was born, despite the Bakers' history.

Tamara shook her head, shaking off the images. Mr. and Mrs. Baker weren't there and she wasn't going to think about them. Likewise, she wouldn't consider having a baby in her life. She knew how she felt around babies. She couldn't take care of one. She had no desire to.

"I don't want it. I don't want anything to do with it."

"You may feel differently once he's born."

"You think they would give me any choice? They wouldn't give custody of a baby to me. They'd be crazy to."

"You're not a proven risk to other children. You acted to protect Amy."

And Sybil's little sisters, though Mrs. Henson didn't know anything about that, and neither did the parole board or social services. As far as any of them were concerned, she was a child killer, and they would be stupid to allow her near any child, even her own.

She wrung her hands. "I don't want it," she repeated firmly. "They can put it up for adoption. I don't care. I don't want it."

Mrs. Henson nodded. "All right," she agreed.

Tamara had been expecting an argument and Mrs. Henson's answer left her feeling let down. She continued to pace, taking a couple of long, slow breaths. "I just want it to all be over."

Mrs. Henson didn't answer right away. She considered

Tamara's statement. "You want the pregnancy to be over? Is that what you mean?"

"No. Yes. I don't know. I mean... everything. Not just having it out of me... I don't want to be here. I don't want to be in prison forever. I don't want my brain to be messed up. I don't want to deal with all of this."

"You sound... depressed."

Tamara snorted. Depressed didn't begin to cover it.

"I guess."

"Are you... considering hurting yourself?"

Tamara looked at Sardis. He was watching her carefully, listening to every word, even though he was trying to look uninterested. She knew he was waiting for her answer. Just waiting to report back to Dr. Sutherland and the medical staff.

"I was already under watch," she said. "I just got off. Dr. Sutherland said these new meds would help. I'm not going to hurt the baby, but..." She trailed off. What was she going to say? That she was going to hurt herself? She would just find herself slapped back into the fishbowl, and she couldn't stand the scrutiny any longer.

"Tamara. If you're feeling depressed and feeling like you might harm yourself, people need to know. It's not your fault and you're not going to be punished. You need help."

Tamara nodded.

There was silence in the room. Tamara didn't know what to say. How to deal with the sucking sinkhole of depression that she found herself in. They couldn't take it away with all of their medications. Tamara couldn't just put her troubles aside and cheer up. She didn't know what she was supposed to do.

"Um..." Mrs. Henson cleared her throat and looked at Sardis. "I know the answer is probably no, but... can I give Tamara a hug?"

Sardis scowled. He was already treading on thin ice by letting Tamara walk around during the visit when he was supposed to ensure that she stayed in her chair. His jaw clenched and he looked at Tamara. Finally, he nodded his head.

"Pat-down first," he said. "Both of you. I'm not supposed to allow any contact…"

Mrs. Henson was looking at Tamara, trying to meet her eyes. "Is that okay with you, Tamara? Can I give you a hug?"

Tamara didn't remember ever having any physical contact with Mrs. Henson before. Maybe a touch on the arm or the hand. She certainly would never have allowed her foster mother to get close enough to hug her before.

"I dunno. I guess."

For a minute, none of them said anything or made any move. Then Tamara moved over to face the wall and put her hands up. Sardis gave her a thorough pat-down and didn't find anything. Mrs. Henson got up and Sardis stepped her through a pat-down as well.

Tamara and Mrs. Henson looked at each other. Mrs. Henson reached out tentatively to touch Tamara on the shoulder. Tamara was uncertain. She waited for the rush of anger and anxiety, but it didn't come. She swallowed once and breathed shallowly, just feeling Mrs. Henson's warm hand on her shoulder. Mrs. Henson reached out with the other hand, reaching around Tamara to embrace her. Tamara put her arms out tentatively, not sure where to put them. The awkwardness was just magnified by the fact that Sardis was watching them like a hawk, just waiting for one of them to make a suspicious move.

Mrs. Henson pulled Tamara gently toward her, and then against her, their warm bodies meeting. Tamara tightened her grip.

"It's going to be okay," Mrs. Henson murmured. "I know this has been so hard on you but it will all work out. Things will get better. I'll do whatever I can to help you."

Tamara nestled in her arms. She hadn't had a hug like that, a real hug, since her Gran had died. So long ago, she could hardly remember it. How it felt to feel warm and safe and protected.

Tears flooded her eyes without warning. She gasped, her diaphragm jumping jerkily. She tried to control the sobs, but couldn't.

"Sh, it's okay. It's okay, Tamara."

"I just want... I want to feel better. Like I used to be. But everything is gone bad. Nothing..." She tried to catch her breath, her chest and stomach jumping with each gasp. "Nothing is ever going to be right again!"

"You're making progress." Mrs. Henson rubbed her back soothingly. "I know it's slow and it's hard to see, but you are. You've had so much to process. You've had so much trauma, and then the pregnancy and psychosis. But you are doing good. You calling me, telling me that you need help? You would never have done that before, would you?"

Tamara shook her head. "No." Her voice was muffled from pressing her face against Mrs. Henson.

"No. You didn't trust me. You couldn't ask me for anything, because I might say no, or I might hurt you and take advantage of you." Her grip on Tamara tightened, giving her a squeeze. "You would never have let me touch you."

Tamara agreed.

"It's better if you can trust and reach out to people. Because people can help. You might feel like you're alone, but there are people who want to help you. I promise."

"What can you do?" Tamara snuffled and swallowed. "You can't make them change their mind about the baby."

"No. But you're almost at the finish line with this pregnancy. At this point, he's viable. You're just giving him a little more time in the nest, to get nice and strong."

Tamara tensed. She reacted viscerally to the thought of the baby getting stronger. She didn't want the life inside of her getting stronger than she was. Overpowering her. It already kicked her until she was sure all of her internal organs were black and blue with bruises. It controlled her thoughts. It made her crave things she hated and get sick from things she used to like. She didn't want it growing and strengthening until it tore its way out of her like some horror movie sequence.

"It's okay," Mrs. Henson soothed. "It will be okay."

Tamara clung to her. "I'm scared."

"Of course you are! Everybody is scared with their first pregnancy. And sometimes scared with every one of them. It's a big, scary thing. And yours is even bigger and scarier than normal, isn't it?"

Tamara shuddered. "Yes."

"I'm going to have to ask you to sit down now," Sardis said. "Before someone happens by and I get in major trouble."

Mrs. Henson helped guide Tamara into one of the two chairs Sardis had left in the room. Tamara sat with her arms around her belly, squeezing. The baby kicked strongly against her.

"Has anyone talked to you about what is going to happen when you go into labor?" Mrs. Henson asked. "I mean... physically?"

Tamara shook her head. "I know, though," she said, and sniffled. "I've seen on TV."

"Well, it isn't quite the same, seeing it on TV and going through it yourself."

"Yeah. I guess not."

"Is it okay if I bring you some pregnancy and birthing books? Would that be okay?"

"They have to be softcover."

"I know. But it wouldn't upset you more? It would help if you knew a bit more about what to expect. You wouldn't be so scared."

Tamara sniffled again and wiped her face with the backs of her wrists. "Yeah. Okay."

"It's scary, but you don't have to go through this alone. I'll help however I can. And so will others."

"You can't be here, though," Tamara pointed out. "When I... when it... comes out."

"I know. But I'll prepare you the best I can and visit often. And after he's born, I'll still come see you."

Tamara took a long breath, trying to settle the hitching sobs. "Okay."

THIRTY-ONE

EVEN THOUGH TAMARA HAD been so impatient to get the baby out of her, labor still came too soon. She wasn't ready. She didn't know what to do. She hadn't finished reading all of the books yet.

At first, it was just back pains, like she'd been having for weeks, only worse. Tamara paced up and down the hall, arching her back and trying not to groan aloud. She stopped and pressed her back to the wall, trying to straighten out the bowing in her spine. She would never take for granted the comfort of not having a backache again.

"Go lie down," Nurse Mary Anne urged. "You look beat. Get some rest."

"I can't."

"Do you need a hand?"

"No. I just want to get this done with." Tamara hunched forward, trying to ease a cramp. She squeezed herself hard, holding her breath.

Mary Anne looked at her with brows drawn down. "Are you okay?"

"Just... a cramp..."

"Come on. I'll walk you to your bed. You should be lying down if you're not feeling well."

The nurses in the units were used to dealing with psychiatric symptoms and minor medical procedures. Tamara had seen Mary Anne and others react competently in situations that made the guards blanch. But they seemed to be squeamish about Tamara's pregnancy. Tamara understood. She, too, was afraid of what was going to happen. What would happen once the invader was out of her. After all that they had done to make sure that she got pregnant and took the pregnancy full-term, they must have something terrible planned for when the baby arrived.

"I don't want to lay down. I want to walk."

"Well... that's not exactly what you're doing," Mary Anne pointed out. "You're kind of stuck here."

"Just... until... it passes." Tamara held her breath as the cramp grew, threatening to split her in half. She groaned.

Mary Anne was starting to look concerned. "Uh, honey...?"

"What?"

"Are you in labor?"

Tamara groaned again. She braced herself against the wall with one hand, her other pressed under her belly.

"No. Just cramps."

The nurse hovered over her, not moving on to do her rounds or whatever other jobs she was supposed to be working on. The cramp started to ease and Tamara took a few deep breaths.

"Okay. Okay. It's fine."

"Come on, let's get you to your room. I have a sneaking suspicion..."

Tamara walked back down the hall toward her bunk, Mary Anne right at her elbow, clucking over her worriedly. Tamara sat down on her bed, then lay down, easing her back slowly into the bunk. She breathed a sigh of relief.

"That's good. I feel fine now. Everything is fine."

Mary Anne stood with her hands on her hips. "Are you sure?"

"Yes," Tamara hissed, exasperated. "I just said I'm fine. Get off my case."

"I'll be back to check on you."

Tamara closed her eyes and waited for the nurse to leave. She'd only been gone for a couple of minutes when Tamara's back started to ache again, so badly that she had to roll onto her side to rub it, trying to straighten it out and calm all of the muscles and nerves.

Then the abdominal cramps started again and she squirmed, holding herself and trying to find a more comfortable position. When Mary Anne came back some time later, Tamara had been through several more cycles of pain and had to admit defeat.

"I think... maybe I *am* in labor," she admitted.

Mary Anne nodded. "I thought as much."

"But... I'm not ready. I don't know what to do!"

"Aren't you the one who has been complaining for months that you just want this baby out of you?"

"Yeah... but... not like this."

"That's the way it works, hon'."

Tamara moaned.

"I'll call the infirmary. They can send someone down to see to you."

"What about... going to hospital? Shouldn't I go to the hospital?"

"There's no point in rushing these things. Chances are, it's going to take a day or two. Having you at the hospital is a security problem. We'll wait until you're ready to actually have the baby."

"But I'm in labor now."

"And probably for the next two days. There's no hurry."

"Two days?" Tamara demanded. "I can't put up with this for two days!"

Mary Anne shrugged. "This isn't TV. It's not going to come

in fifteen minutes. I'll let the infirmary know. They'll send someone down to monitor you."

Tamara attempted to prop herself up, but was crushed by another contraction and fell back. "Tell them I want a C-section! I don't want to do this for two days!"

The nurse shook her head. "You can talk to them when they get here. But they can't do a Caesarian here. That's surgical."

Tamara groaned, both at her words and the contraction. It released its hold on her, and she lay still, puffing and groaning. Mary Anne walked to the door, but didn't leave. She looked down the hallway for someone else. Tamara watched her with a frown, wondering why she didn't go.

Mary Anne flagged someone down. Tamara couldn't hear what they were saying in murmured voices, other than the line "keep an eye on her" as Mary Anne looked back at Tamara.

Burgess walked in. He didn't look any too excited about watching Tamara have her baby. He stood as far from the bed as he could, but was faithful to Mary Anne's orders and kept watch over Tamara.

* * *

WHEN A COUPLE of interns from the infirmary finally got there and looked in on Tamara, she was half sitting up, sweat pouring off her face, as she tried to breathe through the pain of contractions that seemed to come one on top of the other. She didn't have the energy or attention to glare at them for taking so long to get there. She was wondering how she was going to get through the next two days. She was exhausted after just a couple of hours.

Burgess was mad enough for both of them. "What took you so long? I'm standing here thinking I'm going to have to deliver this baby myself!"

"We got here in plenty of time," a black-haired woman said with unconcern.

She shuffled past Burgess to take a look at Tamara.

"How's it coming along?" she asked cheerfully, moving close to Tamara.

"It hurts like hell!"

"I'm sure it does," the woman agreed in a saccharine voice that annoyed Tamara like fingernails on the blackboard. "Maybe we could get the room?" she suggested to Burgess.

"You're welcome to it," he growled, and walked out. He pushed the door shut behind him.

The two interns helped Tamara out of her jumpsuit and pulled a sheet over her; then the black-haired woman was able to check how the labor was progressing. Her manner changed abruptly.

"Uh—we're going to be delivering this baby," she told her counterpart.

"I'll call the hospital."

"You can call them, but we can't get her transported fast enough for them to deliver it. She's having it here and now."

Tamara gasped for breath. "I *told* you!"

"How long have you been in labor?" the male intern asked. "I thought the nurse said that you'd only been having contractions for a couple of hours." He turned to the woman. "I'm sure she can wait until we get her to the hospital. With an ambulance, it won't take any time—"

"What am I supposed to do?" Tamara demanded. "Cross my legs?"

"Sh, you're going to be just fine—" the woman started.

"I'd rather have Burgess deliver it than you! Can you just lose the lovey-dovey voice?"

The woman closed her mouth, looking at Tamara with a pronounced frown. Tamara didn't care how mad she was. She just couldn't stand to listen to the falsely sweet voice for another second.

"You can notify the hospital," the woman told her partner. "That they will be getting mother and newborn, not a laboring mom. And then sanitize and get ready, because this baby isn't waiting for anyone."

The two interns went to work, faces serious. They had brought a couple of medical duffels with them, and had apparently packed well, as Tamara didn't hear any complaints about their missing anything they needed. Not that they needed much more than clean hands, because the monster that had been growing inside of Tamara was soon to make its way into the world, ready or not. For a minute, Tamara lost her breath, worrying about what was going to happen to her after he was born, but she tried to buckle down and focus on the job at hand. She had desperately wanted the baby out, and at least she'd be able to be free of him and his poisonous influence.

"I want you to push the next time," the woman intern told Tamara. "One or two more big contractions, and we'll have him out."

"What do you think I've been doing?"

"Push hard. It won't be much longer now."

Tamara swore under her breath. It was a wonder laboring women everywhere didn't kill their doctors or midwives. She could think of little other than what she would do if she could get her hands on the woman.

"Push!"

"Shut up!"

The intern stopped giving Tamara instructions and just waited. Tamara pushed and labored, sure that she was going to split right open if she had to push any harder or longer.

"There we go," the intern approved. "Here he comes."

Tamara collapsed back onto the bed. She couldn't see what

the two interns were doing. It wasn't like at the hospital where they had mirrors or monitors for her to watch.

The baby's squall was hoarse and deep, nothing like Julie's cries. Tamara tried to see him, alarmed by the noise. There was obviously something very wrong with him. But the intern was smiling as she bundled him up and held him in her arms, as proud as if she had delivered him herself. She didn't give any indication at all that he was monstrous. But then, she was probably in on it. She wouldn't give away to Tamara that there was anything wrong, so that they could go ahead and do whatever weird experiments they had in mind.

"I want to see it," Tamara said. "What's wrong with it?"

"It's a little boy," the intern said. "And he looks like he's perfectly healthy. Here."

She got closer to Tamara's head and tilted the little bundle to show her.

Tamara stared at the baby. The intern was right, he looked perfectly normal and healthy. But Tamara knew that there was something wrong with him. He couldn't have controlled her brain and given her hallucinations if he were normal. He was some kind of mutant or horrific experiment gone wrong. Just because he looked normal, that didn't mean that he was.

The baby's hair was very dark, his eyes blue, open and staring short-sightedly in Tamara's direction. Tamara gulped and looked away, not wanting to get hypnotized or to let him control her mind, now that he was out.

"Do you want to hold him?" the intern asked.

"No," the man snapped, "she's not allowed to."

The woman turned to him, rolling her eyes. "I really don't think she's going to do anything to hurt him. Everyone is just overreacting." She looked at Tamara. "You wouldn't do anything to him, would you?"

Tamara swallowed and nodded. "I probably would."

The woman's eyebrows went up and her eyes got wider. She looked at her partner for some kind of reassurance, but he just spread his hands in a shrug. "She tried to dig him out of her belly with her bare hands," he pointed out baldly. "What is it about that that makes you think she'll behave herself now?"

"But…"

"I don't want to hold it," Tamara said. She held up her hands to prevent any further discussion of the matter. "I don't want it near me."

"Once you held him, you would change your mind. You'd have completely different feelings about him."

"No."

"We're not supposed to," the male intern repeated. "I don't know why you're even discussing it. We were given specific direction."

The woman obviously didn't believe in obeying order just for the sake of it. She shook her head in irritation and headed for the door. "I'll see how that ambulance is coming."

Tamara watched her open the cell door and walk out into the hallway with the baby. She rested her head on her pillow.

"Thanks," she told the man, who had stayed with her.

"We were given orders," he repeated. "I don't know what she was thinking."

"I'd probably kill it," Tamara said.

The man's eyes widened at this assertion.

"But Zobel said I shouldn't," Tamara said in a quieter voice. She wasn't sure if he even heard that part.

* * *

THE AMBULANCE DIDN'T GET THERE for some time, and things were held up as the guards and paramedics discussed Tamara's case and how to best keep her secure for the transport and while she was at the hospital. No one bothered to ask

Tamara if she were going to behave herself and not cause them any problems, like they had when she was going to the courthouse in the prison bus. They knew better now. They knew they had to prepare for every eventuality, because her behavior would be unpredictable and she might try to do something to harm herself or the baby.

"I don't like the four piece suit," Burgess said, speaking of the shackles and chains that Tamara had worn for her courthouse transfers. "It's just going to make it harder for the doctor at the hospital to examine her, and every time we have to unlock her to facilitate a doctor, it's a security risk."

"What would you suggest?" one of the medics asked.

"Handcuff to the side of the gurney. That's the simplest, and it can be left locked while she's attended to."

"I don't know..." Mary Anne said. "I don't like the idea of her having the other hand free. When she gets violent... she could still do damage with one hand free. If she grabs someone or something that she can use to harm herself. She could even flip the gurney."

Burgess looked at her. "What, then?"

"We should at least handcuff both wrists. One to each side, so she doesn't have the freedom of movement to cause problems."

"Can they still do an exam with both wrists chained?"

"I don't see why not. And if they need to undo one hand-cuff, they can just undo one, and then do it back up again right away. It isn't a big procedure like with the shackles and belly chain."

"Does she really need to be transferred?" Burgess asked. "It seems like she's doing just fine. Can't they just keep an eye on her in the infirmary, instead of transferring her somewhere that's not secure?"

"They are not experienced in post-natal," the woman intern chimed in, shaking her head. "I don't want to miss a blood clot or hemorrhage. If everything looks okay, they'll be sending her back within twenty-four hours. I really wouldn't want to take the chance of missing anything."

Tamara drifted a little as they continued to discuss the pros and cons of each method of restraining her, until they finally agreed on the two-handcuff suggestion and transferred her to the gurney in question.

"What about the baby?" she asked. "How are you going to keep it secure?"

One of the paramedics laughed. Everyone else just looked at Tamara, eyes wary.

"The handcuffs won't fit him," Tamara pointed out. "How are you going to make sure that he doesn't do anything dangerous?"

"The baby isn't a security risk," Burgess said, shaking his head and rolling his eyes at the others to express how crazy she was.

"He came out of me. How could he not be?"

"You're freaking nuts, French."

"Exactly."

Eventually, they were convinced that Tamara was secure, as was the baby, and the paramedics wheeled her out to the waiting ambulance. Tamara could see faces pressed to the windows of the General building.

To the paramedics' consternation, Burgess insisted on entering the ambulance first to inspect the interior and drill them on any items that might be within Tamara's reach, limited though it was by her handcuffs. He insisted on riding in back where he could keep an eye on her. It was technically against regulations, but he insisted, and the paramedics were getting so wound up over how dangerous a criminal Tamara must be that they conceded. Burgess was squashed into a corner of the ambulance so that he would be able to take action if Tamara did anything.

After they lifted the gurney up into the ambulance, Tamara

closed her eyes to have a nap. Because she was just that kind of dangerous criminal.

As it turned out, the ride in the ambulance was too bumpy and her body too tender for her to get any rest on the way to the hospital. It was like riding in Gran's old Chevy with no shocks or suspension, and appendicitis thrown in just for fun.

THIRTY-TWO

S HE WASN'T IN AND out of the hospital in a few hours. The doctors there wanted to keep her under observation at least overnight. Social services was taking a long time to get there to deal with the baby, so the two of them were settled into a room in maternity to be watched over by the nurses and maybe looked in at by a doctor in the morning.

Tired as she was, Tamara was restless and anxious about being in the same room as the baby all night. She heard every time he moved. Her body, not in alignment with her brain, thought that she should be nursing him. She would lie still for a few minutes, and just start to relax or to drift off to sleep, when he would start fussing moving in the bassinet, jolting her into immediate awareness.

And when he cried, in that funny, hoarse bass, Tamara went into panic mode.

"You have to stop it," she told Anderson, the guard who had been assigned to monitor her overnight. She yanked on the handcuffs, making them clatter loudly, which sent the baby into louder cries of distress. "Stop it, stop it! Can't you make it stop crying?" Tears came to her own eyes. "Please, you have to stop it!"

"The nurse said she would come and feed him. She'll be here in a few minutes. He'll be okay until then."

Tamara fought against the handcuffs, trying to slide them down the guardrail so she would be able to get closer to the baby to try to quiet him.

"Please!" she insisted. "Please pick it up and try to stop it. Just... just anything. Put your hand over its mouth. Make it stop."

He looked at her, his expression serious. "You need to lie back down. With your head up where it belongs. No more moving around. Just stay still."

"*Then* will you pick it up? Its crying is so loud!"

"He's a baby, they cry. I've heard louder!"

He waited for her to get back into position and then looked over at the crying baby in the bassinet. "Babies are not in my pay grade."

"Please, just do it. Just this once."

"Just this once? You think that he's only going to cry once during the night?"

"Please..."

Anderson went over to the bassinet and slid his fingers under the crying baby, supporting its huge, heavy head and bringing it up gently to his shoulder, trying to find a place between buttons and insignia where nothing would scratch his tender skin. The baby's cries quieted and he rooted around, looking for milk. Tamara watched, terrified he was going to start crying again. Anderson patted him lightly on the back and jiggled, trying to keep him calm. "Dinner is coming, little guy. Won't be much longer now. The nurse is getting you a nice warm bottle and then you'll be happy."

Tamara couldn't pull her eyes away from him. "Do you have kids?"

"Yes. Three boys." A smile that she had never seen before crossed his face, thinking about his little family.

"Wow. Three boys. How old?"

"Four, two, and three months. Two in diapers. They keep us busy."

Three children. Tamara had been run off her feet taking care of two. What if his wife decided that she couldn't manage three that little? Why had he made her pregnant three times so close together? Didn't he understand how difficult it was? Didn't he know what could happen if she got overwhelmed?

"You should..."

He looked up from the baby's head to Tamara's face. "What?"

"I don't know. That's too many. You should give one of them to someone else. You shouldn't make your wife deal with so much."

He raised his brows. "You don't know anything about it. She loves being a mom and we could never give up any of our kids." He shook his head. "People don't just give their children away because they take time and energy to take care of."

The baby hiccupped and made noises, making a knot in Tamara's stomach. Then the nurse finally got there with a small bottle for the baby.

"Well, look at this," she said with a smile. "How about I just give you the bottle and you take care of him?"

Anderson carefully handed the baby to her. "I'm not actually supposed to be doing this."

"He would have been fine to wait for a few minutes." The nurse cradled the baby and offered him the nipple, and he immediately started sucking as if his life depended on it. "You don't need to worry about letting him cry."

"It wasn't him I was worried about."

The nurse's eyes went to Tamara. She didn't know all of Tamara's history, of course. She didn't know what she was convicted of, or the details of her psychosis and delusions. "He would be just fine," she told Tamara, drawing her words out as if she had to speak extra clearly to Tamara for her to understand. "You don't need to worry about us not taking care of your little guy, Mom."

"I just don't want it to cry," Tamara snapped. "I can't... I can't stand listening to it cry."

The nurse's expression hardened. She looked down into the baby's face as she fed him. "Well, he's a hungry little fellow. He's got a good, strong suck."

Anderson looked at Tamara. "Why don't you try to sleep now?" he suggested. "He'll be quiet for a couple of hours now that he's been fed. You need to get your sleep."

Tamara nodded. She closed her eyes and tried to relax.

* * *

MRS. HENSON WAS ALLOWED to visit Tamara in her hospital room. She sat a distance away as dictated by the guard. She talked to the baby in the bassinet, cooing over how sweet he was. "Isn't he just perfect? Babies are such a miracle, they amaze me every time."

Tamara stared at the ceiling, doing her best to ignore it.

"What do you think of him?" Mrs. Henson persisted.

Tamara shook her head. "I don't know why they made me have it. I'm not going to do anything. I'm not going to fall into their trap."

Mrs. Henson raised her eyebrows. Tamara recognized the signal that she was saying something she shouldn't, and closed her mouth, lapsing into silence.

"How are you feeling?"

"Sore and tired. Glad it's out of me." Tamara rubbed her belly, feeling the ropy scars she had torn there. They itched, and she had to be careful not to scratch them, worried she would peel away the skin. "You can hold it if you want." She looked over at Sardis. "If he says it's okay."

Sardis nodded. "Go ahead," he agreed.

Tamara watched Mrs. Henson closely as she slid her fingers under the baby and picked him up. He was starting to get restless and Tamara didn't know how long it would be until the nurse got there with a bottle for him. Mrs. Henson knew all about babies and hopefully, she would be able to keep him quiet until then.

"Hello, little boy," Mrs. Henson murmured, gazing down at him with a gentle smile.

Tamara wanted to tell her to watch out; to guard herself and be sure that she didn't get trapped by him. Not to get pulled into whatever trap they were trying to lay for her.

"Have you decided on a name? Or what you're going to do?"

"No. I don't want to give it a name." That might give it power over her. "And I don't want it."

Mrs. Henson looked disappointed. "That's really too bad. I was hoping that once you saw him, your feelings would be different. Few people can resist the pull of a newborn."

The knot in Tamara's guts tightened. She felt sick watching Mrs. Henson with the baby. "Maybe you shouldn't be holding it..."

Mrs. Henson laughed. "It's okay, Tamara. I didn't mean it that way. He's not going to do anything to me."

"We don't know that. We don't know what they've done to him. He could be some kind of mutant..."

"He's a perfectly lovely little baby. He's not a mutant."

Mrs. Henson was still there, relaxed as she watched the baby and fed him his bottle, when the social worker finally showed her face. She was a narrow, stern-faced woman, who made no apology for being there a day late. She looked over the room.

"I'm Mrs. Arbiter," she introduced herself briskly, flicking the ID sleeve hanging at her neck. "So, this is the little fellow who has caused all of this fuss." She looked the baby over. She was not pulled in by his glamour, Tamara was relieved to see, but remained dispassionate.

Mrs. Henson looked up from the baby and smiled.

"Oh, it's you, Marion." Mrs. Arbiter said with a note of surprise. She blinked, trying to work it out. "Tamara French isn't one of your girls...?" She obviously knew that Tamara was in custody, so she wasn't one of Mrs. Henson's foster children.

"Not right now," Mrs. Henson said. "She was for a bit and I'm hoping that she will make parole in a couple of months and that we can swing things..."

Mrs. Arbiter considered this. "Is she interested in keeping the baby, then? I was given to understand..."

"No," Tamara said strongly, trying to discourage all such talk. "I don't want to see it again."

She saw a look pass between Mrs. Henson and Mrs. Arbiter.

"She may feel differently after a while," Mrs. Henson said. "I'll explain later."

A small nod from Mrs. Arbiter. "Give me a call. And let me know if she makes parole and has a change of heart."

"Of course." Mrs. Henson pulled the bottle out of the baby's slack mouth and lifted him to her shoulder to burp him.

They had a low conversation while Mrs. Henson finished up with the baby, talking about girls and babies they had both known and giving updates on them. Tamara waited, wondering if they would ever take the baby away, or if their plan were to wear her down with their chatter until she could no longer stand it.

Finally, Mrs. Henson gave the sleeping baby a kiss on the forehead and nestled him into the baby carrier Mrs. Arbiter had brought with her.

"Goodbye, little fellow. Maybe I'll see you again..."

Tamara breathed a long sigh of relief as the baby was finally taken out of her room. Mrs. Henson stayed in her seat, her expression distant. After a few minutes, she blinked and looked at Tamara.

"You're probably too tired right now, but we *should* talk about parole before long. You're going to be up before the board again and they'll want to know your plans."

"They're not going to let me out," Tamara said. "Would you let some dangerous psycho juvie out to terrorize the town? They're not that stupid."

"I think things may change." Mrs. Henson shifted and got up. "I should be getting on my way. They'll be wanting to move you back to the facility." She didn't get any closer to Tamara's bed, didn't touch her or hug her before making her departure. "We'll talk again soon, okay?"

Tamara nodded. "Okay. See you."

Mrs. Henson gave a little wave, and was gone.

## THIRTY-THREE

TAMARA WOKE UP AND rubbed her eyes, lying in bed and listening to the sounds of the unit around her. There was yelling down the hall; Brinkley, Tamara thought, still having problems despite all of her med changes.

She ran through the events of the previous few days in her mind, rubbing a belly that was returning to its former shape much more slowly than she would have liked. It wasn't until she had reviewed everything up to her release from the hospital and transfer back to juvie that Tamara realized she had been able to hold the timeline in her head without anything shifting. She sat up slowly, stretching her mind further back, to recall the previous months' events, again with no disorienting changes or confusion.

When the nurse came around with Tamara's breakfast, she found the inmate ready and waiting for her.

"Can I get an appointment with Dr. Sutherland? I think... I want to talk to him."

"I'll put in a request," the nurse agreed. She handed Tamara her breakfast tray. Tamara took the piece of toast and considered the rest of her breakfast, hungry instead of nauseated, for once.

"Can I wait until after I see him to take my meds?"

The nurse frowned at her. "Why?"

"I don't think I need them anymore. If he says to keep taking them, I will," she added hurriedly. "I'm not saying I won't, just that... I want to talk to Dr. Sutherland first."

"I have no idea when you're going to be able to get in to see him. So no, you're going to have to take them now. You have to come off of anti-psychotics slowly, anyway, so even if Dr. Sutherland decided you didn't need them anymore," the nurse's expression clearly indicated that she thought this a very long shot, "he wouldn't let you just stop taking them today. They have to be reduced gradually."

She handed Tamara the little cup of pills. Tamara took it and downed them, showing that she wasn't going to argue or be hard to get along with. The nurse scowled, apparently not impressed. "Let me see your hands."

Tamara displayed empty hands.

"And your mouth."

Tamara opened her mouth, stuck out her tongue, pulled out each cheek, and swiped a finger around the inside of each cheek, demonstrating that she had, in fact, swallowed the pills rather than cheeking them.

"Okay," the nurse agreed grudgingly. "I'll set something up with Dr. Sutherland and he can decide what changes need to be made."

* * *

"WHY DON'T you tell me how you feel about your baby, now?" Dr. Sutherland inquired, folding his hands on his desk and looking at Tamara with piercing eyes.

Tamara shifted uncomfortably in the chair. Still on her cocktail of meds, she was restless, but tried to sit still and prove to Dr.

Sutherland that she was perfectly lucid and the meds could be dropped.

"I don't know..." she said honestly. "I *don't* believe that he is a monster implanted in me by the administration..."

Sutherland smiled. "Well, that's progress."

"But I don't... I don't feel anything for him. I mean, like a mother should feel about her baby. I just don't know..."

"You didn't really have the opportunity to bond, so I wouldn't expect you to have strong maternal feelings for him."

"No?" His words gave Tamara some measure of relief. Maybe she didn't need to feel like a bad person for not having warm feelings for her baby. "I don't know how I'd feel if I saw him now. I wouldn't think he was an alien or monster... but... I don't know..."

"It isn't like you planned the pregnancy or that it was a happy surprise."

"It screwed me up pretty bad."

"Do you blame the baby for what you went through?"

Tamara scratched the knee of her uniform and didn't answer immediately. "I think... I can blame the pregnancy hormones or whatever, and not blame him. I know it's not *his* fault, because it happened once before." She paused, waiting for the paranoid theories to start flooding into her brain. That maybe this was the second time they had implanted this creature into her... but she was able to think it through logically and not spin off into conspiracies. She took a breath and listened to the beating of her heart, calm instead of erratic and trying to pound its way out of her chest.

"You are doing well," Dr. Sutherland said, nodding slowly. "You're much calmer."

Tamara nodded. "I can think. And not be scared and angry all the time. It's like..." she massaged her temples with her index fingers, "like I've got my own brain back again."

"We're going to need to watch for any warning signs. You

obviously have a propensity for psychosis. Things other than pregnancy may trigger it. Stress, illness, sleep deprivation... We may find that you still need a low dose antipsychotic just to ensure your stability. We'll dial it back slowly."

Tamara nodded. Even though she wanted to be off of the meds that made her so tired and restless, she didn't want to take the chance of sliding back into that sinkhole.

"You're lucky," Dr. Sutherland said. "Most people with psychosis don't get to 'go back' to what they were like before. They might get relief through medications but, as you've found, medications have their own set of problems."

"Yeah." Dr. Sutherland was right about her being one of the lucky ones. She knew how it had felt, thinking that she would never be able to be well again. "I just hope... it stays that way. Not like some of the girls who keep coming back to Forensic."

"One day at a time," Dr. Sutherland advised. "And although the delusions seem to be subsiding, you may still have other issues. Mood. PTSD." He shrugged. "We'll just have to take it slow and pay attention."

"Okay."

"That means you need to let me know what's going on in there." Dr. Sutherland tapped his own head with one finger. "You have always played it pretty close to the vest."

Tamara's face warmed and she looked down at her feet. "Yeah. I know."

"It shouldn't take having a complete breakdown for us to know there's a problem."

* * *

FOR HER TRANSFER back to General Population, Tamara had to put up with the full shackles and chains, in spite of the fact that she wasn't leaving the prison grounds, but only being walked from one building to another. Burgess was the one to get her all locked up, and Tamara was pleased to see that the guard from General who had come to escort her back was Zobel.

"Hey," she greeted softly, unsure of how to talk to him after all of the messes he had seen her through.

"French," Zobel's voice was clipped. "I assume you aren't going to cause me any problems this time."

Tamara opened her mouth, surprised by his manner. Zobel gave her a quick grin to reassure her.

"Oh. No, no trouble," Tamara agreed.

He made a show of checking all of the chains and locks, then nodded at Burgess. "I'll take her from here."

He led her from the building and across the compound. "Glad to be coming home?"

Tamara took a deep breath of the cool morning air.

"Yeah. I guess I am. But it's going to be weird after Forensic."

"I imagine you'll get a little attention from the others, until you're settled back in again."

Tamara thought back to the gangs, the posturing, the politics of the unit, and sighed. "Yeah. I guess so."

"Well, just take it easy. Don't overreact. It will pass."

Tamara gave a little laugh. "Are you saying *don't* flip the breakfast table into Lewis's lap?"

Zobel chuckled. "Nice to have you back. Yeah. Little things like that tend to inflame the situation. Lewis is gone, by the way."

Tamara turned her head to read his face. "Killed? Transferred?"

"Released. Finished out her sentence. So she won't be gunning for you."

"Good. Though there's whoever took over the Sharks after her..."

"There's always someone waiting to take over."

"Long as it's not Blacksnake." Tamara looked at him. "It's not Blacksnake, right?"

"No. That girl doesn't have what it takes to be top dog. Despite what she might think about herself."

"All right." Tamara nodded, steeling herself and pretending she didn't feel the tightening in her gut. "It will be good. Everything will be back to normal."

Whatever normal was.

**Did you enjoy this book? Reviews and recommendations are vital to making a book successful.**

**Please leave a review at your favorite book store or review site and share it with your friends.**

Don't miss the following bonus material:
Sign up for mailing list to get a free ebook
Read a sneak preview chapter
Other books by P.D. Workman
Learn more about the author

Sign up for my mailing list at pdworkman.com and get Gluten-Free Murder for free!

# PREVIEW OF VANISHING TEARDROPS

ONE

TAMARA SAT IN FRONT of the parole board, feeling like a bug under a magnifying glass. Everyone in the room had watched her enter the room. She stumbled, suddenly forgetting how to walk normally, too conscious of her feet and legs. Gomez directed her into the lone chair waiting front and center, as if she might not know where she was supposed to go otherwise.

She was in her orange uniform. They didn't get civvies for appearing in front of the board. It wasn't like she had anyone to fool, anyone who would think that she was not a convicted felon. Not like when she appeared in court and they were concerned that the jury not be influenced by the fact that she was a criminal. Though that had never turned out well. Her court appearances had been unmitigated disasters.

They had trusted her to appear in court to testify against the monsters and she had failed, her psychosis worsened by the stress. She didn't know what the verdicts had been in the cases against Mr. Baker and Glock, but she hadn't helped the prosecutor like they had expected her to. But that was all in the past. There was nothing she could do about it months later.

"Tamara French," one of the parole board members said crisply, looking down at the papers in front of her. She was an older woman, probably a retired judge, deep frown lines carved in her face. Tamara had wondered whether she would know anyone on the board, but the faces were unfamiliar to her. People who didn't know her personally and wouldn't care whether she stayed in juvie or got out on parole. They were supposed to be unbiased, but Tamara didn't suppose they would be starting with the opinion that she was a good little girl who had just gotten mixed up in something that was beyond her control. "Convicted of two counts of murder. Released on parole last year, but violated and returned to custody," the woman summarized.

Tamara nodded stiffly and swallowed, a lump in her throat.

Everyone was silent. Tamara looked around, waiting for someone to say something. Her first parole board had been pretty warm toward her. She'd had an exemplary record before her release a year before. But that had all changed and the board undoubtedly knew it.

As awkward as it had been to have them all looking at her when she entered the room, it was worse to have them all looking at their papers and files as if she weren't sitting right there in front of her. Why wouldn't they look at her? Had they already decided, without even talking to her, without even hearing any evidence from anyone else, that they were going to turn her down? If they had already decided, why didn't they just say so and send her back away without going through a charade first?

"Why don't you tell us why you violated last time?" the frowning woman inquired. The way she said it made Tamara feel stupid for not offering up the information herself without prompting. But she had been following the rules she had been given when her lawyer had tried to prepare her to testify in court. Don't offer anything. Wait until a question is asked. Only answer what is asked and nothing more.

"Uh..." Tamara cleared her throat. She needed to sound

confident, not like a little girl, so she forced some strength into her voice. She imagined she was talking to one of the guards or one of the other juvies, not someone who controlled where her life was going to go for the next year. "I made some mistakes… I was contacted by an old cellmate and I didn't say anything to my PO. I was afraid he'd send me back." She shrugged helplessly. "I made a lot of stupid choices. I… didn't think it was going to be so hard."

"And how are things going to be any different this time?" It was a man who asked this; short, balding, peering at his papers through his glasses and then at Tamara over the rims.

Tamara concentrated on not saying 'uh' or 'um' again. They wanted her to be clear and concise, to give the impression that she was being honest and up front and was intelligent enough to change what had gone wrong the last time and over the last year of her incarceration.

"I know I need to use my PO as a resource. Not to treat him as an enemy. I know that he's there to help me, not just there to slap me back in juvie the first chance."

Tamara closed her eyes briefly, fighting back the memories of Glock telling her the system was rigged against her. That the whole thing was just a way to make it look like they were giving felons a chance when all they intended to do was revoke her parole and send her back at the first opportunity. She couldn't believe that. She had to believe Mrs. Henson and Zobel and the other people who wanted to help her. Collins was the one who had told her he would speak for her when she came before the parole board again. He'd had to send her back to juvie after everything she had done, but he said he'd speak for her.

But Tamara had taken a quick glance around the room as she was directed to the hot seat in the middle of the room. Collins wasn't sitting up at the front with the board and he hadn't been sitting in the spectator seating. Tamara's eyes had been drawn to a woman there, square jawed, her blond hair pulled back into a ponytail, who Tamara didn't recognize. She hadn't been able to see the woman's face, only the back of her head, but she wasn't familiar. Mrs. Henson was there. But there was no long-legged, bald black man. If Collins had been there, he would have been obvious. Tamara fought back the disappointment over his no-show. Would the board still consider giving her a second shot at parole so soon if he weren't there to speak up for her?

"Miss French."

Tamara opened her eyes and looked at the board members. The frowning woman was speaking again.

"Your record since you were returned to custody has been interesting... and not in a good way."

"Yes, ma'am."

"I'm surprised that you would even apply for parole again after what's taken place over the past year."

Tamara swallowed and shifted in her seat. It would have been nice if they'd at least given her a drink of water. Surely everyone who sat in that hot seat must have a mouth as dry as hers. Were they intentionally making her as uncomfortable as they could?

"The staff encouraged me to apply," she said. "There should be letters there from Dr. Sutherland about my... problems... and from other administrators..."

A couple of the board members shuffled papers, but everyone had undoubtedly read them already.

"Dr. Sutherland suggests that your psychosis was triggered by your pregnancy. A pregnancy that you kept a secret until it was too late to deal with it."

"I didn't know I was pregnant."

"I see. I've never heard of psychosis being triggered by pregnancy before."

Tamara shrugged. "It's rare." What else could she say about it?

"So that means you're not responsible for any of the

violent incidents on your record during the past year?" challenged another woman on the board. She had long hair in a straight, severe style and slashes of red blush along her cheekbones. She reminded Tamara a little of one of her fifth-grade teachers, a dragon of a woman who had scared Tamara to death.

Tamara looked down the line of the parole board, trying to analyze their reactions. Things were not going well. Dr. Sutherland and the others had assured her that once the board knew that her problems had been the result of psychosis with an identified trigger, there would be no problem. They could ignore those incidents completely.

"I know I did a lot of things that were wrong or bizarre..." Tamara said slowly. "It's hard to explain what was going on in my head at the time... but my thoughts weren't right. I saw and heard things... hallucinations... and I was really paranoid. I thought... there were plots against me... I couldn't control my reactions..."

She had expected further probes from the dragon-woman. Snide comments, disdain, and disbelief. But the woman was quiet, making notes along with the rest of the board members.

"Which brings us to the next point," the balding man said, looking down his nose at his papers and readjusting his glasses. "Your pregnancy."

"If I get out on parole, my foster mom from last time, Mrs. Henson, she wants me to go to her house and to try to take care of my baby," Tamara told him, diverting him from any questions about how she had managed to get pregnant during her incarceration. She turned slightly in her chair to nod to Mrs. Henson, sitting in the chairs behind her. "That's her."

The board all looked up from their papers and notes to study Mrs. Henson. Mrs. Henson smiled and nodded.

"You have discussed this with Social Services?" the man questioned, his brows drawing down as he stared at Mrs.

Henson. "They will approve a plan to put an infant into the arms of a girl convicted of murdering two young children?"

Tamara opened her mouth, unsure what to say. But Mrs. Henson had already been dealing with the prison officials and Social Services on the matter and she spoke up. Her voice was calm and measured.

"Yes, we have been in consultation with Social Services and already have a Safety Plan in place. There is nothing to indicate that Tamara would be a danger to her baby. In fact, even dealing with the psychosis triggered by the pregnancy, Tamara tried to protect him. She asked for help several times when she felt she might be a danger to him."

The balding man's expression didn't change as he stared at her. "This is aside from when she tried to commit suicide or tear the baby out with her bare hands."

The room was silent. Tamara could hear herself breathing. She hadn't been sure how much information the parole board would be given on what had happened over the past year. Obviously, they had been given plenty of ammunition against her.

"Yes," Mrs. Henson agreed. She was still calm and confident, but there was an extra bite in her voice as well. "They changed her meds after that to try to get better control over her psychosis. But more than that, Tamara learned how to ask for help. She learned how to judge when she was losing control and to ask the appropriate people for help."

Mrs. Henson actually made it sound good. Like Tamara had improved and progressed, rather than spiraling further and further into darkness she couldn't cope with. The balding man nodded and wrote something down. Tamara felt like something had shifted in the mood of the room. Maybe the board would actually consider granting her parole?

There were more scribbled notes. Murmurs between the members of the board. Tamara let her eyes roam around the small, warm room. The board. Mrs. Henson. The unknown woman. The rest of the audience she could see without turning her head. She could still feel Gomez's presence somewhere behind her.

"It says here your former parole officer wishes to make a statement?" the frowning woman said, looking up from her papers to spear Tamara with her gaze.

Tamara nodded. She swallowed and cleared her throat. "I don't know where he is..."

"Call Mr. Collins in."

Tamara heard the door behind her open. She didn't turn around to look, afraid they would judge her as easily distractible, impulsive, and unable to control herself. There was another guard there; it wasn't Gomez's voice that called in the larger waiting area for Mr. Collins. Footsteps sounded, the guard and Mr. Collins entering the room. Consuming more of the air in the already-close room.

She wasn't sure whether he was going to sit behind her or stand in front of the board with his back to her. As it turned out, he stood at an angle to Tamara, so she could see his face in profile as he addressed them. He gave Tamara a nod. He gave a casual, confident greeting to the members of the board. It appeared that he knew them. Tamara supposed it wasn't the first time he'd given a statement.

"You were Miss French's parole officer last year," the frowning woman said.

Collins gave a nod. "She had a number of problems, but I believe that if she's willing to communicate with her parole officer, she can successfully reintegrate with society. She did turn herself in. In fact, she has twice. That shows me she has what it takes. With a better understanding of the challenges she is going to face once she's left here and more open communication with her PO, she can succeed."

"Do you really think that things have changed that much since her last release?" the dragon lady demanded, tapping the end of her pen on the papers in front of her. "I'm not sure her behavior since returning to custody shows a positive turn."

"I don't think she had to change much to be successful," Collins said smoothly. "She had a lot of pressure from a previous acquaintance. She was, at times, physically prevented from complying. With Glock Spielman now incarcerated, Tamara's chances of success go up a hundred percent."

"You don't think she's going to allow herself to be influenced by someone else this time?"

Collins turned his head slightly toward Tamara, considering. They hadn't spoken since she had returned to juvie. He didn't know all that had happened to her since, though he had likely seen some of it on TV.

"I think she has the ability to resist pressure. She has a desire to do the right thing, which isn't something that can be said of all of the parolees I've supervised."

The little, balding man wrinkled his brow. He scratched out a few words in his notes. "Do you think she knows the difference between right and wrong?"

Collins didn't hesitate. "Yes."

Tamara waited for him to prevaricate, to temper his statement. Each of the members of the board looked at him, apparently waiting for the same. But Collins didn't qualify it.

"Thank you, Mr. Collins," the frowning woman said.

Collins stood there for a minute longer, waiting to see if any of the other board members had any questions for him. Then he nodded, and he walked behind Tamara to sit in the chairs and watch the rest of the proceedings.

"Is there anyone else who wants to make a statement?" the frowning woman asked, closing her folder.

"I do," Mrs. Henson offered quickly, before the proceedings could be closed.

"You've already had your say," the woman countered, clearly ready to go on.

"No, I only answered your question regarding Social Services' opinion of Tamara taking care of her baby."

The woman rubbed at the lines around her eyes, sighing and nodding tiredly.

"Okay. You've agreed she can be placed in your home, so clearly you believe she can be reformed and is not a danger. Do you have anything else to add?"

"It's important for Tamara to be able to bond with her baby. She hasn't had the opportunity to do that. She hasn't even held him. If she's going to have any involvement in his life, she needs to be given the opportunity to care for him. For his mental health and hers. And caring for a baby means she'll be motivated to make it work. She'll want to succeed for his sake. A baby can have a huge influence on a young woman."

Tamara suppressed a shudder at Mrs. Henson's words. That baby had already had a huge influence on her, taking over her brain for the months before he came into the world. She knew that he wasn't actually evil, but she remembered thinking he was, during her breaks from reality. She had been sure he was a demon, something she needed to fight back against. She struggled to keep her expression blank and not let the board see her thoughts.

"With a baby to take care of, Tamara isn't going to be out partying or looking for excitement. She'll stick close to home. She'll have the opportunity to make friends with other young mothers. She'll have plenty of social supports. We have been working with teen moms for years. Not all of them are cut out for it... but I believe Tamara is. I think she could be a great mom and this could be her path back into productive society."

The dragon lady turned to the others on the board, whispering. Did she think Mrs. Henson was full of hot air? That she didn't know what she was talking about? Mrs. Henson had a lot of experience, but Tamara still had a hard time believing Mrs. Henson knew what she was talking about as far as Tamara's parenting skills went. She didn't know what a pitiful job Tamara had done taking care of Corrine and Julie. It wasn't just that she had killed them while suffering from the psychosis of an earlier pregnancy. Even before that, the Bakers had criticized and berated Tamara, shouted at her for putting the children in danger, and beat her for her errors. If Mrs. Henson knew what a screw-up she had been with the Baker children, she wouldn't be so quick to say Tamara would be a good mother to her own baby.

But it was Tamara's one slim chance of getting out instead of a delay of another year, trying to show everyone what an exemplary juvie she was. If they could be convinced that she wanted to be a mother to her baby, they had to let her out. The baby was already a few months old. In another year, her chances of being able to bond with him properly would be that much lower. Earlier was better. Mrs. Henson kept emphasizing how important it was.

"My baby needs a mother," Tamara said. "I don't want him having to go from one foster home to another his whole life. I don't want him to not have any parents, like me." Tamara blinked tears. "Lots of the girls in juvie didn't have a real mom in their lives. I don't want my baby to end up somewhere like this."

The board members looked at her for a moment, then resumed whispering. Tamara could hear Mrs. Henson shifting in her chair back behind Tamara. She knew Mrs. Henson wanted to be there beside her, holding her hand to encourage her and show the board how sure she was and how much she would help and support Tamara. Mrs. Henson was used to getting her way with Social Services, but Tamara wasn't sure she would have as much sway with the parole board.

Tamara closed her eyes, focused on keeping her breathing steady. She waited for the board to announce their decision.

TWO

Y OU DID IT!" MRS. Henson cheered, giving Tamara a squeeze around the shoulders. "I told you we could get you out. I knew we could do it!"

Tamara put up with the hug for a moment, then wriggled to extricate herself. "Yeah. I didn't think it was going to go my way. I just figured, after all the stuff that happened... there was no way."

"You should pat yourself on the back. It wasn't easy. You did a great job advocating for yourself and telling them you could do it."

"It was all you," Tamara disagreed. "You and Collins. I didn't say that much."

"You don't have to say a lot. You handled yourself really well. Give yourself the congratulations you deserve. If you'd just sulked and not spoken up for yourself, do you think they would have approved it?"

Tamara shrugged. But her face got a little warm thinking about it. Mrs. Henson was right. She had done something for herself for once instead of just withdrawing and saying it was never going to work out.

Mrs. Henson gave her another hug around the shoulders, but Gomez was getting anxious for Tamara to be on her way. "You'll have plenty of time for that later," he said. "If you want to get out of here, everything has to be processed properly. I'm not supposed to be letting you hang around and socialize."

Tamara already had her hands cuffed in front of her, ready to be escorted back to her housing unit. As nice as it would be to just walk out of the parole board hearing and go home, that wasn't the way it worked. There would be paperwork to be processed, interviews with Dr. Sutherland and someone in administration, getting her release date approved and her parole officer onside, and a dozen other moving parts before she actually got out the door and was free.

"Yeah, fine. Let's go," she agreed.

The other woman who had been watching the parole board hearing was standing nearby, watching Tamara and Mrs. Henson closely. She had a hard face. Not unattractive, but not, Tamara thought, used to smiling much. Tamara wasn't sure who she was. Maybe a news reporter, seeing if there were a story to be told. Maybe some victim's advocacy group, though she hadn't spoken up against Tamara being released, so Tamara didn't think that was the case. Maybe it really wasn't anything to do with Tamara or her case; the woman was just a new guard or staff member and wanted to see how it all worked.

She didn't look away when Tamara looked at her. Tamara was used to some measure of respect in juvie. It wasn't respectful to just keep staring at her like that. It was a challenge, and Tamara didn't like to be challenged, especially by someone she didn't even know.

* * *

MRS. HENSON HAD ASKED if she could be the one to pick Tamara up from juvie and to take her home but, for some reason, protocol forbade it. Tamara had to be picked up by her social worker, who had initial custody of her, and then transferred to Mrs. Henson like a courier package. So, just as she had a year earlier, Tamara sat in the receiving room, staring down at her dingy white tennis shoes, waiting for the social worker to sign her out and take her away from juvie.

The social worker had said she would be there at noon. Tamara sat in the hard plastic chair watching the second hand make its way around the wall clock over, and over, and over again, until two hours had passed. Social workers were always dealing with emergencies and were notorious for being late, so she wasn't sure why she had thought the one picking her up would be any different.

Tamara hadn't eaten lunch, and she was annoyed and angry by the time the social worker finally showed up.

She was cut from the usual mold. In a skirt suit, hair pulled back away from her face, a narrow, stern face. Tamara bit her lip and looked away from the social worker. It wouldn't do to start out on the wrong foot. Snapping at the worker for being late was not going to win Tamara any awards.

"All ready to go, Tamara?" the woman asked briskly.

"Yeah." Tamara looked toward the reception counter. "You gotta fill out papers?"

"All done. We can go."

Tamara got stiffly to her feet. The social worker was watching her face. Tamara wasn't sure what was in the woman's eyes. Curiosity?

"You don't remember me?" the social worker asked.

Tamara frowned and looked over her. There was no name tag to help her to recall. But the woman's face did look a little familiar. Tamara couldn't remember where she knew her from.

"We met at the hospital. When I picked up your baby."

Tamara squinted at her, trying to force recollection. It had been a bad time and her memories were foggy and disjointed.

"Sorry," she said finally. "I was pretty doped up."

"I'm Mrs. Arbiter. I have to say, I was surprised to hear that you were going to go back to Marion and try to raise your baby. You were pretty adamant at the hospital that you didn't want him."

Tamara shifted back and forth, uncomfortable with Mrs. Arbiter's keen gaze. "I was going through a lot of stuff," she explained. "I didn't know what I wanted."

"You seemed to have a pretty good idea!"

"I guess." They started to walk toward the door. "But things changed... and I didn't think back then that I'd be able to get out and have anything to do with him. I didn't think there was any point in trying."

Mrs. Arbiter nodded, accepting this. She led Tamara out to her car and didn't try to keep her talking on the drive to the Hensons' house.

Tamara watched out the window as the scenery changed, getting farther and farther from juvie and closer to the house where she had spent those few weeks the last time she was released on parole.

She would do better this time.

She had to.

*VANISHING TEARDROPS,* Book #4 of the *Tamara's Teardrops* series by P.D. Workman can be purchased at pdworkman.com

# ABOUT THE AUTHOR

Award-winning and USA Today bestselling author P.D. (Pamela) Workman writes riveting mystery/suspense and young adult books dealing with mental illness, addiction, abuse, and other real-life issues. For as long as she can remember, the blank page has held an incredible allure and from a very young age she was trying to write her own books.

Workman wrote her first complete novel at the age of twelve and continued to write as a hobby for many years. She started publishing in 2013. She has won several literary awards from Library Services for Youth in Custody for her young adult fiction. She currently has over 60 published titles and can be found at pdworkman.com.

Born and raised in Alberta, Workman has been married for over 25 years and has one son.

* * *

Please visit P.D. Workman at pdworkman.com to see what else she is working on, to join her mailing list, and to link to her social networks.

* * *

If you enjoyed this book, please take the time to recommend it to other purchasers with a review or star rating and share it with your friends!

facebook.com/pdworkmanauthor

twitter.com/pdworkmanauthor

instagram.com/pdworkmanauthor

amazon.com/author/pdworkman

bookbub.com/authors/p-d-workman

goodreads.com/pdworkman

linkedin.com/in/pdworkman

pinterest.com/pdworkmanauthor

youtube.com/pdworkman